I hope you enjoy
my story.
Best wishes
Jerry
Strawberry Day 2010

Join other readers on our website's

Reader's Forum
www.smulron-pub.com

and tell me what you think of my story

First edition, 2008

Published by:
Smultron Publications
www.smultron-pub.com

Character names, corporations, locations and events in this novel have no actual relation to fact, real, living persons, places, or chronology, in any country. This book is wholly a work of fiction.

This book is dedicated to immigrants, willing and otherwise, no matter when, or from where they come, for their courage to brave the unknown, adapt to a new culture, a new language and for having something to offer…contributing and prospering

ISBN 978-0-9789854-1-7
ISBN 0-9789854-1-9

Vallkulla
Book One

G. R. Revelle

ACKNOWLEDGEMENTS:

My Swedish Family

Thanks, especially, to "my family" in Sweden who continue to live in and around Frömansgården, for their understanding and trust in me to tell a balanced story…as much as we know of it, anyway. One hundred twenty seven years have erased all acrimony, animosity and bitterness that must have once existed between our opposing families… Carl's and Brita's, especially in the years just prior to Brita's emigration. To find one's relations in another country after so many years was exciting; but then, to simultaneously learn that when we parted company…with *my side's* emigration to America in 1881, that there probably existed a tremendous anger and bitterness between our families. How would we…the American side, be received when the families met again, after so many years? Knowing my Swedish family as I do today, I could never have doubted the outcome; for they are the kindest, gentlest and most generous people, ever. How could one not come to love them as family?

The Writers Group

Sharon and Bob and occasionally, others, *lived* through much of the early stages of *Vallkulla*, willing and able companions as they were in our little writing enclave. Our twice monthly get-togethers to discuss ongoing and past writing projects proved the value of trusted, writing friends, who unselfishly serve one another as sounding boards to new ideas, themes and dialog and often speaking up fearlessly to criticize, or praise each other's endeavors. Let us hope our invention of the exercise, *Real-Time Writing* will inspire other writer's groups to experiment as we did, in order to prosper in their own creative endeavors and that they, too, will grow from the experience, as I have.

The Photography in *Vallkulla*

I've spent years in the Nordic countries, interviewing, writing, photographing and generally appreciating the beauty of Nordic Traditions, whether music, food, drink, dance or art. *Vallkulla's* underlying theme is probably *fäbodliv*…life in the summer farm. These traditions were common throughout much of the world in earlier centuries; probably the most well known are the shepherds in The Bible, Swiss yodelers and the "Heidi" stories, the latter of Northern Europe. *Fäbodliv* is a favorite subject of study for me. The tradition was nearly identical in Norway, where the girls are called *setter jenta (summer farm girls)*.

But when it came to illustrating the *Vallkulla* cover, posters and advertisements, my personal photography portfolio fell far short...and worse, I had no plans to visit Sweden again before Book One of *Vallkulla* was to be published. Years earlier, as an amateur photographer, I'd attended and spoke at a Gagnef Fotoklubben meeting, in Dalarna Sweden. I'd maintained contact with them over the years, occasionally begging winter photos from them to illustrate assorted Nordic newsletters; they were the first people who came to mind when I recognized that I was going to need some very subject-specific photography to illustrate the *Vallkulla* book series.

I contacted their president, Ragnar Nyberg, a supremely able photographer himself. He put out the word in the club and a member, Therese Nahlbom, came forward, expressing her interest in learning more about the project. I'd previously viewed her work on the Gagnef club's website and Therese, or *Tess* to her friends and clients, soon sent additional samples of her work and confirmed she was interested in taking on the project. After one look at the photos, I emailed several ideas I had for photo theme settings, based on various scenes from *Vallkulla*; several emails crossed the Atlantic until we thought we'd pretty well established an understanding of what I needed.

Therese Nahlbom, photographer

Then we rented a *fäbod*—one of the summer farms near Malung, for a day...complete with timber houses, barns, cows, goats and the clothing and tools needed to provide authenticity on the set. Tess coordinated equipment, gear, models and helpers and on a weather-favorable weekend, set out to do the shoot.

The result, *Vallkulla's* inside/outside cover art and some chapter heading graphics, are only a small piece of the wealth of spectacular photos that came back. If you've visited Smultron Publications' website (www.smultron-pub.com) or attended any showings or presentations related to the *Vallkulla* novels, you've already seen her work. The difficulty to me was that there weren't enough book covers to display the result of Tess' and her crew's supreme effort on the project.

In addition to custom, contract photography, Nahlboms Foto covers weddings, and advertising work. Additionally, they'll soon be releasing a series of specialty postcards and season-specific greeting cards. Tess can be contacted at Nahlboms Foto, Nedre Tjärna 21, Gagnef Sweden, tel. (from USA, dial)—011-46-241-10145; on the web at: www.nahlbomsfoto.se.

Early Readers:

The Løven Lodge (Eau Claire Wisconsin) Book Group selected an earlier novel of mine, "My Enemy's Child" as one of their reading projects; being local to them, they invited me to address their group. When I did, I found their insight, reading skill and perceptions so acute, I invited them to review the manuscripts for a forthcoming novel, *Vallkulla*, promising them only that I would welcome and carefully consider any and all suggestions, but reserving the option to still…do as I darn well pleased. You will find *Vallkulla* greatly improved as a result of their critiques. Thank you Ladies, for your sincere effort, your dedication and your patience; getting together to review your suggestions came to be a pleasurable experience which I always looked forward to.

Last, but not least:

How does a story really come about? My mother and her siblings actually were *vallkullor*, without knowing they were practicing that ancient occupation, when they were growing up on her emigrant parent's farm in Jackson County Wisconsin. To my knowledge, they didn't even know the meaning of the word *vallkulla*. Certainly Mother's parents and grandparents would have, having emigrated from Sweden as children.

In the '50s, I'd heard my grandfather and my mother's siblings practicing the ancient art of singing the *kuja*...calling the cattle, as they termed it in Swedish. Twenty years later, I heard a different version used in Sweden and have now since heard their exact version, older, I think, on ancient recordings, made in Sweden.

I've always loved all things I'd seen and heard about rural Nordic life. In 1983, *enter* a Swedish *dynamo*...Margaretha Hedblom...come to America to record the remnants of "memories" of Swedish-Americans, from my mother's generation. Margaretha was interested in their memories of the Swedish dialect, *mål*...and any surviving Swedish customs still alive in America. Genealogy was another favorite subject for Margaretha and she soon discovered "the story" as she called it. Anna-Stina Malmberg, my great-great grandmother, must have leaped out at Margaretha, while she was doing genealogical research in the ancient church record books, in Nås and Dala-Järna churches in Dalarna.

"This must have been a very interesting woman," Margaretha would hint to me, "...I think you should write about her, Jerry." When I would go to my office, I would often be greeted by mile-long faxes (the days when faxes came on rolls) and in the middle of our night she'd have left long telephone messages (Swedish time) with interesting points about Anna-Stina and other items related to *fäbodliv*, she'd gleaned from the church books. She was relentless and she didn't let up. Whether I was visiting Sweden, or when she was in America: "Have you thought any more about writing about Anna-Stina...?" she would query and launch into another story about the probability of Anna-Stina's adventurous life. Finally, I relented, saying I'd try.

Armed with information given me by Margaretha, from the church books, dating back to the 1600s and my mother's ancestor's genealogy records, I began to examine these documents more closely. I soon came to realize there were some interesting coincidences related to birth/baptism, death and marriage dates. Very slowly, I began to piece together a skeleton, over time—a chronology, surprising me with by the information is suggested, once it began to take shape.

From that information skeleton, I fleshed the *Vallkulla* story. Most of the dates and names (of relatives) are quite accurate; it is only the unknown facts about the character's lives and conversations that I have fictionalized.

I can emphatically state that without Margaretha Hedblom's insistence, persistence and faith in me as a writer and all her other resource material, *Vallkulla* would never have been written; thank you, my dear friend.

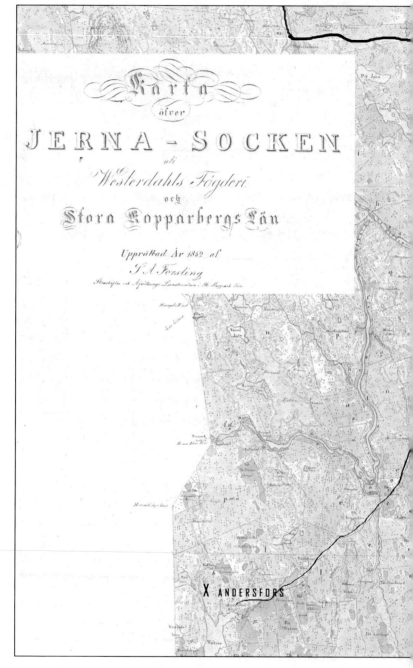

They walked to cumpulsory Sunday church service.

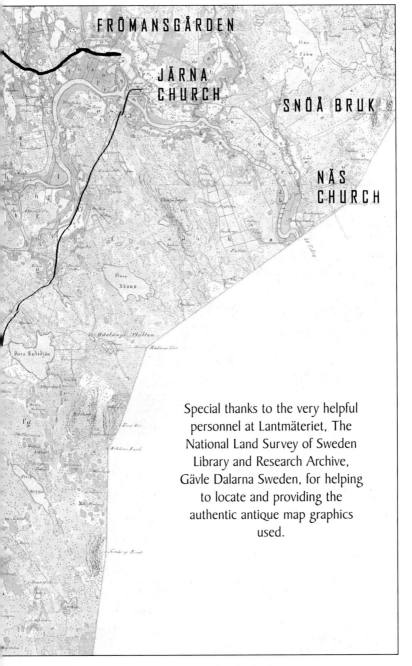

FRÖMANSGÅRDEN

JÄRNA
CHURCH

SNÖÅ BRUK

NÄS
CHURCH

Special thanks to the very helpful
personnel at Lantmäteriet, The
National Land Survey of Sweden
Library and Research Archive,
Gävle Dalarna Sweden, for helping
to locate and providing the
authentic antique map graphics
used.

Map dated 1852

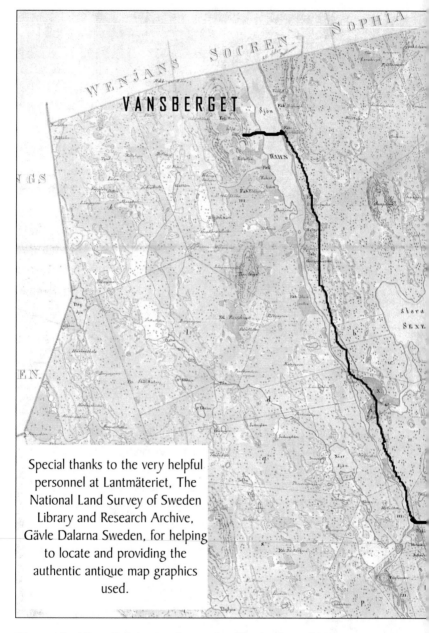

Special thanks to the very helpful personnel at Lantmäteriet, The National Land Survey of Sweden Library and Research Archive, Gävle Dalarna Sweden, for helping to locate and providing the authentic antique map graphics used.

They walked from Frömansgarden to the *fäbod*, a long day's journey with a swim or boat ride at the end.

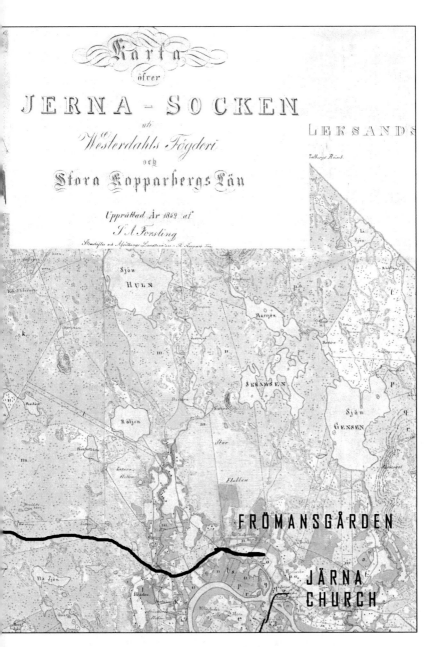

Map dated 1852

Country of Sweden with
County of Dalarna
(highlighted)

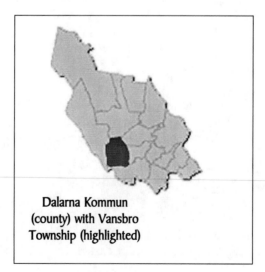

Dalarna Kommun
(county) with Vansbro
Township (highlighted)

CHAPTER I

The Beginning—Karolina
The Farm Attic

"*Ahhhh*...this explains why
I never discovered them, in all
those years of snooping up here
as a kid." I carefully pulled a cracked leather envelope from beneath
a secret compartment in my great grandfather's emigrant trunk and
carried it over by the attic dormer window and sat down on a
battered milking stool, a relic from before they'd sold all the cows.

I'd loved to prowl in my grandfather's farmhouse attic, chocked
full of depression-era stuff as it was—and even older, everything
saved against the day it might be needed again. My grandparent's
remaining belongings were all there: old guns, knives, hand tools, the
wood polished smooth and shiny from use.

Packed with loose trinkets from bygone eras, cigar boxes filled
two large dresser drawers. Nicer items...dresses, hand-embroidered
tablecloths and crocheted linens, rated drawers to themselves. Army
boots, hunting boots, men's and thick-heeled '30 era women's shoes
hung between the rafters beside clamp-on ice skates, along with old
coats, and more tools. On and on the collection went.

My twin uncle's WWII army uniforms were neatly folded in
another dresser drawer, along with other trinkets the two bachelors
had collected in their youth: army medals, matchbooks, photos of
girls they'd met in France and Belgium and, later...Germany, cracked
and worn from much carrying and handling.

C-rations and army-issue cigarettes, still in yellowed
cellophane...coins, dog tags, the boxes went on an on...a young boy's
treasury to sort through. I'd long since become a man and "The

Boys," my uncles, were in their graves, resting at last from their horrible memories of that war. For some reason my grandfather had kept a homemade beehive, but now it was packed with bees that had never flown: canvas bandoleers of .30 caliber army ammunition were folded inside and layered over with even larger shells of a caliber too large to remember. Everything was up there gathering dust and cobwebs.

I had a hideout between the mottled brick, cook-stove chimney and a dingy dormer window. Nearby were cartons containing nearly every National Geographic printed; what more could a curious boy want on a rainy, fall day? But that was years ago.

I leaned back against the cold chimney, hesitating to open the leather envelope, watching the dust motes float through the slanted sunlight. It was early September and the attic was still hot, though I'd opened both dormer windows and waited an hour before climbing the narrow stairway and dragging out the old trunk. Finally unfolding the leather flap I carefully began removing the papers, placing the stiff, yellowed sheets, one-by-one, in my lap, I thought of the conversation with my mother's sister...when I first learned about my Scandinavian family's dubious past.

"Grandma, a...*bast*..." choking slightly I couldn't bring myself to say the word. "A...*bastard*, how could she be?"

Staring aghast across the dining room table at my aunt, this surprising revelation had come slamming into my Southern Methodist upbringing. It wasn't any easier to swallow than inhaling a sugar cookie crumb, which I'd just done. I took another sip of coffee and cleared my throat.

"Somebody like Grandma couldn't have been a...well, that."

My aunt broke a cookie in half and plunged half of it in her coffee: "Well, she was. Mother was only two years old when her mother brought her from Sweden. There wasn't a husband with them." I thought about what I'd just learned. Wetting the end of my finger and dabbing stray sugar granules from the tablecloth I looked at my aunt as if she might change her mind. My mother had died three years earlier without ever mentioning a word about her own mother being...well, anything, but Grandma. I was far from a prude but it wasn't an easy word to connect to someone you loved—dearly. Illegitimate...one might say or, parents weren't married, possibly...even, no father—but using that word seemed too harsh.

"*Yaaah*…well, I prefer the Swedish word, *oäkta*¹. It means the same thing but somehow it seems less accusatory, though it certainly wasn't when it was used in those times."

"I never heard that word: ooh—ek—tah."

"No, we never talked about it…even among ourselves. We were brought up ashamed of it…how it happened to Mother.

"Well…who was my grandfather, then?"

"We never knew…mother never told us—didn't even talk about it. For all I know, she never knew, herself, though I suspect she did; her mother must have said something. But I suppose he was ashamed. In those days people didn't talk about such things, even within families."

"How did you find out?"

"We have these old papers…" she licked some butter from a finger before motioning toward the ceiling, "…the attic…in an old trunk."

"Which trunk…I don't remember seeing anything like that? I've been through that stuff a hundred times as a kid."

"The medium-sized one…with blue painting and a date on it. They're down in the bottom, beneath some of Grandma's old clothes. It's one of the trunks that came over with them; I think the date on it is—eighteen…something."

As my aunt broke another cookie I made a mental note to take another look in the attic.

"Great grandmother Birtha—Mother's mother, probably brought the papers with her from Sweden. I could never understand why she would bring both the child and the evidence. Maybe she needed something to get in…Emigration. I think it was an old fort, then…Castle Garden in New York; that was before Ellis Island. I'd have thought the authorities would have been less thorough. Who knows…anyway, it's all there, written in old Swedish, from that time period—eighteen and something. I can't read the papers very well, but mother could and did…once, to your mother and me."

"Where did the papers come from…I mean, who made them."

"They were official documents, hand written…in those days, from the government or the court: oaths and witness' testimony…that stuff. After she'd had Mother, Grandma had sued a man—a rich farmer's son, before she left Sweden. In the papers she'd said he was the father of Mother, but he'd denied it in his testimony. He didn't want to help her pay for the midwife or for her baby's later needs. She apparently won the lawsuit, got some money in the end, for her trouble and her walking papers too, I guess, to America. That's when she brought Mother and the twins."

"Twins?"

"Your great uncles—her little half-brothers."

"Oh." I'd never thought of those old guys coming as immigrants, let alone as children. They were both dead now; I barely remembered them. "How old were they—then?"

"Uh—I don't know…let's see, maybe eight—ten, somewhere around there."

Alone—they came alone? I mean, with her?"

"Uh-huh, she was twenty-two and brought Mother, who was two, at the time."

That conversation had taken place over five years ago. My aunt died last month and now I'm the last in the family, but for my older sister. After the funeral and everyone had gone home from the lunch, I'd aired out the attic and then dug out the envelope containing brittle brown sheets from the old trunk. I'd never noticed that the old trunk had a false bottom. When I first looked through the old books and school items, I wondered whether my aunt had removed the old documents she'd described that day. That's when I looked closer and sure enough, the bottom lifted out to reveal a false bottom, containing only the folded, leather envelope.

Sitting on a three-legged milk stool in the dusty light of the window, I struggled to read the beautiful cursive script, laid down by an unknown court, reporter nearly a hundred years before. The three separate papers were dated from 1879 to 1881, written in the old Swedish of the time.

That evening, the only person sleeping in the house, I lay listening to a whippoorwill serenading from the apple orchard, wondering whether I would be able to sleep. I thought about the fascinating story the crackling documents hinted at. To think that such heretofore-unknown trauma had happened to my great grandmother, in 1870s Sweden. The court witness's testimony was so graphic. Their descriptions of the incident and the final verdict must have wrought families asunder at the time. It also appeared the Swedish Lutheran

Church had a strong hand in the trial, if that's what they'd have called it, then. I wasn't too certain about many of the old words.

Though I worked most of my thirty-plus years as a business owner, I'd been educated in English/American literature in college, originally planning to teach. I'd always wanted to write something rewarding...a novel, or the like. I had several technical articles to my credit from my business ventures, but they'd brought little satisfaction to my personal adventure muse and I'd retained the yearning to someday write fiction. The revelations in the old Swedish documents sounded like the makings of a fabulous story, I thought; but, how would I learn more?

The following morning I worked my way through bacon, eggs and toast. Sometime between frying the bacon and cracking the eggs, I decided to take a trip to Sweden to see whether I could learn more about my family's origins...where we'd emigrated from. After checking in the office by phone, I asked my secretary work through some dates with me to clear a span of two weeks in early December on my calendar and look up some travel agency numbers. By that afternoon I asked a travel agency get me a ticket on a flight to Stockholm, departing in a little over a week's time. I was unmarried, reasonably successful financially and had no responsibilities beyond my small, manufacturing business, which more or less ran itself with the help of some great staff members.

A few days later I packed, bid goodbye to a surprised John, my general manager, in charge at the factory and phoned my sister in Missouri, to tell her what I planned. She thought the whole idea was a waste of money. But then, she'd never heard of the story about Grandmother and doubted the factuality of it.

The week's preparation gave me little time to research where I would go in Sweden to find the family's original location. First, I revisited the old court documents again in the attic to locate the place where Great-grandmother had emigrated from, with her two year old, illegitimate daughter and younger half brothers. I took them into town and had them Photostatted. I telephoned the US Embassy in Washington for information to wire the US Embassy in Sweden. And after a couple of telegrams, I eventually located relatives of the accused man, the father of my grandmother, now long dead. These came via the Swedish Embassy. I took a chance, had the number located and called them up on the telephone.

To say they were surprised was an understatement. But after struggling to understand my antique Swedish…the version I'd learned hadn't changed since Great-grandma, I had an invitation to visit them at their farm to discuss the possibility that we were relatives. They'd hear the rumor about their great-grandfather, too and were curious about any American relations they might have. They sounded very nice through the static on the poor cable connection we had on the phone.

So, off I went, planning to rent a car at the airport in Stockholm and drive north. Easier said than done; I discovered Sweden was still on the wrong side of the road from America and driving proved not to be an easy task. Slowly, I mastered steering with my right hand and shifting with my left and after nearly a day of careful driving, ended up in the south-central part of Sweden in a province called Dalarna. In a little while I found the community and asking directions frequently, (they smiled at my ancient Swedish) drove into the countryside to the farm of the supposed, distant cousin.

I was immediately made welcome, fed *kaffe* and cookies as the children watched and giggled at my struggles with Swedish.

I'd brought extra copies of the old documents along from the states, which they poured over for twenty minutes, also having a little trouble with the old words.

"If what the papers accuse our ancestors—our ancestor of, is correct," the woman I thought to be my cousin said, after taking a sip of her coffee, "…you and I are second cousins."

"Really…that close?"

"Yes, I believe so. But we didn't know anything about this for certain. Strangely, they—our relatives, never talked about this," she held up the photostatic copy. "I had heard whispers about our grandfather's *oäktabarn*—you know what I mean—a woman and illegitimate child? The one…that had emigrated to *Amerika*?"

I nodded. "My great-grandmother Bertha."

"Yes…Bertha…we say Brita…but we had never given it much thought."

We talked until she and her husband Olle had to stop for chores—milking their cows. But they bade me welcome in their home…there was no place else to stay within an hour's drive. I watched the milking process for a while and then went for a walk down the narrow lane, lined by birch and fir trees, flanked by various-sized, red timber houses with white trim. Sweden proved to be far more beautiful than I imagined it would be.

I hung around the community doing a little research of my own in the church records. There were two towns with churches that had the original birth, baptismal, confirmation, wedding and death records: Järna and Nås. Both were situated on the Västerdalälven, a clear, rushing river that poured from the western mountains and Norway, toward the Baltic, to the east.

The Swedish Church, it seemed, followed the parishioner from cradle to grave. Spending a few days with the books, I was able to trace their side back a few hundred years. Though it didn't confirm anything about my grandmother's legitimacy, there were some very interesting entries made by the Swedish Lutheran ministers of the time; that really set my novelist's mind to work.

After a couple days of discussion with my cousin, we finally determined the information in my documents was rather inconclusive and that we'd probably never know anything for sure, without a living, eyewitness. That's when my cousin had a good idea.

"Why don't you go visit our mother's father's old aunt, Karolina?"

"Oh," I replied, "where does she live?"

"She is in a nursing home—in southern Sweden. She might know something. She is the oldest, living relative to anyone from that time and a sister to our grandfather...the one who is accused in the papers."

"That's a great idea. How do I contact her?"

"Oh...I don't know for sure...maybe you could write to her?"

"Why does he not simply go there to see her—I don't believe she will be going anywhere. Possibly, she could, or would tell you anything she might know."

"Good idea. I'll do that...maybe on Sunday."

My cousin said something quietly to her husband in rapid Swedish. He looked at her for a moment before turning to me.

"Lisa has just made a good point: she thinks you should be prepared to be rebuffed. Karolina's had a falling out with some on our side of the family, some time ago. Lisa wonders whether she is particularly welcoming visitors."

"Oh?"

"Yes…she is known to be rather crabby and is still bitter," he told me, lowering his head in confidence, "and might not tell you anything, even if she knows it." He nodded his head.

So with that encouragement, I got directions, marked my roadmap and departed the following Sunday, driving over six hours and arriving far later than I planned.

Walking down the hallway, the reflection of the nurse's uniform marched a few steps in front of me along the polished floor. From time to time it made a quick turn from one stark hallway to another. Following, I was getting lost. Spotless, white-walled corridors did little to temper the dim, winter afternoon. And the cheerless décor offered few landmarks to blaze a mental trail, back to the front entrance. Noisy children clumped past in large floppy, rubber boots. Urged forward by parents, they were pulling on oversize coats and knit stocking caps as they came. Visiting hours were over.

There'd been a problem at the reception desk. It was late, I was told, and the old woman I'd come to see—Karolina, never had visitors.

"Who are you again?" The bossy receptionist—she wasn't even a nurse—asked, searching down a page in a large book, with one finger. The book slipped and she nearly dropped it, making her even more annoyed. A younger nurse joined her and smiled at me sympathetically, though she didn't offer to help, standing poised in her starched uniform.

"This is my first time…" I told them, hoping to gain sympathy from the new arrival, "I didn't know it was…that visits were over so soon."

Why did you come—and so late…? She didn't actually say it aloud, but I knew she was thinking it, as she glanced over the top of the book. She was shaking her head, mumbling as she turned pages.

So late…you're interrupting our routine…I imagined her thinking…we like routine—we thrive on routine.

It wasn't so unusual that I was regarded with such suspicion, being so obviously an American. Swedes were suspicious people, I'd already learned. They liked order…precision and to them, I must have appeared rather hopeless. I got another sympathetic smile from the young nurse, probably not yet indoctrinated into routine, I thought. The older one looked up at me again.

"You are not in the book," she said with some finality, as if that answered it and ended the interview. But she wasn't finished with me. "The book which says who may or may not visit our people," she said, growing more fretful, "...it does not have your name, *Herr* Andersson."

I stood there not knowing whether I should persist, or give up and leave. Finally, brow knitted, she groaned, shaking her head again as if she doubted my sincerity and taking the book with her, she stood up, opened a door behind her and disappeared. Her younger companion moved closer to the desk, possibly to take the older woman's place. But she stopped just short of sitting down. Glancing toward the half-open door, as if she were having second thoughts, she stopped beside the chair, semi-facing the partially-open door, in case she was summoned.

"She will ask our superior," she said, smiling again and giving me a knowing look. She held a clipboard tight to her chest as, together the two of us watched the shadows extending through the partially open door. Inside, with someone we couldn't see, my fate was being discussed in hushed tones. How could I defend myself...out here? I didn't relish another six hour drive back north, without any answers. My young companion was obviously afraid to intervene on my behalf, though I sensed where her sympathies lay and I couldn't even see my judge, I thought, buttoning my coat again in preparation to depart.

Suddenly the conversation stopped and the woman emerged, hanging her head. I'd won, it seemed. The younger nurse smiled in triumph; as if to be rid of the reminder of defeat I was assigned to the younger woman as my escort to old Karolina's room,.

Smiling, she indicated with a single, "*komma*," that I was to follow her to Karolina Fröman's room. Off we went. I would be able to see the old woman, after all and unbuttoned my jacket again as we walked.

I hurried to keep up. "The old woman is a possible relative...a second—maybe third cousin, I believe," I related as we marched along, single file.

"Oh, I see," my companion smiled over her shoulder.

"She would never have heard of me, of course—doesn't even know I—we exist—our branch of the family, there in America," I added. She nodded her understanding, this time without turning.

As we marched along, I was growing more uncertain about the

idea of barging in. Would she agree to see me? Following my leader's reflection, doubt began to creep in. She'd be surprised—maybe even angry? It was rather late and for all I knew, she was already in bed—old people went to bed early.

"Will she already be in bed?" I queried.

"I think not," came her reply.

Maybe I shouldn't have come...I seriously considered stopping the nurse...telling her I'd changed my mind. But I'd put them through all that effort and I also had a tight air connection, flying back to The States in just two days. If I was going to get any information, it would have to be now. This would be my last and only chance.

Abruptly, the reflection disappeared as the nurse turned left. I'd lagged behind. Timidly, I hesitated, just inside the doorway of a darkened room. In the dimness, the nurse was bent over, talking to someone sitting in a wheelchair across the room. I waited as my eyes and courage adjusted to the darkness. The wheelchair was backed against a wall in what remained of the guttering winter sunlight, facing the only window and the setting sun. The window's mullions cast crisscross shadows over the pair and onto the wall, behind. Karolina sat still in her chair, captured like a prisoner in the mullion's thin shadows. The alternate squares, screened—defined her small environment—a checkered game board. At two in the afternoon the sun's rays were nearly horizontal. In Sweden's near-Arctic latitude the sun would set in a half-hour's time and night would prevail for another nineteen hours of stark, winter darkness.

The nurse fussed with Karolina's clothing.

"Karolina..." she spoke softly, not unkindly, "...you have a visitor. Karolina...are you awake? He has come a long way to see you...especially."

I couldn't hear whether she replied.

"Do you feel like talking to him for a little—yes?" The nurse glanced over at me, nodding and smiling encouragingly, beckoning me to come closer. Despite the fact Karolina hadn't yet responded that I could tell, I stepped closer. I'd thought at first she'd been sleeping. Her head was bent forward slightly. A dark shawl lay across her shoulders. Even in the dimness I recognized the embroidery pattern and colors. I'd seen the same design on the Sunday clothes of my new cousins, up north. The decoration depicted the province of

Dalarna and the particular area from where I'd just driven: sort of, the official uniform. I knew Karolina had been born there. I'd learned earlier from my cousins that Karolina's only marriage had taken her here, in the south. And here she'd apparently remained and it seemed, would no doubt, die.

The pillow plumping finally finished, I could see into the dim interior better now. I'd glanced around the neat room, devoid of all ornamentation that might have indicated current or past interests. Childless her entire marriage, Karolina had none of the usual grandchildren's photos covering the dresser—not even nephews, or nieces, apparently. Maybe she'd disinherited the whole lot of them.

I took another step closer, still remaining a little apart. I'd hoped for something…an ornament, photo, any common bond about which I could start a conversation. The nurse completed her fussing.

"Let me turn you around now, Karolina—so you can see ," she said, rotating the chair to face me.

All this came in gentle, sing-song Swedish. I was now in full view. It seemed the old woman wasn't asleep at all and had cocked her head my way at the nurse's words, abandoning the dismal view of the emptying parking lot.

"*Herr* Andersson has gotten special permission to see you today, even with visiting hours past. Karolina, he has come so far, too…it would be good for you to talk with him, you know… if you feel like it," she encouraged, nodding and smiling in my direction. We both needed encouragement, apparently.

Preparing to leave us, the younger woman straightened, shook her head, frowning slightly and reached across the chair to turn on a small table lamp.

The shadowy bars vanished from the wall. I could see the old woman in better detail. Her features really weren't that old. Her hair, blondish-yellow as only the Scandinavians gray in older age, was done up, but hidden beneath a little, scarf-like *halsduk*[2] in the tradition of the north. She'd probably worn it since she'd taken first communion in the Swedish Lutheran Church. By the old customs, she would never have shown her hair again after marriage—even to her husband. Thankfully, those old fashioned customs were long since discontinued.

From conversations with my presumed cousins in the north, I'd learned Karolina lost her husband midway in their marriage. He'd been involved in the Swedish munitions industry—possibly Bofors, a huge manufacturer of cannons...for the Nazis in WW II. I thought I remembered that his name was Carlsson. Probably, he'd left her comfortably well off, too.

And if my cousin's hunches were correct, if anyone held the key—the answers to my ancestry, it would be this lady. If, in her advanced age, she could still remember anything and if she was willing to tell me, I could be out of here in a short time with all the information she had. I also had a curious question about her own mother that I wanted to ask her—something that had popped up during my rather extensive genealogical studies up at the newly-found cousins. It was a question that might be even more sensitive to her, dealing with her own mother as it did. Karolina, too, was born *oäkta*, as were her three siblings—just like my grandmother. Considering this illegitimacy issue—my grandmother's and Karolina's own, I wouldn't have been surprised if she choose to remain silent after I broached the subject. After all, it was her older brother, if the rumors were true, who was supposedly my grandmother's father. It was really complicated to grasp it all. He would then be my great-grandfather.

In considering these questions as I waited, I found myself captivated by her eyes. They were bright and alert, despite the dimness of the room; there was real fire there. Though she sat patiently enough throughout the nurse's attentions, she must have found it annoying—being plumped, patted and buttoned as she was. Her eyes searched mine, all the while—curious. There is life here, I thought, now almost dreading what might follow; I had the sense of being sized-up, hopefully, not for a battle.

The nurse patted the old ladies' shoulder one last time and started for the door. Beside me, she stopped, leaned down and whispered:

"You can stay as long as you wish—just do not tire her. She may ask you to leave right away, anyway. She is...well, her moods are...unpredictable, sometimes. But the company will do her so much good...you see, no one comes...ever."

I nodded without taking my eyes off Karolina and the nurse closed the door. Karolina stared back, having now tilted her head back somewhat and staring down her nose, appraising me—scrutinizing...like she might say: state your business and leave. There was a slight smile, however. Was it one of expectation or triumph?

She didn't tell me to go; she didn't say anything. She just waited. I tried to smile a greeting, but found it hard to meet her directness and the continued silence. The confidence of old age, I thought. She wasn't helping me much, either. As I said, my mother had taught me the Swedish dialect her parents had spoken, which they had of course gotten from their parents. It was from the rural district and quite antique, as I learned after arriving in Stockholm and from my new cousins. The *Stockholmska*[3] would smile politely behind their hands whenever I'd ordered food, or spoken this—dialect of the Vikings. Younger Swedes immediately changed the conversation to English, impatient, or completely unable to fathom most of the curious, old words I'd used.

Still without taking my eyes off her, I took a deep breath and seized a chair from along the wall and pulled it up in front of her, positioning it at a slight angle. But before I sat down, I hesitated, thinking I'd better mind my manners. She nodded and I sat.

"*Hej, Karolina. Hur mår ni?*" (I'd said: "how are you," using the polite form of 'you' and asking after her health). Receiving no immediate response, I continued.

"*Jag heter Knutes Alex—och Jag ha kom från Amerika...kan jag sitta här?*" (I told her who I was and where I had come from, giving my Swedish *gårdsnamn*[4]—'Knutes').

My farmer Swedish had an immediate effect; she looked a little startled, cocking her head to one side, in obvious surprise. I took this as the possibility that she'd comprehended some of what I'd said and as acceptance so I gave the chair another hitch, forward, in her direction. Her facial expression slowly changed to one of resigned humor. Her face had actually come to life and better matched the gleam in her eyes. Then, she even chuckled out loud and her voice cracked a little when she finally spoke, though it was velvety.

"*Du sproka lika Farfar...*" ("You speak like my father's father"). "*Var comer du från...?*" she asked, "*...Amerika, saga du?*" ("Where do you come from—you said America?").

Before I could answer, she added: "How can you speak old dialect like my grandfather and be so young—and from *Amerika*, too, you said?" She shook her head, smiling. "What is your *gårdesnam*?"

What she wanted to know was the farm name, a sort of a home-place name. In Dalarna, every time a child was born, he or she took as a surname, their father's given name. Johan's son—became a last name of Johansson. If the father was Johan and they named their newborn son, Erik, he became Erik Johansson. A girl's name was treated the same. Her last name would be Johansdotter, until she married. Anyway, to keep everyone straight, they had this unique, sort of, farm-name, which went in front of every given name—and that never changed. My mother's father was *Knutes* Nils Johnson—his given name was Nils. Thus I would have gone by *Knutes* Alex.

"Knutes…" I replied, "…from Wisconsin—in *Amerika*."

She considered this, sort of chewing on the emptiness as she pondered the answer.

"There were Knuters people at home when I was a girl…in Järna," she mused, "…but most of them left for *Amerika*, or died. Tell me…what was your mother's name?"

"Delma Johansson. Her mother's name was Anna-Christina."

Here was my first clue and where I would learn whether she would tell all. Anna-Christina—my grandmother, was the illegitimate child, supposedly sired by her older brother. But I didn't say it. Would she recognize the name?

She did. Her head bent closer and she stared at me as if she were seeking some long, lost facial characteristic in my countenance…something to spark a memory of something, or someone, long in the past; her eyes took on a new gleam, boring into mine.

Very deliberately then, she asked: "And what was your grandmother's…Anna-Christina's *gårdesnamn?*"

She was still smiling, but only slightly. Now, a look of thoughtfulness had slipped over her aspect—like a dark mask ready to descend.

"*Jugas…*," I replied, watching her reaction. "Her mother's name was *Jugas* Brita Andersdotter, from Skålö, in Järna," I added. "And I came here Karolina, to see if you could possibly tell me…do you know who her father was?"

I sort of scrunched up. But she didn't react at all—just sat there. I didn't know what to expect, but I did expect something. Of course, I thought I already knew the answer to my question anyway: her older brother Carl—now, long dead. He was the one Great Grandmother had sued in the Swedish court, so long ago. My research and my Swedish cousins had more or less confirmed this.

I watched the mask change to resignation, and then disappear altogether. She turned her head back toward the window and for a full minute, sat staring toward the nearly-vanished sun. Through the haze of low cloud, the top of the orange orb was just visible, touching the horizon, about to end the chapter of another day. When she finally spoke, her simplicity surprised me.

"Yes—they say it was my brother—Carl," she said, looking disinterestedly back toward me, "as you have probably guessed."

I remained silent, taken aback to some degree by her directness. I expected something more.

"I wondered—if anyone would ever come," she finally added, almost to herself, turning away again. "They emigrated…went away—*utvandrad*. And all those years…never a word from any one of them; so far away…so many of them left that time." She glanced at me: "I often wondered whether they thought of us—we who remained behind?"

I didn't quite understand exactly what she meant. We both sat for a while, looking out the window. It soon became apparent that she was crying; her fingers fumbled in her apron pocket for a handkerchief. She got it out one corner and began dabbing at her eyes, glancing over to me.

"I guess you know we…are supposed to be related, then…you wouldn't be here otherwise," she said quietly, sniffing. "Well, I do not have any money to loan you…or leave you. I have already given it all to the church."

Softly, I said, "I have no interest in your money, Karolina. I have my own business and do all right. I wanted information, only that."

"All right, then…." She began to sniffle again. "I have confirmed what you wanted."

"Yes, I had suspected as much, Karolina," feeling slightly ashamed now for my selfishness. I hadn't thought—didn't consider the possibility my visit might make her upset. In my selfish eagerness for information I'd been rather inconsiderate. I stammered an apology.

"I am sorry, Karolina. We don't have to go into this if you really don't want to talk about it." Her shoulders were shaking gently.

"No, never mind…please, go on," she said, waving her handkerchief lightly in my direction.

I rushed forward then, wanting to get it over. "My mother's family had three old, Swedish court—*trial* transcripts—from the last century…1879. They spoke of a trial held—the *Nås Tingslag*, which outlined the accusation of your brother Carl as the probable father of my grandmother Anna-Christina, by *Jugas* Brita Andersdotter. The witnesses' testimony and the findings of the judges—are all included. It was only recently that I even saw these documents and learned a little of what they contained. I have also been searching the records from the archives of the Nås and Järna churches—births…deaths? In attempting to learn the name of my great grandfather—your brother, I found something else, something which seem so unusual, considering the time and considering, the church."

She nodded, blowing her nose. "And what do you think of it all?" She blinked a couple of times and stared boldly at me again, fully recovered now, head high once again. "Do you not think it is true? Did those…those Free Church People in *Amerika*, did they say Carl Fröman was the father of your grandmother?

Confused and a little defensive, I didn't know what sort of answer she expected. "I really don't know. You see…they never spoke of it—even in the family. In the trial records I found—your brother denied it. I thought you might be able to help me—document it all…for sure. My family is all gone and the cousins up north in Dalarna, they don't really know much about it…only what the court records from the 1870s and 80s show…the same information I have."

She seemed lost in thought, saying nothing further for a moment. "I have thought about it—over and over again during the years. Them…emigrating to *Amerika* and never hearing anything from them again, after that. What has it been—seventy—eighty years? And now you—her—her grandson—you suddenly appear to uncover things…things probably best forgotten. What good will it do anyone…anyway—now?" She fussed a little with her handkerchief and shawl. "You have surprised an old woman—do you know that young man?"

She turned and looked out the window again, her head shaking slightly with palsy. Had I been dismissed I wondered, or was she going to cry again? But she didn't. Turning back to me she adjusted her shawl.

"Well, what did your family think? Did they believe any of it—this story—in the...those old papers? Do any of them even know who Carl Fröman was—or care?"

"I don't know," I said, "I don't believe so—not really...not now, I mean. I am the only one in the family who really had any curiosity—any interest and as I said, they never spoke of it. To them, it was a terrible thing, I believe. If the others—my aunts—mother, had any curiosity—it died with them. And I don't believe any of those still remaining have any idea about your brother; they hardly know we are Swedish—we were Swedish.

She nodded, absently smiling a little at me, seemingly satisfied no one had ever bothered to discover the truth...that it wasn't worth it. I didn't wish to upset her. But my success so far made me decide to venture one last question—my big one.

"Apparently, the judges thought so, since they ruled in favor of my great-grandmother and her child. In the end they believed your brother Carl, was truly the natural father of my grandmother.

"Yes..." she waved her hand with a wry smile, as if it meant nothing, "...they did—but will you ever know for certain?" With the return of the smile, this comment came almost as a challenge; her smile was patient, neither condescending nor intimidating. I was beginning to like this lady.

"And my family...you know Karolina...I didn't even learn of it—these papers from the Swedish courts—until a couple of years ago. My mother, aunts—Anna-Christine's children? They were ashamed of it. And that's why the—the secret was kept so long."

"That is a pity."

"Maybe someday there will be tests they can do to find out who our relatives really are."

"And who are not" she added emphatically. "I do not think too many will wish to take this test—for fear of who they may be relatives with." The wry smile returned.

"So...why then have you come to see this old lady and all the way from Amerika? Just to ask a question you seemed already to know the answer to?" I could see she suspected I wasn't yet finished.

"Well, I did want to ask you another question." I was enjoying her newfound sense of humor.

"Hah..." she snorted, "...the last one alive, too, am I? How convenient."

She turned back to the window, seeming to lose interest, though she was still smiling, her head shaking slightly. The room would soon be completely dark, but for the single lamp. The orange-black glow from the window was only a thin line behind the cloud now.

"Yes, you seem to be, that, Karolina. My last question is not about *Jugas* Brita, or my grandmother."

I was beginning to back-pedal, fearful of her reaction.

"In America, in the rural Swedish community where they settled, they made my grandmother suffer enough for her mistake of birth— my grandmother—her mother, as she grew up. For being oäkta, I mean. In English we say, a bastard."

The old Swedish word again: *oäkta*—it was what the Lutheran minister had written in the yellowed pages of the church book, in Nås, when he'd recorded my grandmother's birth.

"Anna Christine, *född i 1878*, and who is the father of this *oäkta* one," he had scrawled on the page in old, copper-plate script.

Karolina nodded here and there as I spoke, conveying either her understanding, agreement or dismissal. We stared out the window for a while, watching the lights of the automobiles leaving the parking lot. The sun was gone, now. It was night. Suddenly she broke the silence:

"Boxing Day...it was on Boxing Day."

"What do you mean...Boxing Day...I don't understand?"

"She was born the day after Christmas Day—Boxing Day— December 26th...the day when everyone is celebrating—betrothals and all that sort of thing...little Anna-Christine—your grandmother, she was born on that day—in 1878."

"Oh, I see...you actually remember?"

"Of course," she said, casting a glance in my direction, as if to question my sanity, "of course I remember it. My brother—Carl— announced his wedding engagement to his intended—a different woman, on the very day his *oäkta* child saw first light of day. She was born in the barn owned by *Jugas* Brita's—your great-grandmother's, family: Jugasgården, it was."

My heart was pounding, but I remained silent, feeling I was learning more by not asking questions. She seemed to lapse into thought again, but then pivoted the chair slightly toward me.

"Did she suffer a good deal, after she went to Amerika—*Jugas* Brita, I mean...and the little Anna-Christina?" She shuddered then, as if a sudden draft had come into the room.

"Yes, she did."

Bringing the handkerchief instinctively to her mouth she took a deep breath, looking at me again with a sad smile, shaking her head as she settled a little deeper beneath the shawl.

"I believe they both suffered a good deal...at first, based on what my aunt could recall from conversations with her grandmother...*Jugas*-Brita. When Grandmother...Anna Christine, was older, she and her mother were somewhat shunned to some degree in the community. I'm not certain why, but I assume it had to do with the fundamentalist nature of the Free Church community—they were all quite—religious. Everyone in the community knew the child—Anna Christine—was illegitimate. Even though Brita eventually married and bore three more children, it apparently didn't erase the first sin in the communities' eyes. And my grandmother...there was no doubt she suffered, probably mostly at school. I know some of her half brothers and sisters didn't even treat her, or her eventual children, all that well, even though she had raised them, herself—as a big sister."

She considered this. "Such a pity they had to suffer. Sometimes it seems the lot in life for some."

I nodded, again, hoping she would continue. She sat motionless for a long time before speaking again.

"I knew her, you know...*Jugas* Brita? And of course little Anna too...your grandmother, as an infant.

I had to steady my breathing then; my heart was beating in my throat. I still hadn't asked the big question yet.

"How beautiful a child she was, too. When I was a girl, I used to hold her—even pretend she was mine. I was hardly more than eight, then—before it all happened and ages before I was married. They left soon after Anna-Christine was born, left in a longboat, for *Amerika*, rowing up the Västerdalälven in a snowstorm. I stood with my mother and brother and watched them disappear. And then they took the ship to *Amerika* I guess, maybe from *Kristiania*[5], in Norway.

"You saw all that?" I couldn't believe what I was hearing.

"Of course I saw it. I even held little Christine while Brita settled herself in the longboat—the last time her foot touched the earth of

Dalarna. It was so very, very cold and windy; I remember," she said again, distantly. "Not many people came to see them off in that storm.

I began to wish I'd brought in my notebook. This information...I really need to write it down.

"I would often take care of little Anna-Christine, when *Jugas* Brita was in the *fäbod*—the forest—do you know about *fäbodarna*?"

I nodded: "Uh-huh."

"Brita and I were close friends, despite our age differences and even throughout the troubles that came from Carl and the court—and our mother."

Here she trailed off as if she had said too much; or, God forbid, lost interest. I had been literally holding my breath.

"You actually knew *Jugas* Brita—my...my great-grandmother—then?"

I was astonished. This was something I hadn't counted on at all. This woman could be the source of even more information than I'd imagined. My mind raced to grasp it all. Of course, she'd have known Brita, though they came from different social classes—her family being much higher, socially...than mine. They had to have been neighbors there in the farm community—Skålö.

I crossed and uncrossed my legs. Karolina hadn't spoken again for some time. She seemed reluctant to go on. I was trying to sort out these new revelations in my mind. She just stared at the reflection in the window pane.

"Yes...I knew them all," she finally offered, turning toward me again with that wan smile of resignation. "Sometimes, when I really feel...old, I think I know everything—have known everything from the time I was born. You see, it seems so much at times...a burden—the comings and goings—births, deaths, gossips, loves—hates...and there were plenty of all of them, let me tell you...they were difficult times in Sweden, then, for many. Very difficult times."

Here, she seemed to hesitate—seemed to be thinking; as if she'd recalled something in particular. But then she came out of the pensive state.

"You said you did not particularly wish to know about *Jugas* Brita—may I ask why? She was your...great-grandmother. That was the scandal, then. Everyone talked about it—for years—and the trial. Then, when she and that beautiful child emigrated to *Amerika*, all alone, except for those two younger, twin brothers of hers. Oh, what were their names?"

She fidgeted with the handkerchief, troubled at her inability to recall. "She took them with her, anyway. And good riddance to them both, I said then. What were their names? They were terrible to me…in school, they were."

I couldn't remember, either and waited again, for her to go on in her own time. Presently she said:

"Who else did you wish to question me about…I am sorry, I am rambling again?"

I debated once more, whether I hardly dared broach the sensitive subject of her mother. Maybe I should let well enough alone. So far she'd been cooperative—I'd gotten far more than I'd expected, but, just maybe. Taking a chance, I asked her:

"Anna-Stina Malmberg Fröman—your mother? She's the other person I wished to speak to you about, Karolina."

She sat up straighter and leveled hard eyes on me for the first time. "And exactly what did you wish to ask about my mother?"

I hesitated, "She—your mother…had four *oäkta* children, herself, I believe, before she married your father?"

Though her expression remained unchanged, she didn't answer me. She simply turned back toward the window again, with an air of finality. Finally she spoke: "I find I have become…rather tired, young man. I do not wish to continue this interview further. Would you mind leaving now."

So there it was. I was afraid asking something that personal might take it too far and it had. I wasn't particularly taken aback at this change in attitude…I'd already gotten far more information from her than I'd hoped for. But I was also disappointed; no doubt about it. I sat for another moment—praying she might reconsider. I'd taken my chance and it seemed I'd overstepped her bounds. I exhaled loudly—almost a sigh, not realizing I'd been so tense. I stood up. She still hadn't moved.

"I'm sorry cousin Karolina, I didn't mean to offend you. It was just that…I was searching the old records and found so many strange occurrences involving your mother, too. Given the times? The Swedish Church…being so strong, so dominant in all affairs of the community? For any woman to have that many children without being married, I thought—well I thought that possibly you could satisfy my curiosity

31

about how she, of all people, got away with it. None of the cousins up north seem to know anything. There were so many unanswered questions in the dates...things...I thought, I just thought...."

But only silence in return from her. She continued staring into the darkness. I picked up the chair and returned it to the wall. "Anyway, Karolina...thank you once again for seeing me. I'm sorry to have come without...advance notice. And I hope my questions didn't offend you. Believe me, that was not my intention."

I glanced at her again; she seemed more frail, slumped there in her chair—vulnerable. Her shoulders had shrunken beneath the bright shawl. I walked toward the closed door and as I pulled the handle, she said:

"You thought I might give away all the secrets...before I died?"

Surprised, I turned, but didn't know what to answer.

"Didn't you...?" she persisted, this time turning her head toward me, out of the shadow. She was crying quietly. I wanted to walk over, put a hand on her shoulder, and kneel beside her...anything to make up for the sadness my inconsiderate prying had brought. In the short time of the interview I'd come to appreciated her spirit.

"I...Karolina, it's just—it seemed someone should know the truth. There are so many very puzzling questions when one delves into records—disappearing children—questions that bore answering, I thought, for—for posterity—or, I guess, for my own selfish interests, if no one else ever becomes interested." She just stared at me. "Is there something...something so terrible, in the past, Karolina? I never wanted to offend you or your family. I knew Anna-Stina Malmberg was your mother and mother—I—I guess...to my great-grandfather. And I thought...well, because of that, you might be able to sort out the truth for my curiosity. If something was wrong—then—a hundred years ago, should the truth not be told—even today?"

"Mere curiosity...you went to all that work—came all that distance from *Amerika*, for mere curiosity?"

Her insight was accurate; I didn't know how to explain my strong sense of curiosity to her, without looking like the selfish person I had been.

"Well...no, not entirely; I found the mystery, at first intriguing, then...as I learned more, fascinating. Now—I want, more than ever, to write a book—possibly a novel—fiction I guess it would have to be, I don't know...about it...about what happened to my grandmother."

She sort of "harrumphed" then, as if to prove herself correct. "So...you wished write a novel...sell it for money. My family—*your* family?"

"No, not that at all...I'd hoped to make up the hundred year gap in my family's history; nothing more. If a novel or documented history came of it, so much the better."

I now felt the true sadness in my voice. But I went on: "And if it meant finding some answers...yes, you seemed to be the only person still around who could contribute anything, any longer meaningful, unless I found some yet-to-turn-up letters, diaries, or...." I trailed off.

I hung my head in disappointment; I'd come so close. She'd given me a glimpse...and I'd—I'd pushed it too far and now we were both miserable. I turned the handle, swung the door and stepped over the threshold and began slipping into my jacket. I drew a breath, prepared to bid her good by, when she spoke again, so quietly, I hardly heard her.

"Do you know what *hjortron* are?"

I stepped back over the threshold: "I—no..." I scratched my head, wondering at the reason for her question, "...what is it?"

"It is not an it...she replied, a little irritable. "*Hjortronbär*'—berries...*jam?*"

She sat for a moment, staring at her hands, working the handkerchief nervously in her lap.

"If you wish to return tomorrow—at nine in the morning, you can bring some *hjortronbärsylt*. Here, they think it is too expensive and not particularly good for us—because I eat so much of it if I have it. You can find it at the grocer's. In exchange for my story, you can bring a jar to me. A large one," she added as an afterthought.

My heart leaped...she'd relented!

She smiled a wry smile. "I like it on ice cream and I have not had any for...since I can not remember...have you never had it?"

I shook my head, fearful that if I spoke I would wake from the new dream. I thought I'd lost my chance—but she's inviting me back and for an interview.

"You and I shall eat ice cream with a spoon of *hjortronbärsylt* on it. It is very good; you will like it. And I will tell you a little story...tomorrow. And they will make us coffee, too. I will see to it."

"Yes—ma'am—I will be here." I nodded to myself. "With the—with the stuff you said, too."

"*Hjörtronbär*...I do not know the English word for them, but I will ask someone."

"Yes—and thank you for seeing me so late. I—I really didn't think—I didn't know what you would say."

"Nine..." she repeated, again, "...*hjörtronbär*...write it down young man."

"Yes—nine," I repeated, "I will." Smiling and beside myself I left the room quickly with a final wave.

"Yes! Yes!" I said to myself, walking quickly up the hallway, nearly running. "Yes!" She knows! And she's going to trade the answers for a jar of jelly.

IT BEGINS...

The day following our first meeting was Monday. I had no idea what Karolina would be able to relate to me, but what I'd heard the previous afternoon was...fascinating. She certainly seemed lucid— even spicy, near the end of our meeting. But I didn't want to take any chances; I called the airlines and canceled my flight for Wednesday, booking it for the following Friday. I'd been prepared to leave Sweden empty-handed, calling it a unique vacation, but now, I'd at least have an hour or two with her. I also called the cousins up north to let them know I'd met her and that she'd agreed to talk more the following day. I got my cousin Lisa when I called.

"She talked to me, Lisa... took a bit of patience, but she talked about the family and she even invited me back in the morning. She said she had more to tell me."

"The men are in the barn, milking," she said. I will pass along the message. That is really surprising...her talking to you. Good luck tomorrow."

So the next morning I stopped at a small, grocer to buy the golden colored *hjörtronbärsylt*—or cloud berry jam, as I learned it was called, in English. Lucky for me they had one jar remaining. When I commented to the grocer about the low stock gave me another lesson.

"This jam is not rare," the owner related, "but it is seasonal, since the berries grow only in the north. Once they are gone—it is gone for the year."

On the street again, I ducked into a flower shop and grabbed a nice bouquet and headed to the nursing home.

A different nurse escorted me this morning and what a difference, in daylight. She'd been forewarned, too, that I was coming, pointing it out as we strolled.

"How good it is to see Karolina has a visitor—especially from America."

I listened to her comments as we worked our way toward the rear of the building, "...toward the sun room," she'd said. It was a sort of greenhouse wing, jutting from the building's southern side. Encased in glass like a hot house, chairs and tables with umbrellas filled the space. Green, potted plants ringed its parameter, lining the waist-high shelves. Here and there a plant, full of blossoms, flourished in the near tropical heat. But others stood stiff—withered from lack of water and nurturing, or simply past their prime. The sun was just rising above the horizon, at 9:00 a.m.. We were above 60 degrees north latitude; it was near Christmas and the winter solstice; winter days still began late and ended early.

At a table near the center of the large space, Karolina was sitting, with her back to us.

"Does she not look nice this morning…dressed for Sunday visitors, I think? You must be special, *Herr* Andersson," she said, flirting a little and smiling.

"Not many will agree with that." Eager to speak with Karolina and hardly noticing the flirtation, I thanked her at the door and watched her slender figure disappear around the corner before I turned back to my elderly hostess.

Karolina sat in a large lounge, a flowing, gown and robe affair draping each side. In the bright morning light, the difference the colorful garment made in her appearance from the previous evening was startling. Her hair, now tightly drawn up into a bun, hadn't a strand out of place; it was obvious she'd taken special care for today's visit. A good sign; could it mean she would be somewhat more forthcoming toward my questions? I must be careful asking about her mother, I thought   She looked much younger than the previous afternoon. The bright light enhanced her youthful appearance, rather than accent her age and her posture was even better; she sat straight, upright, alert.

In my hotel room the previous evening, unable to sleep for excitement, I'd drawn up a list of questions and was well prepared to query her thoroughly and get out before she could change her mind.

"*God dagen Karolina*," I greeted her in Swedish, walking around the table opposite her, "may I sit here?"

"Good day," she answered me back in English. "Please do…oh, you have brought me some lovely flowers. We will have to get a vase from staff." With a flourish of her blue-veined hand, she indicated the wrought iron chair opposite her and I sank back comfortably into the thick, floral print cushions. She was drinking coffee; a carafe and an extra cup were convenient on the tray. "Would you like *kaffee*?" she pronounced the word in the Swedish style. She leaned forward, preparing to pour, appearing the perfect hostess.

"Yes I would, thank you. I didn't know you spoke English, Karolina? And so well, too."

She removed the cup and saucer from the tray, placed them on the table, turning the cup's handle conveniently to my right. "Yes, for years. You see, my late husband was a businessman, involved on an international scale; we had all sorts of house guests, coming and going, many from Great Britain and a few even from America. I had to improve my English…though I still do not speak it well, but you are charitable to say so." She twisted the top of the carafe with some difficulty and began to pour the bone-white cup nearly full.

"Sounds pretty good to me," I said, watching the strong coffee stop short of the top.

"Certainly better than my Swedish."

With effort and slightly shaking hand, she carefully slid the cup across the glass tabletop, indicating with a flourish and a smile, the condiments, a small cream pitcher and *sockerskål* full of sugar cubes…for me to help myself.

"Thanks—I'll only take a little cream." I tipped a little of the thick cream into the very strong coffee, stirring with a small spoon.

"This cream is as thick as *tjöckmjölk*[8]," I said, referring to the local Swedish yogurt, commonly used on cereal.

"I've rediscovered it since I came to Sweden. They always made it—kept it alive, at my grandmother's home farm in America."

"Really? I wish you could have brought some with you; it is not the same down here. I have not had real *tjöckmjölk* since I was a girl, at home in Skålbyn. Now that you remind me of it, *smultron*[9] seem to accompany the memory."

Her mention of wild strawberries prompted me. "Karolina, I have brought you *hjörtronbar sylt*." I flourished the jar from the shop, unwrapping and placing it on the table before her, as if it were a fine crystal offering, label forward.

"Oh how nice of you—you are so thoughtful," she said, just as if she hadn't asked me to bring it the day before. "I will cherish every bowl of ice cream I have with it and—you must try it too, with me. I only hope those girls in the kitchen won't eat half of it before you get the opportunity."

After glancing over her shoulder, she lowered her head,

confidentially speaking in a lower tone: "They have some thieves here…" she leaned closer, "…I lose articles of clothing all the time—books, too."

I began to wonder whether she was going to ramble along like this making small talk; it must have shown in my face.

"But, here I am chatting about nothing—what shall we speak of this morning?"

I'd already made myself comfortable, placing my note pad on the opposite side of the table. I took it up and peeled back the page covering my list of questions. Before I could get my list unfolded, Karolina began.

"My mother was an unbelievable woman; so much so, I always felt inadequate around her. If she had not been such a caring mother, I would have been envious, I believe."

I was trying to get my tablet arranged and find my pen. She looked down, pausing in thought for a second and then continued dictating like a business executive.

"Mother was born Anna-Stina Malmberg in 1825—June 14th….in Snöån in Järna, Vansbro Kommun, now, but *Dalarnas Lan*, then…Dalarna Sweden. Lars Malmberg and Anna Helgsten were her parents. Lars, my grandfather, was a *hammarsmedsmästare*...such a long word, in Andersfors Bruk—what do you call that trade in English?

"*Uhhh*…a—master blacksmith…I think…iron worker, maybe…?"

"Yes? Well, we had a small house at Andersfors; it was furnished by Stora Kopparbergs Bergslags. Do you know them?" she asked as I rapidly scribbled. Barely glancing up, I nodded vigorously for her to continue, being familiar with the name of the oldest, continuously operating company in the world…which started as a copper mine. She went on.

"My father was Carl Gustaf Julius Fröman. He was about the same age as mother, born the 6th of May, 1823. My father was a fairly well-to-do farmer's son; my mother's father was a near pauper—a blacksmith, as you said, working for wages, for Bergslaget, the company. In January of…I believe it was 1847, mother—yet unmarried, bore a daughter out of wedlock. As you correctly called it, an *oäktabarn*; the child died the following year, in April."

She paused while I scribbled. Finally, I looked up. She was

waiting for me, watching my pen.

"So there was illegitimacy in this family before your grandmother, young man. The child that died...was my older and only, sister."

Again, I nodded, though this was news to me.

"My mother was—raped—in the *fäbod*...Vansberget[10]—you know where that place is? No? It was—is, up the Vanån, on the west side, up the mountain. Mother was a *vallkulla* there in a small settlement...a summer farm."

I nodded again, remembering my cousin telling me about the summer mountain farms. The local women—*vallkullor*, he'd called them, moved into the hill forests in early summer, taking with them their children, goats, cows...even grandmothers, to help. Remaining there all summer, they grazed the animals, gathering animal fodder—grass and even plucked birch leaves for the animals to eat. Lacking refrigeration, the milk from the twice daily milking was turned into butter and cheese, greatly reducing its bulk, so as to be more easily transported down to populated areas, to be sold.

I recalled that as children my mother and her sisters had also been *vallkullor* while growing up in the early 20th Century, in Wisconsin, following the cows around the meadows and woods while they grazed. There were no fences to keep them from straying, so the children had to remain with them all day.

She hardly drew a breath and as she came into the pace of her tale, as I wrote furiously. I wanted to stop her and ask questions, but didn't, fearing she'd loose her stories' thread. Her voice, stronger than the evening before, now settled into a cadence that carried her through to lunch, on for three more hours. She displayed a fantastic memory, the life of Sweden in the 1800s, as her parents had probably related it to her and as she had lived it as a young girl as she continued rather dreamily:

"I suppose it all began at Andersfors, where mother moved with her parents...in western Dalarna, the sort of iron tool factory I told you about."

)

CHAPTER 2

The Walk Home
About 1842

Whitsun dawned clear and warm for the last day of May. Homeward bound to the settlement of Andersfors Bruk[11], county of Vansbro, Province of Dalarna, Sweden, the party of eleven odd families neared their journey's end. The half-day's walk, to and from church, tired worshipers less than the berating they received from the staunch minister. Returning from Järna Church, they gossiped, chided and teased one other as they trod the forest track.

Relieved after the five-hour worship service and divided again as friends, companions and lovers, their excitement grew as their homes drew nearer. Long before humans followed them, the animal trails— rough paths, crossed over hills and wound around lake's shores, narrowing at times, forcing the walkers into single file, then widening again, so lovers could walk hand-in-hand.

By mid-journey the path had narrowed as they trod deeper into the ancient, conifer forest. Where light reached deep enough to support smaller growth, gray moss hung between house-sized stones, strewn about the forest as if left from an undisciplined child-giant's play. It was in such places forest spirits dwelt. One should beware— least troll spring from beneath one of the stones. Ankle deep with gray-green moss, *blåbär* and *lingonbär*[12] plants, sprung from within the carpeted depths to the height of a child's waist, turning the forest floor alternately dark blue in July and bright red by the middle of August, as the berries ripened.

Along the waists of the ridges, clear springs seeped, and then flowed, spreading into forest pools, only to disappear and reappear again further down the valley. To bypass impenetrable, wet areas, flat rocks had long ago been laid to keep traveler's feet dry. Though children made a game of springing from stone to stone, these proved an encumbrance for the old, the infirm, or those burdened with pregnancy, or carrying sleeping children. Clumsy birch-bark shoes did not enhance the walker's step. Some chose bare feet and faired better. There was seldom a pair of leather shoes among the worshipers.

By this time of evening the journeyers cared little for anything but the end of their weekly trek, to complete their home chores, share a family meal and finally retire to the warmth of their hearth, before bed, to enjoy some rest before beginning another week of work in the iron forge.

As the party approached the home settlement, they began congregating once again into individual family units: mothers took charge of tired children, arranging them in the care of unwilling, siblings and potential sweethearts separated and fell back into their respective family units.

The iron workings had been active for at least three hundred years, possibly earlier, beginning when primitive man stepped boldly into the Iron Age, having already mastered copper and bronze. At Andersfors, metal bars were wrought into workable stock, often to be sledded elsewhere for further rework, or distributed to smiths around Scandinavia. As in other locations in Scandinavia, Viking fore-bearers probably mined and smelted the ore, borne by hand, from around the area—one man, one heavy basket of iron-rich rock, carried suspended on the end of a pole over the bearer's shoulder. Smelting and then forging armaments here, Vikings wrought weapons that would conquer half the western world, planting Nordic seed in aboriginal populations as far away as North America.

Andersfors, as it came to be known, sprawled around a small lake, the outlet of which flowed through a small water mill, powering rollers and hammer mills. Thus Stora Kopparbergs Bergslaget, the large iron and copper mining company headquartered in Falun—far to the east, reached far and wide.

The three hour-long Sunday sermons were the same, every *söndag*—sometimes even longer in duration; those who traveled the farthest were anxious for the minister's chiding to end, anticipating the hour of gossip which usually followed outside, weather permitting. An opportunity to catch up on news, it was a special time when the townspeople and country folk alike could barter events of their community and themselves.

Then the long walk home, tiring though it was, came also as welcome relief. The daily work in their forest-factory was endless and a day away from these chores and the small socialization after church was welcome, even when it meant bearing the chastisement of the minister for their inescapable and endless sins.

By church law, all able persons must make the journey and be present at the church service. In the event of sickness, at least one from each family must attend and carry the Message of the sermon home and relate it to the absent family members. Rich or poor, healthy or ill—each and every Sunday without fail, to Järna church and back, they must trod. Had they lived nearer the river, the convenience of a sixteen-oared wooden longboat...a *kyrkbåt*[13], which plied the Västerdalven each Sunday and would have eased their miserable walk; as it was, they lived deep in the forest and could only meet the boat part way.

Trudging beside his wife, *hammarsmedsmästare*, Lars Malmberg was re-living the previous day's meal of boiled potatoes and creamed herring—*potatis och sill*. His wife Anna had prepared more than enough for the family meal; they'd finished the left-overs during today's church service, supplementing the meager offering with flat bread. Lars very much enjoyed potatoes, now nearly the last of the previous summer's remaining crop in the small cellar, dug into the hillside beside their timber house. Soon they would enjoy *ny potatis*[14] from their thriving garden. Lars enjoyed dipping the steaming, white lumps into soft butter, when they could afford that precious commodity. This would leave small flecks of green dill weed behind, to be gleaned with one big finger run round his bowl. Anna, his good wife and mother of his children, made the extra provisions go very far in her family's diet, purchased as they were from the company store...at a premium.

The previous day, beside the spring, Anna had soaked the small, dried fish again and again, rinsing away much of the heavy coating of salt preserving them. She rolled the fish pieces in *råg*[15] and *korn*[16] meal, adding onions, also from their cellar. Then she cooked them in pork fat, adding more coarse ground flour and milk near the end, until she had a thick *völling*[17] bubbling in the pan. This thickened sauce took on the strong essence of the browned fish, onions and Providence knew what other flavors she had conjured to bring out the delicious taste. Feeling appropriately repentant for the sin of greed that so often visited him, Lars now felt very hungry after the three-hour walk. Though he had eaten his share during the church service, he knew he could easily eat again. But it was not to be.

Thoughts of the meal hardly lightened his mood, having been brooding for over a week. After the church service, as his wife and daughters socialized with the other women, he'd taken advantage of an empty place in a cart that was being taken to the nearby Bergslaget in Snöåbruk. He was not surprised that they were modernizing the works, but he was shocked by the extent being taken. He recognized the coming destiny of workers like himself and began to brood over his inevitable fate.

The additions to the giant structure, perched as it was beside the faster flowing stream, carried more head[18] and would have the capacity to shape more iron in a day than could his small anvil in a whole week. He was a simple man but not a stupid man and knew when he was about to be beaten—possibly even replaced.

The need for iron maker's skills from his small home shop would not vanish. So long as there were animals to be shod, gates and hinges to make and repair, he would probably be able to feed his family. But he had none other than these skills. How were they to live, he wondered, without picking up and moving nearer the need for his services? His father had also been a *smed*. Possibly, the company would make another position for him and others like him; this could mean having to join the unskilled labor pool in the Snöåbruk forge. Anders was a proud man and proud of his special skills at the anvil and did not relish the thought of demotion or the cut in his already meager earnings. Worse, yet, to have to resort to being a *dräng*[19].

"Ahhh…" he sighed. There was little recourse but to remove some of the expense from his family.

"Cut the cost…" he had told his wife at the beginning of their walk home from church. "We will have to economize. Maybe some of the children could work out. It would save feeding them."

"Hush!" His wife had shushed him. "They will hear you, Lars.

We can speak of it later, when we are in bed."

Of course she was right and he didn't broach the subject again. But he thought about it: once his oldest daughter, Anna-Stina, went out to work, this would help; possibly, she could even give them some of her wages. At least, they wouldn't have to feed her any longer. Free to take any position she could find, she was fortunate, having already received a generous offer as kitchen maid from the Lutheran pastor's wife in Nås. The position also bore the possibility of her some day graduating from housemaid to caring for the families' cows and goats in their mountain pasture as a *vallkulla*[20]. The old grandmother who had held the position for the last decade had finally died.

Anna and he had discussed the matter the previous week and were relieved at their daughter's good fortune. And she had concluded the agreement this very day. They had been concerned that her headstrong disposition might challenge the minister or his wife's patience. There was also the girl's newly gained, but unfortunate, reputation...as an unmarried mother. But even this had not daunted the clergy folk. For some reason, not apparent to them, the old minister himself had personally requested her. Fortunately, it was probably her superior reputation for caring for livestock in some previous *fäbod*. That and her skill with cheese making had no doubt brought her the generous offer.

Two years had passed since the birth of Anna-Stina's illegitimate daughter. The still-willful girl continued to mourn her daughter's untimely death, which occurred before the child passed her second year. God, in his infinite wisdom and mystery to mortal man, chose to take their sickly granddaughter and as usual, such a young burial brought sadness to the forest community. They had commemorated the child's interment again today at the church service.

Thinking about the job offer again, Providence, Lars mused, only knew how the vicar and his wife came to even know of their daughter, dwelling as far away as they did. When news came of the offer and they broaching the subject with Anna-Stina, they found her eager to accept...eager to flee the forest confines and the remoteness of their home.

Privately, Anna Helgsten wondered whether her daughter's reputation with the *fiol*[21] or *säckpipa*[22] had possibly won her the post; the minister's wife loved music and few could match Anna-Stina's skill and feeling for rendering the old Nordic melodies. She would spend hours tinkering with the *säckpipa*, tweaking the reed, blowing and testing the chanter, then tweaking the reed in the drone, until she had them singing to her satisfaction. Then she'd fill the skin bag with several strong puffs, tuck the bulging bag beneath her arm, turn her pert head to one side and with a far away look, play a melody so plaintive, it was said, it could make cream turn to golden butter without the churn. The notes she struck, warbled and trilled so mournfully, would melt even the sternest heart. Like most of the old tunes they were in the minor key and even the happy songs bore a melancholy chord. It was said of the people of Dalarna—that they even laughed in a minor key.

Aspiring young boys and even older men, having long since surrendered hope of gaining Anna-Stina's affections, renewed their longing on these summer evenings when she played or sang. At other times, the eternal *midsommar*[23] light grew richer as the sound of her violin ranged over the village, bringing many who heard it, to pause and contemplate their purpose in life. And if she sang—more than one husband would roll over in his marital bed, turning his back to his mate and lay listening with a longing heart, hopelessly dreaming of Anna-Stina's strong arms and beautiful eyes...forever beyond his reach.

Anna Helgsten, having learned from her own mother, taught her daughters to play. And before she was hardly able to hold the pipes, let alone fill the calfskin bag fully with breath, she knew Anna-Stina was skilled. Every woman in Anna's family had learned the pipes, for as long as memory served. But none had earned the repute of Anna-Stina and at such a young age. Strange, the young girl had seemed so fickle and capricious in so many other things, but took to music like food and drink.

Where boys were concerned, she seemed to wrap them round like a lock of her hair and then spurn them in a whim, only to choose another. Strange that they never seemed to bear her ill will after the encounters and continued hanging about her, probably hoping for further attention. Likewise, the girl continued to offer genuine care, concern and attention to all the young people, which kept them returning again, as friends.

Her mother could not fathom her daughter's latest plight and pitied her the grief of a lost child. Anna-Stina had never caused her parents trouble, until nearing her twenty-second year. Then tongues

did wag, though and it came as such a surprise—her pregnancy—
since no one in the community could think of any one she cared a
whit about and Anna-Stina was not one to be casual with any boy, at
least to that degree. Thus, her parents were shocked when she
announced that she was with child.

Apparently it had been conceived during the summer in the
fäbod. More surprising, Anna-Stina was totally mute as to the
father's identity. Even with persistent threats, by both parents and
even the minister, she would not reveal her lover, preferring to suffer
in adamant silence, alone in her shame and the scorn of the
community.

And suffer she did. Anna-Stina, shuddered with the cold,
hugging herself as she stumbled home from church, walking alone
ahead of her parents. She still felt empty without the infant in her
arms. For nearly two years, she'd borne the sickly child everywhere,
ever attendant to the poor darling's suffering. But to no end; she
wasn't surprised when the child died—though it was no easier to
accept. The infant seemed wrong from the start—the circumstances
of conception—the birth; a terrible beginning that ended in an even
worse way. But the child's death seemed once and for all, to put to
rest what had begun so terribly; the communities' judgment of her.

She could never forget the *kyrktagningen*[24]—enduring the ordeal
of the ancient church ceremony. Forced to remain in wooden pillory,
standing before the entryway to the church, before and after the
church service, she was publicly shamed for her bastard child. She
alone was punished for her sin. Had she been wed before the birth,
the same ceremony would have been a celebration inside the church.
As it was an *oäkta* child, she and her child were shamed every Sunday
until the deacons decided she had learned her lesson and set
sufficient example for the rest of the younger and more probable
transgressors in the community who might likely stray along the same
path. Three Sundays they humiliated her.

"But I have gotten ahead of myself," Karolina said, looking up.
Karolina's tone broke me from the dream I had fallen into.

"First, you must gain a flavor for how my mother came to be in
this condition and the grief it brought her, for nearly the remainder of
her life."

"OK…" I stammered, still a little caught up in the past, "whatever insight you are able to offer."

"Are you aware of that term, *kyrktagning*?"

"No, I can't say as I am. What does it mean?"

"Literally—I am uncertain, but possibly…caught by the church, or something like that. It is a very old word. In the Church of Sweden, I believe around 1600, the powers in control—the bishops—decided there were too many births taking place, without the benefit of marriage. That was not an unusual happenstance in old Sweden; women have always been strong minded, eager to get a child with a man she liked, marry him if she liked…or not marry him and keep the child that resulted. Even possibly choose a different man. There were always enough family around to take care of her and the child, if need-be: her father, mother, sisters."

"I see. That's a different outlook."

"The church in its wisdom, decided to ban this custom, or should I say habit…what *they* called primitive practice and to impose a sense of shame and sin along with it. Couples found to have a child without being wed, were first offered matrimony, but if it was declined, which it seldom was, they were publicly punished. This took the form of the pillory—do you know what they are?"

"Oh, yes—they used them in the America colonies—along with the stocks. And for the same reasons—church, or community instituting punishment for sins—sins determined by the church minister, or the deacons, if they happen to be more democratic."

"I see, I did not realize that, although…I suppose it was a common European form of punishment, I wonder whether the custom may have come to America from the early Scandinavian settlers, also."

"Yes, possibly—I hadn't thought about that. The first Swedish settlement—in the New Jersey area—only followed the Mayflower—English Pilgrim's colony—by thirty or so years."

"Yes? Well…there you are." She continued: "The parents of *oäkta* children were placed in the pillory before the church entrance as examples of what would come from these misbehaviors. Those pious parishioners, thinking themselves above such sin, were encouraged to abuse the couples—kicking them and spitting upon them at worst, making accusatory comments to them, at best."

"Not surprising, considering the history of much church conduct in the world, to date," I said.

"Because of the ease of denial, the fathers of *oäkta* children were not usually included in the punishment, since it was impossible, without their own admission, to prove they were the other guilty party in the consummation." She paused, silently staring at me at this point. She seemed to wish to emphasize how fortunate we men were to get off so easily, letting the women take our share of the burden. I was unable to meet her gaze and pretended to make another note on my pad.

"Disgusting," I commented to my pencil as I doodled in the margin, shaking my head, but still not looking up.

Karolina continued: "These punishments often took place before the *vapenhuse*—the entrance to the church."

Vapenhus...what's that?"

"The large room on the front entrance to the old churches. It was where the Vikings were supposed to leave their weapons when they entered the church to worship—least they come to blows inside, otherwise.

"Ah—*vapenhus*—weapon's-house, probably, in English."

"Sitting outside in the pillory in wintertime, so soon after giving birth, often killed many young mothers. So they permitted them to be moved inside...to the little room, after everyone had walked past them on their way into the church. Later, when the pillory was finally abolished, the girls still had to sit in the *vapenhus* for several Sundays, before the ceremony, until they were finally welcomed back to the church congregation and permitted to be inside the church with the rest of the parishioners."[25]

I was writing furiously and asking few questions. This was fabulous information—unbelievable. How was I ever going to be able to leave, I thought.

"Of course, you knew the men and women sat on different sides of the church in those days?"

"No. Why""

"Yes...well, things were much different then. People were even permitted to eat food during the service—sermons were so long...and boring," she seemed to add as an afterthought. "It was often difficult to remain awake—sometimes there was even a good deal of conversation, as the ministers preached, trying to reach their flock's conscience. They faced forward and had to listen to the minister's tirades for hours. Should they nod off, they were prodded awake by a designated member the church. The women—on the left side—sat directly before the pastor who was perched high in a pulpit above them. It was as if they, being closest to him—were the greatest sinners and in need of the most warning."

She paused, no doubt to emphasize the remoteness of the male, church population from the minister's chastisements. But I didn't glance up this time, trying not to feel guilty, simply for being a man.

"It may have once been the same, in America. Puritans…they had a long, wooden pole they would use to rap anyone on the shoulder or head if caught dozing."

"Then it crossed the ocean—that—that lack of forgiveness…lack of tolerance."

I only nodded.

"My mother said the first time that she bore an *oäkta* child, she was forgiven the shame of the pillory; but not later.

'Later…?" I asked, preparing to write.

"Yes, later—but, first, I must tell you how it all began."

I took a deep breath. Oh, so much to remember.

"My mother bore four children out of wedlock, including, of course, me." She paused as if waiting for me to comment. I kept my pen moving steadily, refusing to look up. She wasn't going to get me to bite on that theme, again.

"The first child," she finally continued, "a girl…died. The second, Per Gustaf, also died. The third, my brother Carl, you know about and the fourth and last, was me. During this time, at least for the last three of us, we had the same pastor, one by the name of Johansson."

She stopped speaking and when I'd caught up, I glanced up, thinking she was waiting for me. But she was staring at the spoon she had picked up, turning it over and over in her lap.

"In the beginning…he was an understudy, newly-arrived from the south—Uppsala…Stockholm, I can not recall and it was before I was born. But he eventually took the Järna church and began to try to make over the congregation in his own image—not God's. He made his biggest mistake when he tried to do that to my mother—not to mention, falling in love with her…."

Again she paused. I glanced up.

"Possibly, I should have my lunch now...do you mind, Alex?"

I glanced at my wristwatch. Good Lord, where had the time gone.

"No, certainly...I, well, thank you for the information, Karolina. I very much appreciate your taking the time with me this morning. And thanks for the coffee." I rose and began gathering my things.

"Oh—you can just leave those things there."

"What?"

"Your writing materials...just leave them there. For later...after lunch. We will continue."

"You mean...?"

"You can find somewhere to have lunch, can you not?" she asked a little irritable, getting up with some effort.

"Why...yes, certainly," I said, taking her arm and helping her to stand.

"I have become stiff...the peril of growing...well then—return in an hour, can you?"

"You are not finished, then?"

"Finished? Why—I have not even begun, yet. Do you want this information young man, or do you not?"

Now I'd upset her. "Oh, yes...very much. I want it."

"Very good..." She turned and walked stiffly away, leaving me to find my way out.

CHAPTER 3

Meeting the Devil

Karolina was at the table when I returned an hour later. I'd planned to hurry back, compose my notes and be ready for her, so I'd snatched a quick meal from the *smörgåsbord* that the hotel set, daily. She was back in her place, gently swinging one, crossed leg in obvious impatience. I expected we would chat a little about our lunches before beginning.

"The hotel sets a fine *smörgåsbord*," I commented.

She'd nodded, "Yes, I understand they do." She continued to regard me without speaking, until I sat down and gathered up my note pad and pen again. I'd no sooner folded back the written sheets and she began.

"His name...was Pastor Henrik Johansson and he came from money—in the south, as I mentioned. The village welcomed him as sort of a lay pastor, one not yet ordained by the Swedish Lutheran Church. He was clean, polite and bore no end of stories of the well-to-do personages he had been brought up with and who were financing his missionary work among the poor country folk, where my parents and I lived. He'd attended university in Uppsala, I believe and we were his first parish. At first, all the women and girls were curious about such an eligible and wealthy bachelor. And soon, they fawned over him at any gathering where he appeared—anxious for a flattering word in his sophisticated accent, or a lingering glance. After all, he was a bachelor and considered a good match. He had a quick smile for all the girls, which came with every compliment of them. He had a curious way of following his serious thoughts, or comments, with a sort of...'hummm,' as if he was contemplating the wisdom, or possibly the sanctity of his own thought and that you should also. Frankly, it was something I personally found offensive, young as I was."

At first, the young minister's attentions had flattered Anna-Stina. When he made the journey to Andersfors to call, which wasn't often, given the distance, he began to pay more and more attention to the smith's daughter. Though she knew him to be, beneath the carefully cut, black frock coat, merely another man with men's thoughts, he did bring sophisticated knowledge to the deep forest, something she was at first, grateful for.

It was some while before she noticed he was spending a good deal of time at her father's *smedja*²⁶, asking for advice about the malleability of red-hot iron and the different results of dipping the glowing iron in water. What, she thought, did he care about these things? An observant girl, she found all this curious from a city-bred man, but attributed to a casual interest in the alchemy of molding the near-molten iron.

But soon she tired of his senseless chatter of the city life and began to ignore his ever-increasing attentions, bored with the shallowness of his comments. He grew into the habit of lingering late into the day, in order to be invited to stay to the evening meal and then the night, as was the custom. She had to endure his attentions, anew and agreed when her father commented one day in his absence, that they seemed to get more of their equal share of the pastor, for which he was duly chided by his wife. Anna-Stina said nothing directly to Pastor Johansson until he tried to kiss her, against her will. This happened beside the well, when he thought no one else was looking. She came to know his true nature at last.

But even then, she still thought him simply a better educated and better dressed though, still clumsy young man. He differed only from the boys she'd grown up by having a better way with words and being somewhat cleaner about his body.

On that day she'd just walked to the well, with him following from the smith. His attentions had grown more aggressive earlier that morning and he had even attempted to touch her from time to time. She had avoided these advances with growing acrimony. This particular morning at the well, her arms were high above her head as she pulled down the counter-weighted bucket pole with both hands.

Then, taking up the second dripping bucket, she had been unaware he had approached from behind. He put his arms around her clumsily, touching her breasts in so doing as if by accident, before raising his hands to cover her eyes. She still held the dripping pails of cold water.

"The devil will own you if you can not guess your captor," he said, in the obvious chopped Stockholm dialect. Any local would have spoken *Nåsmål, Järnamål*[7], or a combination of the two. His clipped speech was unmistakable. Then he pressed his body tightly against hers, pinning her against the heavy pole beside the well. Then, twisting slightly, he increased the pressure against her, hurting her hipbone.

"The devil seems to be behind me now...but I know my rescuer to be the Lord God—not a rude and clumsy wolf, *bahhh—ing* like an innocent lamb," she quipped. He'd finally made her angry and she quickly twisted from his grasp and with full pails, stood facing him

He was surprised at her strength. A comely farm girl he'd thought to himself. He'd not yet spent sufficient time in the service of the Lord to forget his ever-present hunger for young *kullor*[28]. And as he suspected, licking his lips absently, her breasts were as full and firm beneath the linen frock...as her tongue was sharp. He glanced down at her chest. Her breasts stood firm against the linen fabric, despite the thickness of blouse and apron covering. Her chest was heaving now slightly, in her arousal, he suspected.

Without thinking, Anna-Stina had thrust her chest forward in defiance, as was her habit, leaning backwards and glaring up at him.

Spirit too, he thought, continuing to stare intently at her slightly heaving bosom. He could have seen the warning in her eyes, had he been looking.

Anna-Stina had followed his gaze and now he looked as if he was about to reach downward, again. With a smooth movement, she raised and released the pail in her left hand, dropping it soundly on his instep.

"Oh...look how clumsy I am," she said stepping forward and letting the other pail tip forward suddenly as she did, spilling its' icy contents down the front of his shirt and his somewhat tight trousers.

"*Uhhhhhhh...!*" came with a sharp intake of breath. "What have you...done...!" he exclaimed, springing backward.

"My goodness," Anna-Stina exclaimed, smiling wryly and spinning on her heel, she strode confidently toward the *smedja*. "I must have baptized a lamb—thinking it was a wolf child," she called defiantly back over her shoulder, laughing and smiling broadly at some surprised onlookers, as she strode away. "Do not forget the water pails you promised me you would carry for me, Pastor Johansson; my mother is expecting two full pails."

Henrik Johansson stood still beside the well, dripping in the cold, spring air. The harsh shock of cold water had forced an involuntary intake of his breath before he could stop himself. Now, he stood holding his shirt and vest away from his skin. It was not a pleasant experience and already caused his teeth to begin to chatter uncontrollably. You will deeply regret that my girl, he mused to himself, swearing a silent oath to revenge.

"Du-duh—Do not—bbb-bee too sure of yourself Anna-Stina Malmberg—Gu-guh—God is watching you…Hummmm," he mused to himself with a sneer. "Remember the pruh—pruh—pride—the pride that comes before the fall…Anna-Stina."

She'd seen the shock on his face when she tipped the icy water over him. Secretly, she reveled in the surprise she saw destroying for a moment, his smug countenance. Now, she sensed deep anger in the tone of his voice and when she turned and glanced back, black anger was truly contorting his features despite the ministrations of the two female onlookers who'd witnessed the scene. I have made an enemy this day…I did not mean to make, she thought, but his behavior was growing worse and now, this.

As he watched her walk away, calmness returned to young Johansson. From his point of view, finding Anna-Stina in this wilderness…had been a pleasant surprise—like a flower in the forest. As he came to know her he realized she was a flower in a field of weeds, still a flower, but a very thorny blossom at that. And when she bloomed—oh, what a blush and how she made his heart leap…as none had ever done before. She was intelligent, could hold her own with anyone in conversation, yet knew, most of the time anyway, when to remain silent. In religious matters, she could challenge many divinity students I've known, in her knowledge of scripture. Why…she even asked me those questions about The Text that, at first, even I was unable to answer. Even after referencing the subject in The Book. Not until I spoke to the old pastor did I have the answer for her.

Henrik at some time, probably unknown even to himself, had decided he would marry Anna-Stina. After all, was she not interested in him? A pity though, she would have no dowry. But she would be a fascinating life's companion—to say the least. She was strong, healthy and with the ability to bear him many children, a task he looked forward to beginning, with relish. Her comely ways would make marriage a pleasure and her personality—most of the time—a joy to come home to. He knew he had to civilize her—convince her to cease her evil ways and come to God first, then to him. He would eventually take her out of this God-forsaken place, back to the civilized south. There, her wit, good humor and stunning beauty, coupled with his prowess, would land him an early Bishopsy—at least the possibly even the Archbishopsy, eventually.

Long after the incident at the well, at different times, Anna-Stina noticed the pastor's eyes following her around the village. During the sermons, he would often glance at her and after the church service was always within view, no matter where she moved to on the grounds. During the week, he would appear in the strangest places, watching her all the while, pretending to be on some mission or other. What could he find to do so much in Andersfors? How many souls needed his personal attendance?

It made her feel strange. He did not again openly approach her with his attentions—good or bad and was polite to her when they met in mixed company. She knew he had been promised a post as minister in the neighboring church when his studies finished this year and he completed his internship.

He had perused the various communities in his journeys around the area, while pretending to minister to the poor, wretched people; he despised them for the most part, she believed and scorned them. Why did a man like him wish to take a church here...so far from the fine things he seemed to value most? Things of beauty, wit and sophistication...things only found in the city.

Johansson bided his time. His heart really began to ache for want of the beautiful *vallkulla*. And soon he had formulated a devious plan to have her favors.

Anna-Stina thought more than once of seeking him out and telling him she was sorry for ridiculing him at the well that morning. But the memory of his not-so-clumsy fumbling of her breasts and the ever-present shadowing were enough to put further thoughts of that nature, aside. It would have been pleasant to confide her thoughts, doubts and even spiritual cares in someone besides the old minister. The younger, more understanding Johansson, under different circumstances, could have been that person. She would have considered the younger confessor, but now she knew she dared not weaken herself before him. She would feel too—vulnerable.

I was writing so furiously I hardly realized Karolina had stopped her narration. My hand was aching and several times I'd stopped briefly to massage my cramped fingers. The nurse came to see how we were doing and asked if Karolina needed anything.

Smiling at me, the young lady said, "I will replenish the coffee urn if you would like more?" She glanced at Karolina and back at me. I put my left hand over the cup and shook my head without another upward glance, continuing to finish my sentence.

Karolina said, "*Ney—tack,*" and the woman then left. It was now after three.

"How can you remember all this with such vivid detail, Karolina," I asked, finishing at last and laying down my pen. "It is almost—like you were there."

"My mother suffered a great deal at the hands of this man and the church he represented, both in the beginning and throughout her life, before her marriage to my father. You might say they were rivals during his time as minister, until he was finally forced by the bishop to do his duty and comply with my mother's wishes. That brought matters to a culmination—a conclusion that began with a cart ride and ended—well ended when she got what she wanted from him. His vehemence and ardor for her continued to increase. It was as if he'd struck a new mission in life, one far beyond the one he had already taken on. He seemed to want to reform everyone...take them back to the even stricter time in church history."

I'd been massaging my fingers again; I wanted to take a break, but didn't dare.

"Whenever Pastor Johansson journeyed—Nås to Nöret—Järna to

Skålbyn, visiting in the course of ministering, he never ceased to make ordinary people miserable. Tirelessly, he sought out and addressed their many sins. This increased everyone's feelings of guilt; often those transgressions for which he forgave them were for ordinary little things. Of course the fact they weren't wed—my parents—until the end…was a big part of it in my mother's instance. But it was mostly that he'd made the mistake of falling under the spell of my mother—and once he had, well…ah…I jump ahead of myself again. That story will come later."

I took a breath…more, I thought, but I continued writing steadily.

"My mother spoke often of the young minister. After all, he was a young man, her age…a little older, but she said Pastor Johansson was basically an evil man, down deep, though she said she'd caught a glimpse of good. Ultimately she found herself fighting his influence in the community at nearly every turn, making a good many enemies among the congregation and forever casting herself from any grace with the Swedish Lutheran Church—at least while the minister continued in influence."

"He also drove many ordinary people away from the church and was probably mostly responsible for the foundation of the Swedish Free Church movement that sprung up in our area, around that time and possibly other sects, in Sweden. This you know from your own relatives—that they were among the first Free in Sweden to emigrate to *Amerika*."

I was aware there were Free Church People in Wisconsin when my mother was growing up, but I'd assumed they had joined after arriving in America."

"No, but I wasn't very familiar with their involvement…over here.

"Why would they wish to break away from the Swedish Lutheran Church?"

"It was because of the harshness of the Church, made even worse by Johansson. The parishioners must attend every service—the ministers controlled their every move and in some areas the parishioners weren't permitted to read the Bible for themselves, though most could not anyway, since public schools were not established in Sweden until around 1848. And of course, as always, there was money. The church was—is, very wealthy…the people's money.

The Bible always had to be interpreted for them by the minister.

And of course, every minister interpreted it how it pleased them.
Many *Dalacarlian* people finally began to question this, especially after
the educational system began to abolish the then, widespread
illiteracy. It was a time for change and as usual, the church was not
eager to lose their control."

I glanced at my watch again as she drew breath and continued.

"Mother loved *fäbod* life," she said smiling broadly, "from the
very first."

CHAPTER 4
The Attack

That summer, the marsh pastures and forest meadows in the mountain *fäbod*, were lush…green from the alternating spring rains and sunny days which had continued throughout the summer. Anna-Stina had taken the *Vallkulla* work again. The farmer, who lived on the edge of the village and planted all his fields in rye and barley, paid her well, knowing she would get for him everything his animals could give, though there were not so many of the small, white, mountain cows, or goats in her care. But the family was pleased with the quality and volume of their produce under her care, which they periodically collected from the mountaintop.

Good reports of her herding skill enhanced her reputation, as did her eager assistance to the old grandmothers with their own chores— cheese making, churning and the boiling of *mesmör*, the whey butter. She would often leave her own work until last, putting it aside long enough to lighten the burden of the older women, or mothers with small children to tend. Even the sternest *vallkullor* eventually offered glowing reports of Anna-Stina's Malberg's superlative effort, after her first season in the forest. At first jealous of her good looks and talents, the younger women also soon acquiesced and appreciated her good cheer and helpful ways, soon coming to love Anna-Stina as a sister whom they could count upon.

As the work of the second summer progressed, Anna-Stina forgot the young minister's earlier threats; she had not seen him since before leaving to *bufor*…to walk the animals from the village to the mountain pastures. Now a *vallkulla* for the family for almost a second, full summer, she shared their *fäbod* timber house with another girl, *Torp* Greta. The pair spent the summer together, sharing the heavy work.

One evening, Greta's young brother, Lars, appeared in the meadow with bad news. Their mother was ill and her help was needed at home with the younger children. As the hungry boy devoured a mixture of sour milk and bread before bedtime, the girls discussed the problem. They finally decided Anna-Stina would assume the full burden of both herds, until Greta could return, or send a substitute. That evening, their last together, they could hear Lars thrashing around among the mosquitoes, trying to sleep in the *vind*[29], *above them.*

"Anna-Stina, have you ever seen *troll*[30]...*or Rånda*[31], in the forest?"

She was surprised at Torp Greta's question.

"Why do you ask Greta? But...no—I have not...have you?"

"*Nej*—it is just that I have a strange feeling sometimes...lately. Have you noticed it?"

"No...nothing unusual."

"The feeling is like I am being watched by something. I thought possibly it was a bear at first, but I have watched and looked around...but I have seen nothing—of bears or anything else. Have you?"

"No—none this summer, that I can remember."

"I do not know why I have this feeling. It was especially strong when I went to the spring again this morning—to bathe. I definitely heard something in the forest. You know, a sound that did not belong? I became frightened and took my clothes from the limb and ducked to hide in the bushes. I listened for a while but saw nothing, so I went back into the water. It—the feeling, seemed to circle around the spring, though I still saw nothing. I thought it was possibly someone leaping from one of the large rocks to the next, just out of sight; you were not trying to frighten me were you Anna-Stina?"

Torp Greta had never expressed any particular fears of a spiritual nature, or of the forest life. All *vallkulla* respected and feared the spirits but few dwelled upon them any longer.

"No—I would not do that to anyone. I was with the cows on the other side of the mountain. Remember? And the milking was almost half finished by the time you returned, you lazy *dalkulla*[32], you!"

Her friend smiled at the chiding.

"Anyway, how could I have been away, down at the spring—trying to scare you and still milk all those cows and goats?"

"That is true—I guess I only wished it to be in my fear. Maybe it was just a feeling—but I have never had it before. Take care while I am gone tomorrow Anna-Stina and every night until I return. This was not an idle feeling. There was something…so, lock the *stugo*[33] door and take the ax inside at night—in case it is troll—you know how they fear anything made of iron."

"I will be all right, Greta. Go to sleep now or you will be very tired when you reach home."

Early the following morning, after the milking was finished brother and sister departed, leaving Anna-Stina alone at the small *fäbod*. Before she joined her brother on the path, Greta once more urged caution: "I am usually pretty sensitive to my suspicions, Anna-Stina, be careful, in my absence."

But Anna-Stina merely smiled. "You had better hurry along, or something will find you in the darkness, still on the road, tonight."

They had combined their animals after the morning milking. Anna-Stina now had more animals to manage and kept them in a single herd, for convenience. After she saw sister and brother disappear down the path, she took the animals up into the mountain meadow for the day, as usual. It was quiet with only the wind in the tall pines, waving slowly against the blue sky and white clouds. She knitted as she slowly walked with the grazing animals. During the mid-day rest, she dozed off, sitting against a rock. As usual, when she gauged the time right for milking, double her usual number of cows, she started the herd for home.

The milking finished later that evening with her extra animals and it was getting dark when she finally poured the last pail of warm milk into a crock in the cooling pool of the *källa*[34]. It would cool during the night and in the morning, after she milked the animals again, but before she would take them to pasture, there would be cream on the top to take off and churn into butter. She had been meticulous to keep the milk separate from the two herds, least one or the other owners be cheated.

I will be starting more cheeses again tomorrow she thought, appraising the quantity of stored milk that had accumulated in the

swirling spring. She looked to see where *Torp* Greta's rennet was
kept and if there was enough *vell* [35] soaking, to start the process of
turning the milk into cheese, the following morning. I will leave the
cows in the closest pasture, she though, so I will have more time for
the cheese.

Satisfied at last that all was finished, she returned to the
timberhouse to eat something. She would also need to check the
animals one last time before going to bed. Half way across the yard,
she heard an unfamiliar sound from the edge of the woods and turned
back quickly to look; but she saw nothing. The low sun was circling
the top of the trees, as it did during the long, mid-summer evenings.

A bear, she thought—possibly smelling the milk? Or, she
wondered, had she left food exposed in the timberhouse this
morning? The berries were not yet ready in the forest. Bears would
be hungry from their spring diet of grubs and insects. If one of them
tried for a calf, it could present a dangerous nuisance for a lone
vallkulla. She remembered an older woman telling her that
sometimes the bears tried to take an older cow, or one of the small
calves born in the spring. The stinking goats, they almost always
ignored.

Peering around the spring, she looked for anything that might
serve as a weapon. Mostly there were only dismantled wooden
cheese molds, drying. She spied a medium sized crock. It was a
dear item and the only small stone container the family owned; she
did not wish to risk breaking it on a bear's head. But it was also the
heaviest thing about and if she must destroy it on a marauding bear,
she would not hesitate to save herself, if neither ax, nor another
suitable weapon were nearby.

Hefting the heavy jar, she stood, listening. Nothing showed itself.
She longed for the long, birch bark horn, the *lur* [36], *they used to signal
to the other fäbod* across the mountain. It stood just inside the
doorway of the *stugo*. Longer than the *vallkullor* were tall, the
sounds one could make by blowing a lur would frighten ten bears.
The women used them to communicate to each other in the evenings,
sometimes because of loneliness, or in an emergency.

Cupping her hands around her mouth, *"Yeeeeaaaa-
oooooooouuuuuuuu,"* Anna-Stina shouted in the direction of the
sound, thinking she would whistle in the darkness and frighten away

the thing. After waiting another moment or two and hearing nothing further, she gathered the few wooden containers under her left arm and hitched up the heavy crockery piece in her right hand, holding it ready should the thing follow her.

She stopped to listen twice, again, before she finally leaped up the steps to the cabin, which stood in the shadow of the slightly larger barn. The urge to turn around had been strong. She felt the hair rise up on her neck each time she paused, vulnerable and in anticipation of the thing's hot mouth, closing strong white teeth into her neck. But she was proud and no bear would make her run from her duty, or even turn around to see if one had come running swiftly up behind and was about to grab her.

Not until she reached the relative safety of the stone steps did she finally turn. This she did very quickly—raising the crock above her head in preparation to strike. But there was nothing there. Only her fear and the coming darkness, close on her heels. Far off down the valley, she heard an animal call, too far away to be of concern. Maybe a wolf, she thought. She did not think bears called out, especially at night. She glanced around once more before raising the latch on the heavy door. She would eat something before going to the cow barn for one last look before she slept.

Inside the cabin she picked up the rolled birch *lur* and carried it to the open door. Placing the wide end just outside the door, she pointed it toward the woods, she placed the smaller end to her mouth and gave a mighty blow.

The deep, horn-sound cut through the night, then echoed back from the forest and surrounding mountains. As the last echo died a cow lying in the grass beside the barn answered with a long, low "mooooo..." and two shorter ones. She waited for its echo, too, to fade but heard nothing further. She blew the *lur* once again for good measure before returning it to its place beside the doorway.

Within a quarter hour, she was finished with her meager supper of bread, cheese and milk. Knowing she must see to the animals in the barn before she would see her bed, she got up hesitantly. As Greta had said, the sound she'd heard was not of the forest. It had been an alien sound. Hopefully though, after blowing the horn, she would be able to go and come again, safely. Crossing to the closed door, she reached into the corner and took up a short handled ax and hefted it, thinking it far more threatening than the small crockery piece. She raised it over her head a couple of times, testing its weight and her strength. Then, she opened the cabin door slowly and peered into the twilight. No bear was on the stone step, or in the yard…or anywhere around the barn, that she could see.

She stepped through the doorway, closed and latched the door and gingerly stepped down the square cut stones and walked along the path to the barn. The shadows grew deeper and as she strode along the lane beside the *gärdesgård* [37], she passed her hand lightly along the top rails to gauge her progress by counting the upright support poles. The bark had been removed and she took comfort in the smooth strength of the wood against any intruding animal that might be lurking on the other side.

The eight cows and five calves were safely ringed by the strong *gärdesgård*. Any bear would have to come through, or over that sturdy enclosure. The slanting poles were tightly spaced and would slow any bear's approach to the animals—or herself. As she worked her way along the fence toward the barn, she could see the cows had lain down in the short grass, but were somewhat crowded because of *Torp* Greta's additional animals. The calves had been driven into the barn earlier, along with the goats and as she lifted the latch and pushed her way through the heavy door, she was immediately greeted by a bevy of "baaahhhs."

It was very dark inside the barn, hardly larger than the *stugo* she shared with her friend. At first, she was unable to identify individual animals. The brighter twilight entering from the small window prevented her from seeing into the shadows. She stood for a moment, careful not to disturb the young stock further and start them calling for their mothers outside. The cows would then begin their own lowing and all the animals would soon be awake, upset and calling to one another.

Nothing seemed to be troubling the calves, either, so after a moment, she went back out through the heavy door and turning, closed it firmly behind her. She fumbled about in the darkness for the leather string that suspended the tapered, wooden peg, used to secure and latch the door. It was then she heard another sound behind her…a sound as if something had silently climbed the *gärdesgård* and leaped to the soft, grass-covered ground on the other side. She turned quickly, but saw nothing. She definitely knew she had heard the sound of feet striking the soft earth.

A bear could not climb a fence, she thought, franticly searching with both hands for the leather thong. Her hand brushed the thong, causing the peg to clatter against the door. She slid her hand down the leather, grasped the peg and thrust it toward the latch hole to secure the door firmly.

It was then she was struck a heavy blow from behind. She thought—someone has hit me very hard on the head, but it does not hurt. Am I so strong? But as she turned to confront her assailant— her body was no longer hers to control. The line where forest met evening sky began to tilt wildly. Her ears were ringing as she pivoted and fell...down—down she went, onto the soft earth of the cow yard. She remembered lying there, looking up at the sky beside the roof of the barn, thinking the birch bark of the roof covering would soon need to be replaced and she must remember to tell here employer.

He came closer then...to stand over her, silently staring down, silhouetted against the dim twilight. It was a man, not a bear. For a moment he remained there, blocking the sky, saying not a word or moving. His profile remained expectant—hesitant, as if he might turn, flee. Then he stooped, bent over her and grasping her wrists, began to drag her away from the barn. He is going to help me, she thought. He will help me up. But then she went to sleep.

She awoke somewhere in the midst of a nightmare thinking she remembered someone tugging at her linen frock and pulling her outer clothes. She'd moaned in impatience because each movement hurt her head. Then she returned to unconsciousness and a dream of being in a deep meadow with the cows. The cattle were heading home to the *fäbod* without her and she was frantically searching for some lost article. The cows, usually so hesitant to leave lush pasture, had formed a single line and were ambling away along the path, heedless of her shouted entreaties to wait for her.

The scene blurred into semi-consciousness once again. Through the pain she saw the man rise and stand over her again, outlined against the sky once more, before bending and rearranged her clothing. Then he straightened and she tried to speak to him as he remained standing beside her, but the words didn't seem to come, or she was unable to hear for the ringing sound. The figure raised an arm in a gesture, though he didn't speak, holding out one hand as if to offer assistance. But she hurt too much to rise so he let it fall again and stepped away. At that moment, before she slipped back into unconsciousness, he made a sort of *"harummm…"* sound, turned and was gone. There was the sound of someone again on the fence and one of the cows in the yard gave a single "moooooo" and there was silence.

Karolina sat staring at her feet. She had become increasingly agitated as she related the tale of her mother's fate, so long ago. I was frankly a little concerned for her well being. She'd been wringing her hands and a visible palsy had come into her neck. Her head twitched imperceptibly.

"You see…" she said, "…my mother believed it was Pastor Johansson touring the communities and *fäbodar*. She knew by that odd sound he always made, that harummm…" sound. Surely, it was he who raped her that night and as bad luck had it, also sired her first child…my older sister Anna, who later died. Mother told me that when she was later able to walk, she also found men's footprints around the spring where both she and the other girl had been bathing, daily."

"Did she actually see him—I mean, so that she would be able to identify him? Couldn't she go to the authorities…the police?"

"It was not easy, you see. She was in *budar*[38], with the cows and the other *vallkullor* had gone home. She had no witnesses, even she herself…she did not actually see his face. It would have been unwise, anyway, to accuse him. He was not likely to admit his guilt, was he? And it would have been the word of a penniless *vallkulla*—a dairy maid, against a learned and respected man of the cloth."

"But the habit of his—his moaning…or clearing his throat—whatever he did…certainly that was a sign it was him…wasn't it?"

"Mother certainly thought so—for many years, she never doubted it. She said she would catch him watching her whenever she was in church, or at any of the meetings or celebrations afterward. And once she finally made up her mind—knowing it was him, she sought him out, accused him—not publicly, of course. At first, he would also approach her from time to time about an arrangement—clandestine meetings for—she assumed—sex—but she would have none of him. Each time she would chastise him for the dead, little child…his child." Karolina took another deep breath.

"But he seemed not to care and her rebuffs seemed to trouble him not in the least. Only that she behave in a proper manner, not to have another man, I mean, so the community would know, mattered to him. I personally believe he loved her—in his own, sick fashion— even more than she realized. He hungered after her, rather…in the very least, knowing he could probably never have her. When she came to realize this fact—really knew he was hers—that was when she made a plan and began to institute it—revenge…but I get before myself again." I peeled over another sheet.

"Pastor Johansson was very religious insofar as the community thought. Yet, he wasn't above keeping Mother as a mistress—in secret, though he surely would have readily married her, too I think. But he did not want a single member of his flock to stray, or misbehave. Thunder and lightning would come from the pulpit if there were a single sinner in the congregation that week. He was a very good preacher, you know. He could curdle milk at thirty meters, with his message."

I chuckled to myself.

"Mother was always a scholarly girl. Oddly enough, she was encouraged as a child by the old minister. He immediately recognized her extraordinary intelligence during her catechism teachings. Himself a scholar and a man who took great pleasure in knowledge, he gave her books and regularly helped to teach her to read in the absence of a local school at that time."

"Was that unusual—I mean, to let a woman—a young girl…learn to read?"

"To some degree. I believe it was becoming more of a practice in the south—metropolitan or scholarly communities: Stockholm— Uppsala, Gothenburg…they were soon permitting women in university. As time passed, mother devoured everything he offered her, borrowing and returning texts with every Sunday's church visit. The old minister had begun to make a point to have texts waiting for her…and not only theological works. So it was an intelligent, though informally educated Anna-Stina Malmberg who came to the *fäbod* to live and for the most part, to peacefully coexist with her more illiterate companions. Probably not always an easy task for her."

"I see what you mean, Karolina…playing stupid."

"Yes, exactly and holding her temper. Mother once told me that the memory of her dead children would suddenly spring out at her as she worked in the forest.

"A pain in my heart," she told me, whenever she thought of the first, the infant girl, lying cold in the ground. "No one had warned her—to fear the promises of men of the cloth. In fact, just the opposite; the old minister in Nås church had been a great friend to her, encouraging her reading and studying. He provided her minor works on religion from time to time so she was the leader of his religious studies class. So she had come to love and trust him for these acts of simple kindness.

That trust was there when the young pastor arrived—at first. Had she been forewarned, mother probably would not have heeded the advice anyway, headstrong girl that she was. It was only later that she considered him to be like any young man—after the same end. And of course, he lost any religious piety he may have brought with him, in her eyes.

On Sundays, he had this way of looking around the church. He would settle on the sinner of choice for that sermon, if he knew him—or her...and he would vent—oh, how he would vent. There would be a visible shrinking away from the subject of his ridicule in the pew, by the other congregation members unfortunate enough to be seated around the sinner, until he just sat there alone, isolated, head hanging, shamefaced enduring the preacher's tirade."

"How long did he stay at the church in Nås?"

"I don't remember. I was too young at the time. He eventually became pastor at Järna church, until just after my parents married...he performed their wedding ceremony."

"Really?"

"Yes, eventually...he did. If mother had accused him in public, the full power of the church would have come upon her, unless her proof had been absolute. You do not know the power the church had in those old days. It could make or break a person's family—their spirit as well as their soul, if the right people wanted to do it. As it was, they tried—with Mother."

I shook my head in disbelief.

"Mother was merely the daughter of a nobody. The Church—the church was everything...second only in power to the monarchy—and in those days, possibly even more. Eventually, mother was able to get him to admit he was the...that it was him in the *fäbod*, that evening. She made him do it...forced him, actually. She used the one, single weapon he could not control—the weapon he would do almost everything to make right: his own lust and love for her—sin...hers and my father's—she used it against him, that and his own love for her, or lust, as she said."

She looked at me, triumph in her eyes. "And to think young man—he finally married my parents—can you believe that? That despicable shell of a man—that burning bush—firebrand of religion that was just as weak and as shallow as the rest of us, when you got him wet. Mother finally let him succeed in "ending their sin", as he would have put it...but at a price: the price of admitting his own. Once he was finally willing to do that—publicly, she married father."

"I don't understand?

Karolina glanced at her wristwatch and brushed her brow with the back of her hand.

"I'm sorry—you will have to wait for your answer—we will have to stop for today. Suddenly I am feeling a little tired," she chuckled and struggled to rise. "Do you mind returning again later...tomorrow, possibly? But any day will do, you see...I'm not going anywhere."

As I took her arm to help her up, I answered: "Of course, Karolina, will tomorrow be all right—too soon?"

She smiled and nodded, waving toward me tiredly. "Tomorrow will be good. You are welcome...for the companionship, you see."

"Thank you for...all this," I said indicating the rumpled tablet. "I'll see you tomorrow morning."

I stopped at the nurse's station to let them know I was leaving, but that I'd return tomorrow. They nodded, occupied by other matters, now; far different from the first evening.

As I figured it, I'd be interviewing her as long as she could, or wanted to talk during the day and then going back to my room to transcribe my notes the following morning. I didn't hesitate to purchase a typewriter and worked on the rough outline of the pending novel—the book I really never intended to write.

As time passed, part of the days we would speak of day to day occurrences in the radio news, or happenings in the nursing home—

things the other patients did, or what the staff said. Sometimes Karolina wouldn't feel much like talking about the past—though that wasn't often. When we did discuss modern times, like many older people, she didn't understand the expense of things, the troubles in the world and especially, today's youth, nor did she wish to tackle that one, for that matter.

Staff members would take her into their confidence and she would chortle over the secrets of their love affairs. It was entertaining for her and helped to make her life bearable in the home. She was a very intelligent woman, had traveled extensively abroad with her husband before his death, though she'd never been to the United States. Though she'd not attended any university, she seemed very educated. And, basically, she seemed to be in pretty good health and I think, enjoyed our talks, although at times, it was painful for her to remember. Sometimes, the emotion ran high.

The staff were all pleased to see my daily visits to the old lady; it made me feel a little selfish, knowing my ultimate goal was to extract a story. But I'd been up front with Karolina from the beginning and she was only too happy to talk with me and I was a good listener. Karolina had informed them I was a distant relative, which of course I was, though quite distant, so they were nice to me, giving me special privileges with visiting and letting me stay after normal hours. I was good for her, they said…healthy, emotionally.

And there was also this one person I'd been admiring from afar, not a nurse, but a staff physician. Her name was Anna Olsson. Contrary to what everyone in America thinks, Swedes are also dark-hared. Dr. Olsson was a brunette. Her hair appeared to be long, dark in color and she always wore it up, in a bun, plaited and neatly pinned. Her skin was milky white, but in good contrast. She was quite a striking person, nearly as tall as I and in her long, starched-white gown, stethoscope with a gold pen in her pocket, I would see her sweep down the corridors, smiling and greeting patients and visitors alike with her cheery manner.

It was obvious that she commanded a good deal of respect from the staff—not the bowing and scraping obedience I'd seen in American hospitals. Her's appeared to be earned. For all her stately appearance, I would occasionally hear her joking and laughing from time to time, sounding almost schoolgirl-like, at times. I think it was both her ready humor and quick wit that earned her their respect and love. I later learned, like most who worked with the elderly, that she was also a very dedicated physician.

Dr. Olsson never had any particular need to be attending Karolina, as she had little wrong with her besides "old ladies' complaints," as Karolina put it. But Karolina was ultimately in her care. Dr. Olsson's rounds seemed rather erratic, since I often saw her passing through the home at odd hours. Sometimes we would see her glide past us from the sun porch, or sometimes, she would cross the lawn, preoccupied with her chart as she strolled from one building to the next. At these times, especially if she was passing close by, I occasionally forgot Karolina, momentarily neglecting my notes, in order to watch her go by.

When I returned around ten the following morning, Karolina seemed at first, tired. I had a cup of coffee with her as usual and asked her if she was sure she wanted to go on with the interview.

"Oh...Yes..." she said "...we don't have all the time in the world you know and if I am not doing this, I will be doing nothing...so I may as well enjoy myself and do this."

"OK, but let me know...."

Midway through the session, I got caught. Karolina was finishing a particular narrative and had slowed her speech, waiting for me to catch up on my notes, when Dr. Olsson happened to stroll past. Of course, I noticed, stopped and watched her pass; once she'd turned the corner, I glanced up and noticed Karolina looking at me, a bemused smile playing about the wrinkles.

"What...?" I asked, smiling to myself, knowing she wasn't fooled.

"Are you sure you want to hear this old woman's story, or would you rather listen to one from...someone younger—and prettier?"

"Looks like I lost my concentration," I said, a little embarrassed.

"She's quite a nice person, Doctor Olsson," she chuckled encouraging, "she's very generous and the home is fortunate to have her as chief of staff. Would you like me to introduce you?"

"Well, sometime, Karolina—thank you, but not right now."

By then Doctor Olsson had disappeared anyway. This was news to me—chief of staff. I hadn't put her down as running the place.

"Are you sure you wouldn't like to meet her. She's very pleasant to be around—so young and beautiful, too." this with a smile and raised eyebrows in my direction.

"Maybe another time, Karolina." I continued to smile, shaking my head slightly.

"All right, another time." But she didn't drop it. "She's a member of some physician's organization that once went into remote places that had ongoing wars, famine, or trouble from disasters. The doctors spend their time helping the poor. She told me she'd been to Africa many times. She speaks of the joy in the children's parent's eyes when their children received healing care—medicine and food. She spoke of children who were near death one moment and with the right medicines, they would be smiling and on the road to health in a matter of hours. She likes children very much and would make a fine wife and mother someday."

I continued nodding as I touched up my notes with silly doodles, but not glancing up.

"Strange...no one has seen these attributes and captured her heart." This was said, again with a sidelong glance in my direction.

I didn't reply, but continued to smile at my tablet. But I did want to meet the beautiful doctor.

Karolina smiled at me. "All right, I'll give over...so—where was I? Oh, yes—after the attack at the *fäbod*, mother told how she would dream about it for all the rest of her life. She said it was not the..." and here she looked down as if searching for the correct words, "the matter of the—the intimacy with a man that disturbed her."

I interrupted her, unfamiliar with the Swedish word she had used for intimacy.

"The act with a man..." she explained, seeming reluctant to be too descriptive. "It was not even the fear of it happening again. She said it was a bitter anger she felt for the person who did it, because of what he had taken from her—not her..." she struggled again for words, "her...."

"Her virginity..." I offered, hesitantly, knowing she probably wouldn't say the word if she knew it.

"Yes..." she seemed pleased I'd said it for her. "You know, we did not speak of such things with young men, in my time. Please excuse me if I have trouble explaining some things to you. I understand it is different now—how the young communicate. Nothing is sacred. When I was a girl..." she trailed off shaking her head and smiling, before continuing.

"My mother said that she felt violated; more like a crime against...womanhood? It angered her so much it hurt her to think of it. Years afterward, whenever she would speak of that evening in the *fäbod*, she'd get tears in her eyes. Even after she'd had another three children, she still carried the anger. She didn't hate men in general. In fact...she liked male company very much and of course, they liked her, too. I don't mean, you know, in that way. But she was a captivating person, generous and outgoing, not to mention quite pretty. She was a wonderful musician and could sing well. More than once I have heard the cows and goats in the *fäbod* halt their grazing, just to listen to her *kuja³⁹*...I swear they did."

"Excuse me, Karolina—*kuja*...what is koo—yah?"

"*Kuja?* A sort of talking song—half speech, half chant. The *vallkullor* sang it to the animals while they were in the forest. It's usually high-pitched when used to communicate with other *vallkullor*; often, it has no words—only sounds. When herding, it often includes the names of the animals—the cows goats and specific commands to them. The women and girls did it...playing the sound with their voice across the mountain valleys, playing the surrounding countryside like...like it was their own instrument: echoes, vibrations, hollow ringing. Dense forest would absorb some of the sound; singing beside a lake would bounce it. *Dimma*—fog—would muffle the sound. So they could vary the effect of their voice just by turning slightly one direction or the other. Oh—there were so many things they could do with their voices in the forest valleys."

I got excited then: "Oh yes, I've heard that. My mother and her sisters would do it when I was a child, visiting my grandfather's farm. I suppose they learned it from their mother. They would stand in the back yard, high on a hill, cup their hands and talk to the cows in the marshland, below. The cattle would lift their heads as if they could understand; my grandfather could actually call the cows home, doing it."

"So...the practice crossed the Atlantic?"

"Apparently; I'd like to hear it in a Swedish forest sometime."

"I'm afraid you're too late, Alex, the custom died with the *vallkullor*."

"That's a pity," I said, wondering what else I'd missed by growing up in America, during the 20th Century.

"Mother loved the *fäbod* like all *vallkullor.* She would pine for it in the winter. When the snow was deep and we would sit inside, beside the fire, before bedtime; she would tell us how much fun we would have there, when the spring came. Later, when we actually went along—could remember it, we would accompany her when she took the animals up to the high forest. During the winter she would keep a brass cow bell near the fireplace; occasionally she would ring it during the winter, just to keep the memory alive for us. She would imitate the sound it would make when the cows were grazing, walking, or running. I believe she probably enjoyed hearing the sound as much as we. This was after she married my father and we moved officially into Frömansgarden[40], the house where I grew up—I believe you have seen it?"

"Yes—yes," I said, "your cousin's—there...."

"Mother also believed in the many spirits...old legends, I believe you might call them superstitions, reputed to live up in the *fäbod: skrymt* [41], *troll* [42], *vittror* [43], *näken*[44] and of course, *Rånda.* That was not unusual for the country people, then; but now...you may think it strange for a semi-educated woman of my mother's obvious intelligence?"

"No, not really; there are many unexplainable things in the world."

"I suppose she got that superstition from her mother. Sometimes, late at night, when we were in the *fäbod,* we would hear a strange sound outside. Mother would say, 'I believe *Rånda* is outside—who would like to go and look?' Of course, none of us dared. We would shrink further beneath the covers and our eyes would grow as large as saucers, with fright and we would glance from one to the other to see whether anyone had the courage, but no one ever did."

"You know about *Rånda*...the beautiful woman of the forest— with the fox's tail and the hole in her back? *Rånda* is of course a mystical figure from folklore, reputed to be very beautiful. She has long, black hair, with the tail of a räv—a fox. This tail, it seems, she's quite ashamed of and was always trying to cover beneath the skirts of her long, green dress.

She's a woman spirit, who seemed to live everywhere in the forest, because she was seen in so many places. She would appear suddenly before a traveler, or someone in trouble—a *vallkulla* for instance, who might have lost her cows. *Rånda* could help...or she could bring great harm to the person, depending upon her mood. Men who have encountered her, were captivated by her beauty. But she had this other strange characteristic. When she turned around, there was a large open area in the middle of her back—a hole—that one could see right through. And it was said she would float above the ground, in the forest, her feet hidden from view in the fog and appear, and disappear, quite suddenly."

"It sounds like something thought up to frighten children."

"Believe me, Alex, adults very much feared the appearance of this apparition—in the old days, like so many of the old superstitions."

I shook my head, grinning as I wrote. "I'm happy my parents didn't know about her...the stories they used to scare us were enough."

"My mother used them to frighten us, too, but I think she possibly believed in them; she was afraid not to believe. Her mother's generation completely lived by these spirits. Mother would say it was the troll we heard in the night. Now that I am older, I believe it was only wolves. But we were all afraid, nonetheless, though not mother. She just assumed it was *skrymt* and she would have a remedy for them the next morning—a dance, an ancient chant she'd learned—from Lord knows what old *fäbod* woman, where she may have worked as a child. She wasn't afraid of much up there...just the bears. They could be dangerous sometimes and I think she'd had one or two bad encounters, with her animals. More than one *vallkulla* was killed, trying to take a calf back from a bear that had grown too bold, or too hungry."

"You wouldn't catch me taking anything away from a bear—except maybe myself."

"Every time we went to *fäbod*—always for the whole summer, of course—first thing, we'd dance away the troll, those troll who lived in the cabin, the earth and finally the ones who lived in the forest. We would have to make sure the *stugo* was purified of them before we moved in and slept in it the first night. It was very important we did not offend the troll and *vittra* people—the invisible ones, for they occupied the *fäbod* when we were not living there. They would give us no peace during our summer stay, if certain rituals were not first performed. They could cause the cows to become ill, or the cheeses to spoil...all sorts of ill tidings they could bring upon us."

Karolina paused and seemed to be thinking. I'd learned to take these short opportunities to review my notes before she'd take a breath and press on.

"But nothing could make mother forget what had happened that evening in the cow yard," she looked up. "Sometimes, I would see her staring off into nothingness and this hard look would come over her face and her jaw would take a set. I could tell, then, she was thinking about it...the attack and rape...by Pastor Johansson."

CHAPTER 5

The Sorrow

When Anna-Stina regained
consciousness it was to a bevy of
calves faces standing over her.
Their mouths were ringed with
white foam from sucking the cows of what should have been the
morning's milking. They were blinking bright liquid eyes at her and
slowly swinging their heads from side to side in curiosity. Her face
was smeared and sticky where they had nuzzled and licked her where
she lay unconscious.

"*Ooooohhhh—noooooo,*" Anna-Stina moaned in pain as she
tuned her head. I have gone to sleep and the calves have sucked all the
milk from the cows...there will be no cheeses from that waste.
"*Aaaaahhhh...*" she cried again, as she attempted to rise. The
movement of pushing her arms out and trying to sit up was more than
she could bear. She lay still for a moment, felt sick and turning her
head, vomited. Then she lay back with her head against the cool earth.

She lay panting for a moment, but the bright morning sun, well
above the trees, was burning her exposed skin. Her head and neck
felt as if one of the cows had been standing on her. After a while,
she felt somewhat better and opened her eyes. She was very thirsty.
The calves had moved in again and were tugging on her clothing in
their youthful curiosity. They pulled and prodded at her; with each
lurch, terrible pains shot through her head.

She slowly drew in one of her arms and pushing with the other,
rolled onto her side, facing away from the sunlight. She lay still,
waiting for the new pain to subside. She felt very dizzy. Carefully,
she pushed herself to a sitting position where she remained, eyes

closed…waiting for the dizziness to subside. After another moment's rest, she dragged first one leg, then another, further and further until she was finally able to rise to her hands and knees, but bending her head downward nearly made her faint. Her ears pounded with each heartbeat. She remained kneeling—swaying slightly from side to side. Feeling stronger, at last she began to crawl toward the support post of the barn. There was also shade there. As she attempted to crawl she realized her skirt had been pulled nearly off and remaining on one leg, was caught upon something. Slowly, she moved the other leg instead and the skirt slid free, releasing her.

At the barn wall at last, with great effort, she pulled herself up, grasping each log hand-over-hand. Standing unsupported but leaning against the wall, she struggled to remain upright. When her head stopped pounding, she now attempted to walk along the barn wall. But the movement was nearly more than she could bear; dizziness and pain overcame her again and she feared she'd fall. Her cheek against the rough logs, she clung to the side of the barn, waiting for the nausea to pass.

The overwhelming thirst was foremost in her mind. She knew she must reach the spring, but it was too far. The barn door's tapered peg, still dangled from the thong, twirling to and fro in the wind, occasionally tapping the side of the door casement, emphasizing her thirst. The door to the barn remained wide open from the night before. She wondered who had left it open, then remembered the escaped calves and her attempts the previous night to put the peg in the latch; she didn't wish to think about that, yet. Slowly working her way along the wall again, the moss-packed grooves between the logs offered a firm grip as she crept along the building. Reaching the opening, she stepped over the ax still lying on the ground from the night before and went inside.

Free for the moment of the problems outside, she paused in the dimness. She glanced toward the shallow, wooden watering trough. Nightly, she or *Torp* Greta carried water from the spring to the calves. Some of the calves were too small to drink water.

"Thank God," she said aloud, noticing some water still remained from the previous afternoon. Working her way to the trough, she slumped to the ground. The effort nearly cost her consciousness.

Overwhelmed by an urge to drink and ignoring the pain it

brought to her head, she leaned forward, burying her face in the water. Bits of meadow hay pricked her as she drew in a welcome mouthful, drinking just as the animals drank. She paused for a moment to breathe, then began swallowing careful little gulps again, least she choke. How good it tasted.

Half-lying on the dirt floor, her head resting on the rim of the trough, she paused to rest. Her left eye and forehead were partially submerged. She was breathing through the side of her mouth, nearly unable to move—she could breathe yet…that was enough. Will I drown, she wondered to herself, if I go to sleep again. The pain is so terrible, she thought, closing both eyes for a moment. During the struggle, her hair had come free from her bun and lay in swirls atop the hay and water.

She awoke still slumped over the trough, her head half lying in the water. She heard the lowing of the cows outside, still confined in the small, night-yard. Her head was clearer now. She recognized that the cows were both hungry and thirsty. She sat up carefully and rested. There were several problems she must solve. The calves would have been suckling all morning and would have consumed half the day's milking from the cows; the goats were another matter, but she didn't know what to do with them. She wasn't certain she would be able to do any milking that evening, either, let alone any of the normal work. It's best to let the calves suck, she decided. That took care of that problem for today. Without being milked, the cows would soon dry up completely, but the sucking calves solved that and the other problem of feeding the calves. Arriving at this solution took her many moments in her slow thought process, so much did her head hurt her.

The previous day's milk and cream, cooling in the spring since the evening, would soon spoil, if she did not continue the process, today, of making the cheeses and butter. How will I ever accomplish that, she wondered? When will *Torp* Greta return…or send help? I can not remember…oh, it will not be soon, I'm sure of that. I will think again of it—later when my head is clearer. She closed her eyes to rest again.

After lying still for some moments she slowly turned her head toward the partially-open doorway, wincing at the pain in her neck. The morning was well along, but it is not yet mid-day, she judged.

Possibly, I will be able to do something to postpone the work for a day. I must have some time to recover from this terrible pain in my head; she rubbed her eyes gently, trying to assuage the throbbing. She considered how to get the cattle watered. This was a very troubling problem. If I free them from the confines of the *gärdesgård*, they will wish to forage in the woods as they normally do. She knew she lacked sufficient strength to go with them and knew some would quickly wander off and become lost. They were strong-minded cows; their hunger would take them far from the night pasture, unwilling to remain in the meager forage. Some would likely be taken by a bear or wolves.

There is the problem of water, too. How can I get them to the spring where they can drink their fill? Normally they would go to the spring by the path leading from the *fäbod* and drink there, before they were taken to the forest. She considered the nearby spring, used to cool the milk. It was near by—just outside the *gärdesgård*. But it was crowded with the vessels cooling and storing the waiting milk and cream; butter and finished cheeses were stored there, too. She reasoned she and Greta had accumulated a week's labor there, in finished butter and cheeses alone. The milk from the previous evening's milking would not remain much longer without being dealt with. The cream would have to be skimmed today and churned.

Oh—where will I ever find the strength? The thought was overwhelming. Greta and her brother had taken away what they could comfortably carry of the previous store of cheeses and butter. But a week's work ruined—how could she ever explain the loss to her employer. The thought of her attacker loomed then and she quickly put it from her mind. I must deal with the immediate problem.

She crawled to the doorway and poked her head into the sunlight, blinking and pausing for breath. Slowly, she pulled herself upright and through the doorway and began to retrace her earlier route along the edge of the wall—hand over hand—until she could see the small enclosure ringed by the slanting, *gärdesgård* poles. The fence gate wasn't heavy, but in her weakened condition she didn't know if she would be able to open it, even if she managed to crawl or walk that far.

Hungry and thirsty as they were, once the animals saw the opening, the cows would immediately rush through. She could see the grass of the night pasture had already been cropped short and there were more manure piles scattered around the yard than usual—yet another chore to be done, though it could wait. The animals were growing restless.

She scanned the barnyard and surrounding area for a solution. Suddenly, she thought of the *häskulle* above the small barn. In the spring and fall, they cut and stored a small amount of dried hay up there, for the days when they had to feed the cows in the barnyard. This just might be the solution she thought. She began to traverse her way to the other side of the barn. Rounding the corner, she was relieved to see the door to the *häskulle* was slightly ajar. She could see tufts of hay protruding from the edges of the opening. The door that protected the area was held up with a long, braided birch root rope, wrapped around the wood fastener pegged to the side of the barn logs.

If I can untie the rope and let the door fall open, much of the hay should fall down and attract the cows. That would momentarily solve the animal feeding problem. But how much, if any, is still there? Then, how can I ever get enough water to satisfy them? I can not carry enough for one cow, let alone the goats and the rest—Greta's animals.

Glancing around again—there is a second gate, she mused. It is outside the fence and just before the narrow lane leading out and into the forest. If I can open the *häskulle* door the hay will fall down and keep the cows occupied long enough for me to cross to and open the gate, so they could then drink from the spring. Once they have eaten hay, they will remember they are thirsty but by the time they rushed from the gate, to go to the spring, I would have hopefully gotten the far gate closed.

It will be a challenge. So many things have to work perfectly; if I could only run normally…even walk, it would not be a problem. Once the cows rush from the yard and discovered their way to the forest is blocked, they will turn to the cooling spring where, unfortunately all the milk containers are waiting, full from the previous day's milking. There were cheeses, too. Possibly, some would not be spoiled, she thought. I will save what I can. As another wave of dizziness and nausea nearly overwhelmed her, she resolved to try; slowly, she began to work her way to the braided rope that held up the hay door.

A distance that would normally take her only a moment to walk

now took five. Even then she nearly collapsed from dizziness, crossing
to the building. The sun's warmth affected her head, but at last she
reached the barn. With one last glance at the two gates, she began to
unwind the stiff rope from around the hangar. Her fingers seemed to
have no strength against the stiffness of the braided roots. Rain and
sunshine had caused them to stiffen around the clasp. Dried and
cured tightly around the peg, their inflexibility resisted her efforts.

Leaning over the fence, painfully stretching her arms forward, she
attacked the knotted fiber with vigor. Bending forward, she finally
pulled at the home-made binding with her teeth, but then nearly
collapsed from the effort. Resting briefly, she managed to loosen the
coarse band and freed the knotted roots. As she tugged on the loose
end the weight of the barn door suddenly tore the rope from her
hands and fell down—swinging open against the log walls with a
bang, startling both Anna-Stina and the nearby animals. With it came
a cascade of hay and dust—so much that she was quickly buried to
her waist. The weight knocked her against the log wall. Staggering
to her feet again, in panic, she saw the pile extended out from the
barn by more than twice her body's length.

The startled cows had momentarily forgotten their hunger and
thirst and stood staring wild eyed at her, heads lowered in
anticipation—preparing to flee. But the cascade of beautiful hay
finally reached into their thick heads and one-by-one, they began
pushing forward to sniff, moving toward her warily. Still half buried in
hay, with effort, she waded free and staggered across the yard toward
the first gate, nearly collapsing again with the urgency of her effort.

She reached the cattle as they plummeted toward her through the
narrow lane, parting to either side as she half pushed, half fell
between them toward the outer gate. She was first brushed against
by one animal and ricocheted off another, in the press, as they
passed. She barely kept her footing, continuing to stagger toward the
farthest gate.

Wanting to collapse over it, instead, she lifted the bent wood ring
securing it to the post and swung it open. She immediately headed for
the second gate, another thirty paces down the lane. She shuffled
slowly, wishing she had a stick to steady herself. With each dragging
step, stars burst before her eyes and her ears rang. She had been
stepped upon by one of the cows in their struggle to get at the hay;

barefoot, with bleeding foot, she limped forward, eventually reaching the old gate, which had remained unopened for two seasons, hinged back, folded flush against the fence bounding the cow lane and held fast by the growth of old grass around it. The bottom rail was securely encased by dry grass and dead twigs and intertwined by a season of dead vines. Drawing a breath of resolve, she bent and began struggling to free it. Her head throbbed; she could hear the cattle behind her, probably growing thirstier with each mouthful. She glanced over her shoulder and saw two had already started to follow her.

After a tremendous effort to tear away the dry growth, the bottom rail of the gate loosened. Another painful wrench and she freed it completely—even partially closing it. The effort cost her dearly and momentarily, she staggered and slumped over the top rail, least she collapse totally into unconsciousness.

Recovering once more, she finally succeeded in dragging it closed. The bent, wood ring was missing; the leaning gate would have to stand unsecured until she could find something to bind it. She felt it would hold for an hour or so and leaned on the gate, resting, breathing deeply. With her head cradled atop folded arms, she thought, not yet—I am not finished yet. Still I may save some of the fresh milk and cheeses.

Reluctantly, she turned back toward the spring and the precious commodities that were cooling from the previous night's milking. Hugging the fence for support, she made her way to the stone-lined spring. As she walked, the last of the cows passed through the first gate, necks outstretched, smelling their way to the water. Nearing the stone-lined spring, she planned what to save first, but realized she would not reach the spring before the first of the animals and as they pushed passed her in their haste to drink, she thought all would be lost.

"*Haaaa...*" she pounded the backs of the nearest animals, crowding forward to reach the water. "*Heeeaa*—move...you. Get out...!" she shouted, clapping her hands. Reaching the stones, she fell upon hands and knees. Milky streaks already swirled in the dark pool from the overturned crocks. "Let the milk go," she said aloud. "The butter and cheese is more precious—also some of the tools and containers."

If she could only prevent those finished products from being stepped on, they would survive any number of wettings. Grabbing some of wooden molds containing butter, she threw them behind some stones, out of the cattle's reach. A pair of smaller cheeses rolled from the shelf, landing among the shuffling cattle's hooves. Ignoring them, she snatched up others, planning to place them in her apron and carry them out of harm's way. She realized then, she was still nearly naked from the waist down, so she threw these cheeses, too, behind the stones. Grabbing others, she tossed these into the spring, knowing the cows were mostly interested in drinking and not eating cheese. Once they had drunk their fill, I will be able to control them and can retrieve the cheeses. But as more animals arrived, the struggle beside the spring became fierce and finally, fearing for her safety, she crawled out of the path of the frantic cattle and around the stone wall.

Feeling safer for the moment, she nibbled part of a broken cheese and watched the cattle for a few moments; then she leaned her head back against the wooden shelter and slipped into oblivion once again.

When she awoke again the cows had moved away from the spring and were lazily pulling at the last of the spilled hay. She felt stronger. Taking stock, she noticed some hay still remained in the *häskulle*. A rake handle jutted from the open door. She leaned over the spring and took a deep drink, sat up for a moment and then took another before crossing to the jutting gate and closed it.

She rested a moment before moving on to the barn, where she pulled down the remaining hay. Then she returned to the spring to salvage what she could of the cheeses and butter. When she finished, she returned to the barn, retrieved her torn skirt, then to the spring house, dipped half a pail of water and slowly carried it into the cabin.

In the cold water, she set about trying to wash herself. There appeared to be a large amount of dried blood at the base of her head where the blow from her attacker had struck. She dabbed at the wound through her thick hair. It burned and the blood made the wet linen cloth pale red. Deciding to leave it, she began to wash herself as best she could before putting on her only other dress, the best one, saved only for Sunday visitors.

She sat on the edge of her crude bed. "I will not worry about milking the cows this evening...the calves will suck them all again," she said aloud. "I don't know what else I can do now," she said aloud, exhausted; she lay down in her bed with the cloth on her forehead. She was instantly asleep, though it was only an early afternoon in May.

During this very emotional explanation, Karolina paused several times to take a sip of water. She'd barely touched her coffee. I grew concerned a couple of times and interrupted her, thinking possibly we should take a break, change the subject, rather than continue with such an emotional recollection. But each time, she would shake her head, smile gently and say, "Noooo...I am all right—please let me finish now I've begun."

When she did finally stop, I could see that recalling it all had taken its toll. She was definitely tired. We chatted a while, but I was still concerned when I took my leave in the middle of the afternoon. After helping her from the lounge chair, into the wheel chair I pushed her back to her room and saw her situated in her own chair there and we said our good byes for the day.

It was a Friday— a weekend and I'd planned to go back up north to spend it with my newly-found cousins there at the farm. I promised Karolina I would pass along a greeting to the cousins and would see her early the following week.

As I returned to my car, I deliberately went past the staff office, and spoke with one of the nurses, explaining to them I thought Karolina Fröman had become unusually fatigued today, during our interview and that I was concerned for her health. Possibly someone keep an eye on her. I received an affirmative reply as the nurse made a note. I left, not knowing what else to do.

As I walked out into the spring afternoon, I vowed to call the nursing home over the weekend to make sure she was resting comfortably.

CHAPTER 6
Neglect

As it happened, when I returned to Dalarna my cousin had planned a surprise fishing trip for me, even further up north. We left nearly immediately after I arrived at Frömansgården, driving half the night, up to a remote river to fish for salmon. There, I had no access to a telephone, so promptly forgot my vow to call and check on Karolina.

I did, however, have access to some very nice lax[45]. My fly rod had not had so much exercise since…I couldn't remember when and it was a pleasure to catch my fair share of the beautiful salmon. We spent one night at a cottage along the river, kept especially for fishermen. We ate fresh-caught salmon with a cheese sauce, raw onions, boiled potatoes and some left over cake my cousin's wife sent along. Plenty of strong coffee, made directly from the clear, river water was always the finish to every meal.

So I was pleasantly tired when we returned to the farm, having taken my turn at driving through the winding, mountain roads. I still didn't call to check on Karolina the following day, as I had planned, nor did I bother on the following Monday morning, when I started driving back to Karlskoga. I planned to transcribe more of the voluminous notes I'd compiled, that evening. I would renew the visit with Karolina the following morning, a Tuesday.

As planned, as I entered the nursing home, I bore greetings from all the nieces and nephews to their great aunt Karolina and also their regrets that it was so far to come to visit. I arrived around nine, my usual time, bearing a bouquet; but Karolina wasn't in her room. I knew they got the patients up early, so I headed for the lounge, but found her table empty. I thought this strange and began to worry, so I hurried down the corridor toward the other wing. Near the nurse's station, Dr. Olsson stopped me at an intersecting hallway.

"Mr. Andersson…" Her English was nearly perfect, with just the hint of an accent and a beautiful sing-song in her voice. "I do not know whether you recall—we only met once…with Karolina Fröman? My name is Anna Olsson…I am her physician?"

"Yes…" I said, taken aback by the calm beauty of her at such close range. How could I forget? "…of course I remember, Dr. Olsson. It is nice to see you again. Where is she by the way— Karolina Fröman?"

"Mr. Andersson—I'm afraid I have some rather bad news for you. Karolina suffered an…*incident*, Saturday morning—right after rising for breakfast. We've transferred her into the hospital in the city, for tests and observation. She is well, now and appears normal…but we thought it best to observe her for a bit yet, before letting her return her to the home."

"Oh…." I didn't know what to say. I never dreamed her weakness last Friday was that serious. "What is her condition now?

"She's resting, and responding well to treatment. I understand you had cautioned the staff before you left…about her tiredness?"

I nodded.

"You probably saw it coming, then? She may owe her life to you, since we caught it immediately, watching out as we were. Did you say you were a relative?"

"Yes, well sort of…we're second or third cousins. I've grown terribly fond of her in the last few days. She's going to be all right, isn't she?"

"We believe so…but let me explain her condition: it is our suspicion Karolina suffered a light cerebral hemorrhage. Staff caught it…as I've said, immediately and administered medication appropriately, so that was good. Now, there is only a little confusion, just a little slow response and some forgetfulness, on her part…all of which will pass in time.

"I see."

"Just this morning we contacted the relatives—in the north— a…" here, she consulted a clip board "…a *Herr* Fröman? He said you would be most likely visiting her on your return and if you didn't mind, make any necessary arrangements for her care. It seems, according to him, you are all related to her at the same level and she does not have anyone else, or at least, no one is designated next of kin in her file. So, if you would be willing to assume the minor responsibility?"

I nodded my consent: "Yes—anything I can do to help her—certainly. I feel somewhat responsible...maybe I've been tiring her."

"I really doubt it; to the contrary, your visits, I'm told, have greatly benefited her...emotionally. Initially, she'd lost some of the movement of her right arm and was unable to speak clearly at first, but these functions have already returned. All of these are normal symptoms. She did seem to recognize the staff when they transported her in the ambulance; a good sign. You see, Karolina can be somewhat...testy at times. She rebuked the younger ones, as she usually does, for their care giving. Do you understand my meaning?"

"Oh yes...very much so. I have seen her...moods."

She smiled nodding and glancing at the clipboard again: "She is able to speak clearly now, though...with some difficulty. Those—her speech and limb movements—will completely return, once she has rested and the medication has had time to be effective.

I had been thinking about the remainder of Karolina's story. Now that she'd begun it, it had grown far beyond my dreams. Oh my God, I thought, what if the remainder of the story is lost? But I was immediately ashamed of myself. Had I become that selfish? Dr. Olsson was watching me.

"I'm sorry, doctor, I lost my bearing there for a moment. What more can I do? Are there any arrangements I should make?"

"Not at this time. There are a few papers that would list you as contact person in the event of surgery, should that ever be necessary in the near future. Something of that sort—contacting other family members, just to let them know, but in the absence of an immediate relative, we would normally—the Swedish law permits us to...well, do whatever we deem necessary given the circumstances of an emergency."

"I understand. If you'll guide me, I'll do whatever the facility considers necessary. I want her to have the best of care."

"She's getting that now, Mr. Andersson. But, if you'll come up to my office with me, we can go over the necessary forms; there isn't really much. For the time being, we'll continue to administer an anticoagulant medication and of course, monitor her behavior. If you wish, you can go to the hospital to see her. She's allowed visitors. Please don't tire her out, though. She's had a difficult weekend with the change of environment. She wasn't happy going to the hospital— and she needs all the rest she can get at this point. You can come back in the afternoon for a little while again, if you'd like."

"Thanks, I'll be happy to go. Just tell me what you'd like."

"Come with me now, if you will and I'll help you through the forms."

I nodded and we walked back up the hall the short distance to her office. I noticed how unusually tall she was as she matched my stride in the hallway; she nearly reached eye-level with me. Her hair was arranged a little differently, today. It was very straight, full and put up. When she let it down it must have passed her shoulders. Following her through the doorway of her office I noticed she smelled of one of the perfumes so popular in Sweden at the time—of the scent of woods flowers…really unidentifiable. She smelled very good.

She directed me to sit while she left to fetch the papers. I looked around to see what I could learn about her. It was much like a physician's office in the USA, only larger. Chief of Staff also carried the title of facility administrator, I noted. Diplomas ringed the walls. Photographs, mostly of nature themes, dominated: wild flowers, lakes in the forest, pastures with cattle scattered among the wildflowers— their heads down, grazing in the same direction. I looked closely for any photograph that might indicate any commitment to a husband, or boyfriend, but could find none that hinted at a spouse, or children, either. I'd noticed she wore no rings.

There were a couple of photos of her with four other medical staff, in Africa, or someplace quite primitive. They all had their arms around each other and they were smiling at the camera. They looked young, tanned, terribly thin and tired, but extremely cheerful. Two figures in the photo were males, but didn't look like they had any particular relation to the doctor. There was another photo of the doctor alone, holding thin, hollow-eyed, infant girls in each arm. She had a winsome smile on her face and again, she appeared to be very tired. The children weren't really infants; they were mostly emaciated, which made them look younger.

There was another small, colorful photo on her desk. Where I sat, I couldn't see who was in the photo. I stood up and turned it around just as Dr. Olsson returned.

Seeing my curiosity, she smiled: "My parents."

She paused briefly and glanced down at the photo in my hand. Then she walked around the desk to take her chair. She began to sort through the papers.

I returned the photo. "I didn't mean to pry."

"Oh, that's OK."

The photo had been an older couple dressed in Swedish folk costume...*dräkt*. They were smiling and looked well worn-in together. I had always noticed older couples sometimes took on the same look or actions, the more time they spent together. I'd always thought is a nice trait for long-married couples to assume. I replaced the photo carefully. Dr. Olsson looked up without raising her head and smiled.

"They're attractive," I said, still a little embarrassed that I'd been caught peeking.

"Aren't they though? That was taken at Midsommar a few years ago, just before my father...became ill."

"Oh, I'm sorry," I said.

"They have had a wonderful marriage; over forty-five years. Mother is suffering with him now. It should have been the opposite. Father was far stronger. It's—I believe you call it hardening of the arteries—his memory...premature senility is slowly encroaching."

"That's devastating—to both partners."

"Yes, it certainly is." She came around to my side of the desk, rotating the paperwork in order that I could read it. "Here, have a seat; there's a lot of it."

I sat down and began to struggle with the Swedish legal jargon. Leaning over my shoulder to indicate with her finger where the signature went, the doctor had come quite close. I could smell the warmth of her, beyond the perfume.

She suddenly laughed. "Of course it's in Swedish...I'm sorry. I will read it to you if you would like?"

"No, I can read it—I believe," and squinting, set to scanning the lines, trying to concentrate from both the distraction of her closeness and the difficult words, nearly all medical or legal jargon and most of the words I'd never seen before. "On second thought," I laughed, glancing up into her beautiful face, "if you tell me it is OK, I'll just sign...I can hardly comprehend a thing of it."

She chuckled. "It is pretty formal Swedish, is it not? It's just the normal stuff. In an emergency, we will do whatever we think is necessary...as I said, for Karolina. The law is quite firm about that. So I don't think you will have to worry any. Hopefully, Karolina will continue to improve and we won't have to worry at all. None of it makes you financially responsible for anything."

"OK," I signed with a flourish beside where she'd indicated with along finger and filled in my local address information. She swept the papers into a folder and went back to her side of the desk, put them in an out basket and smiled.

"If that's all, Dr. Olsson, I'll run over and peek in on Karolina. Maybe I can cheer her up."

"Do you have a car here?" she asked as I stood up to leave.

"No, I don't. I walked. I left it at the apartment I rent up the hill, there, on Vensgatan where it crosses Lisgatan." I pointed out her window at the hill leading up from the river.

The hospital isn't far but I don't believe you can easily walk."

There was an awkward silence as I hesitated in the doorway, unwilling to leave and she probably didn't know what else to do with me.

"I guess I don't know much about you Mr. Andersson, except I've seen you come nearly every day to speak with Karolina. It is good to see the change that has come over her since you began coming...your interviews. Did you know the effect you were having? She is younger acting than when she came here, I believe."

"No, I hadn't realized. I didn't know her before...before I started coming. I've only just met this side of my Swedish family."

"Well—you have and it' been very good for her. In fact, one of the therapists has been helping her to walk more again with a cane, unassisted. She now predicts that Karolina may soon be fully mobile again...and she feels it will be because of your interest in her—your visits."

I didn't know what to say. "That would be nice, wouldn't it—walking unaided again."

"Definitely...the exercise will add years to her life. We only hope this incident will have no permanent damage, or interfere with her earlier recovery."

"Yes, I hope not, too." I stepped into the hallway.

She crossed to the doorway. "If you would like, Mr. Anderson, I could give you a ride to your car. I'm going to the hospital to take care of a couple of matters, including looking in on Karolina. Do you know where the hospital is located? Across the river and then around the forest to the edge of town…toward the old airdrome?"

"No, I don't, but I'm sure I can find it."

"If you'd like, I can take you back to pick up your automobile and then you could follow me to the hospital," she said, picking up her stethoscope and an attaché case in preparation to leave. She paused: "Otherwise, you could just ride along with me to the hospital now; I must return and will have to pass nearby your apartment. That way we won't have to go back and pick up your car, which would make it easier. I have to stay for a bit once I'm there. You would have plenty of time to look in on Karolina and visit. Then tomorrow, you'll know the way there."

"Oh—well, yes…if you're certain it won't inconvenience you?" I said stepping aside to let her pass out of the office. I caught the scent of her and my thoughts reeled, slightly, making the thought of riding with her very pleasant.

"Not in the least. Now, if you'll wait by the rear entrance—do you know where it is?

"Yes."

"OK, I'll be out in just a moment. I must let staff know that I am leaving and I must pick up a couple of items, first—then, we will be ready to go."

"Great. I'll see you there.

She bobbed down the hallway with the case under one arm. Did I sense an air of excitement on her part too? Or, was my own enthusiasm getting the better of me?

Outside, it had remained a beautiful day. I strolled along the walk toward the street to wait. The thought of Karolina possibly never being able to speak again, was depressing. And to think, she had just begun to regain her mobility again. Thinking of her suffering in the hospital didn't assuage my feeling of selfishness about pressing her for the story. But I'd imagined my visits were good therapy for her; so we were helping each other, in a sense.

How would I ever finish the story if something happened to her?

We'd explored so many areas now—areas I would never have dreamed existed. In a sense I had the gist of the matter. She had sort of woven an outline for me. But the details she had been able to offer were invaluable. She continued to allude of more yet, to come. Silently, I prayed for her well being. I don't believe it was just for my own selfish reasons either. I'd truly become fond of her in our short time together—she was so enjoyably feisty—probably a good deal like her mother.

This closeness that had developed had created a bond of sorts. Becoming close made the thought of losing her difficult, emotionally and in so many ways, she reminded me of my mother's older sister, Lelah. Although Lelah had never married, there was a sense of oneness about her; definitely a take-charge woman—a woman for all seasons, very independent yet extremely likable to both sexes. She was kind, yet a woman to be reckoned with. There was probably much of Anna-Stina Malmberg in Karolina, her only living daughter and child.

Dr. Olsson, absent the white lab coat, stepped around the building corner, smiled and started walking brusquely down the sidewalk toward me. Without the long coat, she was far slimmer than I had imagined. Lithe, best described her shape; she was muscular—sinewy. Watching her approach was not at all unpleasant; she was all Scandinavian in the simple linen dress, light green-gray with a silk blouse with little pastel flowers. Her easy, long-legged stride was as one accustomed to walking. Just as she took each step, she used her upper torso as leverage to get the rest of her body moving; definitely a different movement, but not without grace.

"*Hej*," she greeted me lightly in Swedish, "ready to go?"

"Yes."

"All right, my car is the white Volvo over there," she gestured toward the street. "I generally park it beneath the trees in the summer…shade you know. I usually arrive early enough; I can choose my place on the street or in the car park. In winter…well, it doesn't much matter. The closer the better," she smiled, "nothing makes a Swedish winter warm."

"Except the Swedish people," I said, not really knowing why I'd said it.

"That was nice of you to say," she said, pivoting and smiling at

me as we crossed the street. She reached across and squeezed my
arm lightly. "You're kind. It's no wonder Karolina is improving."

God—I thought. What is that feeling? We were approaching the
car and she hugged the leather case to her chest as we walked. I
approached, preparing to open the door for her. In my frustration, I
realized I was at the wrong side of the car, something I still did.

"Sorry," I said, turning to the other side; she hesitated, giving me
time to open her driver's door. "My mind is still in America with
automobiles. I'm still not accustomed to getting in on the right side
to drive."

"Thank you," she said slipping behind the wheel. "No need to
apologize. It must be difficult—changing driving and sides-of-the-
road...coming to another country. I've never been to America, or
anywhere they drive on the other side. When I studied in London
and also in Africa, it was the same side of the road as Sweden."

I ran round to my side and got in. "You were in London?" She
started the Volvo.

"Yes, I took my masters at City College there, before deciding to
go to medical school. I'm afraid I was a little undecided. I thought I
wanted to teach—sometimes I still do, but I enjoy my work here very
much. Geriatrics is a field truly made for me...babies are nice, too.
But I so enjoy the elderly. They have so, so much to teach if one
only listens."

She was definitely a kind woman that was easy to see and very
dedicated to her work. The way she spoke of Karolina was a little like
family. We didn't speak much on the ride to the hospital. I'd never
been over to that side of Karlskoga before. I'd considered driving
over, once, because it was the area where the airport was located. As
a private pilot, I always enjoyed the atmosphere around small, general
aviation airports, but not the commercial stuff, which was all business.
The fellows who love to fly and hang around small airports are
enjoyable to talk to and discuss flying and airplanes. In the states, I'd
owned a four-passenger, single-engine aircraft. But because I often
traveled beyond where I felt I could safely fly it—over the
mountains—I'd eventually sold it. It was becoming expensive in
hangar storage and annual inspections and I wasn't flying it enough to
justify the costs. I found it more cost effective to rent an airplane,
when I wanted to fly for myself.

I'd been considering renting a small airplane in Sweden, instead of making the long drive up north to my relatives. Time-wise, I figured it could be better than halved if I flew. There was a small strip within a couple of miles of my cousin's farm, so they could pick me up. I could even walk, weather permitting and there was always a car around there to use.

But I hadn't yet taken the time to visit the Karlskoga airstrip, devoting all my evenings to transcribing my voluminous notes from Karolina's interviews, best done I surmised, while my memory was fresh. Not everyone possessed Karolina's incredible memory.

As Dr. Olsson drove, we passed an airport on her side; I turned, looking past her and out the back window. I noticed there wasn't much activity but did catch a glimpse of a four-place Beechcraft sitting at the end of the run-up pad, evidently preparing to depart the north-south runway.

"That was a nice Beech," I muttered aloud, turning around again.

"Pardon me," she said, glancing in the rear view mirror, "is something behind us?"

"Oh—no...it was that airplane—we passed it back there. It's American—a Beechcraft. I was just talking to myself—admiring it."

"You are interested in aviation."

"Yes, a little. I fly back in The States—or flew. I was thinking it would save me a good deal of time if I started flying here again as well, especially when I go back up to Dalarna to weekend with at my cousin's farm."

"Oh, I see. You are a man of many talents. I, too, come from the north—a little farther, though: Jämtland. Where does your cousin live in Dalarna?"

"In western Dalarna, near Järna...Dala-Järna it's now called, southwest of Leksand."

"Yes, I know it. It's very beautiful there, isn't it, along the Västerdalälven?"

"Exactly...the river...I think it's paradise."

"Really," she sounded surprised. "Many Americans don't like Sweden that much—especially the north. It's too primitive they say—not enough...go. And our dark winters. I'm truly surprised...and impressed." She glanced sideways, offering another beautiful smile. I almost squirmed in the seat. I was beginning to feel like a boy.

We rode a little further before she spoke: "Pilots are quite rare in Sweden, I believe, except for in the airlines."

"Oh? I didn't know that." We rode a little further and I added, "I guess I'm not surprised, though. You didn't have a world war, as did the US, so there were never very many trained to fly and left over, flying for recreation, later.

"My father also flew airplanes—the older ones, with two wings. He hadn't flown any for years—even before he became ill. But he couldn't pass an airport without turning and looking, until it was out of site—as you just did." Again, she glanced at me with a melting smile. "Can you fly here in Sweden? I mean, do you need a different license, or to pass a test?"

"No, nothing—other than my current American certificate."

"Odd. I can't practice medicine in most countries in the world, without first taking a local medical examination. It proved very difficult when I worked with Trans-world Health. Many bureaucrats would rather their countries' children died, lacking proper care, than to permit us to save them, without first being certified by their idiotic bureaucracy. Much of the time we just went ahead and did; and they seldom bothered us. Paper clerks, all of them, worthless—they are the same, in a different way, here in Sweden, too."

I nodded. "The same the world around, I think—government clerks—bureaucrats."

I could see this was an emotional subject for her and I thought of the photos back on her desk. Trans-world Health, she'd said...the Africa she mentioned earlier.

"Anyway...I can fly here in Sweden but I'm guessing I must first be checked out by a local certified instructor, to make sure I know which part of the airplane is up and what part is down. Once they're assured of that they sign me off and I can fly anything I'm already qualified to fly...even to Europe, I guess. So I'll get checked out first, just to be safe."

"It must be exciting..." she beamed that smile again, "...flying by yourself."

"It is...when you're younger. It seems pretty adventurous, but as you get a little older, it becomes simply a means of getting from one place to another—but a little faster. It's still fun, though."

"I was that way about horses as a child," all sign of her previous emotion gone. "I begged my parents to buy a horse, but never got one. We even lived in the country. All the farmers had horses and it was easy to get a ride. But it wasn't the same, sitting on a thick, plodding workhorse, bouncing with its every step. They were so wide and my legs would stick straight out. Can't you just see it? My legs were not so long then." She looked at me, laughing aloud, throwing back her head so I could see the inside of her mouth and the gleaming, even teeth. "It must certainly have looked so strange."

"Every teenage American girl goes through a stage of wanting a horse. My own sister did; it must have been the western movies we saw as children, the Saturday matinees."

"You have a sister..." she said, curious "...any brothers, or other siblings?"

"No only a sister—older, widowed now, with three children. They live in the central US. I see them once or twice a year, whenever I am on business in the area. If it gets to be too long, I make a special trip. The kids grow so fast you know. What about you—family left—brothers, or sisters?"

"I'm afraid I am the spoiled, only child, who the statistics are constantly blaming later misbehavior upon—always having my own way, do you know?"

She'd really loosened up, laughing aloud again, becoming even more animated and she squirmed a little; her eyes sparkled when she was happy. I was feeling very comfortable around her—far too comfortable and I'd started to think I didn't wish to become emotionally involved with a woman a whole continent away, especially, given my rather transient situation with Karolina.

In my work, my company—electronics and engineering—I travel around the world a good deal, mostly the Orient, sometimes Europe. I'd been careful not to become impassioned with any particular woman in my travels. Not that I'd had all that many chances, but now and then I would see someone who, if we were back in The States, or the circumstances were a little different, I would want to explore the probabilities of getting to know her further.

Usually my travel demands took care of it: I would simply have to leave. And I seldom returned to the same area anytime soon. I was beginning to feel this way with Dr. Olsson. But somehow, I sensed she was different. I felt at home with her, as if we'd known each other for years and just come together and assumed old roles—comfortable roles. It was a fine and very friendly feeling, especially so far from home and so long without female companionship.

My Swedish visit had been planned as a sort of vacation research project, only to last a couple of weeks—three at the most. I didn't imagine meeting anyone other than relatives. I'd heard it's always that way: whenever you're not looking, bang, there she is. I was well into my fourth week in Sweden now and I've met an interesting woman.

Dr. Olsson hummed to herself as she navigated the narrow streets. She drove past the hospital parking lot entrance, choosing instead a narrow street that turned behind the rather impressive, brown brick structure. Like many buildings in Sweden, it was difficult to determine its age, but I wondered if it hadn't been used for something else in a previous life. It had a sense of elegance to it…almost palatial opulence; rather strange for a hospital, I thought.

We swung into a small parking lot marked "physicians only" in Swedish. The grounds in the rear were immaculately lain out and cared for in a manner befitting their original planner.

"It's mostly a park today," Dr. Olsson said, seeing me gazing over the expanse of neatly lain out plantings. "Years ago, this was a summer residence for Swedish kings, before the monarchy became more austere," she said. "The royal family would spend time here, before the turn of the century. Eventually, they must have thought better of it and given the facility to the hospital to do with it what they could—tone it down you know. Sometimes I'm a little ashamed to be working in such opulence, but secretly, I very much enjoy the surroundings. We've had to "drab up" the interior a bit, you know—cover the ornamentation a little? It's rather humorous, I think. The patients enjoy it, too."

I held the heavy door for her and we entered directly into a well-lighted area of very organized activity. Staff walked rapidly, to and from a central desk area built into one part of the wall. In the foyer a few robe-clad patients sat or strolled with family members or nurses. It was very nice, with what appeared to be a functional fountain near the double French doors beside the entrance. I followed Dr. Olsson to a closet where she handed me her satchel, removed her jacket and donned a white coat.

"*Tack*, she said, taking back the satchel as we walked toward the nurse's station. I'd helped her with one of the sleeves as we walked and she smiled and nodded over one shoulder.

At the counter, the laughing young woman in the white Volvo disappeared and became all business. I could see the staff knew it, too, as we approached a busy station filled with papers, arranged clipboards and spotlessly-clad nurses. They were prepared for Dr. Olsson and began sifting and consulting charts and answering her rapid-fire questions. I glanced along the hallway while she spoke medical jargon with the staff. Looking toward the ceiling, I occupied myself by studying the Rococo ornamentation banding the ceiling of the one-time palace. No way to drab that up, I thought, admiring the gilding.

Presently, I heard her ask after the well being of Karolina and half listened to the nurse recite more medical statistics as Dr. Olsson paged through another clip board she'd been handed, I assumed, representing the present condition of my cousin. I'd never heard so much technical Swedish before and could fathom very little of it.

"Mr. Andersson, from *Amerika...*," she turned to indicate me, "...will be visiting with Karolina, his relative, while I will take my rounds. Who will be accompanying me?"

The nurse indicated she would find someone and left.

Turning to me and letting her professional mask fall for a moment, Dr. Olsson smiled and said: "Karolina seems to have stabilized nicely. That is excellent news...it shouldn't be long and she can go home again. We will wait a few more days, to see how she progresses. You can now sit with her for a while, if you would like. I won't be too long. Should she become agitated for any reason, or if you notice an alteration in her condition, please tell one of the nurses. I shouldn't be much more than an hour. Will that be all right? Can you stay that long?"

I nodded as a nurse approached and we set off down the hallway. I noticed all the staff we met, greeted Dr. Olsson cheerfully. She returned their smiles with equal ardor, while remaining professional, but with an overall air of friendliness and caring. She was apparently well liked here.

We encountered an older cleaning lady who was mopping the hallway and we stopped. Doctor Olsson examined the woman's bandaged forearm, chatting affably all the while. The woman languished in the caring attention, smiling and demonstrating how well her arm was doing by flexing it.

Further down the hallway, we found Karolina in a ward of five beds. The room, like the rest in the hospital, was very large, with high ceilings. Tall, wide windows made the area bright and airy. Here as elsewhere, an attempt had been made to cover the opulence with white hospital draperies suspended on tracks from the ceiling. The curtains could be drawn around each bed to divide and afford each patient a little individual privacy.

All the beds faced the three, large, floor-to-ceiling-windows, situated on a outward-curving, marble-faced wall. All in all the white drapery lent a rather sterile, but theatrical appearance to the otherwise palatial room. The massive windows were swung open permitting a gentle breeze to move the curtains. It was a pastoral room with the large view of the garden, somewhat like a seat on the stage viewing the audience in the garden, as they went about their exercise and strolling. A gardener and his assistant were working in a bed of shrubbery near the windows and two of the patients seemed to be commenting on their own, preferred planting techniques, thinking they could do better if it weren't for being confined to the ward.

We approached Karolina's bed. She was awake but looked a little groggy, as if she had only just awakened. Her hair was a bit mussed and I knew she'd be ashamed of her appearance if she could see herself. Apparently, she was also abandoning the habit of the old fashioned headscarves. She smiled when she saw Dr. Olsson and her face brightened again when I stuck my head around the drapery.

"*God dag*, Karolina, what have you gone and done to yourself," I said, attempting a cheerful tone.

Dr. Olsson prompted, "You had a disappointed and concerned visitor at the nursing home this morning and he believes that you have forsaken him and claims you owe him an end to a story of some sort. To think, he has come along with me all the way here to see if he should be concerned that he will not get it."

Karolina's hands had gone up to her hair, patting and arranging it. But then, Dr. Olsson interrupted her and began the examination, moving her arms through a range-of-motion and generally prodding her.

"But it doesn't look like there is much to worry about—a little rest, perhaps...yes?" She set about the matter of doctoring while she kept up this disarming chatter to the old woman.

"I am all right now, maybe a little tired, I think," Karolina said, smiling over at me.

I'd taken Karolina's hand and was patting it while the doctor held the other to take her pulse; she seemed happy enough and didn't draw her hand away, even squeezing mine a little. Her voice was noticeably weaker and I detected a slight drooping of her mouth on the right side. And she seemed to have to enunciate her words more slowly and carefully. But her smile was still bright, if a little slow in coming. Tears—the malady of stroke patients—had sprung to her eyes right after she first saw us, but she quickly overcame the spontaneous emotion.

Dr. Olsson stood up, patting Karolina's hand. "Mr. Andersson will be sitting with you for a little while, if you feel up to it Karolina, while I make my rounds. Will that be agreeable, or do you prefer to rest alone?"

"Alone?" she exclaimed, "*Nay...sätt dej...*" she said, smiling broadly, pointing to a straight-back metal chair. She rearranged the bed coverlet around her waist so as to look presentable and at the same time, patting her hair.

"She is doing very well," Dr. Olsson said, leaning close to me to keep her voice low. "I shall return in a little while. I shouldn't be so long."

Her scent was disarming. "Ok..." I controlled the impulse to reach up and touch her cheek, she was that close as she brushed past to slide Karolina's curtain open, flooding the bed with light from the windows. She turned, smiled and waved pertly, then strode briskly out the door of the ward. The other patients had paused in their conversations, nodding and watching her departure.

When I glanced back at Karolina, I noticed she was staring intently at me. I wondered if my thoughts were that apparent in my facial expression. I looked away, turning the chair a bit more toward her and the view of the window.

"So...Karolina. You frightened me when you weren't in the sunroom this morning. I was confused, until Dr. Olsson found me and told me what had happened."

"It was as great a surprise for me—as for you, Alex," she chuckled to herself. "What do you think of Dr. Olsson?"

"Think of her? I've never been her patient."

"Do not avoid the question. You know what I mean."

"Oh, well—she's...she's very nice."

"Yes...anything else?"

"Well...she's pretty."

"Most certainly...anything else?" She was almost giggling.

"Not that I can think of... what is this, Karolina? Twenty Questions."

"I might add...she's unmarried," she said quietly, nodding her head in a matter of fact way.

I didn't answer but smiled at her mischief.

"Where are your notebooks?" she asked, folding the sheet about her waist. "What will you write on?" she asked, fully expecting to continue the interview it seemed.

"Oh, I think we should take a holiday today and just look at your beautiful view. I left my notebook in Dr. Olsson's car..." then immediately regretted saying it.

"Oh...her car? Did you ride here together?"

"No—yes...she gave me a ride...I didn't know how to get here." I wanted to change the subject again. "How lucky you are to have this view, considering you must be in the hospital," I said, hoping I'd not just encouraged her more toward the subject of the doctor. I gestured toward the garden, wanting to keep the visit light.

"It is nice, isn't it? It reminds me a little of home...Dalarna. It is so beautiful in the summer. When I was a child, mother and I would work together in our own garden. We had vegetables...you know, *potatis*, carrots...many others. We always ate fresh things from it. Even in the *fäbod*, we had a little garden. Sometimes we planted potatoes at home and in the *fäbod*. We would have someone to tend to them at home while we were up there, working; so there would be fresh food at both places and for storing in the cellar for winter.

Otherwise, in *fäbod*, it was only bread and milk and cheese, or whatever we could carry up with us in the spring. In the fall, someone would sometimes have to go back up there to dig the remaining potatoes we had not eaten and pull the rutabagas and anything else that took longer to grow. Oh, it was very nice when we did that—sort of like one, last visit to the *fäbod* before it was locked up for the winter, when we brought down any remaining hay. I can still see the cheeses placed in a row, cooling in the spring house with fresh vegetables clean from a scrubbing...red radishes with white tips, with bushy tops, so green in the sunlight, dripping the cold, clear water, onto the stones from the spring.

"It sounds very idyllic," I said, sensing she was starting to get going again. There was a cadence to her speech that, once she got her momentum, just continued until she ran down like a clock spring.

I tried to derail her: "Have you met your fellow patients?" I asked, gesturing toward the other ladies, trying to change the subject.

"No, I've been sleeping mostly, but I heard them talking...wanting to give that gardener advice."

This she offered behind her hand, smiling conspiratorially. We both stared out the window for a moment.

"Anyway...mother and I worked well together. She was such a fantastic person, it was easy for many people to become intimidated by her...but I didn't; I loved her dearly and of course, she loved me...and Carl."

I interrupted her: "Maybe we should talk about something else. You know, I will not be staying very long today. We should not tire you with a lot of visiting until you are feeling stronger and more up to it."

"Nonsense," she said with a certain commitment, "there is so little time and so much to tell. What if I had died, where would we be then with the story...how would we finish it? No one would ever know."

I didn't know how to answer her so merely smiled and nodded. So now it was we.

"I'm so happy you've come. I was getting so bored with..." she waved her hand toward the window and her roommates.

"I will not tire myself and I can always take a nap. I just wanted to finish the story we had started last week before you went home to Dalarna. By the way, how was everyone, anyway? Are they still milking so many cows?"

"Oh, I'm sorry Karolina, I completely forgot...they all send their warmest greetings and love. They said they didn't know when they would be able to make the trip down to see you—with all the animals and work...but I imagine this—your little spell...could bring them down for a visit."

"Don't count on it, cousin and don't you tell them...unless I die. They are a stick-at-home bunch, they are...too much work to do farming...milking all those animals every day. It never ends you know—the work there. Anyway, you and I can talk a little, can't we?

I smiled, shrugging.

"Now that I have begun this, I believe it's also important that the others should know. Not so much them in Dalarna; they don't seem to care much about old history…hah!" She chuckled, "they're living it. But seriously, maybe it's because they are just not old enough.… Someday, there will be others who will see and wonder—like you have done and then it should be there for them…I now believe that."

"I will do whatever you ask, Karolina."

"Yes, I'm sure you will tell them."

"Do you believe it's possibly because they've grown up with the culture—the farms, forest…people. And I—I haven't. It's all new—interesting to me, but they've heard the stories so many times."

"You're probably correct, when I think about it that way."

She smiled brightly. "So…we can talk for a little while anyway…at least until Dr. Olsson returns—can we not?"

"Yes, I rode over with her so I could find the way the next time I come—tomorrow maybe."

At this, Karolina raised her eyebrows, but said nothing. No doubt she was thinking about the doctor and me.

"Well, I certainly hope so…the visit tomorrow, I mean. She is a fine doctor and a very nice person, though I suppose you already know that."

I sensed another unasked question and nodded, noncommittally. The last thing I wanted from Karolina was for her to turn into a meddling matchmaker. I sensed the stroke, or her medication, had lowered her power of self-control and restraint. After a moment she began again.

"She comes from Jämtland—north of Dalarna, you know? I think she has some Sami blood— *Lapplanders*[46], I believe you call them. There's something about her eyes, if you look closely. She also speaks *Jämpska*, the local dialect—*mål* [47]. She's truly striking—don't you think so?"

I was thinking of Dr. Olsson's eyes and had hesitated to answer her without knowing it. When I finally did, Karolina was smiling at me curiously.

"Yes, she is very striking. On the drive over she told me about her home up there—Jämtland."

I wanted to turn the conversation away, somehow. "The staff certainly seems to be comfortable with her." I made another attempt.

"Mother was a little bit like Dr. Olsson—more forward, no...that is not the word: stronger—more take-charge—action. Dr. Olsson...she's strong too, but in a quieter way I think."

I was thinking about the ride over and wasn't listening closely again. Her easy command of the car, shifting the floor transmission with ease, it made me comfortable. The window had been open slightly; we'd never really reached any great speed though her hair had blown loose and waved in short wisps around in her face. Each time, she would push it back around with the back of her hand and a patient smile.

"Mother suffered hardship easily and could take charge of herself...or others, if need be. She was independent, even of father, thought I know she loved him dearly. Resolute, would be a good way to describe her. After the attack at the *fäbod*, she resolved many things in her mind—things which would be different in the future."

CHAPTER 7

A Child Is Born

Much to the chagrin of her parents, their daughter Anna-Stina gave birth to an *oäktabarn*. It was the first source of embarrassment she had ever caused her family. The child...little Augusta, was born on a bitter, cold day in January, 1847; Anna-Stina's mother, Anna Helgsten, sensed the child would be weak from the beginning, because her daughter's stomach was so small. And after the birth she believed little Augusta would die before the week was out. For that reason, with her husband Anders she hastened the child to the church on the first Sunday following the birth, for a christening.

For a first birth, all went well for Anna-Stina. As most things she attempted, her resolution brought her through the ordeal. Her mother marveled at her daughter's resolve, as she assisted her straining birthing. The firm set of the jaw, the fiery, sweating brow and the strength she felt, both surprised and pleased Anna Helgsten, at the same time, remembering her own weakness at her first-birth and she gained a new respect for her daughter. In fact—at times...she nearly feared Anna-Stina's seemingly inexhaustible strength. The firm resolve that remained on her daughter's face now, through the birth pain, was a marvel to witness.

That flame of resolve wasn't without fuel. Anna-Stina, squatting over the soaked pallet at the foot of the bunk, thought of the child's father and the revenge she would one day have. She promised herself, as she bore down with each contraction—with every piercing pain: revenge! Veins marbled her flushed-red face, rolling around the cords in her neck as her muscles tensed. Her lips, tightly drawn over glistening white teeth, could not speak through the contorted grin: revenge. How will I find the way, she thought, attempting a smile to reassure her mother. I do not yet have an answer. But I shall...she told herself. Oh...I shall...gritting her teeth again with the next throbbing onslaught. There will be plenty of time...plenty of time: a lifetime, she nearly sobbed as two small tears broke free, cascading down her cheeks. I will not suffer, she said, gripping the edge of the bed frame, frowning in steadfast resolution, deep within the age-old grip the child's birth had upon her body. At least I could come home, she thought...I do not have to birth this child in a cow barn— in the *fäbod*, like a cow.

It was this final, resolute grimace on her daughter's face that Anna Helgsten witnessed. In complete awe for that moment, Anna even withdrew slightly from her daughter not knowing herself whether is was from respect, or fear of what she saw in Anna-Stina's face.

Within days, Anna-Stina was up and working around the cabin. Her parents wouldn't hear of her attendance at the sickly child's christening, pleading her health and the long journey to Nås church. They knew very well, she was probably able to make the journey along the river ice, in the horse and sled her father had borrowed for the occasion.

Anna-Stina recognized their shame for her plight and consented. She pitied them for the embarrassment she had brought to them in the community. Few of their friends had called at the timberhouse, since the birth. Anna-Stina cared little for the community's unspoken scorn, loving her child and caring for her, daily. The cold of January would keep her confined, caring for the child within the small house. She enjoyed the thought of being homemaker, mother, daughter and sister to her siblings. Being back with her own family again, while her father worked at the *smedja*, was safe. Anna-Stina's brothers and sisters would be at home and she could help them with their studies and let them in turn, help her with little Augusta.

The Sunday of the baptism, her parents passed silently into the church, bearing the bundled child. Though their eyes met, neither spoke as they passed between the pair of wooden pillory mockingly flanking the flagstone walkway. Snow draped the coarse oak top caps where the head and armholes served to emphasize their cruel purpose. It was here the Church dealt minor punishment and where imprisoned sufferers, collared and manacled in ridicule before passing parishioners, received their earthly reprimand.

Her parents knew just such punishment awaited Anna-Stina and the father of little Augusta, also, if she ever revealed his identity. Alone, their daughter would be unable to escape the stock's humiliating embrace and the thought of it was foremost in her parent's minds, during the service that Sunday.

The week following the baptism, a messenger arrived with an official letter from the minister of Nås Church. Her mother had taken it from the boy who brought it and given him some bread and cheese to eat on his long walk back to Nås.

"What is it mother," Anna-Stina asked as she sat, nursing the child, which had contracted an influenza and was suffering.

"I do not know, child—it appears to be from the church—a letter...see, the seal," she said, feeling ashamed at her cowardice, already guessing the document's message.

Herself unable to read, she handed it to Anna-Stina who opened it and carefully read it through. Then she reread it a second time. It was a friendly note asking after her and her child's health. There was no doubt of its' purpose, couched as it was in the kind words of the old minister, who must do the duty the church and custom demanded of him, despite his personal feelings to the contrary.

The letter requested Anna-Stina appear at the church office, an hour before the following Sunday's ceremony, for an interview with the old pastor; it suggested her parents accompany her to help with the child who was doubtless, still nursing.

"What does it say," her mother asked after she had ceased reading and was staring down at her daughter.

"I am to come to the church—early, mother. He wishes to speak to me about some matter," she said, smiling at the knowing look on her mother's face.

Over the years, the old minister had continued his benevolent treatment of Anna-Stina, despite the birth of her *oäktabarn*. He had given her Catechism like most of the children of the community and continued to marvel at her grasp of The Text and all matters spiritual that she encountered. Unlike the other youngsters in his classes, she would openly question the lesson, with intelligence and the reasoning

111

for some of the church doctrine, especially if she thought it conflicted with the Bible. If it were not that she was a female, he might have had concerns with her endless, questioning doubts. She was better suited for the ministry than the *fäbod*, he thought—a pity she was not born a man. She was a born leader and could inspire many to spirituality, given the opportunity denied by her sex.

The old minister knew this bright child had no malicious intent with her endless curiosity—she was more inquisitive and eager to learn. He did his best to further her understanding of the lessons, having, from time to time, discussed other matters—even beyond religion and had loaned her every book from his private library. It was astonishing a girl of such poor circumstances could grasp knowledge as readily as she had, literally devouring them, volume by volume, no matter their content or subject matter. The old minister liked and admired Anna-Stina for her intelligence, maturity and the matter of fact fashion in which she approached all things. And most of all, he liked her genuine, unselfish kindness to others.

When he first learned of it from the visiting curate from Stockholm, Pastor Johansson, the old minister didn't believe the accusation, thinking it some petty jealousy conjured by the local females. But as time and the size of the girl's middle proved, he could hardly any longer deny her pregnancy. He felt no anger toward her for suddenly being with child; he believed in a different sort of holy justice. But at first, he did feel a little bittersweet about the matter, thinking her now trapped, like so many young girls, by the wiles of an ignorant boy whom she would now wed and be trapped in an endless cycle of childbearing. For the life of him, he could not think of any local boy smart enough to beguile a young woman of her obvious brilliance. When he learned of her reluctance to name the impregnator, he became truly confounded and eventually pitied Anna-Stina and her family, the persecution which followed. Like others in the community, he found it astonishing that she would so suddenly be taken with child, when no one seemed able to name a single, likely candidate for the father. And of course, no male came forward admitting guilt. The secret remained undisclosed, to the date of the christening and, unless someone claimed patrimony, it seemed it would be a mystery forever.

Many of the young men in the community had tried to court

Anna-Stina. He'd heard rumors of many rebukes by her in Andersfors and the surrounding communities, as well as when the boys went up to the *fäbod* in the summer. She merely laughed at their feeble attempts, good naturedly, seeming to enjoy them, but apparently not at all flattered by the complement of being sought out for romance.

She appeared to genuinely like all people and was at peace with herself, as with most all the young men around her; when approached, she turned them down gently, retaining their affection and gaining their friendship. The female complement in the community did not take too kindly to these friendly attentions paid her by the boys. But they could do little but complain to themselves, since Anna-Stina chose not to take up any of the many offers made to her—thus offending no one of the girls in particular, leaving them entirely free to accept any forthcoming offers themselves, from the male community. It left little reason for remonstration—yet it remained, nevertheless.

"You see how it was then..." Karolina interrupted my train of thought, "...there was this other terrible thing they did in the Swedish church...to women."

"Yes...?" I replied, my interest perked.

" It was something called *kyrktagning*[48]—in Swedish...I don't know what you would say in English. All women who had born a child were considered by The Church to be unclean, after the birth, but not necessarily in a negative way, if the birth were legitimate. After the mother had recovered from childbirth, usually several weeks, they had to go through a *kyrktagning* ceremony in church, before they could return to the congregation. You might say they had to be cleansed, spiritually. But really—to think that having a child in some way made one impure—I can not understand such stupidity, even yet."

"Really—sounds like the male dominance influencing the church...almost medieval."

"No doubt. For a normal wife and mother, it was supposed to be a sort of celebration...to celebrate the birth and their contribution—gift of life through God and woman, to man—and The Church. The infant was taken as soon as possible after the birth—usually by the grandparents, god parents or relations, to be baptized, lest it perish first, something that happened a good deal, infant mortality being quite high."

"The mother remained at home?"

"Yes, mothers were not expected to travel about so soon after birth, especially in winter. But as I was saying, an *oäkta* birth...those mothers had to first be terribly humiliated, in order that in the future, they would regret what they had done. It also was probably intended to set an example for other women—not to get themselves in a family way and have a child out of wedlock."

There was a moment while Karolina remained in silent contemplation. Finally, "My mother only talked about it one time."

I was searching through my new notes and didn't at first realize she had stopped speaking. Absently, I looked up after a minute of silence. Karolina was staring across the garden with a distant look on her face. I, too, waited a moment, observing her silence.

"Karolina...?" I waited a little longer and she finally turned toward me with a forlorn smile.

"Mother said it was almost the most difficult thing—ever, in her life to endure—the *kyrktagning*. She said it was the most horrible custom in the Swedish church, as far as she was concerned, since witch burning. Thank God, we—women, have persuaded them to ban that custom from the service, forever I hope."

I hesitated to continue on such a depressing vein, but Karolina seemed determined. "Well—what was it, exactly—this *kyrktagning* in your mother's instance?"

"She was made to stand in a wooden frame in the church yard, before Sunday worship and be ridiculed for their sin, by the congregation passing into the church to worship their benevolent God."

THE SUMMONS

The letter, having now arrived, was not unexpected. As Anna-Stina stood beside the window reading the summons for the second time, her illiterate mother watched her daughter's reaction as she kneaded the second bread baking that week. Finished, Anna-Stina let her arms fall to her sides, the page dangling in one hand. She looked at her mother, wrist-deep in flour and dough, the unspoken question in her eyes.

After she related the letter's contents, her mother could do little more than smile ruefully and shake her head from side to side in remorse, the unspoken, but expected ordeal, yet to be witnessed and dreaded, throughout the coming days, until it was finally over.

So the following Sunday, as instructed, Anna-Stina layered Augusta in several wool blankets finishing off with a fleecy, sheep's hide. Her father borrowed a horse and sleigh and with Anna Helgsten along for her daughter's support, they set off cross-country; striking the river, carefully maneuvered along the river ice toward Nås and the church. Despite the bitter January cold, the river remained open. In many places it threatened to spill the sleigh and its precious contents into a black, gaping swirl of water, seen here and there shining in the stark moonlight of early morning. At other places along the shore, great stones, larger even than the sleigh, caused them to skirt dangerously close to thin river ice, open around rushing rapids. From the weight of the fast-stepping horse and sleigh, large cracks shot out before them, cracking like lightning bolts, adding further fright to the already instinctive fear of the danger the horse was being put to. An hour and a half before the service would start, Lars turned the horse up from the river shore and into the town, relieved, despite the gruesome ordeal still lying before them. As requested, the women and child proceeded immediately to the parsonage to meet the old pastor for refreshments and counseling before the service. Lars hurried to put the horse in the barn and saw to its fodder.

As always, when his wife escorted the morning visitors to the parlor, the smiling man of God greeted them warmly. The pastor and his wife made much of little Augusta who had slept warmly through the journey. After serving the men and Anna-Stina, the two older women took the baby to the kitchen to share a cup of coffee together, leaving the minister to prepare Anna-Stina and her father for the ordeal she would soon undergo in the pillory, which were at this moment, being dusted free of the nights' snowfall by the churchwarden. It was his habit, on the occasion of their use, to slowly exercise the top cap hinges a few times to clear the rust and ice from the hand wrought hinge and lock, insuring their serviceability in every way.

Ironically, Anna-Stina's father had himself wrought the ironwork for the pillory, upon his forge at Andersfors and his wife's brother, a *snickare* by trade, had sawn, hewn and shaped the wooden members. Together, they had chuckled to themselves as they erected them, that they hoped neither they nor their own would ever be so hapless to find themselves captive to such crude but strong workmanship; little did Lars know his words would one day haunt him.

Seated beside the parlor fire, after her mother and the pastor's wife had adjourned, Anna-Stina and her father were growing impatient, waiting for the minister to cease his small talk about the baby, the father's work at Bergslaget and other matters about the community and finally get to the point of the visit. Impatient and hardly able to contain herself, Anna-Stina had received her direct manner of speaking from her father; sitting there, neither of them appreciated the tardy reluctance of the minister, despite his well-meaning intention. Finally, noticing their increased agitation, the minister sighed, cleared his throat and began.

"Anna-Stina, you are of course aware why we have summoned you today and the reason I have asked you to be here so long before the service."

"Yes, Pastor, I am aware of the consequences of what has ha…of what I have done."

He regarded her curiously. "You understand, my dear, you do not have to face this humiliation alone?"

"I do, Minister."

"Yet…you remain reluctant to disclose the name of the father of Augusta?"

"Yes…Minister."

"Anna-Stina, the pain you must, by church law, suffer, can be shared…even mitigated somewhat by another of the community…the partner in this…this out coming—or even avoided entirely, should he come forward? This is not the first early birth of an infant in our community, as you know and I know by human nature, it will not be the last. But there is no need for you to bear the whole responsibility for what the church deems. A man who does this willingly, bringing about the consequences of an *oäkta* child, while deliberately remaining anonymous and leaving you to bear the brunt of the shame of the community and the church, is—it is an act of cowardice; nothing less. I am sorry to have to say it to you. But it is cowardice."

Anna-Stina stared silently at the child's woolen wrap draped across her lap.

The minister sighed: "I am afraid, Anna-Stina, that I can not bring myself to respect your…the father of the child for his reluctance to come forward. I consider it the responsibility of both partners in the union to share the repercussion of bringing new life into the world. I have little patience for someone leaving a young mother and her family to the sole obligation of his child's care. It is nothing but…cowardice, as I have said and I can not understand why you persist in protecting someone cut from this cloth."

Neither Anna-Stina nor her father replied, though the minister waited. He had grown frustrated with her silence, expecting something from either of them: disclosure, defensiveness, anger— something, other than this passiveness—this—stoic acceptance. Directing his inquiry to Anna-Stina's father, he said: "Lars…do you not also feel anger at what some man in the community has done to your daughter and your family, yet goes unrecognized—unpunished?"

Lars slowly raised his head; there were tears in his eyes. "I must respect the wish of my daughter, Minister. If she does not want to name the man, how can I make her? Should I beat her—hurt her further for the shame she chooses to share alone?" He lowered his head, brushing his eyes with the back of his hand. "I could not do that thing."

Anna-Stina laid a hand on his knee, but didn't look up.

The old minister sighed again, knowing he would get no further with this resolute pair. Finally, in an attempt to lighten the sadness of the moment, he set about explaining a change in church policy which had not yet reached their community.

"The custom of the pillory as punishment," he told them, "has long been discontinued in Stockholm and Uppsala, where the church and the community are both more progressive. But the old manners die slowly here with the country people; we like our love and our hate in large, well-defined doses. The board of governors for the Nås and Järna churches feel the pillory, even standing empty, are an excellent example to all the youngsters in the community, to mind their behavior. However, the local board even directed me to call the attention of the congregation to this device in the sermons, especially just before Midsommar, in hope of warding off some of the pagan pairing-off...their words...that has traditionally culminated at Midsommar, probably since the first, *majstångar* were erected. Who knows how many hundreds—or thousand years ago that was. If there could be a man also in the pillory here today, his presence would absorb most of the wrath of the church women elders, who are usually the worst abusers of the stocked victim."

He paused looking one last time at Anna-Stina, hoping to see her reconsider, but she sat unmoving.

"Baring the absence of a man, their full vehemence—a passion of another kind—will fall upon you, Anna-Stina, alone...again." A poignant pause: "You will be accused of everything from harlotry to being a temptress to their husbands and sons, no matter the sons are infants, loyal husbands, or toothless old men."

He turned to her mother who had returned, without the Minister's wife. "They will spit upon her, as you know is the custom. And their curses and abuses would continue for two more Sundays from today. I have never seen any single woman endure the pillory without emotionally breaking—by the second, mandatory Sunday. Some even have had to be forcibly placed between the wooden bars and afterwards...helped from them by family and friends, if any dare—these victims become so distraught." Again, he paused, hoping this history might create a chink in Anna-Stina's resolve.

"I recall my father telling me a story of a woman, long ago, who, after enduring the second Sunday in the pillory, on returning upriver, had leaped from the church boat with her *oäkta* child in her arms as the boat was mid way through the rapids. Neither mother nor child ever surfaced. From that time, someone in the church boat has always been appointed to watch out for these special mothers and watch how they hold their children…for it was feared some might even throw the child to the rapids. As you know, the timber rafters still claim they can hear the laments of that mother and child as they pass the point in the river, even today."

Anna-Stina held her child close. The minister continued. "Although, I have never heard it myself," he sighed, "because of the bitterness of the weather, you, Anna-Stina, will be installed in the contraption a quarter hour before the congregation arrives. Once the final bell—calling the congregation inside, was rung…" he turned to Anna-Stina, "…you will be freed and permitted to sit in the *vapenhus*[49] until the benediction is called. You will then immediately be returned to the pillory, to remain until the last worshiper has departed.

Looking again at Lars, he continued: "In this way the parishioners will be able to vent their frustrations upon your—daughter," he said, indicating Anna-Stina with a wave. "In previous times, many prisoners of the pillory did not live to return a second Sunday from having to spend the entire time outdoors in the embrace of the wood. They died of pneumonia before the next Sunday. As it is my child, please take along some additional clothing or blankets from my own house to warm you in the *vapenhus*, for the service will be longer when you are chilled and you will grow cold out there, before having to return again to the pillory."

Turning to Anna-Stina's mother: "You will be caring for the child, no doubt while your daughter remains in the *vapenhus*? If the child becomes hungry or extremely fussy, you may take her to her mother to nurse, or comfort, but you must return with her immediately upon finishing. It must not be seen that you or the child, are comforting her there."

The old woman nodded. She had seen enough of this herself, many times before. If only her daughter would cry, become angry—something, her mother thought.

There came a knock at the door and the minister's wife entered slowly, casting a questioning look at her husband.

Visibly admitting defeat, the minister gave a slight shake of his head and turning to Anna-Stina and her father, said: "It is time for you to bear your punishment, Anna-Stina; may the Lord have mercy upon you my girl."

"Thank you Minister. I shall sustain it—do not fear," and she touched his shoulder gently, smiling. "Thank you for all your kindness, past and now."

She turned: "Father, let us go so you and Mother can be inside with Augusta before...they begin to arrive."

They followed the minister's wife from the study, closing the door.

In a little while, the minister heard them leaving the house; the congregation will soon begin to arrive, filing up the road and coming up the walk to the front door of the church. Approaching between those abominable instruments, they will find to their surprise—and for some—pleasure, my dear Anna-Stina Malmberg, captured by one of them. The other vacant device will at least remain a guilty reminder for someone, of his responsibility, should he come to church today. He sighed mightily and placing both palms on his knees he slowly tipped himself forward and rising stiffly, walked to the window.

A cloudless day brought little cheerfulness into the small, book-laden room. He stood staring out without speaking. How often he had done this—paused in a meeting—seeking inspiration, guidance while gazing at the broad side of the churchyard. Then he saw Anna-Stina and her parents walking along the yard toward the church. Her wrists and neck will soon be captives of the coarse wood, he thought. He shook his head in sadness and leaned his forehead onto the pane of glass, feeling there the cold bitterness that waited on the other side, relentless—without comfort.

CHAPTER 8

The Punishment

The churchwarden was waiting beside the pillory by the time Lars' family crossed the paved path to the front of the church. As they approached he lifted one of the large, wooden caps with its half-cut out holes for wrists and neck. He didn't meet Anna-Stina's gaze at first but looked instead at the packed snow at his feet; she had known him all her life, from attending the church. He was old and a little simple, able to do few jobs requiring skill, but he was not without kindness. She smiled when he finally dared to glance her way and spoke his name kindly. It was not the first time and he had not forgotten.

Her mother and father helped her arrange her heavy sheep's wool skirt over the tall stool before the pillory. This task took a moment before she was finally safely positioned on the slippery, packed ice. Her height was insufficient to stand, bending upright, like a man, for whom the apparatus had been designed. A stool had to be brought from the church and then changed to an even taller stool that better positioned her upper torso for the pillory's embrace.

When she was seated comfortably, Anna-Stina placed both wrists in the openings and slowly leaned forward and rested her neck on the coarse pine of the supporting stock. Her mother watched as the churchwarden slowly and carefully tipped the top wooden cap over first one wrist, then her neck and finally the other wrist. He was careful to smooth the back of her scarf around her neck so as not to pinch into the delicate flesh with the cruelly, sharp wood as the two halves closed around their delicate prize.

But she still didn't sit high enough on one side. They lifted the pillory's arm and had her step down from the stool while snow was kicked beneath the stool's legs in an attempt to raise it. Finally, in frustration, Anna-Stina told them to proceed...that it was good enough, crooked as it was, sitting at an angle.

Again, they delicately lowered the cap around her wrists and slid the rusty iron pin home, securely locking her in place. Anna Helgsten began to cry and turned toward the church door, clutching Augusta to her breast, as she stumbled up the flags. Anders watched the warden finish the closure, swing the iron hasp and slide the lock through the keeper, making the wooden clamp secure. Then he hurriedly followed his wife up the stone steps; his daughter would have to fend for herself, he thought, sadly. She has created this bed by herself and wishes to occupy it alone.

But at the door he paused and looked back, staring long and hard at his daughter, her head turned sharply, facing the tips of her boots. Bent downward as she was, she would be unable to identify her accusers until they were well past her, going into the church with their backs already turned. This way, she would not easily know who had passed her by, without deed, or comment, or who paused and vented both their wrath and possibly their saliva on her, as was sometimes the custom. Lars shook his head slowly, brushed at his eyes and passed into the cold and empty church to take a seat alone on the men's side of the aisle. Shortly after, the old warden followed, taking up his place at the thick bell-rope and began his final bell ringing, beckoning all worshipers to the service.

Anna-Stina settled herself firmly on the stool at the final tolling of the bell. Facing each other, the facing pillories were placed at right angles to the flagstone walkway. She tried turning her head to one side. Despite her thick scarf the coarse edges of the splintery wood cut painfully into her neck.

The tolling of the bell hadn't ceased when she heard the first worshipers approach from the road. She could hear the horses and sleighs; then voices, as the men dropped off family members before putting up the horses in the barn across from the church. As the walkers drew closer, having seen her, they whispered as they passed. She could only see the ground in front of her feet, refusing to turn her head, or attempt to look at them as they approached. As they passed some began to spit upon her. She knew it would be best not to know who among them condemned her, for fear of what she might someday do to one, in the future.

Finally, only the stragglers remained to pass and those were late and cared little to dally before the girl with the bowed head. Many passed without even hesitating. Maybe they too have a secret, she thought, thankful, finally that she was about to be alone once more. And then a few children came as the bell began to toll for the last time. Soon I shall be set free for a while, she thought. That was not so bad, once the first few had passed me, she thought.

Giggling boys and girls scurried past, rushing into the church. One pair were snickering and muttering quiet curses. She recognized the lisp of one particularly disagreeable girl, Olga. Thinking the door would soon slam behind them, Anna-Stina waited, already longing for the warmth of the *vapenhus*. But Olga apparently turned back and running up to the pillory, gave the stool a strong kick, spun round and raced after the boys, disappearing into the church.

Immediately, Anna-Stina was in distress. The stool's legs slipped far to one side, twisting, causing her lower torso to lean precariously. Her body was now far off balance on the stool's edge. She tried to hang on with arms and neck and nudge the stool back beneath her. But it wouldn't move and she soon began to sag. The pillory was tearing into her throat, cutting off her air. She leaned forward and found some relief; but that put her further off balance, causing the stool to tilt further forward. Once again, she attempted to draw herself up and tip the stool back, while pushing one foot forward against the pillory's supporting pole. But the ice let the stool's legs to slip backward even more, as she did; the stool threatened to depart completely from beneath her. Leaning forward again, she took a deep breath, trying not to panic. Then she eased her rump backward again, balancing as best she could with her neck thrust forward, remaining as still as she could while holding her breath, until she had to lean forward again for another.

"Ding! Dong! Ding..." the bell continued to toll.

He will stop ringing soon and come to release me—any time, he'll finish and return. If I can pace my breathing in this way. But each time she leaned forward and rose slightly, the stool pivoted forward, slipping a little further away from the pillory. If the stool falls

I will soon hang myself, she thought. Her heart was racing. The bell continued to toll. Any outcry, should she be able to scream, would remain unheard. Suddenly she heard someone approaching. I shall call for help to them. Surely, they will see what has happened.

She heard the rustle of silks as the party came to a halt beside her.

"There is the Malmberg girl," a woman's voice said. "It is about time she received what was due her."

Anna-Stina tried to turn her head and attract their attention, but the wood only cut deeper. Her attempts to shout came out as strangled gagging sounds. She wiggled her hands wildly, flexing her fingers, but there was no response.

"See how brazenly she defies me," the woman sneered.

"Anna-Stina had held her breath as long as she could and now tipped upward slightly, gasping to catch her wind enough to shout. As she did, the stool fell forward against the back of her skirt and the sharp edge of the lower stock cut into her throat. She was truly hanging now and could neither breathe nor shout. She struggled, whimpering slightly, the sound making only a mere grunt in her throat.

"Look at her squirm," the woman said again. "Children, take note that you do not ever end up in the condition of this poor creature. The Lord in his wisdom has chosen to punish her for her sinful behavior. And a pity, too, the other sinner can not be found out as well to join her across the flags."

Anna-Stina heard the sound of a male voice; because of the blood pounding in her ears she could barely hear what was said.

"Mother…mother, look—there is something the matter with her. See how she sits…has the stool not fallen from beneath her?"

"Nonsense—there is nothing wrong with her. You are only feeling sorry. Hurry now, let us go inside. We are late for service. We have seen enough. Children do not dare touch her or say anything. And if you even look as if you will spit upon her you shall spend the next week without your suppers. Frömans do not lower themselves to such commonality."

Anna-Stina could hear the sound of departing boots as the rustle of silks faded.

It was the Fröman family she thought as the voices disappeared up the flags toward the church.

The ringing in her ears was increasing and she began to feel light-headed. She tried once again to raise the stool with the backs of her heels, but failed. As she struggled, it moved backward completely, beneath the volume of her sheepskin and under-skirt. She hung suspended from the frame by her neck and wrists, with only the tips of her toes touching the ground.

She had about given up hope when a face, turned sideways, suddenly appeared below her own. It was very close. Anna-Stina's only thought was that the children had returned to torment her; but she was far too weak to respond, nearing unconsciousness. As her eyes rolled back in her head, her mouth slowly opened and drool stringed downward from her mouth.

"*Yuckkk…*" Carl Fröman's stood upright quickly, wiping his face. He'd ignored his mother's admonition by returning to determine the stock's victim's condition…and maybe to flirt with her a little in hopes of cheering her up. Handkerchief in hand, he bent forward and twisted his face upward again, this time remaining to one side as he peered up into her face.

"Anna-Stina…are you all right?"

One look at her rolled-back eyes and the veins standing out on her bright, red face was enough to convince Carl she was in trouble. He ducked beneath the stock's crossbar, trying to survey her predicament. He bent searching for the stool he knew must be there…somewhere beneath the heavy sheepskin. Finally, he spied a single wooden spindle jutting from beneath her voluminous skirt. Reaching beneath the edge of her skirt he gingerly grasped the wood, thinking to reposition it without offending her modesty.

He knew Anna-Stina and from a distance had often admired her good looks and charming personality. But he also knew the extent to which his mother's anger would be aroused, should she ever learn he was paying Anna-Stina Malmberg, any favors. Should anyone come from the church now and see him prodding beneath her skirts—a helpless woman trapped and defenseless in the pillory, it would defy all explanation. With one foot, he gingerly pushed back the edge of the stool. But it still wasn't correctly positioned and didn't seem to relieve her suffering. She appeared to be sagging into unconsciousness. In desperation he stepped up beside her and reached one arm around her waist and lifted her up.

He heard a rush of air then as she began gasping for breath. He held her for a moment as she breathed deeply, sucking in and exhaling loudly. He glanced in both directions and then over his shoulder at the church door. But there was no one to help.

He continued to hold her up, trying to determine what he should do; but she was growing heavy and soon began to sag in his grasp. He couldn't hold her much longer. He let her down, bent and with his lower back thrust beneath her abdomen, he lifted her up again, nearly pig-a-back-style; she was not a light burden. He could smell the sweetness of her hair. He held the post of the pillory with one hand, attempting to steady the soft burden. It was all he could do to keep his footing on the ice, between holding her and glancing worriedly around.

After a few moments, her breathing eased altogether and when she tried to speak, only an unintelligible sound issued.

"What—I can't understand what it is you're saying, Anna-Stina."

He lowered her a little, turning to better hear her and see her face. But a strange expression had appeared...a look of extreme surprise was on her face when he peered around the timber. She had been hanging, catching her breath, but immediately began making loud sucking sounds again. As he watched, her face again began to turn bright red. He realized that he had let her sag too far. Quickly he backed and thrust his rump beneath her stomach again, lifting her up and holding her until the slurping, wheezing sounds ceased. As long as he held her so no sounds came out, only normal gasping, so he knew it was about right. This time he held her up until she could speak. At first she began clearing her throat, coughing and spitting, before she was finally able to squeak.

"Lift me up higher Carl Fröman...and stick the damn stool back under my rump!" she hissed and choked in very obvious anger.

He attempted to comply. Unsure how to proceed without letting her down again, he finally dropped her completely, immediately setting off another spasm from the front of the pillory. He walked behind the kicking, bulky skirts, and stood facing away from her. After studying the probable position of the stool, he reached beneath her dress with his right arm and found the stool tipped forward against her legs. He then tried to slide the stool under her rump from that direction. She continued choking, spitting and kicking, at the same time trying to give him orders.

The church bell ceased its tolling; his parents would be wondering where he'd gone. He felt utterly stupid, not knowing how to grab the sputtering bundle without touching her somewhere he shouldn't. Her struggles had begun to slow again. He was concerned she was about to lapse into unconsciousness.

In desperation, he dropped her again. Quickly stepping behind her he grabbed the stool and placed it beside her. Then he grabbed her by the rump, placing an arm around and beneath her, he hoisted her up and onto his lap. He was now half standing, half squatting behind her, holding her around her waist with one arm as he struggled to turn the stool beneath her with the other.

In this position Anna-Stina was more or less sitting on his lap with Carl standing as upright as he could while still supporting her. He'd fished the stool around and managed to get it partially beneath his own rump before collapsing for a moment to catch his breath. His arms ached and he momentarily lowered his burden onto his lap. Immediately she began making gasping sounds again and he realized he was tipping her too far to the side.

After he lifted her, allowing her to catch her breath again, the door to the church swung slowly open. Carl's heart missed a beat. He thought it was his mother come to see where he'd gone. But only the churchwarden wandered out, picking his nose as he came. He spied Anna-Stina and Carl, resting from their recent struggles and hesitated, staring at them, his arm still for the moment in curiosity, having forgetting its' earlier chore. Recovering, he lumbered down the steps and strolled over the flags, stopping in front of the pillory. He stood watching as Carl struggled anew to get a hand or a foot on the stool and right it.

"Kick the damn stool over to me, will you Albert? Otherwise unlock them and let her out…she was choking" Carl strained to hold Anna-Stina upright and at the same time, pointing at the wayward stool.

Albert glanced in the direction Carl pointed, took two slow steps toward Anna-Stina and easily tipped the stool up within Carl's grasp again.

Carl let his burden drop once more, quickly grabbed the stool and reached beneath the stool with one hand pulled up Anna-Stina's skirts above her buttocks and thrust the stool firmly beneath her thighs. Then, with his other hand, he blindly reached back beneath her skirts and slowly worked the stool beneath her as he lowered her again. With a couple of bumps, he bounced her upwards, eliciting an angry gurgle each time from the front end of the pillory. While simultaneously slipping the stool forward and getting out of the way himself, he finally managed to get her securely in place again.

The gagging sound ceased. Carl could tell Anna-Stina was weak because she merely slumped upon the stool and within the pillory. Had she the voice for it, she probably would have cursed him. He didn't back away immediately; he wanted to insure the stool remained in place.

But Albert, his curiosity satisfied, did what he came outside to do and removed the lock and began to open the pillory so the captive could spend the duration of the service in the *väpenhus*. After unlocking the iron shackle and pulling free the rusty lock, he casually strolled back toward the church without a backward glance at the couple. Carl now tentatively walked around to the front of the pillory, glancing tentatively at the still form still perched precariously on the stool.

She is breathing, he thought, seeing her back rise and fall. He bent again, turning to stare upward into Anna-Stina's face. He noticed saliva drooling from her mouth and she gasped slightly from time to time, regaining her breath. Her face was white and her eyes were closed. He glanced around for the misplaced handkerchief, in order to wipe her mouth. He discovered it peeking from beneath her skirt, picked it up and bending, carefully began dabbing her mouth.

Anna-Stina opened her eyes to find Carl staring up at her. His face was very close to hers. She remained slumped and for a moment, both studied each other's features. Her breath came warm and steamy in his face. She couldn't yet speak. Carl smiled reassuringly, while occasionally dabbing needlessly at her face and lips with his handkerchief. She could hear him mumbling incoherent, which she took to be comforting words. It struck her then that it was so strange—this situation—Carl Fröman, the son of the richest farmer in the community, of all people, doing this for me...humbling himself in this way.

Considering the act, despite herself, she began to cry; the tears quickly turned to anger and it took her a moment to control herself and steady her breathing. Out of his concern for her embarrassment, seeing her tears, Carl turned his head aside. He was nearly falling over backwards as he worked.

Anna-Stina finally rasped: "How strange you look, Carl Fröman."

He smiled, happy to see her sense of humor intact.

"Not half as funny as you were...when you fell off your stool, Anna-Stina Malmberg."

"I didn't fall off...it was kicked from under me," she spat back as best she could, angry at his insinuation of clumsiness.

Ah...she does have spirit, he thought, but didn't rise to the challenge.

"I thought you would never put it back, Carl. What were you waiting for...a written invitation? Or, were you trying to see how long I could hang here without breathing?"

"Well, I considered it—but then decided the punishment did not fit the crime."

"That shows how much you learned in your church university schooling. The rest of the community seems to think differently."

"I am not the rest of the community," he mumbled somewhat defensively.

"I can see that, Carl Fröman. And it was nice of you to say so, anyway. Thank you for wiping my face also—I am sorry that— you...you had to do...such cleaning me up."

"You are most welcome, Anna-Stina. Think nothing of it. I am certain you would have done the same, would you not?"

She ignored his question, still embarrassed that a man of his stature would stoop to wipe the drool from a girl such as herself— especially considering her predicament.

"Did you study enough at the university to be able to lift this thing off me Carl Fröman—I believe Albert has unlocked it. I am permitted to sit in vapenhus, now."

He regarded her calmly, even bravely, staring deeply into her eyes. What was it there? A journey of a million miles he thought, tearing himself away from her enchantment. He would not normally be daring enough to look so directly at a girl and would not have, this one, were the circumstances different.

"I feared you might slide out onto the snow, if I freed you too soon," he said with a chuckle, straightening and setting about pivoting the iron hasp, before gingerly tipping the heavy wooden cap up and away from her wrists and neck. "This is my first Sunday back home in Skålbyn; is this your first Sunday—here?"

"My first Sunday—yes and nearly my last. If you had not

returned, Old Albert would have had some news for the worshipers before this service was over. As it is, you have spoiled their fun for today, but kept me available for the next two Sunday's ridicule."

"A pity…I wish…."

"Do not wish anything Carl Fröman," she interrupted, "this affair has nothing to do with you. I accept my punishment—willingly. I do not expect them to hang me however." Did you see who kicked the stool from beneath me?"

"Kicked it from beneath you? I thought you had gone to sleep and fallen off."

When she didn't respond, more reasonably he asked: "Did someone really do that?"

She nodded.

"How cruel—they should be in the other set, there…" he gestured toward the empty pillory across the walk. "For that is a deserving act."

"I believe I know who kicked it. If I find out for certain, she will wish she was in this pillory before I am finished with her."

As they chatted, Anna-Stina had been tentatively massaging her wrists and neck, chafed during her confinement. Noticing her discomfort, Carl had taken each hand, in turn and was examining wrists and then her neck as she finally stepped down from the stool. The flesh had been cut on both wrists and the skin peeled from the cords and muscles of her neck. A twinge of pity—and something else rose upward from somewhere within Carl's boots and rushed to his head.

"You're hurt Anna-Stina," he said, touching her chafed flesh with one finger.

"*Ooww*—what are you doing Carl?" Anna-Stina roared, turning toward him and rubbing the collar of her blouse.

"I…you are hurt…and I just thought…."

He leaned against the pillory at a complete loss for words in the face of her sudden wrath. Seeing how her spiteful words had hurt him, Anna-Stina softened her voice and placed a hand on his arm.

"I'm sorry, Carl Fröman—my quick tongue—please excuse me. I am not myself with this…I know you didn't mean me harm."

He stared intently at the top of her head. Being unmarried, she was not wearing a headscarf.

"What is this in your hair," he asked reaching up and fingering the dampness.

"Please Carl—do not do that…" she said, knowing what he would find in her hair.

With a disgusted look, Carl wiped his hand on his trousers.

"They—show their true selves by spitting upon me. You shame me further, Carl, by—trying to clean it".

But he ignored her protest and continued dabbing at the moisture with his other mitten.

"I'll try not to smear it around," he said pensively. But he was and cleaning it seemed hopeless, short of completely immersing her head.

"Oh—Anna-Stina…they shame all Christians by doing this to you."

"Please…just leave it. I will take care of it later—tonight."

"Tonight…you must stay with this…until tonight?" he said, knowing there was little that could be done, but still questioning the lack of solution.

"These pillories have been banned as punishment in Stockholm for some years, you know. We are ignorant peasants to continue such a primitive practice here in the north."

"Is your father not on the church board, Carl…?" Her meaning was obvious.

He took her arm, helping her around the stool and continued supporting her as she walked unsteadily toward the outer doors of the church.

"Your point is well taken, Anna-Stina. Unfortunately, in some areas I am unable to influence him—this community…and I am sorry to say I can not help you further, here, either. I must now go inside for the service. But I will remain a while after the service and watch as they leave, to see that no harm comes to you again."

"Thank you Carl, but you need not bother. My father will come out and will be there to watch."

"Is there anything I can get you…are you cold…before I go inside?"

"No, I am fine now…thanks to you for your kindness. Please go so no one sees us, least they think you…least someone gets the wrong impression."

"Least they think me the father of your child?" he said, chuckling. "I could not have been, even if you were kind enough to favor me.

Remember—I have been in Stockholm at university for two years?

She smiled at his kindness.

"Keep a tight seat upon that stool Anna-Stina," he said, smiling once more at her. "I will be watching for you...later." There it was again...there, in her eyes. God, what a journey lay there. He straightened, turned and swinging open the massive outer door, entered the *vapenhus*.

"Come now—you can take your seat here. It is warmer and you should rest for...you should rest."

"Thank you," she whispered as Carl turned and opened the inner door and quietly slipped inside the church alone. She heard the voice of the minister raised in prayer as the inner door opened and closed. Her neck and wrists burned. Her throat was sore. She thought about what had happened. He did not ridicule me. He treated it in a silly way so I would not be embarrassed—but I was, anyway. That was true consideration and kindness...even I could not be serious or sorrowful for very long, when he laughed with me—and not at me.

Why was he so kind to me, I wonder, she thought, feeling not at all unhappy, even considering the day? She sat, huddled on the large bench. She'd read about the original use of this part of the church in one of the old minister's books. Here, the Viking warriors were required to leave their weapons, before entering the church to worship, lest fighting break out between warring factions. So long ago, she thought, huddling under in her fleece coat.

I feel like a warrior myself, she mused, battling the will of The Church...and losing. Here, I must spend two more Sundays, to be moved to and from the pillory again. She was not yet growing cold sitting on the bench. Unlike the parishioners within, she did not benefit from the body heat of hundreds of companions around her, so it was only a matter of time until she did. Despite the spittle that lay in her hair, she drew up her wool hood and lay lengthwise on the bench, tucking up her feet neatly beneath her skirt. Next Sunday my head will be well covered, she resolved. If Augusta fussed in hunger, she could nurse her, the minister had said. She occupied herself, thinking of when her mother would bring her beautiful little Augusta to feed.

What a cruel and inhuman thing, she thought, this that they have done to me. The benefit of her education brought about within her, a philosophical objectivity to this most inhumane of punishments. The current custom—being removed during the sermon, was relatively recent, she knew. In the days of old, persons must endure the pillory the entire duration of the sermon—winter or summer. Even today, the custom was still maintained in the summer. Had it not been for Carl, the experience would have been extremely distressing—but not so much so that she could not endure it, she thought, resolutely setting her teeth, assuming the stool remained in place.

Warming a little, she began to relax. The droning of the minister's voice within the church rose and fell with his message. The words they had used...they did hurt. I could not have imagined people felt that way about me. I thought I was well liked in the community. When had I made these enemies? I had never been unkind to anyone that I can remember—except Pastor Johansson. What had I done to make them so angry, now? Just having the child? Could that be some threat? Or did their scorn represent the scorn of the community? All their own unnamed sins—the church and the behavior they thought they were expected to exhibit?

Rationalizing gave her something more to consider throughout the long hours of the service. Her mother finally brought Augusta to feed and seemingly within minutes, returned to fetch her away again—lest the nursing be considered comforting. Anna-Stina understood them—now. She understood them as she never had.

"Damn them," she said, then realizing she was in the house of God. "Damn them..." she mouthed, more quietly, glancing at the ceiling,.

She dozed and awoke again but with no idea how long she had slept. She was quite cold and stood up to exercise her limbs. It was not long before the last hymn was being sung. Yes...sing you holy people, she thought. You, who will soon have your entertainment again, "...come—come..." the music seemed to say—
"...go...go...go to reap their scorn.

She turned as the door opened and Albert strolled through and noisily opened the outer door. The cold wind struck her fully. It was already becoming dark outside. She stood and began arranging her clothes before crossing the threshold and going again to her precarious perch. As she walked out, the inner doors swung open; the final hymn was loud when the door was open: "...go, go..."

Walking down the paved flags, she was stiff with sitting and numb with the cold of inaction. Albert waited patiently beside the pillory.

"This time, fix the stool properly, Albert. I do not wish to hang twice in the same day. When he didn't respond, she arranged the stool, herself. She glanced at the open doors of the church once, before prostrating herself across the beam; but this time, in total defiance instead of fear. As she prostrated herself in the cold wood, Albert lowered the beam, carefully fixing her arms as he settled the beam.

I must be firmly in place this time when they file past. Yes, this time I am ready, armed…give me all you have, she thought, for I can endure it and even more. I know who has done this to me and I shall triumph over him—and all of you if I must, in the end. Just you wait…she thought.

Later, as the sleigh careened homeward in the moonlight, cozy once again between her mother and her father, Anna-Stina cradled her sleeping infant beneath a sheepskin wrapper. Her mother was concerned the child may have caught another cold. Anna-Stina was thinking about the day's event, as the sleigh's runners rattled and bounced over the ridges in the ice. It was not so bad she thought…now that the first one is over. Had it not been for Carl Fröman, it would nearly have been unbearable, now I consider it. She hadn't told her parents about Carl's intervention; it was something she wished to savor alone. Carl Fröman had given her courage. He'd also given her renewed hope and ambition—ambition to stand up for herself and, just possibly, to triumph.

At the church, her mother had seen her gingerly tugging the blouse collar away from her neck, when she was freed from the pillory. Anna Helgsten pulled her daughter's collar back and cried out in astonishment.

"Anna-Stina, what happened? Let me see your wrists," and she grasped Anna-Stina's forearm and carefully, one after the other, peered beneath the bloody sleeves. "Daughter, why did you not say something?" she chided.

"It was too tight, Mother, just a little too tight; nothing more. Nor am I harmed, either—I actually feel strengthened," she said, smiling at her mother's astonished face and thinking again of her rescuer. Her mother shouted above the noise of the crashing steel runners, "Lars—when we come next Sunday—bring your draw knife and see to it that you widen the openings before our daughter is again confined. And if anyone of them objects, you tell me!"

Lars nodded his understanding, smiling biter sweetly.

"...Because I will have your ax, Lars," she said more quietly.

After seeing how his daughter's neck had been chafed, Anders felt ashamed for the roughness of the stock's framework. He and his brother-in-law had constructed the apparatus two years previously, replacing a previous pair, long gone to rot from age. He recalled how rough his fellow carpenter had left the wood after Lars had fitted the irons he'd made. The pair had then joked about how it would feel for the penitent captor, knowing at the time the additional pain it would inflict. Little did Lars know what fowl would come home to roost and the pain their action would one day inflict upon his own. A single tear was caught in the wind and blown backward, freezing as it disappeared into his side whiskers.

CHAPTER 9

The Flame Dies

"It must have been extremely humiliating."

Karolina had paused again in her story and was staring at her hands. She'd been flexing her right hand—the one affected by the stroke, trying to exercise away the stiffness.

"Yes, Mother said—had it not been for Father coming back out of the church to check on her, the ordeal may have turned out differently."

"You mean—she would have strangled?"

"Yes, little question of that. But there was something else, too, a sort of—hope father inspired in her, by caring."

"Hope...how so?"

"Well...imagine...a handsome member of the upper establishment—the class she probably despised at the time. Wealth, power and the ability to so influence her life—punish her for a crime, if you can call it that. Because of her lowly station in life she knew she would be unable to prove any accusations against him and he wasn't likely to take ownership of the child. Anyway, without that hope, inspired by father's gentle caring beside the pillory, Mother said she doubted she'd have been able to endure the punishments that followed. Though they didn't speak again, for a long time, Father was her succor...her encouragement to bear it all; and she did, for two more Sundays. She didn't let them best her."

I considered what she'd just told me: "You know Karolina, I find many of those old practices abominable—those instituted by the old church. Even in America, we had a good deal of witch hunting which resulted in punishment or death…totally unjustified, against innocent women."

"Yes—that happened in Sweden, too—in the old days."

"What did your mother do—after she served her punishment?"

"Her life continued normally, in Andersfors. She continued in her silence—not naming the father of her child. She knew few in the community would believe the true story of her attack, anyway, especially since she'd never disguised her boldness around young men. As a result, she was mistakenly thought to be brazen and forward—although she'd never before known a man in that way."

"Good point."

"No one would have dared accuse her openly. But now, she'd been caught so to speak and would no longer be able to deny a secret lover, if confronted with an accusation…so she had to be careful, least someone conjure up a false charge. The problem they had of course was the absent lover—no one could fathom who the father was and that tormented them. Many women began to suspect their own husbands, especially if they'd strayed before and so…grew to hate my mother without having real cause. Mother could do little but stand strong in the face of criticism—hoping their petty piousness would turn from disgust, to scorn and finally to acceptance of her as who she truly was—a kind person and a potential friend."

"And she eventually brought them around?"

"Well, they did…finally come around, but only from when it became obvious she wasn't interested in their husbands and sons…but I'm getting ahead of myself."

"Sorry…."

"How to avenge the Pastor's deed…that was mother's quandary. She knew there was plenty of time—the remainder of her life, she supposed, because by that time, she assumed she would probably never marry."

"Your mother sounds like a woman of extreme, singularity of purpose—very strong. I wonder, if having had an illegitimate child…that that did not warn away any potential suitors?"

"Strangely, the incident with the pastor's assault at the *fäbod* didn't change her natural attraction for people and young men her age. Even after the birth of my older sister—the Pastor's child, still living with the remnants of the attack in her mind, mother continued to enjoy young men's company. She only seemed now to be more pensive—more…resolute than before. Whenever she saw a young man, even if he wasn't particularly handsome, she told me she tried to smile and regarded him kindly. As a result, many men fell in love with her in this equality of treatment. Personally I believe it—the incident, gave her a sense of…of apparent vulnerability and that attracted many men. Although most young men didn't bear up under her bold scrutiny, many were flattered by it—many, erroneously. Knowing her reputation—a child out of wedlock, some made the mistake to assume she was free and easy with her favors and tried to take advantage of what had never been offered and usually, quickly regretted it. They mistook the vulnerability as inability."

"I can well imagine."

"And sadly, throughout all this, as Grandmother Anna Helgsten predicted, little Augusta did grow frailer and the child became weaker and weaker until she passed away from *hjärtsprång*, a common name for heart failure. She was just over two years of age. As you can imagine, mother grieved—but, openly, only for a day—then she returned to her normal, strong self, working at home, caring for her brothers and sisters and helping grandmother.

"Was that deliberate? Surely, people must have thought her…insensitive?"

"Some probably did. But she grieved in silence for the most part. She had to remain her own woman as there were few to confide in—no family member but her mother…younger sisters. And she didn't wish to tell them what was in her heart, fearing her mother would try to convince her of the folly of her ways, tell her to give up her vengeance and catch herself a good man, before it was too late. She would have advised her to settle down and have another, proper family this time.

But not my mother; she knew her time would come. She knew if she accused the young minister in public, the church board would convene. And in the guise of investigating the allegations, they would simply build a false case against her, if only to save one of their own. No…revenge would be hers; she'd made a promise to herself. She told me that for years, she existed solely upon the thought of revenge.

"I marvel at your mother's strength of purpose, Karolina. She was woman of force, to say the least and for it not to warp her personality, carrying all that hate and vengeance; astonishing, at such a young age, too."

"To say the least and amid it all, still living with a family who were for the most part, illiterate; she had to try to adjust to their place in time—the previous century. Remember, she had, to some extent, an education from the old minister and as a result, was somewhat a woman of the future...ahead of her time, having begun to take charge of life as few women of her time were doing, at least in the rural north. That generation of rural women was very superstitious, as were most country people. The spiritual symbols outside Christianity, from here in the old Sweden, were indeed unique. The *mörksuga*[50] for instance, a visage might be carved and hung in a inconspicuous place in the home. Though no one really knew what the imaginary creature should resemble, they fashioned their worst fears into a small image, of terrible proportions and knew absolutely, that some great harm could come from it if *mörksuga* appeared.

"Yes, I've heard of them—another one of so many creatures of superstition."

"Exactly—strange...yes? And *Näcken*, the legendary naked young man who stood playing the violin in the running waters of a stream or along the lakeshore. He was reputed to tempt maidens as they passed him. Legend had it, if they listened to his playing too long—they would be unable to ever stop dancing.

"Yes—*Näcken* I've heard of."

"He was probably invented by a girl who became pregnant and wanted to blame it on a spirit, rather than the boy, who fathered her child. It's difficult to say how these imaginative creatures came into being."

"That sounds likely."

And *Rånda*? Remember—I told you of *Rånda*...the woman of the forest?"

"Yes...strange—what do you suppose brought about that creature's invention?"

"To the people of the northern forest—she was very real. Indeed, all the legends were centuries-old creations of over imaginative minds. Woodcutters, charcoal-makers and of course the *vallkulla*...all of their duties required they remain alone for weeks at a time, in the forest. After a while they probably longed for a companion, or even a lover and I believe they eventually began to imagine things. One person would tell another and before long, he would imagine he or she saw it too; and the legend was born."

"Possibly the people originally meant to tease a child's mind, but the tales lived on into adulthood for most country folk. There were also rituals about crop planting, having babies, getting married, courting and so on. All my grandmothers—like Anna Helgsten, believed in them all."

"Yes…a good deal of church ritual is based on the incorporation of just such stories."

"Yes, exactly…good point…well, to go on…."

But I interrupted her again: "Karolina—I believe I must leave now—let you get some rest."

"Nonsense," she said, a fire still kindled in her eye from the discussion. "I'll merely lay here and worry. I know when I am fatigued…I'll tell you if and when I tire."

"Are you sure…? I don't want anything else to happen to you."

"It won't, so don't fret."

I still wasn't certain I should remain, but she ignored me and went on.

"Anyway, as I was saying, it was just after mother's first child passed away, she was contacted by the Widow Fröman, in Nås. She was a vicar's wife. Mother was offered the position of *piga*—house maid…kitchen girl. This was an aunt to Carl Fröman by marriage. Her husband was a brother to Carl's father…a former minister himself—oh, it is so complicated—you understand though?"

"And so many of them were named Carl."

Without comment, she rushed ahead. "It was strange and no one ever knew why mother was even considered for the position, let alone, sought out. Later, she always accused my father of extending his family influence through his old aunt, the pastor's wife—which he denied knowledge of. He always thought it might be simply another kindness of the old pastor. It was a huge opportunity for mother and she knew it. Nothing could have kept her from that position. And it greatly pleased her parents; they saw their hoped-for stability returning in their daughter's life. Instead, it turned out to be the opposite.

"For Anna-Stina's journey? It will be the best part of two days to get her there, unless I can borrow a cart," her father said. "I may also try to ask for work from people we may pass along the way of the journey," the smith mused to his wife as they skirted the edge of the lake. "Even the new iron works can not displace my skills as a master smith."

"Shush," his wife hissed, casting a sidelong glance at her husband. "You should be ashamed boasting on the Lord's day." She chided him gently for his sin of pride. "Your favor with the Lord will be sorely needed if what you speak about the *Järn*[51] smelter is as fine as you say it will be."

At dawn on the following day Anna-Stina was ready to leave for her new position. She'd grown up caring for her younger brothers and sisters. There is no husband in her immediate future and now she looked forward to working for the former vicar's wife, who did not have children. Hopefully, there would be a new distraction from the usual childcare of her siblings. There should be interesting persons calling at the rectory in Nås, she thought. Possibly even a potential husband one day.

It was early morning in 1850 and Anna-Stina was more than prepared for the journey. She approached her mother with at smile. "Have you arranged the items you will take," her mother asked, happy for the joy she saw in her daughter's excited preparations. She stood warming the porridge from the previous day's meal, tired and leaning against the small, stone fireplace chimney. For the journey, she'd put several loaves of round flat bread in a linen sack, along with salted herrings and cheese.

"Sit now Anna-Stina—eat plenty so you will not be hungry and have to eat up your mid-day meal, early. And be sure to watch your father lest he take some when you are not looking."

"Yes, I'll watch Father," she answered absently. "I finished gathering my things last evening, mother. There's little enough to take."

She leaned out the door of the small house and shouted to her father: "Let's begin Pappa—or it will become very late for your return...*Rånda* waits for such tardy travelers as you, you know."

She'd packed the last of her few possessions for the journey. All she owned was easily contained in a woven birch bark knapsack; this she would swing over one shoulder and stride confidently into the world. Only her mother knew that the christening dress she herself had made for little Augusta, had been folded carefully and placed in the bottom of the knapsack.

Still, the sounds of Lars Malmberg's anvil rang rhythmically from his shop. Anna-Stina had grown up with the incessant clang of his hammer upon hot iron. It had become an annoyance at times, yet she knew she would miss the noisy comfort the sound brought her, knowing her father was nearby. When she was a girl, there were many visitors frequenting his forge, either to conduct business, pass the time, or both. She welcomed the attention from these frequent visitors. But as she grew older, their random squeezes and pinches came to be placed in different places on her body than when she was smaller. She soon came to avoid the smithy in order to escape certain visitor's coarse gestures, leering looks and groping hands.

Now, as she waited for her father to come to breakfast, she gazed around at the small settlement on the lake. Her father's shop lay adjacent to the outlet of the lake, near the small dam where the small wheel powered the hammer mills. Looking along both shores of the lake, the blue-black horizon where pines met blue sky seemed to shimmer in beauty. Despite its boredom and desolation, Anna-Stina would miss Andersfors. And I will miss the people, too, she thought, thinking of her mother and her brothers and sisters. At second thought she knew she would likely return one day and the thought of her often, ill-behaved siblings seemed worse than the widow's work.

She crossed the garden and entered the smithy to summon her father again. Though the doorway was open, the room was dark, but for the glow of the charcoal forge. Red iron sparks sprung like a newly-burst stars, with each blow of his hammer, as he flattened the work-piece, turned it with the tongs, took another hold, repositioned it and struck it several more blows before returning it to the fire to soften again.

He smiled and nodded to her as he laid aside his hammer and tongs and with his free hand pulled the leather thong attached to the lever arm that lifted the bottom half of the massive, skin wrapped wooden bellows.

"*Whosh—whosh—whosh*"—the glowing bed of coals spoke to her as they were brought to life, releasing tiny fireflies into the room. He rolled the iron work-piece with the continued pulling the bellows arm. Heating the iron, she knew, caused it to soften so it could be worked.

"Softened and reshaped to obey the hammer and anvil—the iron will relax," he once had told her, "like butter in the sun, so it could be put into the shape your mother desires, in the butter mold. Set in the spring, it would harden and retain that shape. The iron we do not melt, completely, or we could pour it into a mold. We only soften it so it will obey my will through the hammer."

She watched, as she had so many times, as he returned the piece, hammered, shaped and turned it again until he was satisfied and dropped it into the cold water to quench it. Steam puffed up, filling the room as the red-hot iron momentarily boiled the water around it.

"The water abruptly changes something about the iron..." he had told her, "...makes it stronger than if we did not put it into the cold water. In the old times, they said the spirits lived in iron worked by man and a smith had to be careful how he worked it, lest he offend them and they leave the piece and weaken it.

With a nod he acknowledged her again, standing smiling at him, hands on her hips. It was a sign that he was finished. "We go now," he said. "It is finished and I will take it along to sell along the way, possibly," he shut the door to the smith. They returned to the house and her mother went inside with Lars.

Together she and her father would set out from Andersfors, going past the long stone wall lining the track away from Andersfors and head east. She looked forward to the journey as she had looked forward to nothing for some time.

Her father emerged with his bag, followed by her mother, carrying Anna-Stina's knapsack, putting them in the borrowed horse cart.

After kissing her mother and the siblings who happened to be around, they began the walk of twenty five kilometers journey to the widow Fröman's large, red house in Nås.

Källeborg, as it was called, when they reached it late in the afternoon, was even larger than the Bergslaget company's factory house in Andersfors. Her father had been there previously, he said on departing.

"Too many women in this house, for me," he'd commented as he kissed her goodbye at the back door. "But figure out how to get along, Anna-Stina, you always do. Don't forget where we are and come home when you can. We can see you in church from time to time."

Anna-Stina watched him disappear around the house.

Straightening her dress and apron and picking up her birch pack, she strode boldly to the door, opened it and stepped across the threshold.

"*Hej...*, she said loudly into the bare kitchen, "*Jag komma över....*"

The widow had four servants in the house and a man who came to care for the garden. One personal maid, Hanna, cared full time for the widow, who still remained busy managing some of the parish affairs. Another girl, Emma, did the cooking. She had a helper named Birgitta, who was a bit simple and had to be told what to do most all the time, a chore Emma didn't seem to mind. She would intersperse her ceaseless chatter with running commands to Birgitta while never turning her attention once from whomever she was conversing with, or the task in which she might be involved.

Another older girl, Marie, took care of the house, with Birgitta helping whenever Emma freed her from her kitchen chores. Marie seemed to work from dawn until dark. Källeborg was such a large house and Marie took her responsibility quite seriously—too seriously, Anna-Stina eventually thought, because she feared even to tread upon the gleaming floors, least Marie would drop to her knees to immediately burnish the scuff with her apron after casting a reproachful glance at the offending foot.

Nevertheless, Anna-Stina liked Marie and tried to become friends with her, though she was never too successful. At first Anna-Stina helped with all of the work at Källeborg and came to know her fellow laborers well. They in turn appreciated her willingness to contribute more than her fair share, demonstrating an overall eagerness to do her own part and help them as well. Her frank friendliness and seeming, well-meaning and sincere nature were a benefit in being accepted in the new station. But there soon came to be petty jealousies, because of Anna-Stina's quick mastery of all their jobs as she filled in and exchanged duties.

She received all her orders from Marie who in turn, was directed by the widow herself. One morning the widow called Anna-Stina upstairs to her study, having sent Marie for her. Marie made Anna-Stina stop outside the room while she inspected her co-worker's appearance.

As she straightened Anna-Stina's apron and hat she smiled kindly and said: "You must look your best, Anna-Stina. This is a chance for promotion to a more responsible position—one I know you will like."

Anna-Stina took a deep breath, smiled at Marie and followed the older girl into the room where the widow waited.

She'd only been in the room once before— that day when she reported for work with her father, after the long journey from Andersfors. Her father had been awe stricken by the surroundings, but warmed to the widow immediately. He was acquainted with some of her relatives from past years and had once repaired some ironwork on the gate at Källeborg. The widow had remembered him and commented upon the quality and durability of his repair, which made him glow.

During the initial interview, with her father standing uncomfortably in the corner, Anna-Stina had sat nervously.

"You will apprentice with the other girls here at Källeborg only until we feel certain you wish to remain with us. We, here in the house, will periodically make judgments about your work performance, Anna-Stina and determine whether we wish you to remain. If that is satisfied, you may be offered the opportunity to take the position of *vallkulla* at the Fröman *fäbod* at Vansberget. That, as you know, is a most prestigious position."

When Marie was finally satisfied with her appearance, she opened the door and ushered Anna-Stina before the widow, where she remained quietly sitting, listening and nodding slightly at intervals as the widow spoke. After an exchange of pleasantries, the older woman began an accounting. She informed Anna-Stina that her work had pleased the family very much. And in less than five minutes Anna-Stina was offered and had accepted the position she had hoped for, for so long. She would be going into the mountain forest at Vansberget, the Fröman *fäbod*, as their newest *vallkulla*.

"Our *vallkullor* are hired—typically for a single year period, from October until the following October," the widow had told her. "Unfortunately, old Emma has passed on and we find ourselves in need of a person to replace her, before the normal end of term in October. I am sure you are familiar with that practice? Yes—all right—each year upon the fall anniversary, you would be given around two weeks freedom to seek work elsewhere if you are not pleased with us, or, if you so desire, to continue to be employed with us for another year. Do you fully understand?"

Anna-Stina nodded eagerly. She'd served as *vallkulla* before, had been attacked in the *fäbod*, had had a child, but was ready to rejoin the loneliness of *fäbod* life once more. She liked living with the older women, but she also enjoyed being alone in the meadows with the cattle and goats, who did not boss her. The other work at the *fäbod* was not as interesting. Cooking the whey left over from churning the milk, making cheeses and butter were not as pleasant as following the cattle through the woods, stripping the birch leaves into her large apron for them to eat and bringing them home in the evening to milk. After milking she always enjoyed hearing from the other women how their day had transpired. And they would listen intently to her recount her own day, if she chose and trade her own stories. Sometimes, visitors would make the long journey up to the *fäbod*, often on Saturdays, or after church and then, Anna-Stina would be asked to play, or to sing for them.

CHAPTER 10

The Doctor

"*Herr* Andersson…Sir…?"

I opened my eyes, confused
for a moment. A nurse was
standing over me, whispering and
gently touching my shoulder.

"I am sorry to awaken you, Sir, but Dr. Olsson had an emergency
and couldn't return as she'd planned. I thought they had told you and
you had already left for the day. I am sorry."

I sat up quickly and looked at my watch. How could I have fallen
asleep? I glanced across—Karolina was also sleeping, apparently
quite soundly, even as the nurse checked her pulse.

"Oh…." I was a little confused. When had Karolina stopped her
story? I didn't remember her starting it again…but a story was fresh
in my memory…perhaps I had dreamed it?

The nurse left and I sat there for a moment, waking up. It was
still early afternoon. The nurse opened the curtain when she left and
I noticed the other patients were discussing the merits of different
bedding flowers.

I looked over at Karolina, sleeping so quietly on the starched
bedding. She really looked older in the relaxation of slumber and the
previous freshness was absent from her face. She had a good color in
her cheeks but her face was drawn.

"Hello—you're still here?" Dr. Olsson peeked around the white,
ward curtains.

"Yes," I said quietly, "we were talking and the next thing I knew,
the nurse woke me up. I guess I just relaxed." I got up and walked
around the curtain.

"I'm sorry to have abandoned you. I had something come up and the other physician on staff was gone. I sent a nurse to tell you but when she found both you and Karolina asleep she decided to let you sleep, thinking you both probably needed it," she said, smiling.

"I'm just about finished. I wanted to examine Karolina again, quickly. Nurse said she seems to be coming up with a slight fever."

"Oh…." I felt guilty immediately.

"Don't worry, it's normal for someone in her condition. She still seems to be improving, though—did she seem strong…was she able to carry on a lucid conversation?"

"Yes, we talked for quite a while, before I…one of us fell asleep."

I wanted to confess my guilt: "I'm afraid…it's so astonishing. She began as usual: talking. There was no stopping her. I attempted to change the subject but she would have none of it—said there is so little time and just kept going. I don't know which of us fell asleep first."

"I doubt you did her more harm than good. Company…someone to visit and cheer her best….of course it tired her. But in her condition, the body knows when it needs to rest…and yours too, from the sound of it," she said smiling kindly. "Nurse said you were both sleeping like children. I wish I'd seen it."

I heard Karolina yawn and peeked around the curtain. She glanced at me and then Dr. Olsson, leaned over and peeked around the curtain, too.

"Oh—did I drop off?"

"We both dropped off, Karolina.

"*Shusssh…*," the doctor said, holding up a finger. She'd taken out her stethoscope and was now listening to Karolina's heart. After she finished, she smiled and stood up, nodding for me to continue.

"Do you feel all right now, Karolina?" I said, feeling a little guilty.

"Perfectly," she answered sleepily. "Shall we continue when Dr. Olsson is finished?"

The doctor answered for me.

"Not a chance Karolina—I think you need to stop for today and I'm sure you need a little more rest, too, Mr. Andersson?" She smiled at me, "no doubt you can return again tomorrow?"

"Yes," I offered, "certainly."

"But—it is…" Karolina glanced over at the wall clock, "…it is only early afternoon…."

Dr. Olsson overcame her protestations. "Doctor's orders, Karolina. By the way, you were really snoring, Karolina—I heard…"

"*Nonsense…*" she interrupted the doctor, "…I have never snored in my life." She tried to sit up straighter: "…must have been him, you heard," she pointed a finger toward me, all the while smiling mischievously.

We all had a good laugh then over her snappy disposition.

"Yes…well, it must have been quite good for you, Karolina," Dr. Olsson said, concluding her examination. She made a few notes on the clip-board and returned it the foot of the bed. Karolina didn't object, which was a matter of some relief to me.

"We can go now—back to the home, if you are ready?" Dr. Olsson said, turning to me.

"Yes, I'm ready," I rose to leave. "Just a moment, though."

Returning to the bedside, I leaned over and kissed Karolina in the middle of her forehead.

"You enjoy the rest of the day and sleep well tonight, I said.

Turning back to Dr. Olsson, I added: "There, I'm ready now."

Dr. Olsson smiled brightly as she held the curtain aside.

"Yes, Karolina…rest and I'll see you again tomorrow morning."

Karolina smiled and wished us both good afternoon, waving.

Walking down the hallway, Dr. Olson laid a hand on my arm. "I'm sure that will do her a world of good," she said cheerfully, "the kiss, I mean."

We walked out to the parking lot in silence, all the while I was thinking of the lightness of her touch. The day was well along and I wasn't tired now, after my nap. I had stolen a couple of glances at Dr. Olsson's ring finger's—including her right hand—where wedding rings were usually worn in Europe; there was still no sign of any betrothal, or promise for the future. I decided to take a chance.

"Doctor Olsson, I get tired of eating alone every evening at the Norse Room at my hotel. The owner/waiter is getting frustrated trying to keep me interested in their limited offering. Would you care to join me for dinner tomorrow evening—somewhere—your suggestion—I know it is rather…sudden?"

I held my breath. She considered it for a moment before responding.

"I'm sorry to hesitate…it is not that I don't wish to accept your invitation…I certainly do and thank you. But I was thinking of your comment….about their limited cuisine? There's really nothing nearby that's any better, I'm afraid. However, there is a nice restaurant across the lake; you might find it a refreshing change, but it's a bit of a drive?"

"Sounds interesting." I was excited.

"It's also a bit expensive. I've only been there a couple of times. Many European tourists dine there and it's also said to have a fine cellar."

"Then it's a date…is that what you call it…in Sweden?"

"Yes, we have copied that term from American movies."

"It's been so long since I asked anyone out I didn't quite know how to go about it…the Swedish protocol."

She smiled away my embarrassment.

"What time should I pick you up—and where?"

"My home…let's drive past there on the way to your hotel. It's not far from the nursing home and you should be able to find it again without any trouble from your hotel. What do you think about six o'clock? Restaurants in Sweden don't remain open late, like Europe or, I imagine…*Amerika*, so we eat our dinner early. But, I guess you know that. My schedule will have been taken by one of the other residents at the home because of what I had to do at the hospital, so I shouldn't have any problem getting free before then. I think it will be a very enjoyable evening and I look forward to spending it with you, Mr. Andersson."

We didn't speak much in the car and she soon turned off the main street paralleling the large lake that lies north and west of the city of Karlskoga and proceeded past the nursing home and directly to her house. It was only eight or ten blocks from the nursing home, as she had said.

"When the weather permits, I walk to the home each morning. It can be a problem if I have to go to the hospital though; then I drive.

"OK, I think I can find it from here, Dr. Olsson."

She smiled at me and pulled away from the side of the street.

"Maybe you should call me Anna," she said, "If we're—going to dinner—on a date? What do you think?"

"All right—but I'm Alex then."

We both seemed a little nervous, but finally left it with a mutual smile and a handshake for the day. Anna put the Volvo in gear again and drove me back to the hotel. I waved as she circled the parking lot and turned back onto the street. I wondered as I watched her heading up the street, whether I had done the right thing. I enjoyed her company and felt a little thrill when we were together. Yet, for some reason I hesitated. Cautious I thought…must just be caution. How long's it been since you went out, buddy, I thought. Too long, my conscience answered.

CHAPTER 11

Expectant Visitors

I brought Karolina a nice bouquet the next morning; I had to purchase the vase separately since the flower shop didn't have anything I thought would look that nice in the hospital.

I'd had a good breakfast, too, since I didn't believe we'd get our customary coffee, like in her nursing home. I arrived a little later in the morning, taking some time after breakfast to organize my notes. I thought I'd naturally curb Karolina's enthusiasm to work so hard at her story when I felt she should rest more. Also, I didn't want to fall asleep again at her bedside.

When I entered the hospital, the staff was finished with the breakfast trays and was bringing individual coffee servings. Karolina already had a cup in her and was sipping from it when I poked my head around the curtain and held out the flowers.

"Oh...how nice. Thank, you Alex. You are so kind and thoughtful."

"Not at all...nothing's too good for my favorite storyteller."

"Have you had your coffee, yet...I can ask whether they'll bring you some, if you'd like?"

"Yes I did; I'm fine. They have better things to do."

"Doctor Olsson was just here...you've missed her today, unless she returns later."

This came with a little twinkle in her eye.

"That's OK. I'm sure I'll see her again." I sat down and began organizing myself. "Feel like talking some more today, Karolina?"

"Yes, definitely; I've been planning just how to relate the next part.

You see..." and she was off.

It was Sunday morning as Anna-Stina finished scrubbing the last of the cheese crumbs from the dismantled, wooden molds. She rinsed them, swishing their insides in the roiling spring water while scrubbing with the tightly bound bunch of fine birch roots. She spread the mold parts along the cut stone that flanked the spring. Lying thus in the early morning sun, by the time the flies became active they would be bone dry in the cool, sunny air. It was time for a quick bath and then a breakfast of porridge.

Her feet squeaked as she walked quickly through the sparkling dew-wet grass, her bare feet leaving a dark trail in the silvery carpet. Many springs ringed the mountainside, some large some small. In succession, they ran from the hillside from one to the next before finally settling into a larger pool, further down the mountain. The water often exited again to meander down the hill, eventually flowing into the river Vanån. But just before that, it became warm enough for bathing.

Today, the early summer sun felt warm on her back. She wore only her long linen skirt and blouse, made for her by her mother. This was her daily costume in the summer, unless it was a particularly cold or rainy day, when the addition of a lighter wool cloak would drive away the morning's chill. The coarse linen cloth, woven from the homespun flax, was durable and easy to wash and lasted forever. She had brought along a clean linen shift to wear back to the cabin.

As she skipped along the grassy path she began to untie the braided strings on the loosely-fitting blouse. She grasped each side and spread it wide...like wings of a white goose, she thought to herself. She spun carelessly round and round as she tripped happily along the path, holding her arms wide. The light color of the linen garment alternately flashing in the sun as she rotated to the rhythms playing in her mind. She hummed quietly to herself as she did the turns of a *schottis* along the path, lost in a dance only she knew the partner of.

The sun's light slanted through the sparse forest cover, falling over the spring, leaving large dapples of dancing light around the shimmering surface, which seeped and rippled from the unseen flow of water from below. Still well away from the ooze and damp that ringed the spring, Anna-Stina loosened the waist braid that bound the skirt and let it fall around her ankles. Deftly stepping over the garment, she continued, nearly naked now, toward the glistening pool. Passing a small birch tree, she flung her clean wrap across a low-lying limb where the linen would be sun-warmed when she donned it again after a chilly bath.

Stopping at the pool's edge, she snapped a twig from a low growing shrub. Giving one last careless glance around, she strode boldly into the muck, her bare feet making sucking noises as she waded toward the warmer, shallow end of the spring. She held out the stick, spit on it, then chanted:

"Take this —and leave me be..." and tossed the twig into the water, knowing, the old spell would ward off any evil the water spirit may wish to put upon her, fixing upon the stick, instead.

She waded further into the pool. Knowing if she went in too deeply, close to the opening in the bottom to the springs, the water would be very cold. She circled the pool's edge, her knees barely below the water, trying to find the warmest part of the shallow pool. Goose bumps sprung to her skin's surface and she felt an involuntary chill. She hugged herself, glancing up and smiling at the sun's warmth.

Finally, she squatted quickly in the water to complete her toilette. The surface of her skin immediately became rigid with goose bumps. Finishing quickly, she stood again, making an involuntary gasp from the cold. Her breasts were shrunken slightly and her nipples were stiff, dripping the cool, clear nectar of the spring, each droplet trailed the other down her belly to disappear back from whence it had come. Cold as the water was, she remained standing in the pool, rubbing herself with a clump of muddy grass roots. The soil would rid her body of the accumulated cow smell since her last bath.

Mostly sweet cow smell all day long, she thought to herself, smiling. But town boys might not like it. The beautiful, gentle cows—her forever companions. Her eyes softened in the contrasting light and she smiled to herself humming another melody as she rubbed and alternately splashed water over her sun dappled body.

She squatted once again to rinse the mud before standing and shaking her hair free of water. She brushed her limbs to rid her body of most of the numbing water. Her long hair hung dripping around her back and shoulders as she finally waded ashore.

She hastily snatched the shift from the birch limb and began rubbing herself with the sun-warmed garment. Goose pimples sprung up anew as the water evaporated.

Finished dressing, she started up the path toward home. As she passed her discarded clothing, she bent and with a crooked finger in passing, snagged each of the soiled garments. She alternately swung and waved them around her as she strolled happily back up the path toward the small collection of timber houses.

She was happy. After all, it was *söndag*[52] and some visitors might wander up from the valley to pass the time with the lonesome *vallkullor* at Vansberget. Maybe, even some boys...come to court, she thought as she approached her small, log house. Her strong body was silhouetted through the thin garment in the sunlight, as she leaped up the stone steps to change into her best frock.

Minutes later Anna-Stina emerged with a large piece of buttered *knäckebröd*[53] between her teeth, spread thick with *mismör* and carrying a comb and a cup of milk. She took a large bite of the bread, sat down on the stoop and began combing her hair dry in the warm sunlight. From time to time, she glanced expectantly toward the path that led from the village. Would visitors soon approach? Surely, soon, if they were coming today.

Sitting on the stones beside the spring-house, around mid-day, some of the younger girls became impatient.

"Ohhh..." Hilma said to no one in particular, "...if any visitors are coming, they should soon be here...should they not?"

"They would have had to miss church to be here by now," another added, "you are too impatient for a man, Hilma."

Ignoring her friend, "They'd have to leave even earlier to be here now and I can't see that happening."

Oftentimes, someone would bring up several people in a cart, stopping on the far side of the Van. Even then, the journey was so far that they ended up staying the night. In those instances, there would be music, dancing and a good time till all hours.

After she'd finished combing her hair, Anna-Stina had dug in to her wooden trunk and brought out her *fiol*, *stråke*[54] and *säckpipa* to tune and play for the other women. It had been some days since she'd taken the time for playing either instrument. She'd always brought them along to *fäbod*, both to entertain herself and others, especially if visitors arrived for a dance. Several of the other women and girls played instruments, too.

Now, as Anna-Stina carried them out into the yard, Hilma jumped up.

"Oh—good, Anna-Stina is going to play. Let's dance together while we wait."

If there was to be dancing, Anna-Stina's services with either of the instruments would be required. At times like this, she often thought, I wish I could be doing some of the dancing, instead of having always to play for the others.

Selecting the *säckpipa*, since it took the longest to tune up, she went out onto the flat stones to one side of the cabin so as not to offend anyone's ears while she breathed moisture into the goatskin sack and moisten the reed. She sat down in the area where the women usually worked beside the spring. Most of the implements had been cleared away after the morning milking. Some cheese molds were still drying.

After a few minutes of huffing and puffing, Emma turned the corner and sat down beside her to watch. "What will you play first, Anna-Stina?" she asked, brightly.

"We shall see," she replied. "Let me first get the bag and reeds moist—then we shall see what tunes it will make."

For a little while the pair sat in the sun while Anna-Stina adjusted the chanter and drone reeds, testing them from time to time, blowing moist breath into the leather sack and dampening the chanter and pipe so the instrument could settle down and remain in tune. It was truly a contrary instrument to tune and play—more difficult even than to play. There was no hurry and she enjoyed the rest and departure from the normal work. The sun was bright, strong and welcoming.

Finally she got the *säckpipa* to sound as she thought it should. She arranged the deflated sack beneath her arm and positioned the drone and chanter. She inspected the reed in each before finally arranging the chanter beneath her fingers. Some of the girls had begun to find places to sit. Another girl—Sadie, came marching from one of the cabins playing a *gånglåt* [55] on her violin.

Anna-Stina placed the proper fingers over the appropriate holes, filled the bag with a couple of strong puffs and squeezed on the swollen sack beneath her arm. There issued forth a couple of hesitant squeaks. She frowned and removed the reed from the chanter and adjusted it yet again. After rotating it round, she grasped each side of the short horsehair drawn beneath the slit in the reed which supported the tongue, raising it slightly to change the sound. Hilma looked over her shoulder, squinting and frowning in the bright daylight, mesmerized by but totally ignorant of what her friend was doing.

Anna-Stina inspected the reed one last time and twisted it back into place and blew again before doing the same for the drone pipe. Finally, with another practice puff or two, she felt the pipe were ready and begin to blow and squeeze her arm against the swollen bag.

After a test note or two, she caught up with Sadie's fiddle. They finished that tune and took up another. The other girls recognized the *Björsköttens*[56] Polska. Sadie tilted forward, violin beneath her chin, and followed, tapping her bare foot to the time.

The sound floated over the hillside. The other *vallkullor*, not yet assembled, paused in their morning toilet to listen, smiling to themselves.

"That sound will bring the boys if anything will," one girl remarked to her cabin mate.

A few of the girls lined up on the flat area of ground before the players and side-by-side, began the easy—step-two-three—turn-two-three of the *polska*[58]. After fifteen minutes, the dust was flying around the bare feet as *hambo*, *schottis* and finally a *vals* were run through by the musicians, with the female dancer's feet and skirts flying around bare feet.

Anna-Stina and Sadie changed tunes several times as the dancing progressed and had even settled into playing Anna-Stina's favorite and old song of the *fäbod*, a nameless melody that was as old as the forest. No one knew the originator of the slow, beautiful piece, played in the minor tones so typical of Dalarna's music.

After a half-hour of exploring various melodies with several variations, she'd completely forgotten about any possibility of visitors and was enjoying herself thoroughly and the pleasure the others derived from the music. They danced in couples, one girl taking the man's steps in each of the dances.

As she started another march, Anna-Stina heard a *flöjter*[58] playing along with her and glancing around, spied the source. A group of young men were laboriously making their way up the rise toward the yard where the girls were dancing. As the unknown player to play while the remainder of the party approached, she stopped to watch four young men bound up the path and leap the rail fence. But who is the flutist, she wondered. She didn't recognize any of the newcomers. As they came closer, one boy held up a *spelåpipa*[59], just as he straddled the top rail of the *gärdesgård*[60]. He immediately began playing again on the other side. Then, she recognized Carl Fröman, her rescuer from Frömansgården. He lived in Skålbyn, further up the river from Nås. Since her embarrassing encounter in the church pillory, she'd seen him only once or twice. And then, it was only from a distance as he passed her in Järna church to sit in the Fröman's family place, far up on the right side of the central aisle.

From time to time she'd remember her timely, Sunday rescue and the recollection of Carl's upturned face, beneath her own, always brought angry emotions, first, but then the warm feeling of appreciation for the young man's caring would triumph. But he was someone far above her social reach. His family connections and place in the local society made her wary; the Fröman family represented the people who kept The Church dominant in society and the government in place, which in turn, kept the common people, like her, considerably subdued and lower down the social scale.

Carl had come to the *fäbod* that day, on a mere dare from his friends. There was little excitement in the community since the completion of the grain harvest. The promise of girls and dancing in the *fäbod* was more than he could pass up; besides, they needed his cart, they told him laughingly. So the four young men had driven his father's horse and cart as far as they could along the eastern shore of the Vanån and had then swam across and walked up the path the remainder of the way. It took nearly three hours for the whole journey.

As they'd drawn near, when Carl heard the bagpipe, he was glad he had brought his wooden *spelåpipa*. He flourished it again with a wave as he strode up the path.

When he got closer, he spied the piper; she'd momentarily stopped playing and was watching them approach. I'm pleased now, he thought, that I've come. There's the beautiful Anna-Stina Malmberg. She stood with her *säckpipa* in one hand, shading her eyes with the other. She was tall, very slender and brown from the sun. What a beautiful *vallkulla* she makes and playing the *säckpipa*, too, he thought and with quite a flair.

Anna-Stina took up another tune as Carl and the boys approached. Carl began comically strutting like a soldier, striding in time to her march. As he reached the stone platform where the players sat, he stopped and began making time, marching in place, trying to play and smile at the same time. He looked mostly at his feet but from time to time, his gaze went to Anna-Stina's face—even more beautiful up close with her summer tan. She was so comely in her light frock with a blue striped apron. Far different from the heavy, winter sheepskin she'd been wearing in the chill of the winter churchyard. I will regret leaving the *fåbod* this day, he thought, staring directly into her bright eyes once again and having his gaze returned with boldness. Yes, I will surely be sorry…if I leave today.

Anna-Stina was surprised to see Carl Fröman. As she watched him playing, over her bagpipe's chanter, she held the pipe with the fingers of both hands, alternately covering the holes which made the small, round reed in the end change its' tune. All the while she squeezed the bag beneath her arm to keep the air flowing steadily through the reeds in the chanter and the drone.

Mischievously, she took the lead by changing to another tune and seizing the advantage: a schottische. Carl struggled to follow her quick move but his confusion showed as he fumblingly attempted to keep up. Seeing this, Anna-Stina decided to have some fun with him. The quick change had been confusing for the dancers and the couples protested loudly for not being forewarned. Ignoring their outcries and hesitating but a moment, she switched tunes again, though she maintained the schottische beat. Carl stumbled again, at first, but this time quickly caught up.

She's a saucy one, he thought, grinning to himself and changing quickly again with her next sudden lead, this time keeping up, since he recognized the tune sooner—even increasing the rhythm on her until he was setting the pace.

But again, she switched to a livelier tune. Carl almost immediately followed and played along, measure for measure, keeping up easily this time. They both knew all the old *Dalecarlian*[61] tunes from the community. It was finger against finger—bagpipe chanter to wooden *spelåpipa*.

By now the tunes were being played far too fast for dancing.

Grumbling, the crowd of youngsters finally stopped, linked arms and formed a semi-circle before the players, watching and listening, bare feet tapping to the heightened pace, satisfied for the moment that there was a contest and each sex cheering for their own champion.

Before Anna-Stina could change the tune, Carl did—forcing her to switch pace to catch up. And she stumbled this time. See how she plays, he thought—she is so quick—so bright.

Let him think he is winning, Anna-Stina thought and followed yet another of his tune changes—but not too quickly, smiling at him openly with a glint of satisfaction in her eyes, teasing him, taunting him openly over her chanter.

What blue eyes she has, Carl thought watching her. See how her body moves to the music; she is at one with the playing—as if she is the only one on earth and no one is watching. Carl made another subtle change in the rhythm, then alternating easily to a new composition, this time, one he had recently learned from his music teacher.

She stumbled...attempted to follow, but then stopped completely. Carl has changed the melody...a tune I have never heard she thought, lowering the chanter. That is not fair...but as she listened she realized the tune was so beautiful...slower and quieter. She tried to follow, sustaining a note to hold her place until she could follow him with the next part of the piece, but it was no good. She still did not recognize the melody and it was in the wrong key for her *säckpipa*.

How perfect each note is, she thought. It was a mastery of music—each note coming exactly as it should and fitting perfectly like the structure of a fence—orderly—stacked—divided and paced. Squared ends fitting perfectly...how beautiful it is—what piece is this she wondered—where has he learned this? Oh...I must listen and remember it.

The tune spanned more than the limited, eight-note octave she was able to play on her pipe; she knew she'd be unable to follow his playing, if the key was the same. So, like the dancers, she was content to remain sitting on the stone step, listening. The chanter she held near her lips but the bag no longer had pressure beneath her arm. She had never heard music like this before. She was mesmerized by the meter and precision of it. She didn't mind that she had lost the contest; she was learning a new tune and taking such pleasure in the hearing of it—and watching the player...and just maybe, falling in love.

Carl had let Anna-Stina have that piece but then switched to play another that his music professor had recently taught him—one which went beyond her *säckpipa's* capability of playing, octave-wise[62]. She will not take this one from me so easily he thought, concentrating in his melody, playing more carefully.

Anna-Stina got up and walked closer to where Carl was leaning against the fence. She paused, listening carefully to the perfectly proportioned sound...but at times, just uneven enough so the effect was wondrous, permitting him to pull—stretch and pace each note. For a second, the music reminded her of some of the very old songs her mother once played for her. This song is made by the same person, she thought. I can recognize him in it, but I do not have enough holes in my chanter to play this. If I had the violin out...she thought, nodding her head in time to the music she smiled and laid down her *säckpipa.* She took up her bow and violin within seconds she was following him. She had the tune now. She even began improvising on the theme. He started over and as they repeated it together, they wove and intertwined the melody and harmony—each having fun with the tune until they had measured its extent, played its variations and exhausted both the tune and finally, themselves.

When he'd changed to the new piece, Carl noticed that she'd stopped playing completely—not in defeat, he recognized, but in seeming wonder, sitting...mouth slightly open, enraptured. He could see her even teeth as she half-smiled and her beautiful face was serious, open with marvel, awe and joy. Almost like that of a child. How vulnerable she looks, he thought as he worked his way through the piece; the music has reached inside her. Yet, how strong she was, risking her vulnerability, exposing her emotion to him. If he hadn't known how strong Anna-Stina Malmberg truly was, he would have thought her weak. Encouraged, he freely gave her the gift of the tune and as their eyes met above his *spelåpipa,* she accepted it gladly. As she took up the fiol he noted how quickly, she then memorized the notes. As he repeated the piece a second time, she took up an improvised harmony and danced within the tune, around him; a gift— merely an exchange—giving and receiving of each other.

Confident again, Anna-Stina glanced saucily over her violin. She has the tune now—nothing can ever take it away. How happy I am that I came today, he thought. For the first time in his life, Carl Fröman did not recognize the emotions that were overwhelming him.

She's so good, he thought. In some ways, she's even better than my professor. See how she pulls at the notes—squeezing three and letting go one, but the basic piece is still there. I wonder if she can compose music. Compose music—I doubt she can even write her name, he mused, reining his thoughts. But then, who cares, with those skills with improvisation. He was smitten, nonetheless.

The dancers had tired of the musical contest and after the first pleasure of hearing them pair play, they'd wandered away to dance to another fiddler who'd started up on the other end of the lane.

Carl stopped playing first, lowering his spelåpipa, his chest heaving somewhat. He waited until Anna-Stina finished her run and had also lain down her fiddle. Then, speaking very softly, so as not to disturb the mood, he greeted her for the first time.

"*Hej*...Anna-Stina."

She returned his straightforward greeting: "*Hej*—Carl Fröman..." smiling at him a little mockingly, "...you play fairly well."

She stared boldly into his eyes as if to search his soul. Carl felt weak with the strength of her silent examination. Neither spoke for a few seconds. Then he retorted, playfully.

"Thank you, Anna-Stina, you are quite welcome."

Neither spoke for a moment. Then to break the seriousness of the situation Carl offered a small taunt.

"I hardly recognized you Anna-Stina, standing up. I'm happy you don't seem to suffer any loss of wind from your sad experience at the church."

"Yes, where I suffered you can not see Carl Fröman, as it was meant to be. But I have never had a chance to thank you properly, for watching out for me on the other two Sundays—when I was in the same...position," she smiled.

"What makes you think I was watching out for you?"

"I caught little Olga one afternoon behind a *stugo*...you know, the girl who kicked the stool from beneath me, the first Sunday? She told me you were watching, but only after I had twisted her ear nearly from her head. She said that you were there—watching over my well being. And later, as she ran away, she shouted that she would have her big brother get me when Carl Fröman was no longer watching. So, anyway, thank you for everything."

"I did not hear from him—her brother, Jonas?"

"Yes, Jonas. But, *nej*—you would not have heard from him. You see, I know a secret about Jonas and well, it's a secret...he knows better than to trouble me. So you wouldn't have heard from him."

"Ha, ha, ha..." Carl chuckled, "I thought Olga's face seemed a little crooked lately, whenever she looks at me. Please, think nothing of it. Those old church customs—they should be banned, before someone really becomes hurt. The pillories are no longer needed...if they ever were. And they're certainly not civilized. They could damage someone physically and certainly, emotionally..." he broke off realizing he was treading on a sensitive area for the girl.

She smiled, recognizing his consideration for her feelings. "I, for one, couldn't agree more."

They sat in comfortable silence for a moment before Anna-Stina spoke again.

"May I ask, Carl Fröman...where did you get those songs? I have never heard such music before—it was...so beautiful."

"It's something I have learned from a traveling musician who my mother paid to teach me—a professor from Switzerland. It's German music, written by a man with the name Johan Bach. His music is now my favorite—after *Dalakarlian* tunes, of course."

"Of course," she added, continuing to smile. "And now mine, too, Carl Fröman, thanks to your bringing them to me—to us, in the *fäbod*."

"You liked the music that much?"

"*Herr* Bach's music is like nothing I've ever heard."

"Good. And your playing...it was also so very fine."

"I very much enjoyed playing with you Carl and listening, too, of course. I hope you did not mind that I changed the tunes. I wanted to tease you a little and also learn whether you could keep up." She smiled up at him, coyly, the serious moment gone.

"And did I," Carl asked, following her mood.

"Yes—most of the time and sometimes...you even changed them nearly faster than I could keep up," she replied, swaying from side to side, her arms clasped in front of her.

Carl chuckled. "Then we could say we are...equals?"

Anna-Stina nodded. "Where did you learn to play the *spelåpipa* so well?" she asked, knowing, as the son of a wealthy farm and merchant family in Skålbyn, it was unusual for someone of his class to play the poor man's pipe.

"I like music and I can play several instruments, thanks to my mother's hired music teachers," he replied. "Oh—I didn't mean to boast," he added in haste. "I only meant that I enjoy very much, playing different instruments, not that I can play that many, or even any of them that well. In fact, I'm not very good at all with the violin and the *Upplänsk*[63] *nyckelharpa*—it completely defied mastery when I attempted to play it at seminary."

Carl felt he could be overwhelming her again with his enthusiasm, for to look at her today, clean in her visiting clothes, sunburned cheeks, her hair tied up in a bun at the back of her head, she looked beautiful. And the look on her face as she watched him play still made him feel powerful.

"Do you play any other instruments?" he asked, before thinking and immediately regretted saying it. What would a peasant girl line Anna-Stina Malmberg know of music? He thought of any way he could cover up his obvious blunder, feeling he had backed her into a corner.

Undaunted, Anna-Stina smiled broadly, "No, nothing at all, but I always sing in the *fäbod*—to the cows. I very much like to sing," she replied brightly.

"I'd love to hear you, one day," Carl beamed back. What a girl, he thought to himself. At this minute, when she smiled at him, he felt he could leap the mountain and swim all the length of the Västerdalälven, all the way back to the village—so happy did she make him feel.

"Shall we go up to the *stugo* and have some coffee, Carl? I think they will soon cook some."

"Do we have to…I mean, I thought we might play another tune…I have another the professor taught me that is very light and pleasant."

"Yes, we can do that. But let's wait and have some food first— or the others will eat it all. I have made a special cake, which I wish to keep my eye on—or it might soon disappear. We can take it…somewhere and eat it—then you can teach me, or play the tunes for everyone, whichever you prefer. I know the others will want some dance tunes, later—all right?"

"Yes, we can eat first."

They turned and began strolling along the cow path toward where the others had collected.

'Embarrassed by the silence, Carl turned and smiled at Anna-Stina: "I am sorry about your child," he said seriously.

"Thank you Carl, you're kind."

"Not at all."

They could hear the laughter ringing through the pine trees as the group warmed up and began to enjoy themselves with some sort of silly, innocent fun. They could hear Sadie sawing out a polka on her violin.

"I have not had anything to eat since breakfast," Carl said, changing the subject back to something less serious..

"Oh…well, we have cheese of course…and milk—and *knäckebröd*—and *flatbröd*—and…and as I mentioned I've made a small *kaka*⁶⁴. There isn't enough for the others, but if you want, we can share it together with coffee, though we will likely be…made fun of—taking it off for ourselves to eat alone; do you mind that?"

"Not at all…let them laugh; I'll laugh with your cake in my mouth. I'd like that very much."

They continued strolling toward the cabins. Then Anna-Stina stopped and turned to him: "Carl—are you not concerned—the others will talk—about you…about us, if we go apart together to eat my cake?"

Such a serious face, he thought. "Who cares—we musicians must have our nourishment, to later play them their dance tunes. If they think us strange—being together—let them whistle their tunes…and try to dance at the same time…that will fix them."

She laughed, looking relieved. "Good—I agree. We can take our cake down to the spring and eat it. Then, when we come back, we can play the tunes you will teach me?"

"Nothing would make me happier."

They joined the rest of the group who were already ahead of them with the food preparation.

"Here they come! Anna-Stina…Per wants to share that cake you made with you!" Greta, one of the younger girls giggled. "We showed it to everyone."

"Yes," one of the boys chided, "I already sampled it a little bit. I hope you don't mind, Anna-Stina. It looked so good, I just could not help myself—the taste I had was soooo...delicious."

She glared at the boy: "Per—are you right handed?" she asked, striding over and stopping squarely before the tall young man, slouching with a silly grin playing about his mouth. She was nearly as tall as he.

"Why—yes, I am Anna-Stina, why do you ask?" he laughed, reaching over and holding the shoulder of a friend for support and possible protection.

"Please hold up your right hand for me, Per," Anna-Stina said, still maintaining a serious tone.

Per held out his right hand and beamed a smile around the group, turning his head and raising his eyebrows in curiosity.

"Must I swear an oath Anna-Stina?" He giggled for the benefit of the crowd, some of whom tittered in return.

She turned and walked toward the *stugo*, but shouted over her shoulder.

"Take a last look at Per's hand," she said, glancing around. "I'm going to fetch my little cake and if it has any part missing—even a finger mark in the top—I shall return with the big knife we use to kill bears here in the *fäbod*. And I will remove Per's hand from his arm. Per...right before the whole group and tomorrow I will feed it to the wolves before telling them where they can find the rest of you, if they liked the taste, which I doubt."

The group roared with laughter. Two of the boys grasped Per's upraised arm and began pulling him around the yard, as he shrieked in mock terror. Anna-Stina vanished through the cabin door, smiling to herself, confident her cake was safe.

The rest of the boys continued to shove Per around the circle, laughing, as he held his arm high above the crowd, now grasping his wrist with his other hand. He moaned and ranted his good-byes to his hand, to the pleasure of the group. Carl smiled as some of the boys began imitating the howl of wolves. Then, someone singled Carl out.

"Carl Fröman—how do you rate a piece of Anna-Stina's cake?"

Before he could answer, Anna-Stina emerged from the *stugo*.

"Because he could almost keep up with me when playing the

tunes and he also taught me some new ones. Anyone like that deserves to have a piece of my fine cake—and only them," she smiled, glancing at Per in good humor. "Your hand is safe for another day, Per. There is not even a fly's footprint on my cake."

Some of the other young men began pushing Carl.

"Give us your *spelåpipa*, Carl. I must have a taste of Anna-Stina's cake. What will you take to let me play your whistle, Carl?"

Two of the boys rushed toward Anna-Stina as she came down the stone step.

"Stand back you fools—I shall drop the cake—and then there will be hell to pay for all of you," she laughed, holding the cake high, swinging it from side to side. "I traded Bras Anna a morning's milking for one of her eggs, for this cake. It is special and you shall have none of it…only Carl and I."

"Let us at least have a closer look, Anna-Stina," Per shouted above the throng, "at least let us gaze upon it—smell it, surely—it is a work of *fäbod* art—or did *Rånda* help you make it."

Anna-Stina smiled, pleased with their attention. She lowered the little cake so they could all crowd around and examine it.

"I do not need *Rånda* to help me bake a cake, Per."

They crowded and pushed to get a glance at her creation. There was a ring of *smultron*[65] around the base of the little, whitish-brown cake. The top edge was ringed with the berries. It was certainly not a pretty sight but the effort showed in the primitive decoration of fruit. In the center, on top, she had placed a spring wildflower.

Selma, the oldest *vallkulla* among them, had remained apart from the group after the music stopped. She was now tending some drying cheese molds at the spring house and had been watching and listening to the youngsters in silence, enjoying the excitement the young people brought. She remembered the days when her own late husband had come courting and smiled at the memory.

"Here, Anna-Stina," she interjected, "let me make some *vispgrädde*[66] for you to put on top of the cake. It will sweeten it up for the both of you and can be my payment for the fine tunes."

"*Oooouuuu…*," the crowd intoned, "are you two ever lucky. Selma will use her precious cream for you."

Selma was known to be extremely thrifty and unaccustomed to giving over to any excessive generosity. Ignoring the chiding youngsters, smiling, she strolled across the lane to the spring. With a small bark ladle she dipped a bit of her cream from a container that was cooling in the water. She began to whip the cream with a birch twig wisp. She liked Anna-Stina for her helpful nature to the older women and young girls and her willingness to seek, listen and accept advice from the older, more experienced *vallkullor*, like herself. Selma knew about the incident at Anna-Stina's *kyrktagningen*, and had heard about Carl Fröman supposedly protecting her from the marauding youngsters while she was in the pillory. At the time, she didn't believe the rumor. It took little to set the gossips to wagging their tongues and it would be unusual that a young man of Carl's social stature would pay any attention to a simple *vallkulla*, for any other reason. Yet, here he was—about to get a share of Anna-Stina's Sunday cake.

As Selma returned from the spring, she stole a glance at the pair. Carl and Anna-Stina did seem to be standing a bit apart—almost as a couple. She wondered now whether the rumor was not true. Carl and the girl seemed, somehow, close. As Selma heaped a white mound onto the cake, the crowd of youngsters set up a cacophony of protest, threatening to "kidnap" the cake. They jumped and danced about the couple as Anna-Stina and Carl started walking up the forest path.

A ring of moving color—the girl's dresses and boy's clothes, began to form around them, shaping into a large, circular ring dance, circling the pair, keeping up, even as they hastened their steps down the path toward the spring. The fiddlers struck a lively march tune. Anna-Stina tossed back her head, laughing and quickly handed the cake to Carl, who lifted it high in one hand, well above the crowd.

With his other hand, he sought one of Anna-Stina's and hands clasped, they fairly skipped along the path, threatening to outdistance the rollicking group who still circled them, singing all the while, until it resounded through the forest. Then, as the path suddenly narrowed, the group had to give in and fracturing, they parted, letting the couple to walk free.

Old Selma thought to herself, the rumor was now substantiated. Could it be true? There would be no good coming from this when Carl's mother smelled it in the wind. She could not find any girl in Nås—or possibly all of Dalarna—suitable for her Carl. There would be trouble from that quarter before the next snow, she was willing to wager.

Carl didn't let go of Anna-Stina's hand as they skipped away along the path. After the group broke their captive, musical ring, freeing the couple at last, they'd shouted after them: "Goodbye—goodbye—goodbye…goodbye Carl and Anna-Stina—take care—do not eat too much cake Carl—be careful that Anna-Stina has not put a spell in the cake Carl." Both turned to wave their mock farewells. "Don't forget to return, you two—we'll need more music after we eat."

The couple set out directly toward the spring, Carl still holding Anna-Stina's hand. She returned the gentle pressure from his grip as they strolled and hazarded a glance at him. As their eyes met, both understood that something unspoken was happening.

Carl carried the cake carefully in one hand; Anna-Stina had brought a birch backpack with cheese, bread and the *fäbod*'s only long-necked bottle, carefully wrapped in a woolen towel to keep its contents of coffee, warm. Tin cups in her ample apron pockets clanked together dully, along with two folding knives, as they walked along the path. Carl smiled to himself at the abundance of Anna-Stina's uninhibited enthusiasm. She was truly certainly full of life, he thought; how refreshing.

They quickly reached the spring, having made small talk along the way. The sun still remained high and an air of freedom and timelessness hung about the afternoon. At the water's edge, Anna-Stina explored the dry, mossy area for any dung piles from cattle, or moose that may have recently come for a drink. Satisfied, she removed a linen square from the back-pack and spread it over the moss. She smiled toward Carl, who had been peering into the spring, looking for fish.

"Come, sit now, Carl. You won't find any fish here—it's too high up and the brook never gets wide enough for them to swim up this far."

"I have seen that," he said, crossing to the pallet, "where shall I put the cake?"

"For now just put it there—on the stone," she indicated a flat rock not far from their chosen spot. Carl did her bidding and returned, licking the whipped cream from his fingers where he had accidentally sampled it.

Due to the size of the cloth, they both sat close together, their knees nearly touching. Carl watched attentively as Anna-Stina assembled the little collection of items. He mused, what a homemaker she is, too…so pleased with these simple offerings. Due to the spare provisions at the *fäbod*, it's almost a feast of simplicity. What would she think of the linen and silver-clad tables I have seen spread, in Uppsala and Stockholm? Could she adapt to that life as easily as she seemed to meet most other obstacles and challenges in the village and forest: *oäktabarn*, pillories in the churchyard, humiliation…no end of problems…he mused, frowning slightly and still gay and pleasant?

Anna-Stina arranged three kinds of small cheeses on rectangular, birch trays, placing a small bowl of butter beside them.

"Carl, would you pour some of the coffee for each of us?"

She rose to a kneeling position and fishing the cups and forks from her apron's pockets, handed them over. Slicing *bullbröd* taken from the backpack, she arranged the pieces on another piece of bark.

"Och—I have forgotten a knife for the butter." Leaning sideways, she drew her *vallkulla's* knife again from the belt sheath and wiping the shiny blade on her apron, laid it beside the bread.

Carl had poured coffee from the bottle and placed the cups beside the knife.

"Mind the knife Carl that you do not cut yourself. It is very sharp."

She treats me like a helpless boy, he thought, smiling and filling the second cup. A natural mother—the way she places everything just so and she is so creative about it.

"I am starving."

"Well then…*var så god…*[67]" she said with a feminine flourish, offering him the largest slice of buttered bread.

"Tack," he said and began to help himself, hungrily.

She took a slice for herself and after Carl had finished with it, sat back on her heels to butter it. She watched Carl add a piece of cheese to his bread and pick up his cup. This is nice she thought— he has fine customs…he eats so carefully.

They continued eating in silence. For the first time in so long— she couldn't remember, Anna-Stina hadn't thought about the death of little Augusta, or the humiliation of the *kyrktagning*. I'm finally enjoying myself again, she thought. Carl does not seem to remember, either, or mind my past shame. Why not ask him the truth, she thought; better to know than to hope.

They sat in silence for a while, glancing at the birds flitting around the edge of the spring and in the branches immediately above. Finally, she summoned the courage.

"Carl—why did you help me…that Sunday at the *kyrktagning?*"

He glanced at her quickly but continued chewing, seeming to ponder her question but smiling at her as he did so.

"Why? I guess…because you needed it. You were in pain—or I thought you were and you might have even been in danger of strangling yourself, when you lost your…your footing, so to speak, on the stool."

She smiled at his sense of humor and the play of words, referring to her *rumpa.*

"Why do you ask?"

"Oh…I wonder how many other people, like you, would have stopped—or cared?"

"I don't know what you mean…people like me. I believe anyone…any Christian, would have…especially seeing your obvious distress. *Järnafolke*[68] are not monsters, despite how some have treated you. Many are quite kind and generous and many speak highly of you—your skills."

"I know, Carl. But..by people like you, I meant…well—not renter-farmers, you know, *drängar*[69], someone like my father, us, Carl."

"Anna-Stina, my people as you say are no different from you— only that we may own more land—and things. We eat, we breathe…" he thought better of carrying the description of their physical and emotional similarities further.

"I am just the same as you—or your father, I mean, being a man."

"I do not think you are; I believe you are different. You are kinder—more generous…not that my own father is not; that isn't what I meant." She said this not to humble her own kind, but to complement Carl; she was somewhat at a loss for words.

"You—you are gentle, Carl. I hope that does not offend you."

"Well, how can I ever live up to that praise, Anna-Stina? Of course I do not mind. Gentle is a nice thing…thank you."

"Carl…you kept that first Sunday, in the pillory…from being very terrible for me. Your kindness and the following two Sundays, also, remaining as you did, to ward off the evil doers…it helped in a way you will never understand."

"I am pleased to hear that Anna-Stina. We can only thank God you came to no harm in the pillory and I am glad to hear you say it."

They sat for a while without speaking.

"Carl, you never asked about the child—my little girl...? You never asked, or pried, like everyone else...and you still haven't."

"No."

"That is another thing for which I respect you, Carl...your acceptance."

He seemed to hesitate. Anna-Stina offered him another slice of bread and then the cheese.

"You see, no one would respect my decision not to name the father of Augusta. I was satisfied to have only her and to forget the rest—to let it drop from memory...to go on."

Carl took a sip of coffee and wiped cheese crumbs from his leather trousers.

"It was not a pleasant—relationship—the child's father, then?"

"I didn't say that," she snapped. Then seeing the look of hurt on his face, reached over and touched his arm. "I'm sorry, Carl, my tongue...is sharp, sometimes."

"Anna-Stina, I, nor anyone else said it was an unpleasant relationship...I merely assumed, from what you just said, that it wasn't pleasant. You mentioned dropping the memory—letting things go and just loving your child?"

"Yes, I did and I apologize for my quick tongue."

"I understand...you do not wish to talk of the matter? We should speak of other things then?"

"No. I mean—I—because you have helped me, I wanted you to know how much that meant and that it wasn't the normal thing between a man and a woman, of our differences. I did not suffer the *kyrktagning* to save some man I love...had a strong affection for—in fact, just the opposite."

"I see—then the experience was not a good one and you wanted me to know that?"

"I guess...yes, but there's more. I wanted to—oh, I can not say it." She was unable to meet his gaze, twisting a corner of her apron. It was unusual for her to be at a loss of words. "Just...please realize it is something I can't speak of to anyone. I have not even spoken with my parents about this—only you, I wanted to try to explain it, but now I find I can not—not without saying too much."

"I believe, even without speaking directly of it Anna-Stina, you have shown me your concern that I should not think badly of you because you bore an *oäktabarn*...and I do not. You have also shown me that— you are very frustrated because you can not—for some reason known only to yourself—speak further of the matter at this time."

"Yes, that is fact—exactly."

"Just by wanting to make me understand—caring that I understand, you show me far more than words could have said."

She leaned forward and laid her hand on his arm a second time. He looked quite serious and put his hand over hers. Their eyes met and held, searching...neither wavered and they gazed deeply, exchanging, seeking...and Carl leaned slowly toward her, lost in the pools of her eyes.

"There they are!" the voice came from the path, "*Hejah*—we've found them—but they are not kissing...yet!"

"I think they would soon have been..." someone else shouted. The group careened down the path waving hats and scarves at the couple and shouting loudly.

"Dancing—dancing—we want to be dancing—music—music..."

The trance between the pair was broken. "I think we had better pick up and follow them—they will not let us be," Carl said.

"You're right," she said, as they began putting their picnic back in her knapsack. "Do you have to go back today, Carl?"

"Yes, I must. Per must help his father finish their harvest tomorrow and my father is expecting me. Why?"

"I didn't know—sometimes the boys stay the night and go back the next day—that's all...I—I was enjoying the...music."

"I also, but no, I really have to go and I am sorry for myself—I would rather remain and have another dance tomorrow. We still have this evening to play for the group. I still have to teach you some of the tunes I've learned from my music professor, if you want to hear them."

By this time they'd finished filling the backpack and Anna-Stina donned it, over Carl's gentlemanly objection.

"I have always carried it," she said "It fits me...let's go now or they will carry us," she nearly had to shout over the noise the others were making again.

Half-running, half-walking around them, the group chided them.

"I think they have become a pair," someone shouted. "They look great together," someone else offered. "*Hooo*...look at Karin—she was kissing Olaf...."

And off they went, following after another, bolder couple who the group had turned on. Oalv was younger than Carl and like Carl, had little experience with girls. Karin had seen this and taking advantage of it, boldly ignoring his shyness, she was kissing him squarely on the cheek several times as they walked back to the *fäbod*, arm in arm. Olaf flushed like ripe currants.

As they trooped after the group, privately, Carl wished it could be he and Anna-Stina. Decorum of age and upbringing prevented it, however—even without his shyness. Carl also had a position to maintain in the community and he knew it. He didn't know what to make of his now, solidly-founded affection for Anna-Stina—except that it existed, now, more than ever. Since the incident in the churchyard he'd thought of her often. Whenever he'd seen her by chance, his heart leaped with pleasure. And today...well today was special.

"My father..." Karolina mused, interrupting my mental reverie as I continued my frantic note-taking, "...often said he was a stranger to women. Even at his university in Stockholm, father had avoided the excesses, which of course included women and drink. His parents— rather, his mother, had chosen the life of a rector for him, probably aspiring for the Bishopsy of Uppsala *Domkyrka*[70], someday. It would have pleased her if he had followed an existing line of ministers in the Fröman family.

Many before him had answered the call to the Swedish Lutheran Church. Grandfather had no opinion in the matter, or suffices it to say, no choice to express it. My father had shown a penchant for things studious—literature, arts and especially, music, early in life. As a result, grandfather had never attempted to foster interests in the family farm, business, or government service as he himself had inherited and chosen for his own career. This left the choice mostly up to grandmother, to sway and convince father to follow those more sensitive leanings toward The Church."

"Your grandmother played a large part in your father's life—early life, then?"

"Father said the seminary school he attended in Stockholm

frowned on any mixing of the sexes during the studies' term. Of
course, there were no females in the school. I believe they even
discouraged visits by female siblings, even on special occasions and
holidays, preferring instead, the boys remain secluded in their rooms,
or the commons room, if they couldn't return home. Many boys
suffered this fate, having been sent from far from Stockholm, many
even coming from abroad."

"That sounds like a recipe for disaster—at least it would be, today."

"For many, it was; but not Father. Although he was left much to
his own resources at school, except for the times he returned to
Frömansgården on holidays, he didn't succumb to the loneliness.
Several of the boys had alliances, but father chose to study hard,
master as many musical instruments as he could and read as many
books. I recall him saying the school's library was quite limited in its'
offerings, dealing primarily with literature suitable for seminarian
students and staff. As his months of study advanced and his studies
matured, some of father's masters recognized his gift of knowledge,
commitment and genuine kindness and offered him free rein of their
personal libraries. There he could choose from all the classics—
opening to him the world of philosophy, normally unavailable to
young students of his level. Even the forbidden novels were secretly
proffered by several of his masters and as with all materials, he
devoured them."

"What would grandmother have thought?"

"Exactly, behavior wise, father seemed to bear no strong feelings
toward any other boys despite the rare instances of personal
transgression. Since he had also worked fairly hard in his father's
farm and business, he was better developed, physically, than most of
the young men and could easily hold his own. The other students
also seemed to recognize in him the role of peacemaker, or mentor
and would often appeal to him in matters, public and personal, where
a neutral mind was needed to decide—to judge, or, failing that, a
strong arm and clenched fist. They knew they could trust his
judgment as well as his discretion—this is something everyone
enjoyed about father. These qualities quickly earned him the full
respect of all the staff, as well as his fellow seminarians."

"Those are admirable traits and rather unusual for a...nearly,
farm boy."

"True. But after that weekend in the *fäbod*, father's life changed. He later told mother that—without ever knowing it, she reached out—all the way to Stockholm. From that day forward, father's thoughts were of Mother—and her in the *fäbod*. And he wrote her endless letters, which she didn't receive until she returned from the *fäbod*, in the fall. She dominated his study of Greek. When he recited Latin, he said, his tongue wanted to speak her name and his lips to shape the undeclared words of love he felt for her. Those revelations, they really made my mother proud for the rest of her life. I read them myself, years later.

"Your parents truly had a unique relationship," I said, sort of dreaming while I took notes.

"Before long, father's teachers noticed the far away look which how often came into his eye. At first, they laid it to delayed adolescence, but when his concentration seemed to grow no better— his absences of mind...lack of attention...the beloved mentors feared for his studies and finally realized it had to be a girl. Yet, when examinations were made, his mental prowess seemed to have suffered little. However, the aesthetic distance remained and it didn't escape the more astute teachers...especially those who knew him best."

"Finally, one semester, father failed to return to the university. A hastily scrawled note from grandfather asked for excuse from the term, blaming family matters—and then, I suppose, they knew they had lost him to some unknown force."

"Or woman," I added.

"Yes, certainly: force," Karolina chuckled, "Mother was that.

"When father's behavior became apparent to his mother, there was soon hell to pay for him. Father told me he didn't contradict her, argue, or provoke her. He simply refused to return to seminary that fall after his tryst in the *fäbod*. And nothing his mother did would convince him otherwise. She even packed his bags for him, but he lived from his travel cases for a week, before she eventually relented. His father secretly admired the new resolve shown by his son, probably wishing himself the same application of purpose in matters dealing with his wife—my grandmother."

"My father said Grandfather took him aside and reassured him of a position in the family business and the farm, or the government, after that. Father chose the farm. For he loved animals and the miracle of regeneration—birth and growth. He thought he would also be able to get closer to Mother, who remained at Kallebourg house, at the widow Frömans in Nås, during the winter months. He assumed she would be a *vallkulla* in Vansberget again the following summer. As *vallkulla* in summer and *piga*[71] to the widow's household in winter, Anna-Stina bore a forbidden avocation and was of a social class from which a man of father's stature couldn't seek a wife. Nevertheless, he was smitten, he told me."

"But Grandmother didn't accept her son's change of mood as anything other than what it was; if it changed once, it could change— or be changed, again. And guess...by whom? It was obvious to her that her son wasn't ailing. He was able to work on the farm along side other men his age, so it must be a girl, she reasoned. Grandmother was no fool and after a few inquiries, she was at first astonished—and then enraged, to learn of the encounters her son had had with the 'Malmberg girl' as she called Mother...a mere servant."

CHAPTER 12

The Cart Ride

The beginnings of the winter ache for the peace of the aloneness, which came to Anna-Stina only at the *fäbod*, had begun to haunt her. How strange, she thought, lonely…for loneliness.

The fall day back in the community dawned fair, with blue skies ringing every edge of the distant horizon, where it could be seen above the giant *tall*[72] and *gran*[73]. She'd been awake since long before dawn, thinking of the excitement of the day. The sun now came later and later as winter approached. Just one week away from the *fäbod* was not enough for her mind, or her body to adjust to her new working schedule. Fall brought the harvest of the *korn*[74] to the valley farms and with it the return of the animals and *vallkullor* to the home pastures. Already she missed the pace of the forest life, the un-intrusive companionship of the other women and the freedom with the animals.

Since the cows were now at the home farm, Anna-Stina no longer need rise two hours early to prepare for the day's grazing. Cheese and butter making, prior to beginning the morning milking, were now handed over to the home farm girls, the *hempiga*[75] at the widow Fröman's, what little of it there was, since many animals had ceased giving milk. Taking the cows to graze in the forest was a thing of the past for another season and a whole winter anyway. Leaving the *fäbod* for another seven months for the boredom of community life was something Anna-Stina did not wish to think about.

Today, however, she was too excited to worry about missing her *fäbodliv:* It was the special day when it was the custom for the community to celebrate the *vallkulla's* past summer's work. In the fall, each year, the community set aside a time for praising their handiwork: the clothing sewn, knitted, woven and fancy embroidering. The quality of the cheeses made for their masters, not to mention the normal day-to-day milking and *mismör* boiling were admired and judged. Much of this was extra work had to be done while they tended the animals. It fell to the benefit of the farmer, or farmers who had hired them. A *vallkulla's* hands were seldom idle as she sewed, knitted or embroidered the agreed upon number of articles for her former master.

During the final summer days in the *fäbod,* all unmarried *vallkullor* took extra care to make several small cheeses, formed in a special shape and were particularly reserved to give to the special young, unmarried men. All the regular cheeses and dairy produce had previously been tallied over the summer and were evaluated, with the result to be read aloud at the festival, in praise of the *vallkullor.*

Aside from the normal practical joking and children's antics, there was a humorous tradition that sometimes occurred at this celebration, done mostly as a joke, especially if alcohol was being consumed. If, for some reason, the young men of the community didn't find a particular *vallkulla* had taken quite enough care with her cheeses, or made sufficient quality or quantity of the small bricks for them to sample, they would capture her and pretend to take her away from the festivities, as a prank.

Always done in fun, several young men would grab her, make a show of placing her in a cart and haul her a little way from the celebration, or at most, start the cart and drop her just outside the community where they would abandon her on the track, leaving her to walk the ten minutes or so, back. More often than not, they'd only threaten to carry out the deed.

If a *vallkulla* had been particularly brazen, or worse, lazy, they'd take her further away and leave her to find her way home. She'd of course, miss the balance of the celebration.

More importantly, she might also miss a renewed job offer or, another such work offering for the following summer, a practice usually negotiated, rejected or accepted on this day, between the farmer and *vallkulla.* It probably was an ancient way of eliminating lazy *vallkullor* from taking up that occupation the following summer but offered a productive woman an opportunity to receive better offers from another family.

Threats of this occurrence throughout the summer, though humorously made among the young girls, were usually sufficient encouragement for even the most indolent *vallkullor* to try a little harder. On the special day, the boys fairly recognized any first-year, younger girl's inadequacies and usually left them alone, knowing they had next year to improve…but only after much teasing and false threats about the quality or small number of her cheeses. This encouraged, or threatened her to do better the following summer, which they usually did. In either event, the young men tended to gain better cheeses to sample as their reward.

And if any *vallkullor* had a particular boy she liked, she'd make and save an extra-special cheese only for him. Many of the young Vansberget *vallkullor* were not yet skilled at cheese making and Anna-Stina and the older women always helped them, as had many, older *vallkullor*-grandmothers done for them. Anna-Stina's superior skills in the *fäbod* had always prevented her from even being considered a candidate for a cart ride.

This particular fall, Anna-Stina made a special set of three small cheeses, thinking of Carl, knowing he'd likely attend the function. One of them was in the shape of a cross, to honor his intended occupation; the other two were oval-shaped and each bore the imprint of an ancient, runic design, molded in place at the time she pressed the soft curd into the mold. Whenever time permitted, she'd fabricated the small, wooden molds, recalling some of her father's skills in woodcraft. Her fingers bled from the hard iron knife she used to patiently shave and form each pine mold, until all the parts fit perfectly. She'd formed the sides into the desired shape after soaking the wood in the spring and then bending it carefully before securely tying it with birch roots in order to maintain the desired shape.

Her cheeses had rested—hidden, in the pantry, wrapped in linen she'd woven and embossed with embroidery. The colorful threads intertwined along the neatly-hemmed edges, in floral and forest patterns. Many hours at *sovhol* [76] were dedicated to the intricate needlework. At every chance she would draw the precious needle from the little *nålhus* [77] hanging from her apron. She'd thread the needle with her own, home-dyed thread and work over the current piece as the cows digested the morning's grazing and chewed their cud in the shade, resting from the mosquitoes and flies.

For Anna-Stina and many other young women, in just a few hours the community would assemble around the central pasture in Skålbyn. Makeshift tables would be set up and covered with pastel-striped, linen from the various households. All the *vallkullor* would spread their prized cheeses and other items and their employers would stand with them and praise their charges for their meritorious summer's work. After all, had they not braved bears, wolves and even troll for nothing?

With her employer, the young women would remain beside their individual displays, offering special samples of her cheese to any passerby who asked. On this day, too, employers renewed offers to re-hire for the coming season; each woman had a week to indicate her willingness to accept, or reject any offers. Many of the girls, including Anna-Stina, had multiple offers. Because of her excellent reputation, Anna-Stina was in great demand.

Usually, the women of the family decided and made their choice of *vallkulla* known; often families who only owned a cow or two, would pool their animals, assembling ten or fifteen cows between them. They'd agree to seek out a specific *vallkulla*, combining their animals for her to tend. She must keep count of the proportion which each family's animals contributed; certainly not an easy chore.

Anna-Stina preferred to remain with the Fröman family. Had Carl not been a nephew, she might have been tempted to change employers. At times she did wish she could see some of the other *fäbodarna*, just for the change. But the lure of Carl and their periodic meetings to discuss the things they both loved, continued to keep her employed where she was. Unbeknownst to Anna-Stina, Carl's mother, who'd gotten wind of the youngster's mutual affection, was out-voted by the other Fröman relations in the choice of *vallkulla*, which infuriated her.

Finally Carl appeared in late morning, circulating among the crowd with a sureness and confidence that came to few who weren't born to generations of influence. At first, he didn't seek out Anna-Stina, but spoke to all the other young people he knew, young and old and especially with every girl he encountered.

Watching and waiting anxiously beside her exhibit with the old minister, Anna-Stina fidgeted and fussed with the display. It is as if it is his intent to antagonize me, she thought, at first, fuming. But as she observed him, she realized she knew him well enough—that he truly loved her…she didn't mind…much. She could easily have turned her back on him entirely and basked in the glory of praise which came from each visitor to their display tables.

As she waited only half listening as the old minister recounted again to a family who were admiring her work, her eyes strayed to the mountains to the north. Somewhere over the hills lay the solitude of Vansberget. The cabins closed now. The pastures empty. The whole scene returned to the spirits who dwelled there in their absence. No wonder we must exorcise them in the spring, she thought. It was their home far longer in the year than our brief summer stay.

So…Carl could have his fun today. She knew his eye returned to her, often enough as he flirted with the other women. During these moments, he'd look over the girl's shoulder, seek and catch Anna-Stina's eye across the crowd and smile.

The Fröman family was, after all, one of the wealthiest, best-connected and most popular families in Western Dalarna. Anna-Stina knew she could only dream of wedding Carl, until certain things changed—if ever. His extended family had already tried to see that the couple did not mix, publicly. If the Frömans—*Fru* Fröman in particular and the sniveling young pastor to be, Henrik Johansson, had anything to do with it, Carl was and had long been, destined for the pulpit and marriage to someone far more suitable.

During these thoughtful moments, Anna-Stina only half-listened to the greetings from passersby. Eventually, at each encounter, she felt the initial surge of pride lessening. Material accomplishments, she thought, really did not compare to the feelings of love for another.

There arose a murmur from the crowd. The old minister, Pastor Håkansson, had stepped away from their exhibit and had been visiting with some of the families just come up river in one of the *kyrkabåtar*[78]. They'd arrived a day early, for it was only *lördag*[79]. Someone had to remain at home to do the daily farm chores, thus missing the celebration. Woe be to the ones who had lost the drawing of straws, for who could go and who must remain to feed the animals and tend the milking. The lucky ones had rowed the boat and would attend the church service tomorrow.

The murmuring grew louder and Anna-Stina craned her neck to see what was happening. She saw her friend Ingrid pushing her way through the crowd toward her, smiling a worried smile, her frown webbing her sunburned brow.

"What is it, Ingrid?" she said as the girl approached. Stepping up and cupping her hand so those nearby would be unable to hear, she said: "They want you to play the violin Anna-Stina."

"All right...I can do that."

"Be careful though—I have been watching Ellen, Helga and some of the other boys. Carl's mother and Pastor Johansson are hatching some plot to spoil the day for you. I heard some talk and...well, I can tell it from their faces. Someone has put them up to something. I believe it to be Pastor Johansson, behind it all. I will watch out while you play. I think they'll do something then—or soon after, though I can't understand why. Do you know?"

"Oh Ingrid, you do worry so...but tack, you are my keeper. Sometimes I believe you imagine a *mörksuga* behind every face. As for Pastor Johansson...well, we must consider the man...," she rolled her eyes. The girls are not really evil—merely jealous and we both know jealousy is a terrible sin and that it's infectious and hard to control. They can't harm us with only their jealousy."

Ingrid smiled at the friend she considered wise beyond her age. She shook her head, frowning, still unconvinced. "Well—I don't trust anyone. So I took your bow and violin to Carl for safe-keeping."

"Oh...tack, Ingrid."

"I asked him to fetch them to you when you need them. He should be here soon. By the way, he was happy to have them," she smiled knowingly.

Just then Anna-Stina spied Minister Håkansson pushing his way toward them holding up one arm. He was smiling and nodding to passers-by as he slowly made his way in the throng. Another *vallkulla*, Alma Petersdotter followed behind him.

"Alma will sing, it appears," Anna-Stina said.

Alma knew the rigors of the *fäbod*, having herself begun as a very young girl and worked until she married. She had six children and was barely half way through her childbearing years. She was a good singer and the pair had often sung in the evenings. Her voice was deep, strong and steady.

Ingrid pointed across the crowd; Carl was coming, holding the bow and violin high above his head. As he nodded and spoke, his eyes returned to the two girls. Seeing him approach, Anna-Stina forgot the festivities and her heart began to beat strongly.

Pastor Håkansson and Alma reached the pair first. Alma glanced around smiling. She nodded her head to Anna-Stina as if to say: "...what a crowd." Pastor Håkansson began outlining the expected performance to her.

"We will have you both up so they can see and hear you...possibly that cart there..." he indicated an unseen cart in the thick of the crowd.

Carl arrived then and the minister put a hand on his shoulder and began to chat idly, while Carl was in the process of pressing the violin and bow into Anna-Stina's waiting hands. For a moment, though his eyes were on the pastor, Carl's hands touched hers and held for an instant longer than necessary and a jolt passed between the couple. Then, the minister had to repeat his words.

"I am sorry...what—what did you say, Pastor...?"

The old man glanced at Anna-Stina, then Carl and smiled, understanding.

"You shall play something appropriate from the *fäbod*, Anna-Stina—I know that between the two of you...Alma has agreed to sing, you can choose something. Anders...where is he? Oh, there..." he said, "...he will happily play harmony for you Anna-Stina."

She smiled and nodded to a familiar fiddler standing near the wagon.

The pastor turned to Carl. "Here, Carl Fröman, get those boys over to help you draw that cart deeper into the crowd. That shall be the musician's platform; then help Alma and Anna-Stina onto it so everyone can better hear and see."

The two followed Carl and within minutes the cart was moved and the two women scampered up, with Carl's help.

"Oh, to be so young and nimble again," the pastor chortled to no one in particular, "just like kid goats."

As soon as they were situated on the cart Anna-Stina and Anders stepped close and began quietly tuning their violins. Alma stood looking out over the gathering, smoothing her dress. Slowly, a respectful silence fell on the crowd. Mothers hastily hushed a few

children. The fiddles were finally tuned and the three young people
stood steady at last, Alma having arranged her dress, folded her
hands and waited, staring down as was befitting a housewife of thirty-
one years. Anna-Stina took a little longer to arrange her violin,
testing and tune the strings once more with Anders. Finally satisfied,
she smiled first at Anders then more broadly down at the minister and
nodded her head as if to ask forgiveness for keeping him waiting. He
beamed, returning her smile.

Nearly standing on tip-toe, as he held onto one of the wagon's
wheels, he shouted above the heads of those around him: "*Anna-Stina
och Anders vill spela—och Alma vill sjunga—fäbod melody*," he
announced, "...an older...and one of our youngest *vallkullor* will entertain
us with one of the ancient melodies of the *fäbod* we all love so well."

By the time they were ready to begin, Anna-Stina had forgotten
the admonishments of her friend Ingrid and was now concentrating on
her playing. The two violins began slowly, playing through the first
part, unaccompanied by Alma, so the crowd could experience the
beauty of the solo instruments. When they reached it, they
emphasized the entry point for Alma, who began to sing. It was an
honest hymn of praise, which made one wish to be in the church and
the *fäbod* at the same time. The ancient melody of the *vallkulla's*
home rolled out to the utter attention of the gathering and Anna-
Stina totally lost herself in the execution of the music. So many
summers singing together in the *fäbod* now showed when the two
performed together.

The song ended as suddenly as it began. There was no
recognition of the superb performance of the two. The crowd
seemed to hang for a moment on the silence that followed the tune.
Anna-Stina and Alma were immediately helped down by willing hands.
Together, she and Carl walked toward her exhibition table and were
immediately lost in the crowd.

Carl nervously began making conversation: "There are so many
beautiful things that came back from the *fäbod* this year."

"What do you see that you like, Carl?"

"Oh...I can't tell...or, I won't get what I want. Like a wish, it's
all quite beautiful, though."

"It must be someone's cheeses—or embroidery...is it someone's
needle-work, Carl?" She was smiling as she pondered the double

meaning of his comment and was about to ask that he be more specific, knowing that he couldn't or wouldn't.

Just then, two young men…Johan and Fredrick, stepped forward and took places on each side of Carl. They were both smiling and making gestures of friendliness, making as if to join the pair's conversation in a casual but mischievous fashion. Carl looked a little surprised and Anna-Stina wished that they'd go back where they came from. They just butted in and began asking Carl about the *korn* harvest. She was about to chide them for their lack of manners, but decided against it, thinking it might make them remain longer. So instead, she humored them by listening to the seeming nonsense they were prattling on about. Suddenly, she felt herself grasped by strong hands on each of her arms. She was pulled backwards with a sharp jerk.

"What…," she uttered, surprised.

Carl, seeing the sudden movement, exclaimed and turned toward her.

"Hey…what…," a look of astonishment crossed his face and he reached for her. But the two men beside him were quicker, turned and swiftly secured him by each arm, pulling him backwards and then down onto the grass. Another two youngsters appeared from nowhere and straddled him. He fought as they attempted to secure his arms and legs, which flailed in opposition to his sudden confinement.

Bystanders had to move aside quickly to avoid being knocked down or kicked. Young pastor Johansson approached and stood over the struggling Carl.

"No boys…" he said condescendingly, pretending to be a peacemaker, "do not fight over these young women," he laughed rather hollowly.

Anna-Stina saw Carl looking up at him angrily, a look of astonishment on his face.

"But Pastor Johansson, I'm not fighting—I'm trying to…."

The young men began to drag him away as Anna-Stina renewed her struggles.

"*Ooch*…Johan…that hurts me," she said, growing angry that the joke was getting rough.

In an appeal to the minister, Carl said, "Save Anna-Stina…can you not see Pastor—they are hurting her."

"Now, Carl—don't exaggerate." He turned toward Anna-Stina

and looked her up and down, sneering slightly.

"What some women will do to lead the young boys on is disgusting," he said with an air of repugnance, glancing over his shoulder as he turned back to Carl. "You shouldn't concern yourself with girls like Anna-Stina Malmberg, Carl Fröman. A young man of your standing—taking up The Cloth...shame, Carl, for wanting to be around someone...."

That was the last Anna-Stina was able to hear or see as she was suddenly sprinted away from the group. Her captors were smiling and laughing at her struggles, making as to be playing a prank on her. They laughed as they half-dragged, half-walked her away. The surrounding crowd parted for the seemly-playful youngsters, no doubt stealing a *vallkulla* in jest.

Anna-Stina couldn't believe her ears after the minister had spoken. Why that...she had thought, but she had other things to deal with. She would worry about Pastor Johansson, later. The troubled and confused look on Carl's face told Anna-Stina she would have to explain what her friend had cautioned her about; Carl didn't realize there was a plot to bring him away from her and to The Church. This would probably mean she'd have to reveal her suspicions to him about the attack on her in the *fäbod*...who she was certain had struck her down in the darkness and raped her.

The boys continued, dragging and pulling her backward, past the heavily laden tables, around the fence, finally turning and yanking her through the thinning crowd. Given the festive nature of the occasion the spectators made way for them, willingly; some cast humorous looks at the fun the young people were apparently having. She glanced at her captors each in turn, smiling and stumbling along between them; she knew all of the boys. They are being a little rough, she thought wondering now whether Ingrid's warning should not have been heeded, earlier. The crowd continued to ignore their progress, satisfied with the success of the summer day and willing to let the youngsters bask in a bit of silliness. Anna-Stina wasn't yet sure of their intentions.

"You have made a mistake if you think to kidnap me," she said, laughingly. The thought that they were serious didn't yet occur to her.

But the boys only leered at her and yanked her even harder.

"I have made very special cheeses for you young bulls—you'd

better taste them again, if you haven't yet. I believe you have gone without the taste of good cheese too long, if you think you must capture me. The other boys—those who remain before the food tables, know their value. They will have eaten them all before you return."

They continued to ignore her and it was then she seriously began to wonder about their motives. And they were not smiling either, but leering, as they bore her on, around the buildings and into the tall trees at the edge of the community. They spun her around, dragging her backwards, approaching a small cart with a single horse hitched. A boy, already seated, glanced backward nervously at the approaching threesome. Because of their boisterous movement, he was forced to hold the horse's reins tighter as they approached. Two more young men had been sitting with their legs dangling out the back. Another was waiting beside it. She glanced left and right at her captors. They still were not smiling nor would either meet her questioning stare. They're serious, she thought—very serious…this has been well planned in advance.

With the help of the others, they unceremoniously picked her up and flung her into the cart. Dried pine boughs covered the cart's bottom and pricked her neck and cheeks as she landed; a cloud of dust and broken needles rose up around her.

Before she could jump up, two of the boys leaped up beside her and promptly swung both legs over her before she could begin to struggling anew. She was pinned, face downward in the sticky needles. The cart started with a lurch, bouncing down the rutted trail, another boy leaped in and sat backwards on the seat, holding her by her wrists.

How can this be happening Anna-Stina thought, feeling a slight panic for the first time? Strong and self-reliant as she was, she wouldn't have believed they dare to do this. Not since her rape, had she felt such pangs of apprehension, humiliation and anger. Her wrath began to build.

Turning her head to one side, she spat dust and bits of dry needles from her mouth. Her flashing eyes were all that betrayed the anger. As the cart bounced, the dried pine needles forced themselves up, sticking her skin through her new, linen dress.

"Where are you three dumb skulls taking me," she asked, still attempting a carefree manner in the mood of the festivities.

"Your cheeses were judged too small Anna-Stina," answered Emil, her nearest captor.

"Lately, you also have had a very bad attitude in the community..." offered Peter, "...and we have been asked to teach you a lesson," he said. And with that, he raised his hand and struck her very hard on the buttocks.

She felt her soft flesh yield at the unexpected blow and her cheek began to sting at the same time. Anger choked her—she became so mad she felt she would burst if she couldn't get at them. How do they dare to touch me in this way, she raged inwardly? But she knew. Once someone had born an illegitimate child, she could never gain back a reputation. No doubt they assumed her easy and free with her favors. Were they going to rape her, too?

Trying to surprise them, she suddenly squirmed and twisted, hoping to break free in surprise. Whack! She was struck on the other side.

"Sit still; or you'll get more!" the boy shouted above the rumble of the cart's wheels.

They are too strong and their weight pressed her even harder. Rage overcame her. Reacting instinctively and without regarded as to what the sticky pitch would do to her, she flung her body sideways in a rolling effort to free herself. Even beneath the weight of their legs, she was able to turn slightly, trying to both protect her backside and to get into a position where she could confront one of them face-to-face...kick, scratch or bite—she cared not which.

"Faaann...! Beware—the *satkärring*[80] will break free," Peter shouted to Emil, flinging himself completely across her torso, trying to recapture one of her wrists, which she had managed to jerk free. One arm free, she made a frantic grab for the nearest boy's face. But as he succeeded in capturing her wayward arm, before she could strike him and in the struggle his other hand landed soundly on her left breast, which he began massaging. He held her that way, which set about another series of squeals of anger on her part. He fought to both restrain her flailing hand and press her now-heaving chest.

To aid his friend, Peter also grabbed Anna-Stina as she had twisted toward Emil. His had found her crotch beneath the thin linen shift that she' d saved to wear for this special day. With his other hand, he pinned her other arm around, behind her head.

"Hold the *satkärring*," he said, "or she'll have our eyes out.'

"Or your balls in her teeth," the other remarked, barely missing being bitten on the thigh. Emil addressed the driver without daring to even turn and look up at him. "Get the horse moving faster before you have to stop and help us fight her too," he shouted.

The cart gave another lurch as the horse increased from a trotting pace, as the driver prodded it with a long stick. Emil looked into Anna-Stina's eyes, but was unable to meet her fiery gaze but for a few seconds.

"We will all be lacking our balls if you don't make haste," he said looking at the wheel that turned too slowly beside his head.

Realizing further struggle would only yield her more pain, Anna-Stina settled down and began to think. She could not determine what direction they were headed. She surmised, from the periodic change in the forest passing above her, that they were moving south and east. Periodically, she would renew her struggle as their hands now alternately roamed freely over her body. Straining to each side, she attempted to look directly in their eyes as they molested her. She watched the look on the young men's faces change from boastful confidence, to uncertainty, to cowardice, until finally, she was certain she saw fear. I have them, she thought; men are so weak when they face their accuser. Though they fondle me, I have planted the fear of reprisal in their hearts...and there will be a reprisal; I vow it.

For their part, the boys had begun to look like they wished the journey would soon end, so they could be rid of her. Emil verbalized this to the driver's back, several times: "Make haste, will you not...fan...we will miss the rest of the celebration!"

Anna-Stina was plotting her various options, already thinking of future revenge. The cart spun around suddenly, turning completely around, drawing to an abrupt halt; the boys stood up quickly and grabbing her flailing arms, unceremoniously dumped her from the back of the cart, where she fell onto the track, striking her head and shoulder hard.

She was free as quickly as she was captured. She barely had time to gain her feet before they were bouncing back up the rutted track, leering and grinning after their presumed success and safety. Someone shouted: "Have a nice walk home, Anna-Stina. Don't hurry too much...you are far enough away that the day will be done before you can return."

"Fools...!" she shouted, "...you dare to do this to me...I shall have more than your balls for this—just wait!"

But she knew her words were wasted against the rumbling wheels. As she stood watching the cart disappear two boys in the back clasped the cart's sides frantically with each turn as it threatened to pitch them out. There had been concern in their faces as they sped away and possibly, she thought, possibly even regret in their backward-glances.

"Bastards...fan...sate...!" she swore, as she attempted to take stock of herself, looking down at her wrinkled, linen shift, with the once-beautiful embroidery. She'd spent hours working the material. The dress' front now had green and brown stains and where she had struck the grass when they threw her from the cart, more grass and pine needles adhered to the pitch from the pine boughs; filthy debris adhered everywhere. I resemble a scarecrow, she thought, bitterly. The simple colors of her frock, she'd woven and dyed with such care...her meticulous embroidery, exquisitely fashioned around the edge of each sleeve, collar and the hem—all now seemed a mockery to her effort.

She'd prepared so carefully for the day, wishing to give her best impression and look her best—not only for Carl, but for the community. Secretly, she also hoped to make the Fröman's proud of their *vallkulla*. She knew she'd excelled at the *fäbod* work—she knew it. But she didn't wish...didn't need to boast of it.

She'd been prepared to reap the harvest of her year of work— pride, she thought, the sin of pride...the minister would have said, shaking his head...the pride that comes before the fall. She looked down at her torn and grass-stained dress. That's what has befallen me, she thought. Aloud, she said: "And now...I shall miss the rest of the *vallkulla*'s day."

Hanging her head, she began to follow the cart. Tears of anger streaming down her cheeks, making clean paths in the grime accumulated during the dusty journey. But it was not self-pity that shown in her bright eyes, blinded and blurred as they were. As she stumbled along the cart track she glanced up the track where the cart had disappeared: it was reprisal.

"Revenge...oh sweet, sweet revenge," she said, sniffing. "I have so much vengeance to dispense."

With that said, her back straightened, she picked up her torn skirts and the long stride of the *fäbod* took over as her pace quickened for the trek back to Skålbyn.

She'd walked barely three-quarters of an hour when she heard a cart approaching. They are returning, she thought, glancing from side to side, before leaping for the cover of the dense wood. "I can beat them this time...," she said quietly to herself, planning to hide completely and choose her moment. "I have warning this time."

With resolution she bent, hefting a large branch that had fallen from a pine tree. Placing her foot on one end, she easily broke it into a smaller size. She crouched, hiding as close to the track as she dared, behind a large bolder. On her shoulder, she held the makeshift club in readiness, waiting until the sound of the cart's wheels rattled on the rocks close by.

Taking a deep breath of resolve, she leaped defiantly from behind the rock and into the approaching cart's path, ready to take off the head of the nearest boy as soon as the horse passed. But she misjudged the sound and instead, leaped in front of the approaching horse. Quickly bounding around the startled horse, she was surprised to find Pastor Johansson as the cart's sole occupant. She could hardly believe her eyes.

Well, she thought, lowering her club, the devil declares himself again. She stepped closer and smiled, anxious for a suitable outlet for her wrath. He couldn't have been better, given her previous captor's absence.

Struggling to hold the dancing horse, the pastor cleared his throat nervously. *"Ahemmmmuh..."* he mouthed. "...Anna-Stina, once again you have taken your evil ways too far."

"Oh...I have, have I...and how is that?"

"Now, you are attempting to steal the soul of someone destined from God's service."

She didn't respond immediately. What was he was up to. This was a new turn. Then he spoke again.

"What devil has gotten into you that you would work your evil woman's ways on Carl Fröman—the way you have been doing? Both his mother and I know he's perfect for the Ministry of God's service—and now...you come along...and cause him to question that Divine Guidance. You are interfering with God's will, Anna-Stina."

He was waving his free arm, as if practicing his sermons, while barely holding the dancing animal with the other.

"Carl has received Word...directly from God. It's not for you to interfere. You should have learned your lesson, when..." he stopped speaking abruptly as if to reconsider his words, "...you learned your lesson—better," he finished, limply.

As she continued listening to his ranting, her anger only grew, kindling the mounting rage within her. Soon, she was so consumed by her rage that it must have shown in her face. It felt good to her and for a moment, she savored the feeling—holding it lightly in rein...teasing it...and herself—barely maintaining her self control.

"What lesson was that pastor...?" she hissed, momentarily interrupting his sputtering.

"What? Why...the lessons of life...the sorry lessons you have been offered because of your evil, sinful...sinful ways, Anna-Stina— your ways with men!" He paused for breath:

"God in His wisdom chose to visit a punishment upon you...took your child from you...made you suffer for your sins...he...."

"He took your child from me—you son of the devil!" she screamed, her words rushing directly from her heart. Leaning forward, she grabbed her skirt and leaped toward him, her next words coming as a harsh rasp.

"Youuu...dare to speak of sin...after what you did to me— you...she was your child—yours! And...after...after what you did to me, youuuu...!"

The first rush of anger, once she finally freed it, immediately exhausted her. She could little more than stammer anything further as they faced one another. He, standing in the cart—reins in one hand—holding onto the cart's side with the other, glaring down at Anna-Stina where she had leaped so close to the cart. With trembling fingers, she clutched the iron rim of the wheel to steady herself. She'd sprung at him so suddenly, grasping the wheel beside him with such agility and surprise that he'd started backward at the vehemence of her passionate onslaught.

She had absolutely no fear of him now—none at all, now that she'd confronted him. In fact, she reveled...a hateful way, in the pain the anger now brought her. She actually desired to be close to him and to better see his face, best witness his reaction to her mounting accusations.

"What do you speak of—my child…? How dare you accuse me
of lying with you—getting you with your bastard. I could never—
never bring myself to even think of such—such sin? Even to touch…"
he fell off in a sputtering, consternation of meaningless words.

But he was visibly distraught, Anna-Stina noticed and he had
finally to sit down on the opposite edge of the cart, he was trembling
so much. The horse had of course sensed, seen and heard Anna-
Stina's rage and for the moment the animal wanted only to be far away
from her abrupt movements and shrill voice. It had alternately shied
and danced between the shafts, as she berated the minister, waving her
arms and shouting all the while. Pastor Johansson was struggling to
hold the animal as it alternately backed and pranced sideways, confined
by the narrow track and the thick forest on either side.

Anna-Stina noticed the minister's eyes kept returning, again to
her bosom. Looking down, she noticed that one side of her blouse
had been badly torn. A sleeve hung from the shoulder and the
frock's front gaped, partially exposing her bosom's pink flesh,
blotched now with pine pitch and dirt, bare between the torn pieces
of delicate embroidery. With even greater pleasure she released yet
another flood over him. It burst from her then as if it had lain,
waiting for this moment for millennia.

"Youuu…" she exclaimed leaping onto the wheel's hub and
reaching down with her free hand, she yanked the thin, flax lacing
holding what remained of her blouse's bodice. To the minister's
wide-mouthed astonishment, she slid one arm free of the sleeve and
then the other, dropping the garment forward to her waist. Her taunt
breasts trembled with the effort and each nipple hard—jutted forward
and upward from her internal rage.

The minister stood, legs braced, watching her; his was mouth
agape as he looked down in total surprise—first at her right breast,
then the left, before looking up at her face. Leaning forward against
the wheel's rim, she cupped one arm beneath both breasts, stood on
tip-toes and thrust her upper torso toward him, a gruesome leer on
her face. Involuntarily, the minister had already begun leaning
forward, before finally realizing what he was doing. Checking himself,
he glanced alternately at her breasts and at her face in astonishment.
His mouth opened and closed, but made no sound. Joy and

repugnance—all emotions seem reflected in his expression.

I have found the key, the thought flashed through her head—the lock has fallen open—with the sound of thunder—all of his emotions betrayed a secret to her—his secret is his lust.

Leaning forward again, steadying herself with a foot on the wheel hub: "This is what you want," she purred, thrusting her jiggling breasts toward him over the high cart wheel. But he visibly shrunk from the offering. His fingers were trembling violently. The reins had fallen slack across the seat.

"I...! I...!" he intoned, saying nothing coherent and appearing as if, like the horse, he might bolt any moment. Though the horse had calmed somewhat, it continued to prance between the shafts and Anna-Stina had difficulty remaining on the wheel hub.

"You lusted for me even before you attacked me that night in *fäbod*. You lusted for me—it was you who struck me in the dark— like the coward you are—and then—and then...you raped me. And you still lust after me—you evil, evil man. You are weak! Weak! But now I know that and I can control you...with that. And I will rule you—rule you—until the very day you die, Pastor. I will use your uncontrollable sin of lust to control your every emotion, henceforth."

To emphasize her newfound control, she again cupped her breasts toward the minister's pouting lips.

"I shall be your private Satan—your constant reminder of your cowardice and your human weakness. That frailty in your body and my will to control it will only grow in you until it consumes even your sanity. You shall continue to lust after these..." she gestured again, "and the rest of me. Eventually you will even fear me...for I will feed your lust like the savage animal you are...fattening your sinful craving at every meeting...until the day you will die for me—you will wish every day to have me again. From this day forward Pastor Johansson ....you are mine!" she said, with a final, defiant gesture.

His eyes had hardly strayed from her beautiful breasts. Her breath now came in gasps and she had to lean backward to keep from falling into the cart. Her chest heaved with the exertion of clinging to the cart and the effort of shouting at him. Her breasts continued to dance with each gasp. She watched him beneath lowered lids, as his eyes followed her prescription. And then, more quietly, she intoned:

"You shall regret ever seeing Anna-Stina Malmberg. I shall make the rest of your existence hell—a hell like you have condemned me to—a hell that I have known since you stole my virginity—my reputation...stole my life. I have known my hell so long and so well, that now I embrace the loss. And I will use my new-gained power against you—you, evil, evil being. Furthermore—I will take Carl Fröman from your precious church. Yes! I shall take Carl from God—and—keep him for myself." Her voice had become so weak; the last words came as only a growl.

"And one thing more...I vow to you...one day Pastor, you shall marry me to Carl Fröman in Järna church. And the day you do that—you will also confess your lust for me. You shall do this before all of the wedding guests in the church. And you will confess to them your sin of lusting for me, attacking me and impregnating me with your child...the poor, dead child...child of lust—your sinful, uncontrolled desire who God took because of your sin."

When he didn't reply, she concluded. "I shall see you make that confession before you die, Pastor Johansson; I now know that I have the power to make you do that. So prepare—Pastor Johansson— prepare to live a slow, lustful, but unsatisfied, life—a consuming death in life, on this earth, among my people and in my community."

With that, she leaped from the wheel and began walking up the road. She knew he would have to turn the cart around and pass her on his return. Walking, quickly, she put her arms through the sleeves of the blouse again and re-laced the torn bodice as best she could, before finally giving up in frustration, letting it fall and flap open as she stumbled over the rocky track.

As she walked she marveled that she now knew how she would do it—carry out her threat, if she lived long enough. Though angry tears had started again, she smiled through them—this time, a smile of triumph. She reasoned how she would shamelessly take Carl for her own, also. Neither his mother, nor The Church nor even God could have him now, until she had finished. He was to be hers. She could do anything she wanted. Carl himself had to be willing—but she believed he already was, or soon would be. And she would destroy this Pastor Johansson in the process—and with such pleasure she would accomplish that. Thinking to herself, she smiled bitterly as she strode resolutely toward home:

"He has not yet passed me; the more time passes before he

does, the more strongly I have affected him—so he must recover, before starting."

It was at least a half hour before she heard the sound of the cart's approach. She stepped well aside, into the woods, least in his terror or anger, he run her down.

The figure that stood in the cart as it passed was a visibly shaken man. She saw him from the shelter of her hiding place as he passed, glancing nervously from side to side...and even over his shoulder, as if some *Rånda* of the forest would leap out and take him. Yes, she thought, I am *Rånda*, today. I am and will be his *Rånda*, forever.

"So you see," Karolina said, smiling wryly, "it was the young minister—as mother always knew. She told me long after he finally fulfilled her prophecy and married my parents. That was many, many years later—when I was old enough to understand and well before she died."

"So he did marry them then, in the end? That seems so strange. One would think once he'd been confronted with the—the attack, he would have moved to another church to be away from her and the reminder—the threat of it all."

"Oh no...not Pastor Johansson; she gauged him precisely. He despised weakness of character; possibly, that was why he was so weak himself when it came to my mother. He couldn't help himself. He was a normal human being beneath it all—a man of lust. Had he not been, my Mother would never have been able to rule him."

As an afterthought, she added: "...please, no offence...?

I shook my head as I continued to scribble.

"And Mother quickly set about to teach him that he couldn't live with the torment of her. It was nearly as simple as that—he loved my mother. She went out of her way to see that he continued doing so...fanned the fire on every occasion."

I didn't want to say anything at this point, preferring to remain on the safer ground of silence. And Karolina went on.

"He wanted to flee, but, oddly, to his credit, his religious zeal was overpowering, forcing him to face his weakness. I sometimes wonder whether he might even have received a rather sick pleasure from the emotional pain the ensuing punishment brought him. After a while, I don't believe he could bear to be parted from it for very long. It soon became an addiction which he fed upon and eventually, was consumed by it. But it almost consumed my parents in the process; especially my mother. From that day forward, she never let up on him—until the very end, of course and it nearly cost her everything...her husband, her family, her sanity."

I nodded, catching up on my notes; Karolina seemed lost to the quiet of remembrance, sitting placidly, saying nothing and resting after the emotion of her tale.

Glancing up at last, "Hur mår du?" I inquired, concerned with her silence. She seemed a bit tired but it may have just been a pensive mood.

"Jag mår bra," she answered positively, with a smile. "Bra—and I was thinking about it all...you know? Considering everything—it turned out pretty well, up to the point of their wedding and even after that, for a while."

"You mean your mother's accusation of the minister?"

"No—well...yes, the fact that at this point in time, she'd turned the tables on The Church for the first time and began to sway the world in her favor. I believe the encounter on the road with the minister was the turning point—even though it was nearest the beginning of my parent's relationship. It eventually became the upward turning point. Without it, my parents may never have married and Johansson and The Church may have triumphed. Mother determined the course for almost the rest of her life, at that single point. And with her strong resolve, she carried it out—stubbornness, or persistence, throughout all the trials yet to face her."

The day was slipping by. I had a date with Dr. Olsson; I didn't want to cut Karolina short, but I didn't want to offend Anna either; Karolina had noticed my sudden preoccupation.

"You seem distracted, Alex. Am I boring you now?" Karolina was looking at me with a smile.

"Oh, I'm sorry. No, I was daydreaming about what you'd said. It's almost more than I can comprehend."

"It is more than I want to talk about any more today. Do you mind if we stop?

"Not at all, you've read my thoughts it seems. I have to be honest, we—Dr. Olsson and I, have a dinner date tonight; so it would be convenient for me to stop here. I planned only a short day today."

"Oh...I didn't know. But, how nice; I hope you two enjoy the evening. What are you planning to do, if you will humor an old woman who is far too nosey, but too old to mind being rude?"

"Not at all," I chuckled, "we are just dining somewhere near here, down at...I've forgotten, I'm afraid—a restaurant Anna—Dr. Olsson knows...around the lake."

"*Hummm...*I see. Well enjoy yourself and I'll see you tomorrow. You can tell me all about it then."

I got up and kissed her forehead. At the corner I turned and waved once more before turning through the doorway.

CHAPTER 13

The Date

Dr. Olsson...Anna, opened the door almost immediately after my knock. I was a little surprised and it must have shown.

"Oh...you're right there?"

"I was waiting for you," she replied seeing my confusion. "I had no problem getting away from the facility—so I had plenty of time to get ready. It didn't take me very long and I was a little excited to be going out; it has been a while and I've never spent much time around Americans, so...?"

I smiled involuntarily at her forthrightness.

"I'm sorry; maybe I shouldn't have said that?"

"No...no...it's just—not very many women—American women, have been so honest."

"Maybe I shouldn't have been so...truthful, saying what I felt. But, I don't do this every week—hardly at all, actually. I found myself looking forward to being with you—eating a good meal and well, just being on a date again; some intelligent conversation. Anything, but sick old people, for a change. Do you not, also...won't it be enjoyable?"

"Well—yes, I do. And it will be fun—I'm sure," I said, hardly able to match her enthusiasm.

She cocked her head to one side and smiled mischievously. She hadn't invited me in. Reaching around the door she retrieved a small evening bag before turning and inserting and turning a key in the double lock.

"There. Ok...ready?" She was, true to her word, ready to go.

We walked down the flagstone walkway side by side. I held the car door for her and she slid in.

"Thank you," she said, smiling. I walked around and got in. She turned toward me in the seat: "I think, possibly, when I'm happy, that I reveal too much of my true emotions,"

"Nothing wrong with that."

"No…Swedish women are frank—is that the word—the same as a man's name?"

I nodded. "Yes…it's the same. It's…well, it's refreshing—your frankness, I mean."

"We speak our minds and I am afraid, I'm doing it again—you see and we're honest in our relationships, too. I find no reason to pretend otherwise."

With that said, she sat back and nodded her head matter-of-factly, smiling somewhat to herself as if self-satisfied with the turn the events were taking.

Well, I thought. What have I here? Certainly a complicated one—and self-assured also, to say the least. I must admit, some of my own self-doubt began to creep in. I'd never had a relationship with an aggressive woman. Do you really want to get involved again, I asked myself as I backed from the driveway? Are you ready—prepared—for someone this strong?

Getting out of town was easy with her along, giving directions. And it was a pleasant drive toward the restaurant. As about anywhere in Scandinavia, Swedish countryside has a contest-winning photograph waiting around each and every bend in the road. We both enjoyed the scenery and spoke little. Anna pointed out the odd, interesting view and gave me my headings. It required several turnings before we were there, winding around to the other side of the lake. I knew I would have had trouble getting back home in the dark, had she not been along. There were few markings for the turns. I attempted small talk hoping to keep her from being bored.

"What sort of food do they offer at this restaurant? Do they have a…specialty?"

"Oh…I think their menu probably changes somewhat with the season, as with most of the better Scandinavian restaurants. Of course they prepare the usual Swedish menu—*körttbullar*[81], *potatis och sill*[82] creamed with *potatis*—other fish—*lax*[83]…that sort, you know? I understand they also keep a lively international cuisine going, too—at least they did…many sorts of beef: roasted, steaked—and they have a Armenian shish kebab affair, that I've never tried. Let's see," she mused, "I seem to recall wild game is another of their specialties: deer—probably from Finland or Russia and of course, our local *älg*[84]. Those they usually offer roasted in a sauce—French style, with currant or other berry-based sauce—quite good. Have you ever tried *älg?*"

I shook my head, "No, but as a kid I ate quite a bit of wild game…everything from squirrels, in the south, to grouse in the north. I've had deer and antelope…but never any moose."

She nodded. "Otherwise, I've also had very nice sole there—I prefer it almandine—all that butter." She grinned and patted her stomach. "But they will prepare it any way. There are prawns in many styles…I like shrimp. With lots of garlic and butter—Scampi…*uummmm*." Here she smiled impishly at me. "My second favorite is *kräfta*…I don't know what you call them in English?"

"Where I grew up, they're called crawdads, but mostly they're known as crayfish. I ate them occasionally as a kid but not since. How do you cook them in Sweden?"

"Oh, just boil them; maybe some treat them differently, I don't know. They're very delicate. We Swedes have them many ways at the summer cottage, in addition to just boiled—in salads, or as a *smörgås*, you know, our open-face sandwich? Usually, we take them with a light cream sauce and some fresh salad—not your salad—ours: lettuce, thinly-sliced carrots, a little celery—all in a light cream sauce."

"You said they had a pretty good wine list, too?" As she went on about the wine, I thought, she can cook, too, I'll bet. I was warming to the conversation and the person.

"Yes, a fine cellar. They take special care to keep a good variety of vintages—which is rather unusual outside Stockholm. You'll be hard pressed not to find the type of wine you prefer, assuming it is European. That's what they keep—mostly. We don't have any Swedish wines. I understand you're developing some very fine wines in America—in California, though?"

"Well, I'm not so sure about that. They're trying to, at least. They certainly have the climate for it…if not the soil. I guess that plays a very important part in viniculture, as well as experience; that we probably still lack somewhat."

"If you speak to the French, real wines can only be grown between Spain and Germany, the English Channel and the Mediterranean, but mostly in France."

"But French is best, right?"

"Right. They're extremely snobbish about it though, aren't they?" she chuckled

"Yeah, they don't like to be reminded of when the vine blight struck their vineyards in the last century, they were forced to import new vine stock from America, to replace most if not all their infected vines. Our plants were resistant to their fungus, so they could restore their own dead and dying vines. Want to make a Frenchman mad, just mention that America saved their wine industry with American root stock."

"Oh—I didn't know that...but I think it sounds like a conversation to avoid. Do you have a favorite?"

"Don't think I can say I prefer a single wine, but types...reds, certainly...I drink them, mostly. I seldom just drink wine; I think it needs food to be really enjoyed but you're really talking to an amateur, about wines. What about you, Anna?"

"Exactly. I believe you cannot simply drink wine. Wine is like a sauce; it must complement the taste of the food. You can drink several wines with a specific food, or eat several different foods with a specific wine. Like friends I think. Some work together—some don't," she said pertly, tilting her head back and smiling again so I could see her teeth.

We rode in silence for a few more moments, lost in our own thoughts. My impression of her as adjusting; I hadn't known what to expect from the little exposure we'd already had at the hospital. I guess I thought she'd be different from what she was turning out to be, but I didn't really know in which way. Now we'd talked, she seemed far more sophisticated than I'd originally thought she'd be...even if she was a traveled physician. Yet, she was also down-to-earth: unsophisticated, not snobbish. She certainly knew a bit about food and wine and seemed to appreciate both. Though you'd never really know it by her body, I thought, glancing across at her profile. She was slim, but not skinny. Her arms were lithe with a hint of muscle—like she did some physical work of some sort.

She caught me looking and smiled, then suddenly pointed: "Turn left here," she held up her arm. "I'm sorry, I was lost in thought for a moment."

I braked quickly, "OK, not a problem."

"I believe it's just down here…along the lake."

We drove slowly for a moment before seeing a sign: *Restaurang-Servering*, painted on the side of a long, weathered, wooden fish. I eased into the dirt drive the way the fish pointed, dodging a few pine trees and found a space beneath the leaning trees. I eased the Volvo in between a Mercedes and another Volvo.

"It seems we're early, or there would be few diners this evening."

"You may be right; but I don't think we're early."

The large car park was nearly empty. I got out, walked around and opened her door. Anna smiled as I took her hand and helped her out of the car. The touch was delightful. How long was it since I'd held a young woman's hand? We walked through the carpet of pine needles to the wooden stairs leading around one side and the entrance. The structure was located near the lakeshore, with the dining room running along the full, lakeside exposure, up on the second floor.

As I held the heavy door, somewhere in back, sleigh bells rang. The lobby was rather dark and deserted. Intimate, one could also say if one were in the mood and had a partner of the same feelings. I was concerned after the sparseness of conversation in the car. I'd rather hoped for some surrounding company to lighten the conversation load, as we became better acquainted, but it didn't appear that would be the case. A woman came smiling from the kitchen area and apologized for keeping us waiting.

"Have you reserved," she asked.

Of course we hadn't thought of that. "No…we have not. It doesn't look as if it matters?"

"No matter, you are fortunate; there remains a single table for two…along the window, if you would like to sit there?"

"Yes, please," I replied, raising my eyebrows at Anna in surprise; we fell in step behind the woman.

"The other dining room will fill as the evening progresses. It is still a bit early for most of our customers."

We took the proffered table. I held Anna's chair as she settled into the upholstered seat. Circling the table I took my own seat and smiled across at Anna, who was glancing around. I took notice then of the interior. There were clean, beamed ceilings, varnished so the natural oxidation of the wood could be seen. This was a welcome freshness to the smoky interiors of many restaurants in America, or some the heavy German eating establishments I'd had the occasion to dine in during my business travels.

Some of the walls were paneled in a lighter, denser-grained wood—possibly birch or poplar, I couldn't tell. Being unstained and only slightly oxidized, the wood was still fairly light-colored, making the room very bright—even at this time of day...totally Scandinavian, inside and out.

Some of the walls were wainscoted; surprisingly I thought, for Sweden. There was plaster above—painted an off white, with attractive wallpaper beneath. These two, different materials were divided by a horizontal board running the length of the wall, about a yard from the floor. It had a molded shape on the top and side and tended to break up the room and make the ceilings seem higher than they actually were. During the noonday, this dining room must be dazzling, I thought, with all these windows facing the lake.

Anna quietly continued peering out the window: "That's Karlskoga over there," she pointed out the window to the broad expanse of dark lake water.

"It must be twenty kilometers or so. When it gets darker, later, we will be able to see the lights shimmering across the lake. Sort of romantic, with the moon, too tonight, I think."

I nodded, not knowing how to take the romantic side of her remark. As usual, she followed it with a pert, mischievous smile.

"Yes, it's quite pleasant."

Before she could say anything else, a man appeared with two menus under his arm, carrying a small tray with napkins.

"Good evening," he said, smiling and nodding to both of us in turn. "Welcome to our restaurant. We hope you have a pleasant dining experience with us this evening. My name is Erik and I am the *maitre'd*. We are quiet, so far tonight, but it will soon become very busy, so at this point, you will have the entire command of the kitchen staff—at least for a while.

"We have—I have never dined here before," I said.

"Then doubly welcome. I have brought menus to provide you an idea of our offerings." He smiled at each of us in turn as he offered the menus. "Of particular popularity this time of year is the grilled älg with currant sauce. There is also a very good selection of Baltic lax and some sole that was just brought up on ice today from The English Channel. I had one for lunch and can highly recommend it. We can prepare it any way you wish—we have a rather nice assortment of sauces available—here, in this section of the menu..." he indicated these on each of our menus. "I can go over each one with you individually, if you have any questions."

With that good news he stepped back, smiling at Anna first, then me and asked: "Since neither of you have been to our restaurant before..."

Anna interrupted: "Once—I was here, a long time ago. My...friend...has never been."

"I see...then—welcome back..." he said with a slight bow to Anna, "...and again, welcome to you," he repeated the bow to me. "We have a custom in our restaurant of welcoming each new guest with at cup of hot *punsch*[85]. Do you remember it from your last visit?"

"No, but it was a long time ago."

"Have you ever had it?" he said, rubbing his hands in expectation.

I looked at Anna. "I've heard of it, of course, being Swedish," she said, smiling questioningly at me, "but I've never had it. I'm willing if you are Alex."

I nodded, "Yes, we'd like to try it," I said smiling questioningly at her and nodding at the waiter.

"Very good. It will only take a moment."

He bowed slightly and disappeared.

"What's *punsch*," I quickly asked, bending over the table.

"A liquor of some sort—yellow...sweet, too, I think—they heat it and it is drunk very warm—nearly hot—traditionally with pea soup in our country, I believe."

I raised my eyebrows, "Pea soup...?" and made a wry face. Anna smiled back, gesturing with her hand that I should remain silent, as the man was returning again, carrying the silver tray which he placed on a small serving table he had earlier unfolded beside our table.

From a small, thermos he carefully poured two miniature, clear-glass cups of an amber-colored fluid. A strong aroma wafted over us. Placing the cups on the tray along with a napkin over his forearm, he turned back to our table. Bowing slightly, he served Anna's cup to her right and carefully turned the handle toward her. Doing the same for me, he nodded to us both.

"Be cautious…it is quite warm. I do hope you enjoy it and again…welcome to our restaurant."

"What is that aroma?" I asked.

"It is arrack, the primary flavoring of *punsch.*"

I was leaning forward looking into my cup when he made a quick movement with his napkin, or tray, startling me. I looked up quickly, thinking he may have burned himself with the little thermos.

"Excuse me," he said, turning to me and folding the napkin over his forearm. "I will return in a few moments to take your order. If you have any questions about the menus, please let me know. I will just be over by the bar, there," he indicated with the little tray the small bar in a corner of the room. We nodded our thanks.

"Some service," I said to Anna, who was watching me attentively. "Well, shall we?" I raised my little cup and holding it with two fingers by the little handle for a moment before matching Anna's typical movement of the Swedish toast, bringing the cup up and forward in the direction of the host, or guests and looking her directly in the eye.

"*Skål,*" I said raising and dipping the cup slightly to her.

Our eyes held as we both took a tentative sip. It was certainly warm. Delight shone in Anna's eyes. I felt the warm and sweet liquor coat the back of my throat as it slid down.

"Ummmm…I think I could grow to like this," Anna said taking another bigger sip, smiling again and dabbing her mouth with the large napkin. "It's not that hot."

"Not bad," I commented, matching her enthusiasm. "We may just have to have another before the food comes," I quipped, "If you're game."

"You bet," she said, American style, "I'm free all day tomorrow and the next day…and I'm not even on call for a change. So I don't have any responsibilities…I can do anything I wish."

"Then, let's get at these menus and decide what we're going to eat. No time to waste."

Her enthusiasm was contagious and I began to catch on to her carefree mood. I glanced around for the *maitre'd*, who standing by the end of the bar and as if to anticipate our moods. When I raised my arm, he smiled and tray-under-arm, strode boldly over, beaming at us—particularly at Anna, as he approached.

"How did you find the *punsch*," he queried, eyebrows raised in question to her.

"Very good," I answered and meaning it.

"Is there something else I may bring you?" he asked.

Anna smiled rather impishly at him; I must say her mood was festive.

"Yes, we would like another of these before we order."

"Absolutely, sir," he said, seemingly pleased with our appreciation, "I am happy you find our customs so—tasty," he said bowed again slightly and vanished in the direction of the bar.

Anna watched him go. She had both elbows on the table leaning toward me and cupping the little cup in her hands. "We must be careful, she said, smiling over her cup.

"Careful? Of the *punsch?*"

"Yes, there is a very high incidence of alcoholism in Sweden. We don't want to be mistaken for a couple of drunkards. And we'd better order soon, or—speaking for myself—we will be unable to speak coherently enough to do so or prove false any suspicions of our condition, otherwise...if that made sense?"

I laughed, enjoying myself. "Add yet another stigma to the American stereotype; we can gesture, surely and they'll understand so long as we remain stoically serious?"

"Oh, no," she said, feigning a serious face. "Americans are known for being carefree and fun loving. That's the mood we're projecting. He thinks we're both Americans. I can tell because he's catching the mood also. You see, we Swedes...we are such...how do you say it—branches in the water—no—that's not it?"

"Sticks in the mud?" I offered.

"Yesssss, exactly! Such a queer expression...almost Swedish in its ambiguity? Anyway, please pay close attention to the man. When we entered, he was very proper and formal—though friendly, still quite discrete. That is Swedish! But now, now he is beginning to relax and take on your mood...that is very un-Swedish—American—iz—a—tion."

"My mood? You're the one who has convinced him we are carefree and fun-loving, Anna. I'm an old sober-sides— businessman—an original stick in the mud."

"Oh, noooo, not at all; being out with the American Culture, that's what is at work here. That which is turning the stiff, formal and professional Swedish girl's normal upright, physician-demeanor, into that of a lighthearted American...possibly?"

"I think you've been watching too many American movies, Anna," I laughed, "but let's not disappoint him, I'll begin by ordering and it will include a bottle of wine. Do you think we might ruin our reputation as Americans if we are too Continental—the wine choice, I mean—French, maybe...voulez-vous verifi...," I said, offering her the wine list and at the same time, butchering the French language.

Laughing, Anna said: "Not likely with that accent. Where did you learn to speak French—somewhere that they neglected pronunciation, I think."

Here she smiled mischievously, reached across and squeezed my forearm, possibly thinking I might have been offended by her playful manner.

"I take offense at your criticism of my accent. It's genuine American Midwest high school French—bigger than the whole country of France. True, though, the wine's not as good," I added, to show her she hadn't hurt my feelings.

Another twinkle came to her eye and she had a pert little way about how she held her head when she was having fun—almost a movement of restraint, that joy and fun were liable to burst out at any moment. I felt she was partially correct in her self-assessment and it was as if she weren't accustomed to giving in to humor. She was guarded, knew it and was working hard to let down the guard. This I found curious—and at the same time, flattering, that she was trying, just to please me.

Being a bit silly myself, I picked up my menu with exaggerated flair and held it upside-down, pretending to read, if nothing but to encourage her. She snatched up hers miming my movements, but then glanced in the direction of the *maitre'd* and was unable to carry it through. She held the menu to her face, like a mask, just below her eyes and glanced from side to side mischievously.

"Pronounces the same this way, too," I said turning my menu

back over. I continued the charade, turning slightly sideways as if to deliberately ignore her and regard the menu with exaggerated interest.

She bowed her head a little toward me to depict mock shame, then looking directly at me, lowering her menu to reveal the biggest, most open co-conspirator smile I'd seen yet. Careful, Alex, I thought...this is getting dangerous. The thrill of budding affection found a home where none had lived for so long.

"You play the part of the serious Swede too well. I believe we'd better order now," she said sitting upright as if to make amends for her misbehavior, "...or the man will become annoyed with us and let our soup get cold."

"OK," I added, picking up my own menu, "but...must we eat soup?"

"Serious, now," she said with a mock smile of recrimination, "...remember."

"Ok. This...have you given it any more thought?"

The menu proved bountiful as we pondered it, head to head, before settling on our meals among the multiple choices. I was hungry and could have ordered anything at the time, eaten and liked it; I was also becoming enraptured by this woman.

"I liked the sound of the sole," she offered, thoughtfully. "I think I'll see if they'll make it *almandine*—and maybe take some asparagus. That's in season now...with butter and some—uhh, some...carrots."

"That sounds appetizing. I considered the sole too; we don't get fresh sole in The States. However, we don't get fresh moose, either...so I'm going to try that. It will be a first for me. Is it common to eat currant sauce with it?"

Yes, we usually have sweet sauce with red meat. In Swedish it's called rödavinbär, from the red wine berries.

"We say currant sauce."

"We have also *svartavinbär*[86]...black wine berries...also currants."

"As do we. That's sort of like when we eat cranberry sauce—like your *lingon*[87]...we have it at Thanksgiving and Christmas."

"What exactly is Thanksgiving? I understand the word, but not the meaning."

"They're really the same. It's a holiday we celebrate near the end of November—to be thankful for our blessings and a good harvest from the previous summer. It's something that supposedly came from the first harvest by the Europeans who settled in America...they invited the Indians—the native tribes-people, too, supposedly."

"I hope they did not serve lutfisk...to the Indians I mean," Anna laughed.

"Maybe they did and that's why the fighting began. I don't blame the Indians, if they had to eat that," I said, holding my nose.

Defensively, she said: "Oh...it's not so bad, especially when compared to our little *surströmming*—the small, rotted, tinned-herrings...have you had those yet?"

"Rotted herring? Not that I know of, at least willingly."

"You wouldn't forget it if had; they are put in tins and permitted to ferment—you could say, rot. The cans actually swell and bulge with power—literally."

"Really sounds appetizing."

"Well...it's something we have only when celebrating special happenings. Not holidays—but others, like engagements, birthdays and so forth. But don't believe those people who say they taste delicious. They're truly awful—*ughhh!*" She laughed, pinching her nostrils, shaking her head. "They put them in a bucket of water to open the tin so the odor won't escape."

"Yuck...I think we should order the wine before we change our minds," I said.

As the *maitre'd*, with perfect timing, brought the seconds of hot *punsch*, he served them with the same care and deliberation. True to form, he was extremely attentive and once he had pleased himself that all was in order with our drinks and our table he stepped back a step, bowed slightly again and asked, "Madame—Sir—have you found something on our menu that tempts you?"

Anna smiled up at him. "More than we can choose from."

"Yes, thank you. We try to keep a respectable offering."

I set about ordering the meals with deliberation, as Anna looked on, smiling and hopefully, impressed. That took a couple of minutes since the *maitre'd* was even more exacting in knowing our pleasures as to preparation, sauces and accompaniments and offered a couple of suggestions not listed on the menu. Then he turned to the wines.

"Do you have half bottles," I inquired?

"Yes, certainly sir, but not for all our vintages. Did you have something particular in mind or would you like me to suggest something?"

"A white for the lady's fish…something fairly dry," I asked glancing at Anna with a questioning look.

She nodded her agreement.

"May I recommend a *Poulle' Fuise'* for the sole—I don't believe you will be disappointed with it," he said glancing questioning at first me and then Anna. She smiled broadly at both of us, unwilling to give up the charade of American pretense to the *maitre'd* by speaking too much.

"I believe the *Poulle' Fuise'* would be fine—and what did you have to offer in a red to enhance the *älg?*"

"Of course, sir, there are all the varieties from the Italian and French—others, less known, too. Have you any particular preference?"

"In America we do not have a great variety of European wines available where I live. I would certainly consider something new…can you make a recommendation?"

"Absolutely, Sir." He paused thoughtfully for a moment and said: "We have a very full-bodied red, rather of the Burgundy family, but Hungarian in origin—fairly heavy—possibly not the word…in their country I believe it is called Black Burgundy. If you have never tried it, I assure you—with *älg,* you will find it complementary, Sir. Many diners here have found it to be so and we keep an ample stock in readiness?"

This fellow was really working for his tip.

"How could I resist after that introduction—yes, please."

"Is there anything else, before we prepare your choices, sir?" He looked questioningly at both of us, smiling and definitely enjoying the fact that I'd accepted both his recommendations.

"We look forward to the meal," I said, smiling.

"I will bring the wines, then." he said and left again.

We didn't speak for a while. With the coming darkness the window beside us had slowly turned to a mirror. Anna shaded her brow with one palm and peered through the glass.

"I believe I can see the lights now," she said, tossing me another dazzling smile before leaning forward to peer deeper through the glass.

I didn't follow her glance, choosing instead, to stare at her profile. Her small nose was a bit upturned and it was easy to see the *Samer* blood Karolina thought she detected in Anna's features. Her eyes had a slight slant, characteristic to *Samer* and they sort of wrapped around the side of her face, a bit like the Finns, I thought. She was truly a beauty. Not classical Greek, although some might consider her so, but more wholesome, hometown, with a couple of wisps of her dark hair that escaped in front of her ears. And she was also tall, which I liked.

She caught me staring at her and smiled a questioning look across the table:

"What...?" she murmured, turning her head to one side in a captivating gesture and frowning slightly, "...you looked so serious just then Alex. What were you thinking?"

Before I could stammer an answer the *maitre'd* appeared with the wine accompanied by a waiter he introduced as Johan. I only smiled back at Anna's question.

I began going through the wine ritual with them. Offering me first Anna's white, the waiter turned the bottles' label so I could verify it before he drew the cork for an approving taste. I nodded my approval when presented the label, tasted and nodded again. It went the same for the red, which had an unpronounceable Hungarian name. I merely smiled and shrugged at my lack of knowledge as he presented the label before me. He drew the cork and poured a half inch of the near-black liquid in a fresh glass. Taking up the goblet I inhaled the headiness of it before trying a taste.

With great expectation he watched me intently: "It is the variety I recommended, Sir. If you are displeased with it we will find something more palatable."

But the taste more than verified his high opinion of the wine; its full body would more than complement my moose. "Your suggestion is excellent; a wonderful wine."

With a satisfying nod and smile he helped the waiter gather their paraphernalia before they disappeared, leaving the two bottles open on the table to breathe.

"Well, that's that," I said, wiping my mouth and returning my napkin to my lap.

Anna was watching me rather quizzically over her cup of *punsch.*

"Are both your parents living," she asked.

"No—neither of them. How about you—those snapshots in your office?"

"Yes—both mine are alive."

"You are fortunate to have them, still."

"Yes, I realize that. I tell myself—when father's...condition is causing us some sadness, he's still here and he's not really so unhappy. His problem—mostly irritates those who must be around him, those who love him, more than it irritates him."

"That's unfortunate."

"Sometime, I'll tell you about him. I think you would have liked him the way he used to be...it's not that important—nothing I wish to go into tonight—simply life—old age—we all come to it. I've seen that, in health care."

"Well—what can we talk about...*hummm*....let's see—ever been married?"

I regretted asking the moment the words left my lips. She'd looked strangely at me—so strangely, I thought she wasn't going to answer for a moment. How could I have been so stupid, I thought, wishing I could take back the words.

"What dismal subjects to speak about on a first date," she finally said. "It's your turn to tell me about your life—have you ever been married?"

"Yes, I guess you're right and I apologize for my...stupidity."

"Oh, I don't know if I would go that far, but I accept it. So, answer the question," this with a smile to show she wasn't offended.

"Well, yes...yes, I was married when I was very young. Too young, to be honest—both of us. Our marriage endured for about three years before it died of boredom. We sort of got tired of each other and eventually split up—amicably. I haven't heard from her since."

"Do you regret it?"

"No—not really, well...maybe. It was nearly four years wasted, unless you want to put it down to experience; I regret that."

"I suppose you could look upon it as a learning experience—and you've graduated?"

"It's a useful way to regard it; fortunately there were no children. What about you, Anna...?"

But before she could answer, the *maitre'd* returned with two waiters in tow and began to juggle our plates and other items. True to *maitre'd's* word, as Anna and I had been quietly talking, the dining room was filling. I gestured to a party that was just now being seated. Swedes, it seemed, dressed richly for dinner as some couples wore formal attire.

Each of our servers carried a huge silver tray and waited while the *maitre'd* set up a folding stand. He removed our plates again and one of the waiters set about opening covered chafing dishes while the other began de-boning Anna's sole, before pouring the steaming almond sauce over it. We watched in anticipation as they did a beautiful job with her fish.

My moose was a little more primitive: a large chunk of charred meat in the chafing dish, *cognac* on top, light the fire and pour a thin, rich sauce around the edges with the flaming plate placed before me for effect. And it certainly did have that, especially the aroma. Anna and I both loved the service. Some of the newly arrived diners seated around us smiled along in appreciation and friendliness, no doubt, anticipation.

Once the staff departed, Anna looked rather mischievously at me: "Do you suppose our servers are required to sleep with those trays in waiter school?"

"Wouldn't surprise me a bit."

We both laughed and the light-hearted mood was on again. We didn't talk much during the meal other than to utter several, intermittent *ooouus* and *ahaasss*…we both ate and drank with appreciation for the excellent preparation and variety of flavors, textures and effects our individual meals offered. We sampled each other's entrées and sauces, following immediately with a sip of each other's wines in order to gain the effect with the food. It was an excellent meal and lasted well over an hour as we followed it with dessert, *cognac* and coffee.

Walking out to the car after I'd paid the bill, I said: "Anna, did you notice how intense the *maitre'd* was when we first sat down and how jovial and personal he had become by the time we received the check."

Anna was feeling her *punsch*, wine and the cognac:

"Yup—I sure did—must 'a been the money."

I laughed at her Saturday matinee western-movie lingo: "Money—you mean tip. But he did work hard for his money, though…didn't you think so?"

She surprised me by taking my hand as we wound around the darkened path and through the crowded parking lot.

"No doubt…it was your American, culinary sophistication."

We laughed at her exaggeration. She turned as we continued to walk and put her arm through mine, folding my arm up with her other hand.

"And your French *pro-nun-shee-aaa-shun*—try and say that one three times, quickly mister," she said, deliberately slurring the syllables.

"Now, silly—none of that," I said as I opened her door. Once she was seated and before I closed her door, I took a risk: "It was your sophistication and beauty. Probably thought you were one of the royal family—out on a lark with the peasants," I said, accenting the word and slamming her door before she could answer.

I walked around the rear of the car, opened my own door and slid behind the wheel. Oddly, she didn't comment as I started the Volvo and carefully backed it into the gravel lot. Anna seemed uncharacteristically quiet and for a moment, I wondered if she'd taken offense from something. Surely my remark was meant to be flattering.

I glanced at her sitting with one arm up by the window, staring straight ahead, an impish look on her face. As best I could tell, in the darkened car, she appeared to have a secret she wasn't about to disclose to someone—without a lot of persuasion.

"OK—so what's so funny," I said, taking the Volvo out of gear and turning in the seat? You look like you're gonna' bust if you don't let it out."

And she did. She threw back her head and laughed heartily. Leaning forward to catch her breath, she put both hands against the dashboard. I watched, amused, but unsure exactly why, as she attempted to gain her self control. After a minute she slid across the seat toward me, still snickering and shaking her head from side to side.

"What…? Come on—what," I said, taking her hand. She put her hand on my forearm but could only shake her head and begin laughing even harder.

I turned off the engine, then the lights. "I'm not moving another inch—centimeter—until you own up. What did I do—or, what did you do—come on?" I said, starting to chuckle myself caught up in her infectious glee.

At length she sat up straight, sincerely attempting to control herself. After one more outburst of laughter, she finally seemed to be capable of talking. Sitting up, hands pertly folded on her lap, she looked over at me and said: "I winked at him."

"You what?" I exclaimed, not believing I'd heard her. "Who? Winked...? The *maitre'd?*"

By all impressions, another outburst was coming and she was struggling for self control, shaking her head, smiling, choking on her mirth.

"I winked at him...that stuffy *maitre'd*" she choked, "...when he served the first glass of *punsch*—I gave him a wicked smile—looked him square in the eye and winked at him...."

"You didn't?" I said unable to believe she had the nerve.

"I did! And he nearly dropped his little tray....remember?"

"Yes," I said thinking back, "but I can't believe you did that?"

"Why can't you? I was playing the American."

"I—well—it's so...so—un-Swedish?"

"That was the idea."

"Weren't you worried about what he would think—about you? It's...it's not—Swedish, you know, the Swedish conscience?"

She shook her head from side to side, not daring to speak again. She appeared to be in real pain. Her lips were pursed as if she were holding her breath. She had also squeezed her arms against her sides—ready to explode with laughter. She finally gained enough control to squeak again:

"And—all the while, you—you, Mr. Sober-person...you went through that ritual they always make the customers observe—to make it look so sophisticated. He wanted your money and was willing to cheat the waiter out of the tip you gave him..."

"He wouldn't have...?"

"He would! And I'll guess that he did. I simply wanted to deflate him a little—so he wasn't so pompous. And I think I did."

"You certainly did, but...?"

"But...but..." she mocked jokingly, before completely losing control again; she leaned forward, poked me in the ribs lightly, before bursting into another peal of laughter—unable now even to maintain her hold on my arm. After a moment, tiring somewhat harder, she turned back toward me and leaned her head on my shoulder, trying to control herself, body still shaking, her head wiggling in mirth. I grumbled a little under my breath—not feeling a part of the humor, or, on the wrong side of it, but liking the smell of her hair and the warmth of her nearness. Far too soon, she sat up straight and nodded to no one in particular.

Hoping to make her feel badly, I started the car again and put it into gear, steering it out onto the road for home. I said no more about it. From the occasional giggle that erupted in the dark from time to time, I figured I failed there, too.

It was such a surprise, I thought as we drove in the dark. It seemed so uncharacteristic of what I thought she'd be like. I'd gotten a little perturbed at first, but it was difficult to remain angry with someone as open as Anna. I'd really grown to enjoy her company. After a mile or so of my grumbling and muttering under my breath, she began teasing me out of my hurt feelings; we made up and had a pleasant ride back to her home. Then I'd gone in for *kaffe och cognac*...and she'd let me kiss her goodnight...I think she let me, anyway. Maybe she kissed me goodnight.

CHAPTER 14

A Pledge to Revenge

Even after going to bed I couldn't put the evening with Anna out of my mind; I could still hear her bubbling laughter, feel and smell the closeness of her. Anna...she was some lady. I finally decided to review my notes from the day's interview with Karolina, so I got up, turned on my little bed lamp, grabbed my tablet and crawled back into bed. As I began reading what Karolina had related that day, in a little while, her steady rhythm began to flow.

"My father was frantic after those boys kidnapped mother...and took her away. She said he'd told her later that, after he was freed, he'd rushed around looking for her. Of course she was nowhere to be found. He asked several friends whether they'd seen Anna-Stina, with some boys. One old woman recalled seeing a family leave by the north cart track and thought that was who Carl sought, so he took his horse and rode a couple miles without seeing anyone, before finally realizing the old woman must have seen someone else.

Anna-Stina had to walk the entire distance back to the settlement. Halfway home, she began to meet carts with families returning home from the festivities. Ashamed of what her captors had done to her, each time, she deliberately stepped into the forest to hide until they passed. Her frustration grew with each step, angry that she must hide in shame for something, once again, which was not her fault, for which she had no part in, other than being the victim.

Looking down through angry tears, her beautiful vest and blouse were badly torn. The debris from the tussle with the boys and when they'd flung her from the cart, was stuck fast by the pine pitch. Had those returning families encountered this disheveled vallkulla, she thought, they would only think the worst, seeing me walking home alone from the forest. She was no stranger to false shame—but still was unaccustomed to the shunned feeling...there goes that Malmberg girl again...they would say...look at her clothes—it is easy to see where she has been lying.

And each time she was forced to hide, it cost her time; it was very late when she finally approached the edge of the village. She then cut cross-country through the fields and finally managed to reach the house without being seen. Evening chores were well underway when she entered the barn, in her work clothing again. The only sign of her gruesome afternoon was a small bruise on her shoulder where she'd struck the stones when they threw her over the wheel. She'd hidden the pine pitch-encrusted clothing beneath her bed, intending to bury it the next day, or throw it in the fire when no one was watching. She thought, feeling sorry for herself, so many hours of work, wasted.

But her strife made her resilient and she grew stronger; after the unfortunate incident and set about instituting her plan of revenge. She knew it would take three things to bring it about: first, the minister's infatuation with her. She was fairly certain she already had and could maintain that and hopefully, even increase her emotional control over him further, if she cultivated it; that would be the difficult part because she'd grown to hate him so.

Secondly, her affection for Carl Fröman: there was no doubt of that continuing, given the proper field and fertilizer. The third and most uncertain part was Carl's affection for her. She was quite sure he liked her a good deal—possibly even loved her, at this point. But to take that affection to the next level would be difficult under the circumstances, without more opportunities to meet and grow to know one another better.

The physical and social distance separating them were seemingly insurmountable impediments; it prevented them from meeting or cultivating a mutual affection. She felt especially frustrated given her lack of mobility. It appeared always to be only random chance that brought them together, up to this point. Finally, the greatest to overcome was that of social distance: his family had already expressed their extreme displeasure in their behavior toward one another.

The arranged kidnapping during the *vallkulla* honoring day and her ensuing cart ride, were example enough. She knew she must be wary and tread carefully around anyone with social or emotional connections to Carl's family, especially Pastor Johansson. Any defiance of his family must be instituted by and come solely from Carl, when it comes, she thought. I must not even plant the seed of defiance in him, but merely see that the ground remains fertile; he will decide—and whether it is to flourish. He must come upon the idea himself and implement it, in the end.

She did not know when she and Carl would next meet, but she resolved to try harder to make the change in their relationship happen, when chance encounter presented itself—though at this point she wasn't exactly sure how. She hoped Carl carried very strong feelings toward her; God help her, they were mutual.

What Anna-Stina could not realize was how very strong Carl's love for her had grown. His preoccupation with this *vallkulla* was the source for many daydreams. As he mastered the skills of operating and managing his father's farming and business interests, he would often find himself thinking of her beautiful eyes. When he saw any woman, he immediately compared her to Anna-Stina Malmberg and the woman inevitably came up short. Even if they happened to be fairer, in someone else's eyes, Carl felt there was little comparison with the special characteristics of his wild and strong-headed girl of the forest.

He realized the serious nature of the objections brought about by his family, particularly his mother and now fanned by this assistant minister, Johansson. Carl didn't like the man, although he tried very earnestly not to let his dislike surface in their various associations. The old pastor often had Carl's family to tea or Sunday dinner and of course, the young minister would inevitably be present.

Carl found him—old, for his age and to be too severely smitten by book religion, very nearly akin to that of an elementary, seminary student. At times he resembled a fire-brand. And he was only Carl's age plus five years or so. Usually, that early, the burning enthusiasm for The Teachings had been sufficiently tempered by time and knowledge, replaced by a more mature, studied point of view. But not Pastor Johansson; he flamed with his religious education. He would turn every conversation to it that he could, manipulating the discussion toward the subject of man's sin and God's punishment, a habit that made all but the most ardent believers avoid him. No one could tolerate a constant theological conversation—about self-guilt.

Carl often wondered whether the young pastor even had the word forgiveness in his vocabulary, or knew the meaning of charity. And although Carl, too, had attended seminary—a far more prestigious one even, than Johansson—he didn't complete his studies and therefore felt it would be unproductive, even unwise to enter a conversation debating the obvious differences in their individual philosophical approaches to the relationship of man and God.

Though the minister often attempted to draw Carl into the discussions he resisted; his ability to argue from a philosophical point of view equaled the minister's, he knew. Carl also knew that espousing them would only lead to further debate. Already, a raft of new tribulation would soon come floating down the river—Anna-Stina Malmberg would be sitting square atop the raft, if the minister had anything to do with it.

Carl found these Sunday meetings with his mother and Johansson for discussion very boring. He found himself thinking of Anna-Stina. Had the young minister been able to proffer and discuss a less severe approach to man's relationship to God, as did the old minister, Carl might have enjoyed the challenge. But he knew the harvest it would reap, in this rural venue, would be spare. Thus, Carl merely let his mind wander, appearing the dolt. Today, he found himself concentrating on how he might conspire to meet Anna-Stina again; the sooner the better.

Winter passed and spring arrived with intermittent snowstorms and sunny days. The first flowers would bloom only to be covered with late, wet snow, followed the next days by sunshine, melting it again. But the sun was another day higher each time and a new greening and yet more blossoms were promised in the fresh scented, southerly winds. The unpredictable weather kept Anna-Stina in and out of the barn, preparing the home farm animals for the departure to the *fäbod*. As always, fodder grew in short supply and the animals were weakened from the long winter's confinement. Whenever she was outside she would glance toward the northern mountains with longing, wondering whether the grass on the southern sloping meadows was greening up, or how much work there would be to do in the small, timberhouses. But it was still too early and she would busy herself again, knowing the day would arrive, soon enough, when it was finally time to *buan*—to return to the *fäbod*.

But finally the day arrived. As always, those in the community who would remain behind, also turned out to wish the departing women and children a safe and uneventful journey; many of these, husbands and sons, would return to plant and tend the crops of rye and *korn* after helping make the trek. Their duty would entail helping to open the *stugo* and barns to receive the animals and their human tenders.

Before departing, the community prayed for a good summer, a reward of many cheeses, much butter and fat animals returning home again at the conclusion of the summer's grazing and monstrous loads of hay to sled back home during the following winter.

The march to the mountains went well. There were few injuries to humans or animals and they arrived late in the day; each cabin owner set about practicing the rituals to clean the cabin of any evil beings who might have occupied them during the winter. It was known that each fall, after the women departed the *fäbod* for home, that *vitrafolk*, invisible people, quickly took back possession. It was necessary to practice certain spells to persuade them to once again, move aside for the summer to permit the human occupants to move into their home. Care had to be exercised, lest the *vittror* be offended; otherwise. a summer of misery would follow the ill doer, wherever she went about the *fäbod*.

After the first week everyone had settled again into the normal summer duties of rising at half past four to milk the cows and goats. Build the fires to begin boiling the *mesmör*; churn the cream to butter, prepare milk with rennet to making the cheeses…the tasks were endless. These home chores were preferred by the older *vallkullor*. Superintending the animals, while grazing in the forest, the more strenuous of the tasks, was often preferred by the younger women or girls. This was Anna-Stina's first choice and she usually set out for the high meadows as soon as the morning milking was completed, or when she was no longer needed for other duties.

Two weeks after arriving, Anna-Stina sat daydreaming at the *sovhol*, watching the cows as she knit a stocking. The animals lay quietly digesting the new meadow grass. Their backs were dappled in partial sun and shade and butterflies circulated lazily round, seemingly aimless in their fluttering from blossom to blossom.

From time to time Anna-Stina would glance up from her stitches to regard the animals; their contentment never ceased to offer her a sense of well being. Seeing the colorful butterflies circling in pairs, she thought they must be courting. They don't seem to be taking any nourishment from the few plants with blossoms, she mused, but prefer to circle about each other again and again, hardly touching or alighting. She thought of Carl and herself and wondered when—and if, he would come so close to her. She had been waiting so long for him. With each passing day, doubts crept deeper into her thoughts as to the success of her plan; she even awakened during the night, dreaming and wondering. When will he come? When will they meet again?

Anna-Stina had been considering courses of action which might move their relationship forward. What she'd finally decided to attempt would probably be the death of her, in both this life and the one to follow, she worried. After carefully considering the possibilities available, she resolved to tempt Carl Fröman to make love to her. The consequences were that they would conceive a child, which would bring trouble to his family. She didn't have an immediate plan to marry Carl—she knew better than that. His family would never permit it, at least in the beginning. She felt the disparity as this act absolutely necessary, in order to force Pastor Johansson's hand.

Like a carefully banked fire, this most serious mission burned within her and she was careful to fuel it well. With this resolve, she considered various opportunities which might present themselves; as the cattle grazed around her, as she milked them, or lying in her bed in the *stugo*, for the few moments before she fell fast asleep, she considered her options.

She was still uncertain how to maintain the delicate balance between Carl Fröman's initial infatuation with her and an eventual lust and love she planned to cultivate. After the lust was satisfied, she worried, it could be difficult to maintain the love, over the period it took to convince Pastor Johansson to do his duty, admit his guilt and marry them.

Scheming toward this delicate balance didn't come without the fostering of a certain degree of regret for the callous manipulation it required of the young man she'd come to love. Guilt for misusing their mutual affection, more than once, nearly caused her to abandon the scheme. Using one's love in this way was a dull tool with which to begin to carve a life together.

She knew any sort of what the young minister construed sin would immediately drive him to launch a personal mission to cure and alleviate the sin in that particular parishioner, like a physician's resolute desire to heal a diseased patient. If the sinner resisted, or for some reason seemed unable to overcome the particular transgression…like drunkenness, Pastor Johansson's vehemence would only intensify.

From her own personal observation, Anna-Stina believed Pastor Johansson couldn't tolerate any congregation member's straying, disobedience, or repeated sins, let alone persist, blatant or outright defiance, as she herself anticipated. He would do practically anything to prevent, or correct the contravention—even to the extent of eventual destruction of the defiant sinner, or possibly, even himself, if need be. That was the minister's character strength…and the weakness which Anna-Stina hoped to leverage—his absolute inability to cure her sins, the only woman he loved. Plant the seed of sin in me Carl and I will nurture yours and the minister's love, taking them both to the highest pinnacle I'm able. Get a confession from him and you as my husband…and I will then have my sweet, sweet revenge and my lover for a husband.

Yet, Anna-Stina remained concerned with the possible consequences; she knew banishment of the sinner from the community wasn't beyond the power of a minister of Johansson's ilk; the community would forgive, but he would not. So, carefully planning, Anna-Stina determined the course she would chart: to be that defiant sinner. She hoped for sufficient personal strength of resolve to carry out her goal. Nothing short of her life, her families, Carl's, or the yet-to-be conceived child would come between that determination and her vengeance.

Once Carl's family became aware of what she and Carl had done…were doing, his mother would be unable to withhold her approval of their courtship and would eventually urge the minister to offer his blessing. Then, they could immediately marry, thus lending legitimacy to the yet unborn child.

Two weeks passed without news from Carl. Anna-Stina began to worry, for fear his mother or the minister had at last convinced him to leave off his infatuation with the farm maid and return instead to serious study at the divinity school. This doubt and fear continued to plague her for another week. She'd grown quite downhearted by the time the weekend came, with still no word; the day to prepare for possible visitors had come and now nearly gone without any sign he or anyone would come up to the *fäbod*. She felt so terribly lonely and abandoned.

I wonder if my daring words have reaped a moldy harvest, she thought. Glancing up at the dim light penetrating the tall forest, she saw it was growing late. I should take the cows back to the *fäbod* and then bathe. The others will be finished with their own milking and ready for visitors by the time I finish and return. I wonder...she mused, turning the cows down the familiar path.

Carl had his plans foiled time and again by either his mother, or the minister and for two weeks he'd planned to escape, no matter what they organized to keep him at home. He was certain they had a conspiracy against Anna-Stina and him. He was not far from the mark, though his father was not a part of this miniature connivance, feeling they were too petty and an utter waste of time.

"The children will do what they will do," he told his wife. "Let the boy do as he wishes—what's important is that Carl has made a choice—he's come home to take over the farm and the business, instead of attend the divinity school."

This fact, his father was more pleased with, than he dared disclose to his wife. Some would simply hang about with the simpering wastrels in the church crowd, avoiding real labor; but not his Carl.

"Religion was all right," he gave them, "we need it to maintain order in the soul, as we need government to maintain order in the society and among nations—but let someone else's children do it this time. Frömans are not always suited for the cloth."

When he learned his wife and the lay pastor argue in favor of, and were themselves planning to select a bride for Carl, without his knowledge, *Herr* Fröman rebelled.

"To stoop so low as to choose a mate for my son...no, that custom has long since died," he said, daring to utter the thought aloud. Back to the time of his own youthful marriage, he'd wondered at the suitability of his own family selected mate at the time, a mate whom he had not been able to choose. In more ways than he cared to admit, he'd been disappointed. This herder girl of Carl's, she seemed comely enough and of good temperament, too—everything one needed in a wife. The aunt spoke highly of her work skills, too. And...she had spunk, he'd heard; something lacking in this family for a while. And the boy loved her, apparently.

"We Frömans have stature enough in the community; the Kommun and perhaps the whole country can tolerate our own renegade in our midst, now and then. Keep the blood balanced—like our livestock," he told one the assemblages called together by his wife after a church meeting. In his excitement, he had been waving his arms and spilling the little cup of coffee on his trousers and the carpet. The young minister smiled condescendingly and regarded at the ceiling demurely, but his wife glared at him, her lips a thin line of displeasure.

"Carl will be the better off for it. A partner, she would be—a true working partner, who understood very well the animals, if not the fields. But Carl could see to them, well enough. Yes," he said, confident now in his tack, "she might be just what we Frömans need. The community speaks well of her—fine *vallkulla* I'm told. If only she hadn't thrown off that *oäktabarn*—pity, too—the child died. For a moment he pondered whether his son could have been the father but then, remembered Carl was away at seminary—far to the south. Not a chance, he thought, no chance. The young pastor was given over to a good deal of "*harummmmming*," having caught something in his throat with the tea he drank, incessantly, when visiting Frömansgården.

Finally, in utter frustration and longing to see Anna-Stina, Carl grudgingly resolved to tell a lie to his mother. In the past he'd spoken with his father about Anna-Stina Malmberg and was surprised at the lack of resistance there—almost, but not quite, he had felt encouraged by his father. That door is unlocked, if not open, he thought, afterwards.

So, that day he'd told his father of his intentions to get away from the work for a few days and asked for the time away from the farming duties. His father waved away Carl's concerns at the workload encouraging him to have a good time.

"Where will you go," his father asked as he arranged some recently repaired oxen harness.

"I—I had not given it a lot of thought, Father. I wished to learn whether we could spare my absence from the work, before I decided."

"How long since you have gone visiting to Albert's," his father asked.

Albert's, Carl thought, why would I wish to go all the way to Mockförd? "I can't remember, Father—it's been some time— probably with you and Mother."

"The fishing's quite good along the way—to Mockfärd, that is. And you might want to stop of at the *fäbod*...Vansberget? Check on the animals, you know? Can't always rely on the women to see they're getting enough to eat—talking, you know—talking all the time...don't pay proper attention, sometime."

He'd even given Carl a knowing wink then, before returning to his work. Mockfärd was no where near the *fäbod*, Carl thought. Why would he suggest Albert's? But it wasn't long before Carl concluded his father's purpose, unaccustomed to deception that he was. That afternoon he spoke with his mother.

"Mother, I want to do a little fishing tomorrow and shall possibly travel to see Cousin Albert, afterward, at Father's suggestion and spend a few days with him. It's been busy for the last half month but we're ahead of schedule with every errand and chore. I feel I deserve some time away—and Father has agreed."

Her son's daring surprised and pleased his *Fru* Fröman. "Yes— your father said he told you to go visit Albert's family—said it would do you good. " At least, she thought, he is not demanding to see that *vallkulla* again. The cart ride must have convinced him of other's opinions about that person...as if pastor and I haven't done our best.

The fact that Mockfärd lies in the opposite direction should make it safe enough...and it isn't as if Carl is a child any longer...although I sometimes wonder, she thought. God, please watch over him in your infinite grace she said to herself. Let him find a suitable wife, soon.

"Be sure to tell Cousin Albert I'd like to see his mother more often—but just do not have time. And be sure to tell her I'm sorry about her illness...what was it anyway—now I have forgotten. Honest...?"

"She broke her hip I believe, Mother," Carl replied with the patience of someone who knew he would get his way if he just waited.

He knew his mother despised his father's sister, cared little about her afflictions and would never verify his story of the feigned visit until it was too late, or she just plain forgot about it.

Carl had never lied to his mother to this degree. And she had no reason not to believe his destination wasn't Albert's instead of Vansberget *fäbod*, where his love lay dreaming. But, he felt guilty for the deception, nonetheless.

The early morning's work left Carl grimy; I won't bother to bathe before leaving. The road grime will have to come off anyway. No one was the wiser when he brought the leather traveling bag downstairs, packed the night before and had saddled his mare. He kissed his mother's cheek and mounted the waiting horse, waving goodbye to the kitchen girls. He knew he'd likely have to swim the Vanån anyway, before he reached Vansberget—there was plenty of time.

The ride along the Västerdalälven was a pleasant reprieve from farm work. Carl took his time, not wishing to arrive too early and appear to be as eager to meet Anna-Stina as he truly was. He knew she'd be somewhere up in the forest. Best to time my arrival with her return to do the evening milking.

As he gave the mare her head, he mused, contemplating Anna-Stina's qualities: She was so generous; he couldn't comprehend why his mother disliked her, so. She hardly recognized Anna-Stina when she did encounter her. It was more likely she felt Anna-Stina stood in the path of the collar for me, he guessed. But I really don't believe I ever truly wished to be a pastor. I wonder if God had ever actually called me…even though Pastor Johansson tried to convince me it had truly happened; the old minister always told me I'd definitely know. True, I've had one or two moments when my mind and body—it was as if they left me in ecstasy in contemplating The Word, he thought, when they rose above me and the circumstances of my life. All the trivial things and people…but was that God? If it did really happen that way and if that truly was a Call, why…then, should I later choose to take up the collar, Anna-Stina would be a good minister's wife. She is kind, understanding and God-fearing, I believe.

But would I have to return to study again? Many ministers I have heard did not have the formal education of any seminary, let alone a prestigious institution in Uppsala or Stockholm, as I have done. They were very powerful speakers and powerful believers and probably had not completed their studies. Pastor Johansson has been to Uppsala, though, but he's not a very powerful speaker; he's loud when he is full of The Spirit...but he isn't very powerful.

Sometimes, I feel he's even rather conniving, Carl thought, but then felt guilty. Well, maybe conniving isn't the word...he is...well, I don't trust the way he is sometime—the way I see him looking at Anna-Stina—he's, well...strange. And why does he have such strong distaste for her, too? It was almost like it is personal. Yet he could never remember seeing the two quarreling, nor had Anna-Stina ever mentioned anything. Probably, it was because of the child Anna-Stina had borne—without naming a father, or with none stepping forward to claim their blood and take their responsibility.

After turning away from the Västerdalälven and up the Vanån, he rode north and then began seeing boats going downstream, no doubt to spend the night in Järna with relatives or friends and then to church next day—Sunday. He waved at each of them in turn, wishing to share his exuberant joy at being free for a few days at last and pleased with all he saw around him. To the few other travelers he met from time to time on the stony track, he nodded in greeting and wished them well.

He welcomed the thought of foregoing church attendance the next day...Sunday, though he guessed he'd feel a little guilty. Maybe Anna-Stina and I can have a quiet spiritual moment together, or with the others, in the morning. Maybe I'll be asked to hold a small worship service...speaking for them, if they would like me to do it. He'd given inspirational talks of this type before, in the absences of a formal minister. He was a good, unrehearsed speaker, he knew; his kindness and gentle nature were pleasing. The common people liked his simple messages and since he wasn't ordained, they felt little threat from him for their mis-behavior. As the son of one of the wealthiest men in the area, they hadn't yet come to respect him as they did his father.

The narrow path leading northwesterly along the swiftly flowing Vanån continued along the steep, easterly shore bordering the river, with occasional passages through dense forest. It was mid-afternoon when he finally approached the area opposite the river and Vansberget *fäbod*, high on the mountainside, opposite. The Van, as this lake-like portion of the river Vanån was called, was nearly at its widest, here.

In the absence of any passing boatman whom he could pay for passage across, Carl's sole option to gaining the other side was a long, cold swim, clinging to the horse's mane. He didn't particularly mind this in the summer; he even found it a challenge. Impatiently glancing in both directions, he waited perhaps a half-hour, but no boatmen approached. I can wait a while longer to see whether any boats pass, he thought, or I can begin to swim now and possibly see Anna-Stina even sooner.

He finally stood and began removing his clothing, double wrapping it all in an oilskin, brought for the purpose. This, tethered to a long line from the horse's neck, would float free as the horse swam.

He stood naked, gazing across at the forested mountains on the other shore. The westerly-ly--ing sun was warm in his face and the light breeze crossing his bare skin, stirred a feeling of eroticism in anticipation of seeing Anna-Stina. What if she could see him now...from where she was? Across the broad expanse of water, he could barely see the smoke above the forest from the fires of Vansberget. The older women would be boiling the whey to make *mismör*. And somewhere above, to the right or the left, Anna-Stina is tending her herd.

Hesitating no longer, Carl stepped into the water, leading the horse carefully behind. Before the depth reached his waist, the horse lunged forward and began swimming, turning downstream with the current. Carl, after a few strokes along side the horse's head, got her turned westerly again, toward the far shore.

On the far shore after the twenty-minute swim, Carl unrolled his clothing bundle and quickly dressed while the horse stood in the sunlight, dripping and shaking with fatigue. Man and beast dried quickly in the gentle breeze as Carl rested the mare. The sun had not quite crested the top of Vansberget. After half an hour's rest the mare had regained her strength and Carl dressed and remounted, turning her up the narrow path. It has been a long ride, he thought and the mare wasn't with the same spirit as when we departed. Pitying her finally, Carl dismounted and began leading her up the track. The way soon became steeper and they were forced to skirt many areas where springs surfaced and seeped toward the Van, below. Once, Carl stopped to let the mare drink her fill. Then they continued the upward climb.

Vansberget *fäbod* was a collection of six family grazing areas, with as many little, red *stugo* and miscellany of barns and small sheds. Slanting rails of several *gärdesgård* bordered the lanes that wound up the eastern slope of the mountain.

After the evening milking, the goats and cattle would be held in another, fenced area, where they would be handy for the morning's milking before another day of pasturing. Early each morning the cattle and goats were taken to daily-assigned areas of the forest to forage, never far from the watchful eye of their particular *vallkullor*. The grazing areas were rotated to prevent overgrazing and to give each family, fairly, a chance to graze the best spots.

Carl removed his satchel containing extra clothing and the gift he'd been keeping for Anna-Stina; these he placed on the ground and swung the gate of woven branches open and led the mare into the enclosure. Within moments, he'd removed the saddle and bridle and freed her to graze. He closed and latched the gate and laid the saddle on the ground outside the enclosure, near the path, so he wouldn't forget to take it to shelter in case there was *åska*[88] later in the day.

The climb up the mountainside had been strenuous. The long swim had removed the dust from the track but the struggle up the mountain turned into another sweaty endeavor. Reclaiming his satchel, Carl started another slow climb further up the path to where he knew he could have another bath in the privacy of a deep spring. Somewhere up in the forest, he thought, glancing from side to side, is Anna-Stina. I wonder what she is thinking right now. What a surprise it will be for her that I've finally come. It's been so long since I have seen her—I long for the shape of her face against the sky…her dark eyes. She is so beautiful and makes my heart feel like God is truly touching me when I look at her and when she smiles and speaks to me. How can it be as wrong as the minister and my mother say…to feel so strongly about someone in that way? One who has never done any harm to anyone?

Carl wandered up through the small collection of cottages and barns, seeing no one about. The whey fires were only smoldering, already having served their purpose for the day; the old women's cooking tripods stood empty, where they had recently held the massive, iron whey kettles. It was still mid-afternoon; most everyone would be up in the pastures somewhere taking advantage of the lull of mid-day and the mid-afternoon heat.

The old women were probably napping in the *stugo*, he thought. Carl passed completely through the dwelling area without seeing anyone. He proceeded up the track along another trail that led south along the side of the mountain, avoiding the steep rise of land. Anna-Stina had shown Carl its location on their first visit together, a quarter hour's walk off the main path. There would be no one there this time of day. He would swim once more and bathe, before changing into his fresh clothing. Then he'd return to the timber houses and wait.

He was perspiring heavily by the time he finally reached the upper ground. There it is, he thought, pausing at the break in the dense forest; the slanting, evening sunshine illuminated the clearing and the rivulets of sparkling water as the spring flowed downhill. The larger, stationary pool was like shimmering glass, reflecting in reversal, the top of the surrounding forest and the beautiful sky below and toward him. Carl stood for a moment, catching his breath and watching the clouds sliding across the mirror of the water, enjoying the peaceful vista. The left side seems the driest area, he thought; it's there I'll wade in to take my bath.

He edged around the main pool, at least as wide as two barns and three times that long, with a dog-leg in one end where the pool reached around a corner, extending out of site. Since it was on the side of the mountain, it turned the corner, following the brow of the hill and was shielded by a dense growth of young pine and alder. This end will be the warmest he thought, knowing the pool's bottom was dark with the silt of the surrounding drainage and the ancient rot of the forest. It would have drawn the heat of the sun down into the water throughout the day and kept the water warmer. He remembered the other end was the deeper, though and planned to swim to that end.

He dropped his satchel on the moss, opened it and removed clean trousers and a shirt, hanging them on the *lingonbär* bushes around the area. He removed each boot, then his stockings, before removing his damp vest and shirt. With barely a glance around, he slid his trousers down to his ankles and stepped free, naked again in the sunlight. Hesitating only a moment, he waded into the shallow edge of the pool.

"It's not so cold..." he said aloud as he walked, arms outstretched for balance. Taking three bold steps toward the middle of the long pool, he finally let his body fall forward and began to paddle. "*Oooohhhhh,*" he cried aloud. "*Det är källt!*" he shuddered, his breath partially taken away. *Ouuueeeeee!*" he exclaimed again, swimming a few strokes to offset the shock of the deeper water's chill.

After *sovhol,* Anna-Stina had taken the twelve cows to the top of the mountain, since no one had grazed that meadow recently. Everyone at the *fäbod* must obey the proper order of grazing so no one family received more than their fair share of the new pasture. She'd worked the animals around the side of the sloping pasture in the morning. Earlier in the day, she'd stripped several apron-loads of birch leaves into her linen apron to supplement the animal's meager forage and carried them to the waiting cows. The goats she left to fend for themselves and shooed them away whenever they tried to rob from her labor, meant for the cows. They'll never starve, she thought, not necessarily fond of the troublesome goats.

She'd been careful to see that each cow received an equal share, with a little extra for those who had sucking calves, since they need the extra strength. For Butternose, the boss-cow and her favorite, she fed several handfuls by hand. The cow had received her name from Anna-Stina because the end of her small, upturned muzzle and nose was a yellowish brown, although the animal's body was completely white. She was always friendly to her mistress, but took no nonsense from the other animals.

Like all the animals, she was a small cow and through her strength of character and intelligence, had asserted her leadership of the herd. The effort required in maintaining order in the herd wasn't without occasional action for the boss-cow. She tended to be thin, also and controlling some of the larger, more unruly cows cost her no small effort. She had strong, sharp horns and never hesitated to use them to maintain order among her larger and more stupid herd mates.

She was a trustworthy cow and because of her responsible attitude and leadership qualities within the herd, Butternose had earned bell cow honor. With seeming great pride, she'd worn the large, brass bell around her neck, suspended from a woven, birch-root collar and symbol of the herd's leader. The bell signified her higher status. Only that spring, right after arriving at the *fäbod*, Anna-Stina had woven a new collar from birch roots and once again entwined the bell, the symbol of authority and pride for the wearer. With each lumbering step, the bell clinked and clanked, declaring her presence, lending both unexpressed discipline and safety.

During the mid-morning grazing, Anna-Stina had worked the herd back toward the *fäbod*, planning to rest the animals while taking her mid-day meal. Since it was Friday, she'd carried extra clothing in her knapsack, planning to bathe before returning to the evening milking.

The animals had had their fill and lay in the edge of a partially shaded meadow. She heard Butternose's bell clank from a sudden movement of her head. Not unusual in the fly season, she merely glanced up from her knitting. With a concentrated expression, the cow continued to gaze intently in the direction of the spring. Lying as she was, with her ears forward and her head up, she looked as she might suddenly spring up.

A bear, Anna-Stina thought to herself, mildly concerned? Surely not in the middle of the day? She had her walking stick with her and a small knife at her belt. She continued to watch the cow's behavior; she has definitely heard something. But after a moment the cow's head went back down and she languidly began to chew her cud, seemingly unconcerned. Anna-Stina went back to her knitting and her thoughts.

After some seconds, she heard another noise—a human sound…of wailing, something? The cow's head jerked again and the animal looked alternately in the direction of the spring and as Anna-Stina stood up, watched her to see what steps her mistress would take next.

Anna-Stina picked up her stick and began walking toward the sound, passing among the cattle and calling to them in turn in a soothing voice, pausing to scratch the root of Butternose's tail to calm her and scratching others behind their ears as she passed each one. The cows rotated their heads with pleasure at the attention, pointing their noses skyward and rolling their eyes.

She listened intently during these ministrations, but heard nothing further. She spoke a few more calming words to the cattle before she began to make her way through the large boulders, weaving her way

along the trail in the direction of the sound. She was a little
frightened.

Who could be at the pool, she wondered, having come to the
conclusion the sound was made by a human. No other *vallkulla* was
supposed to be grazing up here. It was not the sound of a bear, she
thought...or was it, wishing for a moment she'd brought her hand ax.

Because of the very dense growth, her progress slowed as she
approached the pool. From this direction she knew she'd be
shielded. Leaving her stick in the thick growth, she stooped and
began crawling toward the pool. First, dense young birch sprouts
obstructed her progress, then the thick stems of the alders, which
grew right up to the edge of the spring. Nearing the edge of the
pool's opening, she gingerly poked her head through the leaves,
carefully peering in both directions. The pool's surface was calm and
empty and there was nothing on the opposite bank.

No bears here, she thought, sitting back in a kneeling position
and no people, either. As she carefully arranged her long skirt and
turned to crawl back, she heard the sound of splashing around the
corner of the pool. Oh! She thought, backing quickly, there's
something there. She hurried back the way she had come, intending
to retrieve her stick, skirt some of the dense growth and approach the
pool's edge from the further side.

The first thing she saw when she poked her head through the
brush was a fine leather satchel. Strange, she though, no *vallkulla*
would own such an extravagance. Who could it be who has left that,
she wondered, losing her fear now she knew it wasn't a bear? Then
she saw a man's clothing strewn about atop the bushes. She peeked
further around the alders, parting a branch in each hand. Carl
Fröman turned just then and slowly began to swim back toward the
corner of the pool from where she had just come.

He's come, she exclaimed to herself, feeling her excitement and
heart begin to beat rapidly. He's come for the weekend, she thought.
Leaning back on her haunches, she sat, thinking. What should I do?
I can go back to the cows and wait. He'll probably return to the
fäbod to wait for me. Oh, how wonderful, she thought, he's come
again...at last.

Sitting, thinking, she was undecided. This could be my chance
she thought—but am I bold enough, barely able to continue to

240

review the plan that had suddenly sprung to mind again. What will he think? He's a man—but what will he think when the shock of meeting me is over. Oh, how shameless you are Anna-Stina Malmberg—as shameless as your reputation, now, surely.

She continued sitting on her heels, her hand upraised to her chin; pensively, she chewed her lower lip in thought. Will I drive him away, or will I capture him forever, she wondered. Will I be able to live with myself afterward—with Carl? I believe I have the power to take him now and bind his heart to me for the moment, but will it be bound for all time, or will I destroy any chance for the future, binding only his body. Lust today, cold shoulder, tomorrow—once the prize is nearly won, it could be as easily lost?

Finally, hesitating no further, she turned back to the thicket. Grabbing her stick, she half crawled, half ran back around the cover of the birches, around to where she had peeked onto the pool earlier, in the direction Carl would be swimming again. Standing upright, she dropped the stick and hastily began unwinding the cord holding her long skirt, dropping it to the ground around her birch-bark-shod feet. Off came her vest and then the blouse was quickly unlaced; soon, her breasts were bare. She felt her nipples stiffen as a shudder of fear ran up her spine…a feeling of half-fear and half-excitement. God…forgive me, she thought; make his heart mine.

The linen underskirt dropped about her ankles as the cord came free in her hands; she stood completely naked now, her body dappled by the slanting sunlight where it streamed through the birches. She resembled a spotted lynx slinking through the forest in search of prey. A cat's spotted coat—a coat a man might wish to caress forever.

Committed, down she knelt and began to make her way to the pool's edge. She parted the branches at the bank; Carl had not yet turned the corner of the pool, but she could hear him swimming. He is singing as he swims, she thought, smiling to herself in surprise at the sound of his bubbling pleasure. It made her feel somewhat better about what she was about to do.

Truly, Carl had been humming as he leisurely, crisscrossed the length of the pool, paddling rhythmically. When his nose was out of the water a tuneless song was evident, but he was blowing bubbles like a child as he turned his face and his nostrils passed underwater for the other stroke and a breath on the other side. The water felt so wondrous and cleansing. He was happy and expectant.

Anna-Stina waited behind the shield of greenery until she thought Carl had turned in the water to swim back toward the pool's end where she knelt, half-squatting above the water's edge. She saw the ripples from his wake splashing against the roots along the far shore. She pivoted her body on her knees and holding the roots along the shore, eased backward and let her legs slide into the deep water of the pool. The cold crept up her naked limbs, then around her belly, causing her to shudder, though her heart didn't slow its' rhythm.

She was accustomed to bathing in the spring water and the excitement of the moment would have warmed her heart a thousand times at the thought of what she was doing. I am gambling my future and my heart, she thought as she settled into the pool. Kicking easily away from the shore, her body now craved action—movement, to throw off the anxiety and to warm herself—to keep pace with the quickening heartbeat. With no further hesitation, she took steady, quiet strokes toward the middle of the pool. What should I do now, she thought. Can I be so forward to swim to him? Oh, I wish I hadn't done this now, she thought, suddenly and turned in the water, planning to return to the shore, momentarily losing her courage. I can climb the bank before he sees me she thought and increased her stroke and kick in her impulsive panic.

Just then, Carl turned the corner of the pool, having planned to traverse its complete length for the last time before ending his swim. Anna-Stina realized that he hadn't turned back, as she'd thought he would. Having now reached the far bank, she reached upward, stretching…trying franticly to grasp the exposed birch roots she'd clung to when she descended into the pool. Her nerve, now entirely gone, she wished only to escape before she was discovered.

Carl kicked each leg hard, paddling strongly in expectation of turning at the far end; as he brought his head up, fanning the water forward in a wake, he glimpsed an apparition in the water ahead of him. There was something—a person…swimming? He slowed his stroke, treading water for a moment. To his amazement he recognizing Anna-Stina, head wet with tendrils of long hair streaming on her shoulders. As she reached the far bank, she grasped the dangling tree roots and began pulling herself from the water.

"My God!" he exclaimed. "Anna-Stina…how did you get here—

what…were you swimming?" This…while she seemed to be trying to escape.

"Oh—I…*fan*[89]!" she cursed, forgetting herself for the moment. She'd attempted to pull herself up, but the root parted suddenly and she tumbled backwards. Surfacing, she coughed and cursed again: "sate…" she sputtered.

Alarmed by the first sight of her and thinking her some sort of woods spirit, Carl had watched, astonished, as she'd swam the few strokes to the far bank and began pulling herself from the water. "She's naked," he exclaimed to himself in disbelief. The thought leaped into his realization as she'd began pulling herself from the pool, the sun flashing on her hips and thighs as her lithe arms began to draw her up the bank, when the root parted. Like a bolt of lightning, the warmth sprang to his loins and he dove forward toward her.

"God, Anna-Stina…" he sputtered, half to himself as he swam, "…God!"

A few strokes brought him to her side. She was struggling and choking, having inhaled water when she went under.

Carl stopped just short of her bobbing head and shoulders, presented with a quandary. The impropriety of touching the naked woman, sputtering, or not, in the water, momentarily confused him. Finally, he reached for her shoulders and for the second time in his life, Carl did not know where to put his hands to help Anna-Stina. Changing his mind, he reached to grasp her waist. She'd inhaled a good deal of water and couldn't touch the bottom of the pool to catch her breath.

Carl felt for her waist and realized one hand had found her breast. Immediately reaching lower, he found her navel and waist and lifting her somewhat, himself kicking in the deep water, he held her fast as best he could at arm's length as she continued to cough and gag.

Water streamed from her mouth and nostrils as she felt strong hands above her hips. She was having trouble breathing. Her racing heart and gasping breath were no help and after several strong coughs and a blow or two from her nostrils to clear them, she finally relaxed somewhat in Carl's grasp and placed both hands on his shoulders. She released one hand to pull her hair away from her face. Realizing her breasts were bobbing on top of the water, she lowered her arms, this time resting them on Carl's forearms, as he continued holding her by her waist.

When she'd surfaced, Carl had seen the water streaming from her nose. Instinctively, he'd let go with one hand to try to help her with her hair, but when he did, their hands collided as she reached down. She tipped sideways and sank from his grasp again. Groping again, Carl found soft flesh before again successfully circling her waist.

As Anna-Stina went off balance, she'd tried to save herself by kicking violently with her legs and reaching upward. In doing so, her knee rose and struck Carl in the groin.

Carl's expression changed momentarily as he involuntarily let go of her completely a second time and grasped his testicles. In agony, he realized he'd dropped her again, but only for a few seconds, he was unable to help her.

Anna-Stina reached for one of his arms, steadying herself with the other on his waist. She had felt the soft flesh yield above her knee as she'd kicked her feet.

"Oh," she'd said, alarmed, "what have I done, Carl..." she sputtered, unable to reach the area to offer comfort.

She placed one of her hands on his chest to help hold her body away from him and somewhat balance herself again. She recovered from her coughing, cleared her nose and brushed back her hair. Cautiously, she glanced into Carl's face for the first time, daring to sample his mood. He'd remained relatively motionless after she had struck him with her knee.

"Did I hurt you?" she asked coyly, looking directly into his eyes. Their bodies bumped lightly together. Anna-Stina now had both her hands on his shoulders again and with her feet she kicked just enough to maintain buoyancy and some clearance between their bodies.

"No...I am well...I...I'm sorry I touched you," he said glancing downward.

She smiled up at him, relaxed, calm again at last. She felt more assured and confident, the earlier confusion gone. She knew the course she must now carefully follow.

"It does not matter Carl." She grimaced slightly in the effort to stay afloat and maintain the body separation. Her thigh brushed his carefully...an invitation.

Carl reached higher on her waist again to steady her. His hands were just above her hipbones. He could feel the unbelievable softness of her body, but there was also firmness. Never before had he felt a woman in this way—how could anything be so soft yet be so shapely but also strong. Their thighs touched again. Anna-Stina looked down coyly and turning her head slightly to the side, deliberately coughed once more, rising slightly from the water as she did and exposing the tops of her breasts.

Carl briefly glimpsed her taut nipples, erect from the cold water. He had seen women nursing children many times, but that had never excited him, as now did Anna-Stina's nakedness. He moved his hands higher to steady her further.

He nearly touched me that time, she thought.

Carl could feel her ribs through her muscular back. The muscles of her belly fairly rippled beneath his hands.

Anna-Stina tipped her head back and to each side, letting the water drain from her ears. As she did each side, each, opposite breast rose partially from the water. Conscious that Carl was looking, mouth agape, she smiled and relaxed her grip on his shoulders.

"Sorry..." she said and smiled, settling lower in the water again, temptation withdrawn.

Carl let her slip downward and her breasts now touched the top of his wrists. *Ohh*—God! Carl thought, frozen—not wanting to move his hands, but beginning to grow cold from the spring water.

This transpired in less than three or four minutes, but to both, it seemed like an hour. Each was near bursting with arousal. Anna-Stina was in control, though Carl didn't know it.

Careful, Anna-Stina planned her next step. She was enjoying herself as she, more or less, followed her body's instincts. She was still confident she had not yet gone too far.

Carl seemed uncertain of everything, stammering in his confusion. Aroused as he was he didn't know he was being manipulated, or where they were going with their water play. He'd begun thinking he should slide his arms further upward, increasing the pressure on the underside of her breasts.

As he was about to, Anna-Stina sensed she should act again, saying, "I'm all right now, Carl." And pushing free, she kicked away, just out of Carl's reach, teasing him. As she did, one breast came completely free from the water when she rolled over on her side to swim abreast of him. There was a flash of pubic hair as she turned in the sunlight to swim past him again.

"What do we do now," she said, treading water again, frankly not knowing what else to say to take it to the next level, growing cold herself.

"I wanted to surprise you," Carl blurted, conscious still of their nakedness but not knowing what else to say.

"You did that, Carl," she said, hoping she would not have to explain how she came to be in the pool with him.

She turned on her side again and swam two strokes toward his satchel. As she rolled in the water Carl saw the shape of her breast again and the sun flashed on her hip and flank as she kicked away.

"I'm getting cold, Carl...I think I want to get out of the water now. What were you doing here, anyway...swimming?"

"I was—bathing—before coming back down to *boda* and—I'm sorry...I didn't know you'd be here, too." After a moment, he added, "I don't know what to do either." He could feel his arousal, despite the cold water, strong and near bursting.

"Yes, you said that Carl. It seems we've gotten ourselves into a small problem but I don't blame you, Carl—you shouldn't feel badly for finding me swimming...this way."

She felt crafty, but ashamed for insinuating the guilt upon him. But the game was very big and she went on boldly. "But I don't think I can climb back up there..." she gestured to the steeply-eroded bank, "...by the birch roots, without falling in again. If I wade out of the pool down there," she said, indicating the end by his clothes with a quick wave of her hand, "may I use some of your clothes to cover with while you come out?"

"Yes—certainly—Anna-Stina...I'll wait."

"You must promise not to watch me, Carl; will you do that...promise?"

Carl was nodding before she even finished speaking, his face a mask of eager innocence. "Yes—no, I'll not look, Anna-Stina. You can use my clothes—no, better yet—there is a blanket in the satchel...you can cover yourself with that."

"All right; I'll find it. Close you eyes now Carl. Put your hands over your eyes."

As they had discussed these options, she had been working her way toward the far shore and had reached a depth where she could now touch bottom. Turning and glancing once more toward Carl, she said: "Now don't watch me, Carl," she commanded him, knowing full well that he would probably disobey…planning that he would. "I'm wading out now…so keep your eyes covered."

Carl put his hands over his eyes as bidden, his heart racing. He was nearly choking with arousal and numbing cold and his heart hammered to supply a body bursting with desire for her. He could hardly restrain himself to remain in the pool. He heard splashing sounds as Anna-Stina waded slowly toward the shore and somewhere, he heard the faint clanking of a cow's bell.

He parted the fingers of one hand slightly and saw Anna-Stina had stopped wading and was glancing in the direction of the bell. After a quick glance back toward him, she took two more steps and her back emerged with its long, beautiful depression running down the center—from her neck to her buttocks, little-by-little, rising from the water, a beautiful woman's body emerged. Inwardly, Carl moaned.

As she continued slowly wading from the water, Anna-Stina drew both arms over her breasts crossing her wrists as if to cover herself somewhat. She'd become nearly numb from the spring water and was having difficulty walking evenly on the stony bottom. The sun was behind her, so it wasn't difficult to see where she was wading. As she stepped out onto the soggy moss, she stopped, turning to glance back at Carl. He hadn't moved. He stood chest deep in the pool, his hands still covering his eyes. Has he looked—her self-doubt haunted her. Will he be too good? I hope not, she thought—I sincerely hope he will not.

Carl had indeed looked…and his resulting arousal combined with the numbing spring water, was causing his legs to jerk spasmodically, seeming, of their own volition, to want to leap from the pool toward the naked Anna-Stina. As Anna-Stina had turned back to look toward him, Carl saw the full front of her, one arm at her throat, the other extended out from her body for balance as she gingerly picked her way through the stones to the water's edge. Her groin was covered with hair just as was his own…something he had only heard the other boys speak of. The smooth curve of her belly, the shadow of her navel, the long muscles of her thighs were beautiful, making him ache so with longing to touch her.

Anna-Stina bent, searching Carl's satchel for the blanket. Her beautifully shaped backside was directly facing the pool. Finding the linen blanket, she brought it out with a jerk and unfolded it. Oh, what have I done, she thought? The memory of the rape at the *fäbod* flashed before her and the old fear returned. But she swallowed hard, putting down the emotions. There is more here, she thought and I must take care to nurture and grow it. He is worth every risk.

"I have it Carl—now..." she shouted over her shoulder, "...you can come out." She flung the cover around her body, hugging the front to barely cover herself. Carl was already splashing toward her. Still with her back toward him, least she see his nakedness, she said: "I will fetch my clothes back with the cows by the birch grove." And with that, she started for the forest edge.

Carl had been able to control himself; beginning to run from the water, he was like a raging, bull-moose...only the cow in his mind. God himself could have appeared and Carl would not have slowed his rush. His nakedness was nothing to him now.

As Anna-Stina turned toward the forest she seemed to stumble, entangling her foot in a branch between the stones, pitching forward onto the moss. The sudden pain in her foot made her cry, "*Oooowwww...!*" When she spread her arms to cushion her fall, the blanket slipped from her shoulders. Recovering quickly, she grabbed it and sat up, pivoting and pulling part of it over her nakedness. Then she tried to free her foot from the pain of the limb.

Carl was suddenly on his knees beside her, bending to free her foot, oblivious to his own nakedness. She couldn't keep from looking at his nakedness, though the fork of the branch was painfully pinning her foot so that she had to lay on one side, twisting her foot to relieve the pressure and pain. The blanket only partially covered her and she didn't bother to draw it closer. One leg and an arm and part of her chest were bare...flashing bold and bright in the sunlight, as Carl ran up.

Bending the branch back Carl easily snapped the limb that bound her ankle, gently freeing her foot. She looked up in gratitude, rubbing her ankle and mumbling her thanks. Their eyes met, stared for a moment...and then they were lost each to the other. The world around them disappeared in the emotion of their mutual longing.

Still clasping Anna-Stina's foot, Carl moved his hand slowly to her calf, then her thigh as he lay down beside her. She moaned quietly beneath his touch and reaching up, circled his neck with her arms, letting the blanket collapse around her. Carl leaned over her as he slid his hand up her thigh, as her arms circled his neck; her soft breasts lay with the weight of steel anvils against his chest. Carl's hand moved to her pubic hair. Tensing, Anna-Stina reached for his hand, half to stop him, half to guide him. Then she laid back and pulled him to her, their arms circling one another.

Moving her hands up his muscular arms, Anna-Stina slowly drew Carl down to the moss. Carl had not been in control of himself since he came from the water. Anna-Stina didn't' know what was happening to herself—inside her body, her desire was uncontrollable. The Devil surely has me now, she thought, panting in panic that Carl would not be in time. All memory of the rape was forgotten, as they rolled on the blanket. I do not care—may God forgive me—I no longer care, she thought, spreading her legs around Carl's trembling body as he rolled atop her.

Within seconds, Anna-Stina reached her climax, groaning with ecstasy—a long wail escaped her, muffled slightly by her firmly clenched teeth. With her eyes closed, she grinned in ecstasy, behind curled lips…a mighty grimace of pain, passion, or both.

Carl became frightened, seeing her eyes rolled back and her contorted face. He knew he had been caught in a vice of his own body's making—himself struck rigid by his own climax, it momentarily prevented him from speaking. Anna-Stina's body had arched upward against him. One final time she thrust herself upward and then collapsed.

Carl had been staring down in amazement at her flushed face.

"Anna-Stina, are you well?" he said, concerned that he had brought her harm.

"Have I harmed you?"

Although she heard him, she was unable to immediately respond. With eyes closed she could only smile and shake her head vigorously; she patted his shoulder in further encouragement.

Carl had taken the weight of his body from her, lying to one side with one leg across her thigh. He was waiting for her to speak first. Though his own breathing had calmed, Anna-Stina's chest still heaved. Carl watched her heart hammering against her bare chest as he lay beside her, staring, marveled by her naked beauty. One of her hands lay on her abdomen, just below her navel—the other she had flung back and over her forehead, partially shielding her eyes from the bright sky.

Carl stared at her magnificent breasts, each quivering slightly with each beat of her heart. Leaning on one elbow, it was the first time he had seen a woman naked, other than a nursing mother's partially uncovered breast. What beauty her body possessed. Her long, lithe legs and flat stomach where a marvel; she was all curves, rounds and shapes, each more beautiful than the next. Her nakedness no longer made him withdraw in shame, nor was he any longer ashamed by his own uncovered body. It and curiosity drew him closer. He wanted to take her all in, from the top of her head to her muddy feet.

"If this were not sin," he said aloud, suddenly breaking the silence around them, "I would believe God had touched us, Anna-Stina."

She smiled up at him.

"I can not believe He didn't touch us Carl—and that we are not damned for it, either. We have only participated before marriage. Many couples do it," she said laughing, "...and after marriage it is not considered a sin. That is when the babies come short. Didn't you know that?" she said, reaching up and touching his cheek tenderly. She had opened her eyes earlier and noticed that Carl was staring at her, down there. Circling his neck with the hand, she pulled his head onto her chest and smiled up at the clouds.

He lay still for a moment, one hand cupping her breast.

"There are noises coming from inside you, Anna-Stina."

She tilted her head up, kissing the side of his head. He lifted and turned his head to smile at her. Reaching up she pulled his mouth down on hers, kissing him long and hard. After a few moments of touching Anna-Stina, Carl became aroused again and began to mount her.

"Here...Carl...," Anna-Stina's passion had also blossomed. This time she attempted to control his spasmodic movements as he slid atop her, settling between her parted legs once more. But unschooled in the intimacies of lovemaking, as they both were, Carl was beyond control, it seemed. In a fit of part passion—partly pain, she abandoned her restraint completely and flinging her arms around his shoulders, began to meet his thrusts—again and again.

Their bodies came together with such force; the swampy ground quaked around the edge of the pool. They finally reached a mutual pinnacle—both moaning and shouting in abandonment, such that Anna-Stina's grazing cows, far up the hill, raised their heads in wonder at the strange sound from the voice they new to be their mistress. Butternose's bell clanked when her head came up and she stared intently in the direction of the sounds, recognizing Anna-Stina. Sniffing the air, the animal lowered her head, snorted, giving her sharp horns a violent shake and as her bell clanked, she let go a long bellow, drowning the sound of the lover's passion.

CHAPTER 15

A Welcome Gift

In my dream I heard an automobile passing—I could hear it, but I didn't want to wake up. The strange dream seemed reluctant to leave my sleep-dulled thoughts. I'd heard the car even before I opened my eyes, wanting in vain to return to the dream— willing it…the car, morning, daylight…all to go away. But it was useless; I was awake for the day, having fallen asleep the previous evening, while reading my notes from Karolina. They'd slipped from the bed, sometime during the night and lay strewn on the floorboards.

Trying to organize my thoughts, I listened to the sound of the community going about its' day. I slowly came to consciousness, remembering the evening with Anna and thinking about the day we were to have; it was Saturday. Anna and I had a very late night. Arriving at my room after leaving her house, it was half-past one. I'd collapsed into a wonderfully, peaceful sleep somewhere in the midst of Karolina's story. Then that dream intruded…and what a dream.

While shaving I felt sexually aroused, just thinking about it. I simply couldn't purge the scene of Anna-Stina swimming naked in the spring, from my thoughts. I couldn't recall when I'd ever had such a sexually explicit dream; certainly not since adolescence. Was this a sign of middle age, or worse, old age, I wondered, chuckling to myself?

Last evening, Anna had finally managed to get her funny-bone under control. During the ride home she even apologized for making me the butt of her minor flirtation with the *maitre'd*. I really didn't mind, once I'd understood it and told her that and it had certainly lightened the remainder of the evening—although at the time it wasn't that funny. I could already foresee difficulty with my seeming ability to keep up with her bizarre sense of humor.

She'd certainly bested me, probably without intending to; she'd just sort of rolled with the opportunity, I think. Of course, I kidded her that she'd had a head start—that was why she'd succeeded, especially since I hadn't even known the game was running. But I warned her to watch out...I might yet get even. I felt comfortable with the idea that she could feel that secure around me, already—to pull off such a silly stunt.

"Royal family," she'd chuckled and then tickled me to show me she was still joking, but that I'd better watch myself—I wasn't going to get away with this one. I'd liked her touching me that way, too. She was a warm person and she did that a lot—touching...a hand on my arm, touching my shoulder in the car to emphasize a point and then finally, tickling me. A childish little habit and I loved it, especially when I smelled her hot breath coming so close to me.

Anna was truly a woman to be reckoned with, I'd decided, by the time I left her at her house last evening, or rather, this morning. I was unaccustomed to being with women of her intellect. Many American women were not so open—accustomed to speaking so directly. They seemed to either shout, or plied their wiles—having to get their way by other means, up until that time: trickery, deception, special favors—even tears, usually through no fault of their own. I'd laid it down to the female species, possibly mistakenly and maybe a little unfairly, but with Anna...it wasn't the same: she was extremely bright.

Anna had just gone and done it. No apologies, no forgiveness—forthright and honest—but brutal to the unaccustomed, American male ego.

After a late breakfast I charged through the parking lot and entered the wing somewhat tardy and still a little tired. Karolina sat in the chair beside her bed, her legs propped up on an adjacent chair, reading a newspaper. I crept up behind her and stepped around the curtain, leaned over and gave her a kiss on top of her head.

"What was that for...?" she asked, surprised and smiling broadly, folding her paper as I took a chair.

"Oh—nothing special. I just felt like it. I thought you deserved it."

"You must have had a pretty good evening with Dr. Olsson."

"It was…OK, now you mention it; she's nice…fun." Karolina looked at me and smiled but I didn't say anything further. Women's intuition, I thought. Karolina was definitely improving; I'd noticed she seemed to have little difficulty holding the newspaper, holding both arms outstretched. She'd been keeping up well with the physical therapy—lucky lady, I thought to myself, to survive a stroke without any lasting damage, other than a little slowness with one foot. Anna had said that the slight dragging of her foot would also disappear as Karolina's therapy progressed.

Lucky me, I thought. There was still so much to learn about the old family. And also lucky me, thinking of Anna and our evening's dinner and drive home, followed by coffee and cognac for a nightcap. That's when I kissed her, or she kissed me, I still don't remember which. I certainly started it—still a little upset with her…joke, but she definitely finished it as we were both soon breathing quite heavily and hadn't even drunk all our brandy.

Breaking into my thoughts and my second cup of coffee, Karolina asked: "So…how was your evening…aren't you going to tell me about it?"

"OK, I guess…and no, it's none of your business."

"Ouch," she replied giggling. "I must have touched on something close to home. You say only OK, but I surmise there was more, or you wouldn't be so…so testy," she replied, smiling having taken no offense. "I should have thought it would be wonderful to be out with Dr. Anna and a good deal of fun, too?"

A little annoyed, I got up again, stepped over and sat down on her chair's arm and took her hand.

"It was, Karolina, but…," I glanced around the curtain just in case Anna was near, "…don't you tell her Karolina, but…Anna got the best of me, last evening."

"Got the best of you…how, what ever do you mean?"

"*Shusssh*…yes, I was…acting too…too prim and proper—her words; she sort of put me in my place, but in a nice way, I guess, in retrospect."

"Prim and proper? My, that certainly doesn't sound very promising. Should I speak with her—tell her to mind her manners, as it were?"

"Oh no…of course not, Karolina; don't you say a word now, promise? I have to be able to hold my own with her, or I'm no one…can't you see?"

"Oh…" she sighed, "…men!" But she winked at me. "Where did you take her?"

I returned to my own chair. "We went to the restaurant across the lake from the city and enjoyed some…," I had to recall the menu again, "…some well prepared fish and moose with some good wine."

"Oh—that sounds lovely—certainly better than the food they serve here. Did Dr. Olsson enjoy the evening also?"

"Yes…and at my expense, too, as I said."

"I—I don't understand. You mean…you paid for the meal; is that not normal for the man?"

"Yes…no! It's just a private joke," I interrupted her. "Yes and both of us had a splendid time, really."

I thought I'd change the subject from the date with Anna. "Maybe you would like to go out some afternoon when you are feeling stronger, Karolina, just you and me? I'd like to take you to that restaurant when you're feeling stronger—we could make it a working lunch—continue the interview, if you felt like talking and I can bring my notebook."

"Yes, that sounds pleasant. I can't tell you when I was last away for a decent meal. Sometimes it's easier to just settle into a routine. You call it a rut, I believe; we say *slentrain* in Swedish—or did you know that?"

"No, I didn't."

"Well, I think I would like to try it—leaving my *slentrain*," she said, chuckling to herself, "So Dr. Olsson enjoyed herself—I don't know whether she goes out very much, but I don't believe she has many friends?"

"Really, why do you say that?"

"Oh, I don't know—just a feeling. Sometimes, she seems so—so…lonesome…and I've heard the staff talking."

"Do you think so? Well, she seemed to enjoy herself last evening—least-wise, she said she did." I couldn't help smiling, waiting to see whether Karolina would take up the role of matchmaker I'd glimpsed yesterday. But she only smiled pleasantly. I thought I'd tempt her natural, female inclination:

"We went to her house for coffee and cognac, afterwards," I said, feeding Karolina tidbits.

"Oooh...the perfect way to top off an evening. I don't think I could enjoy cognac any more, though; it would probably make me silly or sleepy...but a little wine with dinner—now that—that might be quite nice."

She wasn't going to meddle, it appeared. I was surprised and pleased, I must say. I was ready to rebuff any really probing questions about my evening, but Karolina remained circumspect.

"Let's ask Dr. Olsson," she said, suddenly looking up and smiling.

"Hello, you two." Anna approached carefully carrying a tray of coffee and smiling brilliantly. "Ask me about what?"

"Karolina wants you to begin serving wine with the meals here," I kidded.

"I do not!" she responded, slapping at our hand lightly. "We were talking about lunch someday and maybe, some wine when I get out of here."

"Would a glass of wine hurt Karolina if we go for lunch, after she's feeling better?"

"I should think not, but don't let her drive after," the wry smile crept into the corners of her mouth.

"Well, I can see you're still primed for humor...from last night," I said, taking the tray from her and starting to set up the three cups.

"I thought you might not make it here so early Alex, so I went after the coffee for us. Just before you arrived, Alex, we were having a nice chat without you."

"Oh...Karolina didn't say you'd been...already." I glanced down, realizing I'd been bested again. I didn't know what to say for a moment, taken aback. So, she and Karolina had been conniving; not matchmaking, my eye.

"I had a couple of things to do before we went on our picnic today, so I thought I'd get going early."

"Well, so did I. Anna and I are going to the beach and I didn't have a swimming suit. I had to wait until the shops opened to pick one up...that's why I was late."

"Yes, I also," Anna said, "and for this afternoon—snacks and *korv*[90] and we're going to cook them over a fire, Karolina, American style."

She made a wry face, obviously not the charred wiener type. "I'd prefer your fish and moose that you mentioned Alex...and wine."

We chuckled at that.

"But no matter if you want to eat burned *korv*. Dr. Olsson was telling me about your evening. We've also been discussing what to take on your outing this afternoon. If I was feeling better, I would try to butt into your holiday party, Dr. Olsson...invite myself along. However, as it is," she said stretching languidly, "I'll gladly rest in the sun, instead."

"And welcome you would be, too, Karolina," Anna responded. "But...I believe you need another week or two, resting here. Then, we shall see."

"See...about what," Karolina sort of snapped.

"About the wine, Anna answered."

"Oh...I see. I'm not concerned about the wine," Karolina said, laughing, "but I will take the lunch date," she said smiling over to me," as soon as I'm able...and permitted."

"You're on...as soon as Dr. Olsson gives the word." Anna began pouring coffee for three; Karolina broke up some of the almond Danish pastries Anna had brought and we enjoyed the coffee, rolls and small talk.

Finally, Anna sighed and got up. "I must do some paperwork if we are to have the rest of the day...I'll pick you up at one o'clock," she said, putting a hand on each of our shoulders.

"No, I'll pick you up."

"No...I insist. It's only fair that we share the driving and the food expense."

I was to bring the wine and she the food. We watched as she disappeared with her long-legged stride.

"She is such a fun person," Karolina said, "and strange, is it not...she's never married?"

I searched her face for some sign of what she was thinking, but saw only her matronly smile. I didn't reply, thinking it was best left that way, but I suspected the hint that lay behind the comment.

"So...how was your evening Karolina? All we've done is talk about my evening. Did you rest well?"

"Oh, I was fine—boring...but about the time I realized how boring it was, I was ready to go to sleep. This..." she frowned, massaging her left arm, "...this affliction has taken my strength—I can tell. Dr. Olsson says in a few more days I should have it back and will be ready to go home."

"Well, that's welcome news."

She sat quietly for a bit, rather pensive. My mind, too, was elsewhere as I assembled my notes. I was still a little tired from the night before and couldn't forget the dream. Seeing Anna this morning, for some reason, renewed the sexual arousal. Karolina interrupted my amorous reflections.

"You know, before you came, I was thinking about how things really began with my mother and father. I'm not really certain when they first met...let alone fell in love. Mother once told me father was mad about her from the beginning, but of course he had to deal with his family's disapproval. Father's aunt, my great aunt Maria Andrietta Fröman died in 1853, in the fall. This was while mother was a *vallkulla* in the summers, living at Källeborg—in Nås, during the winters...you know Nås—south of Järna...down the river about ten kilometers?"

I nodded.

"Well, after that, mother said the widowed pastor—she was keeping house for him, during the winters, then—was in such a state of grief, he didn't pay much attention to what was happening around him. Mother said Father came to Källeborg, very often that winter. That is when they tried to get married the first time."

This time, Anna-Stina was quite certain. She recognized the signs nearly immediately, remembering what she'd felt like with Augusta. She knew she was pregnant from the first month. Her body and she were very close; between being late with her monthly cycle, to the immediate swelling of her breasts and the beginning of the daily sickness. The next time Carl came to Källeborg, she told him she was pregnant with his child. She did not suggest marriage. He could have denied it. But to credit this father, he put his arms around her and thanked her and God, for giving him a child.

"It's what I have wanted for a long time," he said, holding her face between his hands. "Now, they can not deny us; I will go to see Pastor Johansson this evening and plead our case before him. I don't believe he will discourage our marriage. I believe he'll even ally with us to help persuade mother of the senselessness of her continued interference."

Anna-Stina listened, appreciating Carl's devotion to her. She was secretly thankful their naked swim hadn't taken the opposite turn. But she doubted both the willingness of the minister, or an alliance with Carl's mother. There would be no easy approval in the matter and she told Carl so. She didn't want to wed him this way, as much as she wanted to wed him. After all, there was still her revenge against the Pastor…and his confession, yet to be made, something she hadn't yet told Carl about.

"Carl, I believe we should look elsewhere for allies. I really doubt Pastor Johansson will help us. I believe we must seek stronger affiliations—someone who can convince your parents and persuade the minister. Didn't you tell me once, you have the acquaintance of one of the bishops in Stockholm, or Gothenburg?"

He thought for a moment. "No, I have no associations there, but that's a good idea, nonetheless. There is Uncle Johan; he's well connected there, but I'm certain he would side with mother against us." He looked alarmed: "Anna-Stina, we can not let them come between us…we now have our child to consider; it must have a father."

She put her arms around his neck. He smiled down at her, a gentle, kindly smile. She rose up on her toes and kissed him, long and hard for that reassurance. "You don't know how much your commitment means to me, Carl. There are many in your station…many who would put their tail between their legs after what I just told you—and flee like a cowardly dog. But you—you kiss me and call a blessing on us…how fortunate I am."

"Nej—I'm the fortunate one," and he kissed her again.

Later the same month, Carl had been calling at the old minister's again. That afternoon, the house was quiet and already dark. Anna-Stina rolled over on her side. They were in her room at the rectory, crowded into her little bed. In order to face Carl in the dim light of the March afternoon she had to lie on her side near the edge, her head propped on one elbow. Carl had ridden down from Järna and was tired. They'd immediately made love and he'd fallen asleep. She had longed for him since their last meeting. It had only been three weeks since she told him of the coming child. Since then, he'd tried to come to her at every opportunity. The news of his fatherhood only encouraged him. What a man I have, she thought.

She watched his facial profile in the flickering candlelight. She welcomed the warmth of the bed, even though it was still afternoon.

The fires must be dying in the fireplace below, she thought. I must rise soon. The old parson would need nourishment and want company again, sitting in his library, reading in the light of a single lamp. He will soon come looking for me if he becomes too hungry— or worried. She'd often watched the old man as they sat together after the evening meals, wondering whether he really saw the pages, or was merely lost in thought of the years past.

He'd confessed to being so lonely before she came; though Anna-Stina didn't say it, she thought, to the point of becoming a bit deranged. Sometimes he spoke as if Maria Andrietta—his late wife, were still alive. Once he had even told her to ignore his ramblings about the past and not think unkindly him, but that he sometimes pretended his wife was still alive since—for a little while anyway—it made the pain a little easier if he could think she was still there.

Anna-Stina came to realize Carl's visits were good medicine for the parson. Sometimes the pair would talk beside the fire for extended periods and the minister would completely forget his sadness, debating and joking with Carl. And the parson didn't even seem to realize the impropriety of Carl's visits, or he completely ignored the obviousness of the two of them. She didn't know which. He welcomed Carl each time and was as sorry as Anna-Stina to see him depart, later speaking of him often and with fondness.

During one of these conversations, he spoke to Anna-Stina about Carl finding a suitable partner: "Anna-Stina—do you not think Carl Fröman should get married soon?

Her heart began hammering in her throat. She wondered at first whether he was hinting about Carl's regular visits and at first she didn't know how to respond.

"I have not really thought about it Sir," she said, hoping he would be more explicit.

"I was thinking…when Carl was last here—married…he ought to be married. We should invite some of the eligible young ladies from the community here to Källeborg, to dine with us. Carl needs some urging…more exposure to young ladies, ladies of his class who would be eager, I should think, to marry a young man of his stature."

Her heart sank. I thought he was talking about us…Carl and me. What a fool I am to still believe I would ever be accepted by this family…a mere cow-woman from the *fäbod*.

"Anna-Stina? Are you listening? Why don't you help me think of some names? Do you know any young women who would be suitable for Carl?"

"No one in particular comes to mind, sir," she replied, trying to keep the emotion from sounding like a sting in her voice. "But I'll put my mind to the task and see what I can think of if you wish it, Sir."

"Please do…but do not reveal it to Carl the next time he comes to visit us," he chuckled, "or he may stop coming. I do so enjoy his visits. He is such an intelligent and charming young man. If Maria was only here…she would know just what to do and who to ask…ah, Maria," he sighed, already losing the thought.

She watched it recede somewhere out the window, a far away look already in his eye. Yes, Maria certainly would have, she thought and none of them would be an ironworker's daughter who smelled always of cows.

Carl was still asleep beside her. It was growing darker in the room. I must rise, she thought. The old man will be hungry. I can prepare the meal, if Carl is there to eat and talk with him. Carl's visits served more than one purpose, she thought, reaching beneath the covers toward the sleeping form to find him, soft and warm. Once more and then I will go to prepare the diner, she thought to herself, sliding closer across the cold linen toward the warmth of her lover.

"Carl, my love, wake up *kära du*…I have something for you dear one—and I have a promise to keep."

Pastor Johansson turned the horse cart from the Järna road, heading toward Skålbyn. He'd been planning how to get his way in this afternoon's confrontation. By the time he turned down the drive toward Frömansgården, he knew. He planned to confront Carl in the presence of his mother. He would challenge Carl about Anna-Stina's now very obvious pregnancy. Secretly, he seethed with animosity; imagine, Carl Fröman having the single thing he himself desired most. The pastor did not live well with this disturbing emotion. Anna-Stina Malmberg, defying the law of God and the church—and even me, he thought. What sin. If only—if only I could get to her…the inner her and banish the evil which certainly must possess her. Imagine…that she would lay with this—this farmer, Carl. Oh…he thought…*ohhhhh*. The idea of that dolt having her and why would he even want a woman like her, the daughter of a smith and a lowly *vallkulla*, hardly fit for the animals. They never had been anyone and never would be.

She could, however, be the wife of a vicar one day, if she'd only see the reason of the argument. Elevation of her families' status, should she marry me, was permissible; but for a Fröman to marry down to that level was unthinkable. He was going to suggest this in rather strong terms to *Fru* Fröman, this very afternoon.

He tied the horse to an apple tree in the yard beside the barn. The children of one of the hired men had been running about but now stopped, for the moment in deference to the tall man in black, frightened, least he should chide them in his thundering church voice. They waited for him to knock and enter the house, before deciding to go to the other side of the barn to continue their play.

Pastor Johansson noticed their dirty condition. It was time he touched on the subject of cleanliness again, in the Sunday service and its' relationship to Godliness. In a future sermon, he thought, especially among the coming generation...I must bring it up. He approached the door of the red log structure and lifted the iron knocker.

The *piga* Ulrika opened the door and quickly curtsied in difference to the minister.

"*God morgon* pastor Johansson," she said stepping aside to let him enter first. He remembered her from his last call at Frömansgården. He didn't realize how...well, she'd grown up. He noted the swelling of her new breasts beneath the hand-me-down shift. Even the apron didn't confine their newfound life and freedom. Time to find an older sister's dress he thought, or burst the seams of that one, tempting some young man to roll with her in the barn. And then there we would go again. These thoughts distracted him and he had an immediate passion to take her aside and chastise her...heal her, as he followed her through the house and into the parlor. His eyes hardly left the swaying, round hips as she left the room to call her mistress.

The little Jezebel—she knows I'm watching, too...how can they do this—all of them? Continuously touting their wares...is it no wonder we have so many *oäktabarn* in the parish? The need for another sermon was noted as he took a seat, glanced around the room, taking inventory since the last time he was there.

The stone fireplace was in the old style: like in a primitive *fäbodstugo*—possibly this was once one, he thought, wondering at the age of the community. The heavy, smooth fieldstones were cleft in seemingly random shapes, but were arranged so as to need little mortar; despite their odd shape, they fit together well and stretched up through the ceiling to the second story and beyond.

A thick, hand-wrought, iron rectangle sat atop the hearth. Something—pastry, probably, was raising beneath a striped linen towel. He verified this, lifting one corner with the end of his stick; bulging rolls, no doubt secreting an extravagance of newly-churned butter between their rolled layers...beckoning him.

Choosing a small settee, he sat down, but then, remembering the urchins, he promptly turned around and peered through red geraniums in one of the windows. Looking toward where his cart was tied, he scanned the yard. They have left it alone, have they, he thought, well...they had better have, "...they had better," he said aloud, turning back to face the door.

Arranging his cloak and stick on the settee beside him, he leaned back, surveying the room's furnishings. A tall blue clock in the corner matched a blue-painted cupboard, bearing the date 1765. An antique, he thought and it was groaning with glassware, silver and some pewter plate, along with assorted candelabra. No doubt the drawers were equally filled with sterling tableware.

"Hummm..." he mused. This kind of wealth should be giving more to The Church, he thought, again making a mental note to urge the Fröman family to increase their share—*Fru* Fröman, that was.

He hoped the elder Fröman, who made him nervous, would not be at home. He seldom was. As a merchant-farmer, he was away, traveling for something or other...about the farm, the iron works at Snöån or, simply making business and more money, from the looks of it. Pastor Johansson had heard rumors of the senior Fröman's adventures in other communities. Best not to think of them, he thought. What he does away from the parish is his business—and God's, he thought in justification, reluctant to confront the powerful man with his rumored improprieties. The Fröman family was one of the largest contributors to the church, as it was and they fed most of the communities' poor. People were starving all over Sweden; but in Järna, they were merely going hungry, gaunt and dirty, he thought, remembering the children outside.

Just that morning, the old pastor had given his blessing to the latest emigrant departures. They would soon be in a train of carts, headed to Kristiana, in Norway and then by ship to the port of Hull in *Stårbrittannien*[91], for the voyage to *Amerika*. Many were selling everything to emigrate. They had to have the Church's approval to depart the parish; pastor Johansson did not approve the free nature of the old minister's grants, giving away the church's future income. In order to help the old man, that very day, he himself had reluctantly taken down the massive book from its' cupboard and stricken the three families' names from the church rolls—*emigrerade*, he wrote. Gone forever, he thought…good riddance. The parish is not growing, despite the number of children being born. Will this emigration never cease—until we have no more souls to save, he wondered? Pity we cannot send away the evil ones…instead of those who are going. This thought made him consider what his duties would be without parishioners. He never once considered following them; to tend their spiritual needs there—in *Amerika*, would surely have its' share of sin redemption, would it not?

Considering the unpleasantness which would no doubt accompany an adventure of this type, he immediately discarded it as a fool's missionary.

His stomach rolled over again at the thought of butter dripping from one of the lightly browned buns, yet to be baked. He'd wash them down with several cups of good coffee, which only the Fröman's could afford in abundance. He stood, walking over to check the progress of the pastries; they would have coffee with these…surely? As he bent to raise one corner of the towel, *Fru* Fröman entered.

"Pastor Johansson…oh, what a pleasant surprise to see you."

He spun around and straightened as *Fru* Fröman swept up to him, removing a long, linen work apron as she came to shake his outstretched hand.

"When Ulrika said you had come to call, I was so surprised…and pleased. And just in time to enjoy some small *bulle med kaffe*. They should be baked in less than an hour. Can you stay…surely?"

"Well, I shouldn't stay—you know, I have so many calls to make. With all the hunger about, there are many who need…comfort," his eyes went to the linen coverlet on the buns.

"Oh, please stay a little while, Pastor. I'm alone today, except for
Ulrika. My husband is away again for some of his business dealings
and Carl has gone to Nås to see old pastor Fröman. I wonder that
you didn't meet him on the road? He has not been well since the
death of my sister in law, Maria Andrietta. I believe he finds Carl a
comfort in his loneliness. And of course, he continues to help us
groom Carl for the calling, I am sure, but it is a pity—I fear it is
hopeless."

He opened his mouth to speak, but she interrupted him again.
"We lose not our hope, Pastor, though the chances be sometimes
thought slim...no?

"That is excellent, *Fru* Fröman...that you should bring this up—
exactly the subject I wished to address with you today. I had however,
hoped that your husband and Carl could be here since this matter
concerns him also...somewhat. Possibly, I can remain long enough to
have our discussion and enjoy some of your ever-wonderful
hospitality."

"Oh, that's wonderful...shall we sit down Pastor?"

They crossed to the settee and the minister removed his cloak
and stick, placing them on the floor and remained standing, waiting
until his hostess had seated herself. He looked at the ceiling as if to
ask God's grace in composing what he would now proffer.

"You are exactly correct about Carl's gifts..." he began, but
thinking about the gift of Anna-Stina.

"Yes, I still believe there remains hope for Carl to yet answer the
call. He's such a kind and thoughtful son, you know; he will make
such a grand but humble servant of the Lord's work."

The pastor smiled and nodded as he finally sat down.

"What was it in particular you wished to discuss, pastor?" she
asked, turning in the seat as her companion arranged his coat.

"It is a matter of some delicacy, *Fru* Fröman. Can you be assured
we will have complete privacy?"

"Ulrika is here, but I can send her away for a while. If you can
just wait one moment, I will dispatch her upon an errand that will
keep her away for an hour or so."

He nodded and she left him alone in the room again to find and
instruct the servant on some task. He stood again, turned and
walked to the window and peered through the sparkling glass and into

the yard. The skinny children were piling small snow mounds on the fenders of his cart and running around the horse. Little urchins, he thought. Why don't they go make their mischief elsewhere.

He heard a door close somewhere in the house and then the servant girl, Ulrika, emerged from the back door and stepped into the yard, tying her wool scarf beneath her chin as she hastened to avoid the nearly accurate, snowy missiles from the young boys. But she was smiling. After they exhausted their ammunition in vain, she turned toward the children and smiling, motioned for them to approach. The pastor leaned closer and saw her remove a large folded napkin from beneath her clothing, squat before them and unfold it on her lap. They gathered round, leaning forward in anticipation. Ulrika handed round something to them—the pastor couldn't tell what and they began to eat whatever it was. She quickly gathered up the napkin, wet the end of her finger, dabbed the open napkin and then licked her finger, before finally folding it into her apron pocket, standing up and hurrying down the road.

The children walked in the other direction, still eating something…whatever it was she had taken it from the house. She has given them some buns, he thought, angry at the waste. Thief! Pastor Johansson said under his breath: sneaking thief, stealing from the house that employs you—the hand that feeds you! I must speak to that girl after Sunday service and ask her to call on me for a rebuke, he thought, making another mental note. The parlor door closed.

"There— I have sent Ulrika on an errand to Ilbacken. It will take her a while," Carl's mother said, breathlessly, coming back into the room. "And I have prepared a little something for us to nibble on while the *kaffe* is cooking. There was plenty of this dried fruit bread. I felt Ulrika needed something to sustain herself on her walk there, so I let her have some slices to take along…least she feel weak on the return."

The pastor's mouth opened and he glanced toward the window, but said nothing.

"Now—Pastor Johansson—what was it you wished to discuss with me." Carl's mother settled herself opposite him and offered him some heavily buttered bread from the small, silver tray she'd brought.

Taking a large slice from the middle, the pastor cleared his throat and began.

"Anna-Stina Malmberg has been caring for your brother in law, our dear friend and my old associate, Pastor Fröman, since his wife passed to God."

"Yes, I can not understand why they—he keeps her on, either, other than she is the best *vallkulla* that has been around, in anyone's memory, I am told."

"Yes, I have heard that rumor also, although I believe it is somewhat pretentious, personally. I find the girl adequate in many ways and all together coarse in others; she appears to be a hard worker—but in need of something…more, at this time in her life."

"Well, I hadn't really thought that much about her. There are so many families on the farms here around Frömansgården that I had enough to worry about without thinking about a servant girl down in Nås. What, exactly did you have in mind, Pastor Johansson?"

"Anna-Stina Malmberg is with child, again," he said quietly.

"*Vad säger du…!*" she said, "…that girl? Do you know who the father of this one is, Pastor?" At this she slapped her hand on her lap quickly. "It could certainly not be Pastor—my brother in law, there in Källeborg, could it? Certainly—he is so old?" Her voice trailed off, expectantly, looking at him for reassurance.

The young pastor took another slice of bread from the tray between them, before he answered, calculating his time to make it most effective.

"I believe the father to be your son and my very dear friend, Carl."

The shock in her face was as if someone had smitten her with an ax.

"What!" she exclaimed, leaping to her feet as best she could, nearly spilling the tray of bread, which the pastor barely saved from falling, butter-side, on the floor.

"Carl—my Carl! He would not do…how could he? Thinking of…if he…?" She was shocked and placed a hand on the pastor's arm.

"I believe if we confront him, as God is his witness, he will speak up and give us the truth, *Fru* Fröman."

You can certainly expect I shall confront him, Minister, immediately upon his return—why…."

"However—madam, bad as that news is, that is not the immediate problem. Unfortunately, I believe Carl also wishes to marry the Malmberg girl…marry her and bring her home—here…to live as his bride and wife…one who would soon be mistress to all in your house."

"Well…he certainly will not…how could he even think of such a thing. The servants? She would be little better than a servant."

Pastor Johansson stood up beside her, shaking his head slowly and looking very sad. Then, Fru Fröman seemed to rise up in anger, becoming agitated again.

"Pastor, are you most certain of your facts in this matter? Are you aware of whom you are accusing of these sins?" she exclaimed, now hurt and taking his revelations personally. Her anger began to replace her wish for sympathy and he was the messenger she might be about to shoot.

"Madame, please…*Fru* Fröman, how could I be absolutely certain? But I am not, completely, of course. Though I believe there is little doubt of the truth. Anna-Stina Malmberg is with someone's child and I believe it truly to be your son's. Knowing Carl, I am certain he will not only accept responsibility, but will actually acknowledge the child, if he is made to do so."

"Why on earth would anyone try to make him acknowledge the child Pastor?"

"The mother would—certainly, hoping to have him as her husband, or, lacking that, at worst, a large sum of money in exchange…"

She interrupted him: "Marriage? To that…Anna-Stina Malmberg? Why, it is out of the question. If Carl is the father, whom I highly doubt, we will certainly make appropriate amends to her, but marriage…absolutely unthinkable."

"I have the impression your son wishes to wed the woman, *Fru* Fröman—that both of them probably desire it."

"Carl…how could he? What has gotten into the boy? We shall certainly see about that."

With that outburst, she broke down in tears of anger and shame. "Oh Pastor Johansson, what shall we do? Mothers try so earnestly to bring up their sons to be kind, loving—decent…and then along comes a—woman…oh, I can not abide the thought of her in the family—after this. I should simply die—just die. And besides, what would people think?"

"I have had some sufficient time to ply this matter with thought, *Fru* Fröman," he responded wisely. "Firstly, I think your son need not even be accused, thus no embarrassment need come to the family.

We can threaten her to make her leave of her own will—accuse no one. And make her take herself and the unborn child with her, or else—"

"What sort of or else, Pastor Johansson?"

"I believe that since this is the woman's second *oäkta* child, I can persuade the bishop, with you and your husband's help, to petition the court to have the child removed from her custody. Since she is obviously an unfit person and about to be an unfit mother...again— forgetting not, this is the second brat. Presented with this petition, how can she remain among us?" It seemed to be too much for *Fru* Fröman.

"Oh Pastor...I find this to be, to be overwhelming," she held both hands to her head. "I believe I would rather be alone, if you don't mind, to consider the matter. It has come as a surprise, you see." She stood up. "This is all too much for me to comprehend. I feel—feel a headache coming on. Would you mind—seeing yourself out? I fear, I must go upstairs and lie down. Now—where is that girl Ulrika when she is needed?

A surprised Pastor Johansson bid adieu to *Fru* Fröman, escorting her from the room. As they passed through the door, he cast a backward glance at the fireplace silently mourning the pan of *bullar* that remained unbaked on the hearth. Sighing quietly to himself, he donned his cloak.

In the cart again, where the driveway met the road to Järna, the horse turned around the circular graveled drive and broke into a trot, recognizing the homeward journey and a warm stall.

During the journey, the pastor regretted missing the *kaffe*—the delicious kaffe. Angry at his own impetuosity, he wished now he'd waited to broach the subject of Anna-Stina until after the maid had served the food. Ah, one must pay, he thought, for the trials of being a spiritual guide to the community. I will not make that mistake again, he thought. The unbaked rolls haunted his thoughts during the hour's drive to his Järna parsonage, while most of the timber dwellings he passed, had little or no gruel for their children's many mouths. I shall summon Anna-Stina first he thought to himself, his plan already made.

CHAPTER 16
The Picnic

We stopped her narrative just before lunch. I could see that Karolina was still willing, certainly able to continue, but I decided to break it off, but over her protest.

"Yes, I can see you are still strong Karolina and that's why we should stop for the day. If we end before you tire, you'll gain your strength even faster and that's our ultimate goal."

"Oh, I suppose you are correct. A little nap wouldn't hurt anything anyway," she said stretching. "The evening will be boring though. Maybe I can find someone to play cards with."

"That's the spirit. You know this is Anna's weekend off? I promised to occupy her whole weekend, starting with dinner last night, a picnic this afternoon. Tonight and tomorrow, well…we'll see what that brings. She only has a free weekend once every month, she said. I personally think it ridiculous, for the facility director; but anyway, I want to give her a good time."

"Off with you, then…get going. If you two get bored, come by, I'll beat you both in cards, or something. These old people will be no sort of challenge—and they go to bed so early."

Earlier that morning I'd been rushed in order to make my purchases: some bathing trunks and a bottle of wine, which I promised Anna I would pick up…something light. She said she would bring cheese, bread, some vegetables and whatever else she could find. So I headed for her house as soon as I left the hospital.

"Hi…" Anna greeted me as I jumped from my car, dancing down her steps with a picnic basket. She must have been watching for me from her window.

"Hello...."

"I didn't get a chance to ask you this morning...did you wake up early, too?"

I rushed to help her but she beat me to the car door.

"Oh yes," I said opening the door. We sparred a little about who would drive, before I won. She claimed it would be easier if she did, since she knew the way. I won, claiming I should, since it was my car.

"Here—let me help," she said from her side of the seat, leaning close and thrusting a small bundle into the back seat and settling beside me.

"I just wondered..." she teased, "...it was pretty late when you left last night. We could just stay here if you'd like—go into the back garden and have our picnic there?"

"Yeah...and have all your neighbors watching, I suppose?"

"Well, that's true...they'd find it most interesting, since I don't have too many men calling on me."

She'd turned around again and was rummaging through the paper wrappings in the back seat. In the mirror, I saw she was reading the wine label. Her cute rump was bobbing beside me.

"At least none that buy such great wines."

I had started the car and began to pull away. Hanging on, she turned and held open the paper parcel containing my new swimming suit.

Settling into the seat again: "Hey, look at this," she held out the little blue bathing suit between her thumbs and forefingers.

"Pretty sexy—yes?"

"It was the only one they had that fit me—well, that I thought I could wear. Some of them were really small." Skimpy was what I meant. The shopkeeper had difficulty finding any I considered my size. She took nearly ten minutes to come up with the box of them and they were all mixed up, size-wise. I almost had the impression she wondered what I was going to do with it, she'd acted so disinterested."

"That's because nowadays, many Swedes don't wear any clothes at all at the seashore, or lake, especially if it's remote...like this one will be," she added, mischievously. "Bathing with family or friends, one doesn't need a suit—we're brought up to believe that, now. Likewise, if there are strangers around, one doesn't know them...so it doesn't matter anyway."

I glanced toward her, trying not to show my American astonishment.

"Do I shock you?" she asked, laughing. "I do believe you're blushing, Alex."

She must have seen my jaw drop. "No—it's not that," I protested lamely, though it was. "I knew Swedes were pretty liberal—compared to Americans, but for a moment today, as I was digging through the shopkeeper's box of little suits, I thought the clerk was going to just give up on me and the suits—just let me to go without; honestly, I did," I laughed at myself.

Anna smiled, sliding a little closer to the middle of the seat.

"You Americans, you're so—so...naïve—is that the word—in English?"

"Not naïve...I think you are looking for—modest, maybe...or prudish? I told you my family helped organize a very conservative Swedish fundamentalist church in Dalarna, before they emigrated— were urged to emigrate. They helped contribute to that American Puritanical outlook."

"Modest, I have heard...proo—dish...I have not. And what is pur-i-tani-cal?" She had trouble pronouncing it. She'd turned sideways toward me; in her slacks, her legs appeared very long. She put her right leg up in the seat and her arm on the seat back, hugging her knee. Her hand was behind my shoulder on the seatback.

Careful, I thought...here you go again, Alex. She doesn't mean anything by it. It's just her way—naturally effusive and outgoing...the physician in her.

"Puritanical comes from the religion of some to the original English immigrants to America—Calvinists, named after—John Calvin, I believe. Some of the first anyway, who had strict religious and social behavior ideas...pure thoughts—ideas, thus, Puritans. A lot of it still lingers in America, today, especially in rural areas and in the southern part of America. Actually, Anna, the Swedes were right behind the Puritans—arriving in America around thirty-some years after the English, founding New Sweden—near New Jersey; in sixteen—sixteen something."

"Oh, I see," she said, smiling up at me—again with that impish expression. "And which one are you, pru—dish, or...pur—i—tan...I can't remember the rest of it?"

"I haven't decided yet," I joked. "Maybe some Swedish women will help me decide."

"*Oouuu*," she said rolling her eyes and touching my shoulder lightly.

"I'm afraid you will find none of those in this part of Sweden. You'll have to go to the north—back to Dalarna, during Midsommar when they raise the *majstång* and drink lots of *brännvin* and think about the old ways—the not so *proo-dish* old days. Those times of renewal of...well, some sort of pagan things that have lingered over the years, having to do with fertility. They still practice them up there...in the forest, you know." This she said with the eagerness of a schoolgirl answering her teacher.

"Sounds exciting; maybe I won't need to bring my bathing trunks—err...suit, if I go there."

"Definitely not," she laughed. "There are more naked bathers in Dalarna on a hot weekend day than there are mosquitoes."

"Where am I going anyway," I said, interrupting her, having come to a tee in the road? She'd been giving me hand directions and we were now beside a lake.

"Oh—turn to the left and let's go around to the other side. There'll be fewer people there and we're more likely to find a place with some space...to ourselves," she added almost as an afterthought.

I swung the car to the left and began weaving between walkers and bicyclists, slowly working our way around to the right along the shore road. I drove in silence for a few moments, concentrating on the unusual pedestrian traffic until it began to thin and the road narrowed to a track.

"Do you like to bicycle," Anna asked as we passed a couple cycling side by side slowly, holding hands as they pedaled?

"I haven't ridden one for years. But, yes, I'd enjoy that."

"We could sometimes take bikes for a day, if you'd like. I'm sure I can borrow one for you."

Anna certainly had something about her personality. I glanced at her profile, but she caught me, her look turning quizzical, tilting her head.

"What is it?" she said.

"Oh, nothing, Just thinking about the picnic. What did you bring to eat, anyway. Some of those herrings you were telling me about last night at dinner, the ones with the swollen lids? I thought I smelled fish."

"Are we celebrating something?" Again the devilish smile.

"I don't know—should we be?"

"Remember last night...I said we only eat *strömming* at special celebrations?"

"Yes, I guess you did."

"All right...so today, we have *lax*...salmon, to you—but still fish, nevertheless. Actually, Baltic *lax*...that has just been smoked. How dare you insult such a noble fish as the *lax*...calling it herring. If you weren't an American and didn't know better, it would be unforgivable," she laughed, playing with me again. "I was going to purchase *korv*...wieners."

"I can just see we will have to find an occasion to have *strömming* some time."

"She looked down at her hands, twiddling her fingers: "Remember, only at special celebrations," she said coyly.

I glanced sideways at her; she wasn't smiling.

"Like pregnancies."

She tapped me lightly behind the neck, leaning forward and showing her teeth in feigned indignation. "No, silly—more like...oh—like if you pass your exams, or, publish a book...something like that."

"Hummm...well, don't think I'll be graduating from anything anytime soon...hope that's all behind me. But, I might write a book. If Karolina and I can put it all together that is."

"Yes, I have been wondering how it is going...your book. That would be a suitable cause for celebration. Karolina told me that you were possibly working on a book, when you first began to visit. She said she was only planning to tell you a little of what you wanted to know and then turn you out on your ear, but it seems she has really gotten into her story, or gotten into you?" Here she looked at me with a very nice smile.

"I have to admit, I genuinely like the lady and enjoy Karolina's company. When we're together, I don't know where the time goes. Hours later, I leave after what seems like only an hour, with a notebook full of notes to transcribe. I was concerned at first that she would do just what you mentioned—turn me out. But we soon got lost in the story, both of us. We get along so well, too."

I thought about her lying ill the hospital and felt a little guilty. "We must make her well again—that's our job," I said turning to her and smiling.

"You now play nearly an equal role in that quarter, Alex" she replied, "I know she has grown fond of you, too. That's good therapy: the need to get well—wanting to, something to finish...something to keep on living for."

We hadn't seen any pedestrians or cyclists during the discussion and I must have driven over a mile. "Maybe you should give me a little hint of when we will be leaving the main road, Anna."

"It isn't too much further I don't believe." She glanced around as if acquiring her bearings. "I didn't pay proper attention while we talked, Alex. I'm sorry. But you did say you didn't wish to picnic at the regular public beach, so I chose this one; I often come here now that I've found it. Privacy is easy to achieve in Sweden, you just have to go a little further around the lake. Don't worry, I'll give you plenty of warning."

We drove on in silence for some time. As we approached a dense forest, Anna gave me directions to turn.

"There—to the left now, just past the two girls. Coming up a narrow road were two teen-aged girls wearing only the bottoms of their swimsuits. I was surprised but said nothing. I as I turned I noticed Anna glance at me, but she didn't comment either. I thought possibly that she was testing me. I'd heard about the Swedish lack of inhibition.

The road went to narrower gravel and after a few hundred feet, became sand. Now, really not much more than two tracks, it was smooth and level for the most part, just a dip here and there along the way. Eventually I pulled up where Anna indicated, in a grass clearing beside the lake.

There were two cars already parked there, seeming to have also just arrived. The adult members were sorting their picnic paraphernalia and some children were running around the cars. I assumed the two girls we'd seen were a part of that group. The picnickers stopped what they were doing for a moment as if interested to see whether they knew us. They stared curiously, smiled and then went back to what they were doing. I eased the Volvo up beside them, turning carefully to park on the side of the clearing.

They seemed to have come together—at least they seemed to know each other and were chatting back and forth. The men were joking with the women about how warm the water would be. Turning around in the seat, I fetched the wine I'd bought, got out and followed Anna 'round back to help her lift out the picnic basket. I put the bottle in her basket and waited to pick it up. Anna had a cloth bag of some sort with personal items she carried over.

The families had been helping the children undress for the beach. One of the men turned his back to us and dropped his trousers, flung them on top of the car and began rummaging in the car. I stole a glance at Anna, who was still browsing the contents of the basket; she didn't seem to be paying any attention. The wife of the other man came around the back of their car, talking to the man about his misplaced clothes. She wasn't wearing a blouse, or brassiere. The man backed out of the car to get out of her way, but instead, she thrust her head into the trunk and immediately came up with a pair of men's swimming trunks and waved it in his face with a knowing look. Shaking his head, the man slipped out of his underwear and stood, turning the trunks around, before finally pulling them on.

Still, my mouth was open, though I was aware Scandinavians weren't known for their modesty. Turning back to the car I watched as Anna stepped away from the other side of our car and slammed the door. She was also now bare above the waist; this time my eyes must have gone out on stalks. One of the men from the other party shouted something over my head, addressing Anna in quick Swedish. I couldn't catch what he'd said. She laughed and answered him, glancing toward me. The other woman said something else and they all laughed together. I heard Anna mention the word *Amerikansk* , meaning the American, but still didn't catch the subject.

I couldn't concentrate as the conversation changed rapidly. The second woman appeared around the car carrying a small child. Both of them were completely nude. I ducked down myself and began poking around for the parcel containing my swimsuit. Anna had wedged the package against the seat on her side to cushion my wine bottle.

It appeared time to join the Romans; but somehow, I couldn't bring myself to. Anna stuck her head in the back door window, opposite the seat from me.

Smiling, she said: "They were here yesterday and said it was beautiful on the beach, but the sand got really hot. So you'd better wear your shoes—or at least, bring them along. I've brought a blanket for us to spread out."

Still bare above the waist, she returned to rummaging in her bag, apparently looking for the top to her suit. As I was gathering my wits at last, Anna slid her slacks down and stepped out of them. I turned away—not meaning to be a prude, but it was automatic. Partially averting my eyes, I fumbled with my buttons, trying to take off my shirt. But unable to resist, as I unbuckled my belt and hesitantly stepped out of my trousers, I glancing over my shoulder. Anna had her head inside the car again, rummaging in her cloth beach bag. She eventually came up with a pair of cotton shorts, which she examined carefully before deftly stepping into them. Before she slammed the door again, Anna removed a towel from the bag, folded and placed her clothing back inside and drew the strings. She then flung the towel over her shoulder and with a quick smile toward me, began walking around to my side of the car.

"I'm ready." She held out both arms, palms upward, she said, "feel that sun...it will be a day to get sunburn, so we should be careful."

She stood there like a goddess for a few seconds—arms and face uplifted, eyes closed. I felt a tightening in my throat. Gulping—too late, I quickly slid down my underwear, rather clumsily as it turned out. My back was slightly averted as I stepped into my new bathing suit with a bit more agility. Anna stood waiting and watching me.

"You have nice thighs," she said, smiling. "Did you once do a bit of running, or gymnastics?"

"No, I didn't," I said, without turning, "but I've worked with some of our construction crews in the engineering firm. Now and again I join them on the job site and let them know the boss knows how to do that type of work, too. It's hard, physical work and the exercise is good for me. I enjoy the camaraderie, too keep up with the other side of life, so to speak." I prattled on to the point of babbling.

She waited me out. "About ready?" She smiled up at me pertly and completely unabashedly.

"Guess so," I answered, not looking at her, "lead the way."

She fell in step beside me, indicating the way with her folded towel. "Shall we follow them for now to see where they go?"

"Yeah, OK."

"Once they've settled, we can pick a spot beyond them. They were here first so they should have first choice."

"That the Swedish consideration?" I asked.

"I should think it would be common consideration, anywhere."

"You haven't been to Chicago...the beach on Lake Michigan," I retorted, chuckling.

We followed the family safari along the sandy shore of the lake as it wound alternately among the pines and hardwoods, emerging now and then closer to the shore. It surely was a beautiful day. There was hardly any wind. One of the men in front of us commented to their group that there would be thunder and lightning in the afternoon, if the heat persisted.

"*Åskvader...*," he said, turning and smiling toward us. Anna nodded. We passed several other bathing couples, singles and a family as we trudged along the sandy path. Where their cars were, or how they'd gotten there, I'd no idea. Presently, we emerged in a long stretch of the beach where there were few trees and lots of coarse sand, stretching quite a ways back from the shore. There were a few pieces of driftwood and we passed a place where someone had recently had a fire. Here, the other party stopped and began circling as if to remain there.

"Let's go a little further on," Anna said, "they'll stay here I believe. Will the children annoy you if we are too close?"

"No, I like kids, but I don't want them on the blanket with us."

A couple hundred yards further along the shore, Anna stopped beneath a lone pine tree. The low swept branches offered some promise of shade if we felt we needed it later.

"How's this?"

"Looks great," I said realizing I was looking at her breasts. She'd removed the towel draping her shoulders. I squatted and put down the basket, then sorted through the items, feigning curiosity. I didn't know where to look. Her body was beautiful and she didn't seem to be at all ashamed to be top-less. She didn't actually flaunt her nakedness; she just sort of...was undressed. We might as well have been in downtown Stockholm for the way she carried herself.

"Here, take one end," she said holding out an edge of the blanket she'd unfolded from the basket. We backed away, facing each other arms outspread.

"Shake it first," she said waiting for me and then giving her side a couple of vigorous shakes. "It's got sand in it from the last time."

We did and then bent together, letting the blanket settle onto the dry sand as the air cushion escaped from beneath it.

"There," she said stepping back and regarding the square's placement on the sand. I brought the basket and the wine over.

"I think I'll put the bottle in the water to keep it cooler—the sun...," I said.

"Good idea," without glancing my way. Anna had sat down, removed her clogs and leaned back on her elbows to watch me walk over to the beach where the water met the sand. I dug a little depression and put the wine in the water, burying it partially in the sand to keep it from rolling in the gentle motion of the waves.

When I turned, Anna had closed her eyes from the glare of the sun. It was behind me so I could watch her as I approached the blanket. She began unbuttoning the waist of the white shorts when I was still ten yards away. At five yards, she pulled apart the waist. And as I sat down beside her, she wiggled a little and lay back again on the blanket, putting one forearm over her brow to shade it, looking at me.

"Hurry up," she squinted in my direction, shading her eyes with the back of one hand and showing her teeth, "you're missing the sun."

I stood on one leg and removed my tennis shoes, one at a time before collapsing on the blanket. "That feels better," I sighed in pleasure, turning toward her.

"Ummmm." She didn't open her eyes, lying with her forearms over her forehead, shadowing her eyes. Small beads of perspiration had sprung out on her upper lip. I noticed the small wisps of hair in front of her ears were damp and matted against her cheek from the effort of the walk. It was getting hot.

I couldn't see the families over the brow of the dune from where we lay, but now and then I could hear the children. Anna still had her eyes closed, unknowingly affording me an opportunity to look at her near nakedness without it being so obvious.

"Are you hungry for some herring yet," Anna murmured, tipping her head toward me, cocking one eye open; she wouldn't let me forget my herring mistake. I realized she'd probably been watching me watch her, but hadn't turned, or offered to cover herself.

"I can wait for the salmon, if you want to."

"Let's let the wine cool a bit, if you don't mind."

"Sure."

We lay for a half hour soaking in the bright sun. It continued to grow warmer, despite the light wind.

"Feel like a swim yet? The water won't be much warmer this year, than it is today."

"Sure," I said, opening my eyes, happy for the distraction. "Let's go." I stood up, offering my hand.

"Just a second."

She reached for the waistband of her shorts and humping up her rump, slid them down and lifting her knees, pulled them completely off her legs. She was as naked as the day she was born.

"OK," she said, "ready now," offering me both hands to pull her upright.

I hesitated before heaving her up and didn't release her hand as we started toward the water. Where the waves met the sand, she stopped, turning toward me.

"What...is it," I asked?

"Are you going to wear that...in the water?" Her hands were on her hips and she looked like she was trying not to snicker. I glanced down. She was pointing to my bathing suit with her other hand.

"Oh..." I answered, confused, "...I guess—I never thought..." I lied.

She giggled: "Oh—I'm sorry. I hadn't thought about it...you're not accustomed to us—when the sun shines. You see, we're brought up as children to be...naked—without inhibitions, around members of the other sex, at home and in even in public places, so long as it doesn't offend anyone. Are you offended, Alex?"

"I—no, certainly not." I was finally able to smile without averting my eyes.

"So we don't really think too much about it. We have so little sunshine and the winters are so long. When summer and the sun finally come—we go a little crazy, I think, maybe reverting to our paganism. But, you may..." she indicated my skimpy suit with a wave of her hand, "...keep it on—if you really want?"

That sounded like a challenge. From where I now stood with my back to the water, I could see the other families down the beach were also without clothes, not just the kids; the adults were also cavorting...a game of volleyball without a net.

"No—I won't." I bent and slipped my suit off and flung it toward the blanket. Looking Anna in the eye, I said, "Let's get wet."

When I'd straightened, she hadn't been looking at my body, but was smiling directly into my eyes.

She shouted: "Last one in is a spoiled cheese," and leaped with surprising agility for the water, emitting a squeal of delight as her legs pumped. In a single leap, it seemed, she was ten feet away, with me in quick pursuit. She glanced back once as I closed the distance, but I was able to catch her by the time she splashed knee deep in the cold water. Then, with me right beside her, we dove headlong into the water and began swimming strongly toward the middle of the lake. I followed and with only a few strokes managed to draw up beside her. She smiled at me between turning her head and took time to sputter.

"Race you!"

I nodded my head and let her start, setting the pace and direction. We swam side by side for several minutes and surprisingly, she hadn't even begun to tire. But after another few minutes, her strokes weren't as strong and eventually she was beginning to wallow, swimming so close to me that our hips and shoulders brushed each other a couple of times, a fact that immediately brought the image of my dream from the previous evening.

Finally, Anna gave it up, ducked her head for a second and came up, flinging her dark hair back away from her eyes and sweeping it backward with both hands, kicking hard to stay above water.

"*Ooooh...,*" that felt good, didn't it?" She breathed heavily. "I could swim for miles in this water."

"Yeah..." but I was a little out of breath.

"Ummmm...it's great...but the water's a little cold...don't you th—th—think...?"

I was shocked at how cold it was, even after the strenuous swimming exercise.

"Other than collisions...I wa—wa—watched for winter ice...in case we ran into any." I had trouble speaking, my breath kept trying to leave me.

"*Ooouuuhhh...no...it's...really...nice,*" she sputtered, her own

chin quivering, "you should swim in the spring, when the water is
really cold."

She was partially dunked then by a wave, filling her mouth,
choking her starting her sputtering. She put her hand on my
shoulder and began treading water beside me; I stopped paddling,
myself and took hold of her waist to steady her, kicking hard with my
feet to maintain our mutual buoyancy; the dream, again.

She tipped her head to the side and hit the side of her head
lightly with the heel of her hand to extract water from her ear, still
coughing. As she did, she twisted for balance and I felt a breast
bump against my hand. Again, I had the feeling of *déjà vu*...Anna-
Stina Malmberg swimming with Carl.

"That's not very—very, er...physician-like," I laughed, indicating
her head banging, my own jaw quivering. "Is that the recommended
method?"

"Well..." she changed hands, "...one must make do with what is
at hand. Have you had enough?" she said, paddling again.

"Sure, let's go back," I said and set the pace, wanting to get to
the blanket ahead of her.

Despite the cold of the water, I'd become somewhat aroused, or
at least, I thought I might be. It was too cold to really tell, under
water. With a few last second strokes, I managed to beat her in,
planning to fling myself on the blanket before she could see my state.

Behind me, I heard Anna panting. I glanced back as she dragged
herself from the water, exhausted from the exertion. She called
toward me.

"There are a couple of towels in my bag, there."

I bent, quickly opening the drawstring on the nearest canvas bag,
managing to paw one of the towels free from the jumble. Standing
up, I shook it out and quickly wrapped it around my waist and tucking
it in, before pulling the other out for Anna. She was still standing half
way to the water's edge, hands on her hips, head down and breathing
deeply. I strode over and held out the towel. She was pulling her
hair backward, twisting it up in a sort-of knot; I stood waiting, trying
to look to one side, despite her upheld arms and very erect nipples,
chilled now, by the combination of the wind and sun.

"You took mine," she said, suddenly, jerking my towel from
around my waist with a swoop.

"*Wha…*," I stammered, grabbing, but too late. With a wicked grin Anna turned to run for the blanket.

"No, I didn't," I said, quickly tossing the towel I had brought at her retreating figure and grabbing for hers as I closed the distance between us. She pivoted, trying to dodge. I caught her just as she reached the blanket and we both collapsed into a wet, cold, slippery heap on the sun-warmed blanket. We lay there for a moment, too tired to struggle or separate, both savoring the warmth and closeness.

"You forgot your towel," she finally said, indicating the direction of the lake with her head. Still maintaining her hold on the stolen towel, she rolled onto her side, facing me, clutching the towel in front of her breasts. "I got mine she said," glancing down and giving it a slight tug against my grip.

Rolling toward her a little more—our forearms and other parts were now touching between the entanglements of the towel's folds; I tightened my grip, tugging back with one hand.

"We'll just have to share this one, I guess," I said gently.

"I guess we will at that," she said, snuggling a slight bit closer to me our upper bodies and thighs still not quite touching. Only our arms and her breasts remained tangled within the wadded towel.

I freed one arm with some effort and reached over her and put one hand on her slender waist. She smiled. "Ummmm…you're warming up quickly…" she said, rolling slightly onto her back, "…from the sun, too," she added wickedly, glancing over at me.

I followed her movement with my other arm, reaching my other hand around the small of her neck and slid closer. She let the towel fall between us and reached up and forward, putting both arms around my neck, coming closer. I looked into her brown eyes. I know my chest was touching her breasts somewhere in the hot-cold, sweaty, sandy tangle of towel; a chill ran up my spine. I shuddered slightly. For several seconds, we stared into each other's eyes, neither daring to move and destroy the moment. Finally she tilted her head toward me slightly and shifted her gaze to my mouth. She wanted to be kissed.

And we did, very gently, tasting each other…holding the closeness, savoring the feeling that only comes with first-times. Shy but insistent, she kissed me back. Her hand explored the back of my neck and hair…then she trailed her fingers slowly down my spine.

Stopping just at the top of my buttocks, she slid her cool fingers up and then back down again, tantalizing close, so that each time, I wondered whether her hand would go lower. But her fingers only played a soft tattoo, before moving ever so gently on again.

Experimentally, I edged my tongue between her lips. She opened her teeth slightly. I explored the space while she pressed her lips together along each side of my tongue, gently biting it from time to time as I progressed around her mouth.

I brought my hand around between us and carefully clasped her jaw, gently squeezing the sides of her mouth as I explored deeper between her lips. My forearm pressed her breast gently.

A soft moan escaped her and I felt a slight shudder in her shoulder. She began to respond to my kisses with more insistence; I reached behind her and grasping the small of her back above her buttocks, exerted pressure to edge her even closer to me. The towel was molded between our bodies. I'd forgotten time and place and didn't notice at first when the bits of sand began to fall on us, subconsciously, probably thinking it was the wind.

But then a large clump hit the top of Anna's head and she made a startled sound and jerked backward in surprise, brushing sand from her face. Two children were standing between us and the lake. They alternately scooped dry sand in their little tin shovels and tossing it high into the air toward us, with a conspiring look between them. I was about to shout a warning when, from over the hill, I heard one of the mothers approaching, calling them to come back.

Anna rolled onto her stomach and I followed. We remained on our elbows facing each other, heads down and smiling devilishly.

The woman said, "Excuse me..." to our backs and taking the children, chided them for not staying close and for disturbing the man and the lady.

"Well," Anna said, "that was close." She was smiling now and had turned on her side, leaning on one elbow. I didn't know for sure what she meant and the usual impish expression she was attempting to master left some doubt as to the double meaning of her statement: sand, or sex?

"Was it?" I said, feigning surprise, "I didn't really notice." I reached to brush some of the caked sand from her hair. As I did, she leaned upward on one elbow and kissed me soundly on the lips, sticking her tongue deep into my mouth. Before I had a time to respond, she slid from beside me and jumped up, dropping the towel.

"Time to picnic," she exclaimed, bending deftly and stepping into her shorts again. "You shake the blanket and get the wine."

Anna began unpacking the picnic basket while I shook the sand from the blanket and spread it out again beside her. I fetched the wine while she laid out the upturned basket cover and put two broad rimed glasses on it, serving as our table. She'd brought wax paper parcels containing smoked salmon and some freshly-peeled cucumbers and raw carrots. There was a jar of herring in a sweet mustard sauce. She had a loaf of fresh bread, butter and some cold, boiled, dilled-potatoes.

"A feast good enough for a king," I said looking over the spread she'd laid on.

"And a queen," she said, smiling up at me. She only put on her blouse, but hadn't buttoned it and I couldn't help but watch her as she worked; she was perspiring slightly in the bright sun.

We ate ravenously after the swim, cleaning up everything but the wine. The bottle still had an inch or so still remaining in it; Anna stood up and taking the bottle to the lakeshore stood up very straight, holding the bottle over the lapping waves.

"I offer this drink to Odin, that he may find peace with us in our supplication, in eating his food and living beneath his sun."

With that, she tipped the bottle and slowly poured the wine into the lake.

Returning to the blanket, she said: "There, that should take care of us for a while."

"What was that all about?" I asked, chuckling aloud.

"Don't laugh...I'm serious about my Nordic gods. I was just appeasing Odin; we must give them something, or we could come to regret it if they should find disfavor with something we do.

"I see. Rather like the *vittror* and *troll* in the forest, huh?"

"Oh...you know about them? Yes, nearly the same, but older. Odin is the primary god, he rules the universe—over all those others, which are actually more spirits, than gods. They're just minor characters in his larger drama."

"Rather like us?" I questioned.

Anna only smiled sweetly and nodded.

"Are we going to do something…which they would find fault with?"

"I don't know," she said, mischievously, but didn't offer anything further.

We sat for a while discussing the day and Karolina. It grew late as we languished in the sun, enjoying the simple conversation. I was certain Anna was enjoying herself. Presently, though, she grew quiet, preoccupied and I noticed a little frown had crept onto her pretty face. I didn't say anything, but I watched her closely as we talked. Finally, she said she must return home soon, because something had come up earlier.

So I got up, shook and folded the blanket while she packed the basket; we gathered everything and started back to the car. As we walked she said she'd tell me more, later. I didn't know there was going to be a later, but was pleased at the thought of not having to break off the day. The other families had left sometime earlier. When we reached the Volvo, there were two shovels of sand placed on the car's hood, side by side. The two urchins had exacted their revenge for not getting to watch the show on the beach.

We didn't talk much on the ride back; when we arrived at Anna's, at her direction, I carried the blanket and picnic basket into the kitchen, following her in, putting them on the pine table where she'd pointed.

Her house was neat and well decorated in the typical airy, clear Scandinavian pastels that I never ceased to find pleasing, in Sweden. Her kitchen was bright, despite being on the north side of the house. There were many, very Scandinavian cooking implements lying or hanging around…on the walls, in baskets, and suspended above the little cooking island, something I thought was very un-Scandinavian. I'd never seen one of those in Sweden and had hardly even seen them in The States. Anna returned then and saw me looking more closely at it. It contained a wood burning stove on one end and gas jets on the other.

"So you've discovered my secret," she said, now wearing cotton slacks and buttoning a clean blouse.

"I was just looking around, trying to figure out how those herrings came to taste so good."

"Afraid I can't take the blame, or credit for those. The potatoes were all mine, however."

"Well, I suppose I should be going back home to bathe and maybe transcribe the notes from the morning discussion with Karolina."

I was hanging back a little, still thinking about the mention of later, but not wanting to push her either. But she walked over by the door where I lingered, walking right up to me and put her arms around my neck and leaned fully against me—not sexy—but sexy. She didn't intend it that way, but that's sure enough how it came off.

"I wanted to thank you for today—*tack för idag…*" she said, "I really enjoyed myself—in fact, I can't say when the last time was that I had that much fun. You're fun to tease, Alex."

She tilted her head backward and gently drew my head down and kissed me long and hard. Again, not sexy but more like a promise.

"Thank you," she said with sincerity, leaning back her arms still around my neck.

"You're welcome…I'm sure."

"I'd like to ask you to come for dinner tonight. Or, do you think we are pushing this too much?"

"I—well, I hadn't really thought about it, Anna," I lied. "It certainly is going pretty fast, but I believe I can keep up—if you can."

She smiled and nodded. Oh, I can.

"And I know I'd like to see you again tonight, so…yes, please— what time and what can I bring?"

"Come around seven-thirty; you needn't bring anything. I'll make something simple…shrimps with pasta—some vegetables, maybe. Does that sound all right—you like shrimps?"

"Shrimps would be great—I'll be here. Sure I can't get some more wine?"

"No…I have plenty. I'll have some wine ready, so—just bring yourself and your appetite. We can have a drink first, I'd like that. I bought a new dress last month and I'll never get to wear it at this rate, the summer will be gone, if I don't create an occasion—so tonight's it; be prepared."

"Ok—then…I'll wear my jacket too…see you at seven-thirty."

I believe I actually skipped down the sidewalk to the car. And back in the apartment, I somehow managed to pass the time organizing some of the older notes from the last two days with Karolina and then gave that day's work a lick and a promise. I was very pleased with the way the interviews were coming and looked forward to each morning, afternoon and sometimes, evening—whether it was re-reading them, or re-typing them into the draft.

The direction the day's outing with Anna had taken was somewhat disturbing to me. I thought she was being a bit forward, especially for a professional person. Granted, she thought I was somewhat a sober-sides (and I guess I am) but it seemed somewhat out of character for a woman who'd hardly just met me. I was thinking about the picnic: surely, the other families were also nude. In Scandinavia and Europe, for that matter, it wasn't that unusual to see naked people at the beaches. Many of the women went without their uppers at the beach; it was quite common.

So why had this afternoon taken such a hold on me? Certainly, Anna is a knockout. It's the matter of fact way she handled the whole afternoon, not simply the beach thing. She's mature—yet a little girlish...and I really like that about her. She's professional, yet she's considerate and kind while doing it, softening her physician's technique and skills. She holds back...when it makes sense, I guess; but can also be bold and assertive. And she's certainly proved it with our relationship, so far.

Why then...am I beginning to run scared, I asked myself? I've had other relationships with women; they didn't necessarily come this far, this soon. But Anna and I—well, although we didn't have intercourse this afternoon, that scene on the blanket exceeded many bedroom endeavors I'd had in the past. Possibly, it was her frankness...without seeming brazen.

Nonetheless, I was feeling that little twinge of conscience that haunts oneself and I didn't understand it. My emotions seemed to be out of my control when I was with her. I could tell myself: slow down, Alex. But that didn't seem to slow me down. Probably...I decided, because I didn't really want to. I really, really—really, liked Anna.

I stared out my window, my notes momentarily neglected. I've looked at other naked women, become aroused—excited, but Anna was different. I wanted to consume her...like a commodity. Not with disregard for who she was, or to cast her off afterwards, I didn't mean that, but to experience her. Yes, that's the word...experience her, fully, like a—a beautiful piece of music. Only another human being can offer another a meal of that sort—and it must be freely-given, in order to be enjoyed by both.

Leaning on the kitchen table, I watched the vanishing day until I finally decided to get up and enjoy a bottle of beer and take a little *knäckebröd* and cheese before getting ready. Seven-thirty was still two hours away and I'd gotten hungry. As I prepared my snack, I slowly came to a conclusion that I was probably falling in love with Anna. How else could I explain that feeling? I hadn't felt that way— God…since I was young. But there it was…back again. Just like I was eighteen, fresh as ever when holding the hand of a girl for the first time, I shook my head in wonder. There was something about the feeling of touch…someone else's hand, especially when you hadn't even touched someone, beyond a handshake, for a long, long time.

"Can you believe it, sober-sides?" I said aloud.

Since my failed marriage, I hadn't really connected in any relationships. I'd never had time…taken the time, I guess, to make the occasional, accidental encounters, blossom into anything more. First thing I would know, the woman would be gone, tired of waiting for me. Those who did hang around, my few, assorted affairs, I'd permitted to run their course, meandering and eventually finishing in a drought of emotion on both parts—probably because they'd simply not worked out, rather than any particular disappointment in love. But there was always the element of time behind them—pushing, tugging—prodding. There was usually no rush of feelings at the end, on one or the other's part; simply a drought. And like all neglected things, they ceased to be important in the end.

"Better get it moving," I said, again, "or keep it moving." Considering my one-sided conversation, I replied to myself: "…or what?" Continuing, I added: "What's different then…about Anna?"

I considered that: aside from the quite obvious things, like looks, personality, occupation—stuff like that…I guess I couldn't say. Possibly, all of the above characteristics, maybe, I don't know. Should I be worried about falling in love with her?

I mulled this over until it was nearly time to head out. I'd had a quick bath by then and as I was about to dress, remembered: she's wearing her new dress.

"Damn! Almost forgot," I said.

So I pulled on different slacks, dark socks and a light blue shirt. I sorted through my four neckties before I came up with one I liked with the jacket I'd bought in Stockholm, but not yet worn. I made a mental note to plan additional time in Stockholm again, soon, to spruce up my wardrobe, most of which remained in The States and wasn't anything to write home about, anyway. Maybe Anna would like to come along?

That was a pleasant thought, too, as I rolled up her street a little before seven-thirty, resolved to maintain my self-control. Above all else, maintain control, I thought but really wondered whether I would...or could.

Control fell in the face of the new dress; oh, what a dress, I thought when Anna met me at the door. Did I say she could be seductive? I don't remember. She not only can be—she is. At the door she handed me a gin and tonic.

"You remembered," I said, taking the glass and leaning forward to present the cheek she obviously wanted to kiss. I'd mentioned sometime I liked a G N' T. She'd now gone to the trouble of finding the ingredients—not an easy task in that part of Sweden, I guessed. Before I took a sip she leaned forward and gave me the kiss, just a peck and a smile...but, that all-knowing, devilish smile.

The dress...ah...it was long and beige—sort of rich cream colored, with just the slightest bit of brown piping running diagonally down the front, on the bias, crossing just beneath her right breast and down across her left hip and on around. I don't know why it was so striking, but it was. It was cut low at the bodice and suspended with the thinnest of spaghetti straps, across each shoulder. Though I would have thought her bust sufficient to suspend it, the straps slid somewhat loosely on her shoulders. The material appeared very sheer and light and fit her snuggly and seemed to fit he well...it certainly suited her figure.

It was a semi-formal dinner, or party dress; almost too formal for going out to any restaurants in that part of Sweden. That's probably why she didn't wear it the night we went across the lake. Stockholm, that would have been the proper venue for a woman like Anna wearing that dress...a fine restaurant somewhere in Gammalstan, in Stockholm. I'd like to take her to Stockholm for an evening on the town, sometime; maybe if we go clothes shopping together, I thought.

She took my hand and we strolled through the house. I had my tonic and she carried a glass of white wine. It wasn't a very large house and she pointed out the various rooms; finally, we ended up in the back garden. Small and very intimate, considering she was in the city, there was plenty of privacy. Someone had spent a good bit of time working in it and the proportion of blossoming flowers, vines and other shrubbery were well balanced. I recognized some of them— some I didn't and had to ask.

"They're near tropical, some of them. It's the rather temperate winter here, unlike many other parts of Sweden, with the Gulf Stream coming up across Norway, it warms us; we can winter certain species that would perish in many other countries south of here and inland, in Europe."

"Oh, I see. I've seen that effect from the Japanese current on the west coast of America."

"Are you hungry yet, Alex? I don't have everything finished, but I can rush it?" she asked.

"No. I can wait." I thought of the *knäckebröd*, glad I'd snacked.

She was having some trouble with the dress and seemed to be continuously fussing with the shoulder straps. It seemed to be trying to come off, shifting in one direction when she stood one way, the opposite direction, if she sat in another, always offering me a tempting peek inside one side or the other. After a while, I found it very distracting. One strap would slide down at the oddest moments. Anna appeared also to be annoyed by its misbehavior, but didn't say anything.

"I thought we could have a drink or two before going in. The pasta is finished; the sauce, too. I just have to heat it with the shrimps. It is so nice outside yet, I thought we could talk for a while."

"Sure," I said, sitting back in anticipation, trying to ignore the allure of the wayward dress.

"Actually, there was something I wanted to speak with you about." She hesitated for a while, seeming to search her memory and my face for words.

"I don't know if I mentioned that I have to go home next weekend...to northern Sweden."

"I don't remember...but I don't believe you did."

"Well, I do...for a couple of reasons, really."

"Oh?" I said, sipping my wine.

"My father's not well—I believe I told you he suffers from—what do you call it, hardening of the arteries? He began to forget things and now, he can't function without someone in constant attendance— my mother. And it causes him distress, you see, not to mention her."

"That's understandable."

"My mother finds it difficult to cope and keeps getting annoyed with him—reminding him, trying to put his memory back, each time he forgets. But of course it won't remain and he forgets again almost immediately, which frustrates her even more; it's a vicious circle. This isn't uncommon behavior for spouses in situations like this, especially when they're older. It doesn't make it any easier for families, though. It annoys mother and confuses Father. The two feed off each other, unfortunately, sometimes in a negative way."

"That's unfortunate; I suppose there's nothing that can be done?"

"Work a miracle," she said, glancing over at me over her wineglass and smiling bitterly. "No, there's nothing. I'll have to arrange for someone to come in to help my mother. It will let her get out, do some things for herself and at the same time, offer father a rest from her nagging and fussing. One doesn't have a lot to look forward to sometimes, in old age."

"I understand. Karolina is fortunate to have all her faculties and also has her memories; but, she has no one to share them with."

"There is you, now—*you* show interest?"

"Well, certainly, but isn't it more for the sake, on her part, of recording the past. And on my part, originally, purely selfish a reason, until I came to know and love her. Getting the truth written down, before it is lost to future generations, returned as a goal, but by then it had become a goal of secondary importance."

"I suppose so, but she hadn't written it down, before you came, or showed the inclination. You made that happen, Alex."

I thought about that for a while. "Maybe. You mentioned another reason...for returning home, Anna?"

"Yes, there is...another..." she hesitated as if gauging the moment.

I waited. She seemed to struggle again.

"I wasn't concerned with this—about this particular matter until, well, until we went out for dinner and then the beach and picnic today.

I—well, I thought I had better tell you something before—we...."

She trailed off again, so I prompted: "And...we—what about we—us?"

"I'm married."

It hit me like ton of bricks. "Married...?"

"Yes...I have a husband."

"Oh." What else could I say? It really grounded me.

"Harald is—*was* a physician too.

I tried to calm my pounding heart.

"Like you?"

"Yes, we grew up together—medical school together, from start to finish. It was love at first sight...then."

Once she began it just rushed out and it left me feeling hollow.

"We moved in together and traded shifts, hours, classes—from graduation, through internship—all the way. He was posted to Central Hospital in Stockholm and I was in Uppsala at University Hospital. We even bought a house in Sigtuna and rode the train every day, in two directions."

It seemed to pour from her, as if she would appease me for the deception by just letting it out. However, it served the opposite purpose.

"It was a storybook romance for a couple of years—and then Harald's behavior began to change for...." She paused, seeming to gather her thoughts, breathing deeply at the same time, before going on.

"You don't have to tell me this, you know Anna. If you'd rather..." I found myself becoming strangely jealous, an emotion I was unfamiliar with.

"No, I should tell you. I think it's important and if you don't mind, I'll feel a lot better, too."

"Ok," I said, thinking, but not saying, I won't feel any better at all—in fact, I'll probably feel worse.

"We were both from Alfrenberget, up in Jämpland. Our families knew each other for years. It was as if we were destined to marry. But, as I said, things began to change—with Harald, afterward. No one really knows what is wrong with him, if there really is—was. Anyway, he became—sexually, semi-violent, until...until they finally institutionalized him. They put him away."

"Sexually violent...with you, Anna?"

"No...,"she put her head down and raised her hand to cover her eyes. Her shoulders gave a little shudder and my heart went flip, flop. I wanted to hold her. But I was still smarting—stunned by her revelation.

"I'm sorry, Anna," I said crossing to sit beside her on the settee. I put my arm around her shoulder, pushing up one of the straps that threatened to slip off the edge.

"I'm OK," she unconsciously pulled the other strap up, "I just wanted to tell you now—before…"

"Before…before what?"

"I felt I owed it to you, since—well, what's been happening."

"You thought that if I was beginning to become emotionally attached to you?"

"Well, yes—no! I mean, I didn't want to mislead you…in case…please, Alex," she reconsidered, "…don't believe I didn't want to be presumptive, it's just that, ever since it happened, I've had to curtail my relationships with other men. Because…not that there have really been any, but because, well they…a man would likely be disappointed if it were to go that far, I mean…us. I didn't want us to be disappointing, Alex. I…I think too much of what little we've already had—up until tonight. I didn't want to mislead you…hurt you, later."

She looked at me for some help, but I just sort of looked at her.

"I've never let anyone to get very close since…but this….our…we—seemed to have gone a little beyond where I'd gone with anyone since Harald…since I left him.

I gave that some thought: "I suppose that's perfectly understandable, Anna, but I believe you're making too much out of this for a…for just an apology. I'll admit…too, things have gotten a little complicated."

Her brows knit at this.

"Well, a little more than complicated, then. But why don't we take this one day at a time and let things, sort of happen."

I became a little concerned at this point. I didn't want to overplay the calmness thing, because the sick feeling inside me hadn't begun to subside. Yet I didn't want to make her think I was head-over-heels, which I wasn't—well almost wasn't.

"You realize that…since I'm still married, there's nothing I can do. I mean, if I did meet someone else, I'd have to—we could not— I would have to divorce Harald and I would be afraid to do that, right now; his treatment is very sensitive. The doctors say, in balance, I am told. And I still...feel responsible for him—I think...somewhat?"

She really broke down at this point and began to cry. She cried quietly, actually, elegantly, as she did everything else. Her right hand shielded her eyes so I couldn't see her embarrassment and with her left fist, she lightly struck the chair arm a couple of times. There were no hysterics, no blubbering—sobbing heavily, just strong, quiet, unashamed tears.

I moved over to her and drew her nearer. Enfolding her in my arms she really began to unburden herself; with her head pressed hard against my chest she sobbed and sobbed. I had the feeling then, that she hadn't had the chance to really cry...probably since all her problems with her father and this...husband-thing, had begun. My feelings were in the tips of my fingers as I reached around her, caressing her back and the side of her face.

Once she'd cried for a bit and seemed to be getting her breath back, I wanted some more answers: "How long has Harald been institutionalized?"

"About three years." When she said this, she finally looked up at me. She was even more beautiful with a red nose and tearstains. "Do you have a handkerchief?"

I handed it to her. "Are his relations—family...involved? Do they help you, come visit him, make decisions...you know?"

"No, his parents are both dead and he had no siblings and that makes it more difficult for me. I'm really all he has, now."

I thought about this as she continued.

"His father lived the longest and Harald, being the only child—I think it broke his father's heart. He was very supportive to me for about eighteen months and then he died, suddenly. Before he died, his father told me I was his daughter, now that he didn't feel he had a son any longer. It really hit him; also, he didn't have time to forgive Harald before he died. Since then, it' s been only me and Harald's doctors."

"What is the prognosis for your husband's recovery?"

"They—the doctors, psychiatrists actually, keep talking about stabilization—then control—then cure. So far they've barely reached control. Personally, I don't believe there's much hope. That's why, when you—when I met you and you asked me out to dinner, I thought, why not—it's been three years. Total denial of male companionship for three years—almost four; I felt I owed myself...*that*. I'm sorry I chose you as my first...experiment. I guess I'm not much of a martyr and I really didn't believe it would...get complicated...you know, meeting you? I don't mean this to sound like the time was up and any old port in a storm; you are more than that, Alex and I think you know that. I've never told anyone about Harald—even the staff at the hospital don't know; only my board administrator, so please don't tell anyone—*Katrina?*"

"Well, no, certainly not. Anna, I'm sorry and I don't really know what else to say. I guess...where does that leave us? What do you want me to do? Hold you at arm's length? Put you on a shelf? Visit and look, but don't touch? I don't like the sound of that. And I don't think you'd like being treated that way, either."

That came out echoing the anger and frustration I felt. Embarrassed, I stood up at that point. Damn, this jealousy thing was really getting to me; I hadn't been this upset since—I couldn't remember. I wanted to leave...hide.

"Please, Alex, sit down again and continue to be reasonable for just a little longer. I want to talk to you about it...the future. You've been so kind, listening, so please—sit...," she patted the sofa cushion, "...just for a little longer, please? Beside..."one of the dress's straps had fallen from her shoulder and she absently pulled it up, "...I still have your handkerchief."

Feeling like a little boy with my feelings bruised, I sauntered back over. Pouting a little I suppose as I sat down.

"Oh...*hell*!"

"Here..." she leaned toward me and gave me a long, gentle kiss, one hand on my shoulder, "...I'm sorry." I tasted her tears and felt the flush warmth of her face. "You are such a reasonable guy. I wanted to tell you that and—and let you make up your own mind—up-front, so to speak. I didn't know I would—we would...well, that there would be so much emotional involvement, or I might not have begun it—accepted your dinner offer."

"I've never fooled around with—whatever you call it, with a married woman."

"I am not surprised by that, Alex."

"I like you, Anna." I almost said I love you. What was getting into me?

"Thank you Alex; I like you too. You know, I've also have had a grand time these last few days with you—a really grand time."

She didn't do, or say anything for a while, just looked down at the garden flagstones.

"Anna, what do you expect me to do now—with us, with what—we've started?"

"I don't know, Alex." She looked like she would begin to cry a little, again.

"When I decided to tell you, I didn't think it through, far enough, I guess and I didn't know what your reaction would be. I especially didn't wish to deceive you and I didn't want to go further into any relationship with you, without your making your own choice, knowing all the facts. Am I making any sense?"

"Sense...*yes*, solutions...*no*. But in matters like this I doubt there's much sense to be made." I stood up again. "Why don't we have something—some dinner? A man can think better on a full stomach. I don't know about a woman."

"Oh, I'd completely forgotten, Alex! I'm so sorry; you must be starving?" she jumped up, dabbing her eyes and handed me my handkerchief. "Better keep that handy."

"Yes, that's a pretty good description of it and I either need another gin 'n tonic, or some wine with the shrimps."

She turned toward the kitchen with me close behind, but then hesitated in the doorway, turned and again, leaning forward on tiptoes, pecked me lightly on the lips. The left strap of the dress slid off her shoulder and the bodice cocked at a crazy angle.

I almost held back, for the briefest split second, I nearly backed away from this spontaneous demonstration of affection—it was instinctive. I don't think she noticed, but she'd just hurt me pretty badly. This was the last thing I was expecting I'd have to do tonight—control my emotion of not giving in to her, when she couldn't give herself to me...figuratively speaking I mean. I felt a little...*used* right at that moment. She turned toward the kitchen and for a while, I just stood watching as she tossed the pasta back in the steaming water and put the sauce back on the burner.

"There are a couple of bottles of wine down there under that cupboard..." she said, indicating the corner cupboard nearest the back door, "...if you'd please take them out?"

I bent down, reaching for the door.

"Uh-uh—other side," she said, licking stray sauce from the side of her hand and pointing to my left, when I turned.

I found a couple of reds and three whites. After looking them over, I chose a red Portuguese that I had never heard of.

"Red ok...?"

"Fine. You'll find the corkscrew in the drawer to your right. I took her directional queue for the corkscrew and retrieved it. Within minutes of opening the wine, we were wrapping steaming pasta around forks, pivoting them on the spoons in the delicious sauce she'd conjured. The meal proved as tasty and I was hungry. I never did handle *female* emotion well, let alone on an empty stomach. I felt much better after we'd eaten.

Not discussing the Harald matter again, we rinsed the dishes together and left them in the sink. On Anna's orders, I carried a tray with a pot and two cups for coffee into the parlor, put it on a little table and took a seat on her divan—*collapsed* is probably a better word. Anna followed after a minute with two large glasses and a bottle of brandy, putting them beside the tray and sitting beside me. She smiled and poured the snifters a third full. I handed her one and then took mine and we settled back.

"All we need is a fire," I mumbled contentedly.

After a moment of sipping and silence, Anna asked, "Better?" and leaned back onto my arm.

"Absolutely...I never could negotiate when I was hungry."

"Negotiate...was this a negotiation?"

"Hardly, but emotional stress—you understand?"

"Certainly...again...I apologize, Alex. In retrospect, I believe I should have told you when you asked me to dinner—you know, the first night?"

"Oh?"

"Yes...we could have avoided...well, misleading you, if I had."

"I don't know whether it would have changed anything, but you're probably right. I should've known. Then I'd have only myself to blame for the way I feel now."

I think I stunned her a little with that remark, because she glanced up, looking pretty serious; so I tried to temper my remark. "I'd have probably continued to rush in anyway, Anna—head first."

"You're a dear in your honesty, Alex; the way you maintain your balance in a situation many men might have either become very angry about, or flown from. You keep both your sense of proportion and humor."

I was running out of steam; maybe patience, too, feeling as if we'd pretty well run the course we were intended to with the subject of discussion. The brandy, on top of the wine was making me feel a little careless and I was afraid I might say the wrong thing. To hang around further would probably only make me feel worse, so I stood up again, planning to leave.

"On that complement, it's probably best I take my leave. There's a lot of Karolina stuff to go through yet in my hotel."

She stood also, looking a little hurt. "Alex, I didn't intend to ruin your evening by telling you about Harald; I hope you understand that. But...waiting would only have made it more difficult and far worse for both of us, in the end. Please, stay for a while longer. Honestly, I don't want you to go away feeling as I'm afraid you do."

Saying that, she took my hand and sat down, patting the cushion. I thought for only a second before sitting down. With a surprising move, she slid so close, I opened the arm that didn't contain my brandy glass and she put her head on my chest and snuggled. Snuggled...like a damn schoolgirl, tucking her legs up under her.

"I wouldn't have been able to forgive myself for not saying anything sooner, if you went away hurt, Alex."

I don't know what she had intended but, the smell of her hair, the confidence she belied by making herself so comfortable—so vulnerable; it was disarming and my earlier reluctance fell away in another seventh grade surge of emotion.

I think she was almost purring, she made me feel—like I was valuable, not that I lacked self-esteem, no more, or no less, than the next guy, but that gesture...that closeness, made me feel something—more. Something between being loved and accepted to being needed. Necessary was the word...I couldn't adequately describe it. But it was very, very extraordinary. And then those damn spaghetti straps slowly slipped down onto each arm.

Lifting her head, she glanced first at one and then the other, making a small sound of disgust as if she was regretting having purchased it. She wiggled her torso, attempting to settle in to the garment, but the dress disobeyed, moving in the opposite direction she intended. She shifted again, but the dress didn't—only gaped. She slid down—the dress slipped up threatening to come off one side.

She glanced up and looked directly in my eyes. "It seems to have a mind of its own," she said, glancing up at me and smiling slightly as if we were both innocent observers of the phenomenon of the dress.

"One would think when one pays that much for a gown, it would at least obey the purchaser's desires. Think, if I were wearing it in...Stockholm."

She'd read my thoughts. Maybe it's obeying mine, I wondered, with a touch of bitterness. She pushed herself upward and squirmed again. The gown remained where she sat on the divan and both her breasts came nearly completely out of the bodice. She sat up quickly, covering herself with a forearm.

"Yikes..." she exclaimed. Then glanced over at me and said: "*Shit*, I think I will take this back to the shop. I will never own it—it is bound to own me, from the looks of it.

I leaned over and circled her neck with one arm and bending, kissed the hollow of her shoulder. "What are we going to do," I murmured to her collarbone.

"Make love, I hope," she said, reaching her arm back and pulling me forward to meet her embrace. "I have needed someone to love me so badly, Alex and you are...very attractive."

"Are you sure you want that," I asked. "I'm not so certain myself?"

"Scruples have gotten me nothing more than loneliness, for more than three years. I've never been with another man...since Harald. You'll have to decide for yourself, Alex, whether you...do. `But...I do, I *really* do—and with you. I decided that today; that kiss on the beach. I knew I had to tell you first, Alex—to be fair. I despise deception and didn't want to begin our relationship under a lie...an omission which was the same as a lie."

"I see." I wished she wouldn't talk so much; my emotions were in a storm of contrasts fueled by heightened passion.

"Let's finish what we started today on the beach," she said, leaning forward and reaching behind to unzip her gown. She settled back in my arms and looking up at me. "Are you having reservations, Alex?"

"Uh-huh," I murmured, nodding slightly, not daring to look at what the gown's bodice might have done with the zipper down.

"I...well, we think I should think about this a little more."

"I can't say that I can blame you for that, though I regret it; are you sure?" She sort of slumped then, sadly, as if she'd lost a yet another battle with herself.

"Anna, I'm going to tell you something my better judgment tells me I shouldn't, but I will, anyway."

"Don't do it, please...if you feel you will compromise yourself."

"It's not that...it's, well, I—no one likes being vulnerable. You women—*ladies*, don't seem to mind quite as much as we men; you know, male...ego? Anyway, we find it hard to expose ourselves emotionally to a woman—I guess, to anyone, for that matter— anyone who can take the information and use, or abuse us with it. Am I making any sense?"

"I think so," she murmured, noncommittally.

"I'm old enough and experienced enough and it shouldn't do much more than sting for a little while, afterwards, if it backfires— sorry, fails."

"Now I don't think I am following you."

"Anna—I have begun to fall in love with you...up until you told me about your husband. I haven't really been involved with anyone— in an enduring relationship for, well...," she interrupted me.

"That's not what...."

"Wait! Please let me finish. I have to get this right. I have never remarried. I have never really come close enough to that—again. Without sounding *vainglorious*, I can say, usually, when a woman came that close to me, for some reason, I usually terminated the affair, either because I began to feel it was going to go nowhere or, by remaining in it, the woman would only be hurt. I guess I just never clicked with anyone, until now, that is."

She was listening attentively.

"But I clicked with you Anna. In the short time we've been seeing one another, more has happened to me, emotionally, than has happened with any other woman, possibly ever. You've excited me emotionally as well as sexually. What you...what I hope you felt at the beach; that was genuine on my part and I was feeling it too, like a teen-ager, but I was feeling it."

"I felt it too, Alex..."

"I know…," I interrupted, "…I thought I could sense it and it didn't feel shallow—contrived…it was mature, intellectual, advanced—hell…I don't know how to describe it, but it was good! I've been taking it stride-by-stride, swallowing each morsel, as it was offered; no rushing, until—well, until tonight. Right now I'm more angry than hurt, although the hurt will come later, I'm sure."

"Yes…?"

"I want to strike out at the something that has—what—ruined us? I feel as if I've been cheated by fate because I still care for you, Anna."

"Oh, Alex—I feel exactly the same. I feel fate has cheated us both. I feel my circumstances have been cheating me for three years now and I want it to end, but I don't know what to do beyond what I'm already doing. I still feel responsible to Harald. I pity him and…probably love the Harald that I married so long ago, the one I haven't seen since…oh, since a long time, Alex. It's not his fault he…his head is the way it is. I despise the psychoanalytical jargon so, used to describe his…*condition* and after this long of dealing with them—I've come to *despise* those who dispense it in my profession."

"I can't have sex with you Anna, as much as I wish to, I can't. It isn't a matter of respect or anything noble. It's…for right now, anyway, it's a turn-off—emotionally. That dress…that's really some dress. The way the thing keeps shifting, exposing, or almost exposing this—exposing that—very distracting. In fact, I would suggest you don't wear it anywhere, unless you want to be assaulted."

Anna smiled and reached back and laid the palm of her hand on my cheek.

"You're sweet. You want to assault me?" she kissed me lightly.

Another gentle offer, I thought.

"…don't you?"

I didn't reply, considering the double meaning of her remark. Assault, or assault—love, or anger. She didn't say anything more; we both just sat there. I, rolling my glass of nearly untouched brandy. She, twirling her fingernail over the upholstery pattern on the settee arm. I supposed we were both considering what had transpired in such a short time, sat for a while in the twilight, each lost to our own thoughts. And then rather abruptly, I thanked her for the day and evening, got my jacket and went back to my apartment without a backward glance.

CHAPTER 17

A Proposal Refused

"I see you have sunburn,"
Karolina said, smiling as I came up
the walk toward the sun porch."

"It was a beautiful day," I
said, reaching down and patting her shoulder. I didn't feel like it
was...not after the evening I'd had with Anna. I didn't want to talk
about it...not even think about it. Instead, I said:

"How are you feeling, Karolina?"

"Oh, I am much stronger...you know..." she said, turning to me
"...you were correct."

"Correct...?"

"Yes—resting...stopping the interview short...yesterday, it made
a world of difference. I had so much energy later in the day. So I
played cards until nearly nine o'clock last night and this morning I feel
spectacular!"

"I didn't think I would see anything of you today," Karolina said,
tilting her head against the bright sunlight. "Weren't you supposed to
have this long weekend free...with Dr. Olsson?" This good-natured
chiding was probably directed toward Anna.

"How could I neglect my favorite Swedish woman, I said?"

"Well then, don't. Come and sit here," she indicated one of the
cushioned wooden lounge chairs at the small table. "We can talk a
little while."

"Thanks," I said, just having noticed Anna walking along the side
of the building, clip board in hand. She gave a hasty wave as she
crossed the corridor. Karolina followed my gaze and we watched her
together, the long legged stride as Anna went through the open
French doors of the lounge.

"She is a delight—that one," Karolina mused, glanced at me.

"That she is," I said, not caring if Karolina heard the disappointment in my voice. But she only saw the fondness in my gaze and smiled as we watched Anna disappeared into the dark interior hallway.

"Well," I said, saved for the moment, "what shall we do today? Or, would you rather just sit and visit?"

"If we wait too long, I'll forget the rest of the story. I've been trying to sort out the part where mother lived at the big Fröman house, Källeborg, in Nås. The times were near enough together and changed and I have always been a little bit confused anyway, with when she was here and when she was there," she waved her hands in annoyance. "When mother became pregnant with my brother Per Gustaf, she was in Källeborg, where they moved after living in the vicarage. Källeborg was a single house then; not divided into apartments as it is today. The man...a relative, who once lived there, the father to the old minister, was manager of the large iron fabrication concern, near Järna, called Snöå Bruk. You have seen the ruins?"

"I nodded, remembering the massive stone arch and thick walls, standing in weed-grown ruin. Some of it stood crumbling along side the clear millstream and pond. It was truly a lovely site. Wildflowers bloomed merrily where impoverished men had worked in near slave conditions a hundred years before.

"Mother said," Karolina interrupted my thoughts, "that after the minister had her in for her thrashing, that she didn't see my father for some time. She worried that his mother and the minister had finally been successful in convincing father to forsake her and the coming child. She was troubled...very troubled, indeed. More than once mother doubted the wisdom of her decision to force Pastor Johansson to confess. She believed she would succeed, if she could maintain her course, emotionally.

But, as you know from your genealogy research—or, as I will tell you, I guess, it took the birth three more children to finally bring resolution to the matter. And by then...other problems were looming...but that is later.

Monday, Carl left three hours before the sun rose. The old parson was still in his bed and Anna-Stina had the kitchen of Källeborg to herself. She was planning to mix bread dough and set it aside to raise and bake before the day was done. The parson and some of his poorer neighbors would have fresh bread with their supper.

Later in the morning, a messenger arrived. By then the bread was raised and ready for the oven. She knew the man as someone living in Nås who worked for the Kommun and sometimes, the churches in Järna and Nås. She invited him inside to warm himself and say *hej* to the old minister, who had recently taken to ever-increasing bouts of loneliness. The man had nervously refused and left immediately after handing her a document.

After wiping her hands on her apron Anna-Stina examined the exterior of the official-looking paper. Her name was written boldly on one side and it bore the seal of the Järna Church. With her thumb nail, she broke the dark, red seal and folded open the stiff paper. Carrying it over to the window, she began to read, absently brushing flour from her apron. It was from Pastor Johansson...what does the devil want now, she wondered as she scanned the script. The letter advised her she was required to present herself to the Rector of Järna church in three days time.

So...she thought, he has got word of the coming child. What sort of devilment has he concocted to punish me? I must be strong and play this game carefully...boldly. He holds all the strength. They can all control me. But, they cannot stop the child from coming now, nor can they deny the fact that it is Carl's, especially if he freely admits it. They will have to let us marry, now. But will the evil one ever admit his guilt? I must make the journey into darkness—again, into the unknown...to listen to that evil one, claiming to be a man of God.

Later as she continued her work in the kitchen, she worried about the possible consequences: I must be strong. I must persevere—no matter what. She imagined the conversation that would take place in the parsonage. The pastor was summoning her to demand that he be allowed to immediately marry her to the father of this one. She was determined to once again present him her own ultimatum: marry them...yes, but first, admit your own sin of carnal lust, assault and rape and claim the now dead child as your own. If he refused, she would not budge in her resolve—he owed her this admission. It was little enough to pay for what he'd done to her.

Barring that, she would not marry Carl...or anyone. That stand

caused her a spasm of emotional pain. She would stand
defiant…shamelessly remaining in the parish with yet another
oäktabarn—a reminder to all of Pastor Johansson's ineffectiveness as
minister to his flock. But most of all, she decided, she would
increase her effort at taunting of the minister himself—driving him
even further toward the madness she knew was waiting inside him—
waiting for the proper combination of circumstances to bring it out.
She'd seen it in many animals and also men. She knew it was
smoldering there, locked in his psyche; hopefully, she had the key to
unlock it?

Karolina was silent for a moment and when I glanced up, she was
looking across the table directly at me.

"That madness—which is inside all men, mother would
manipulate to serve her and my father's ends. They would bear child
after child—including me, lastly, until either Pastor Johansson
complied by marrying them, the minister died, or they killed or
imprisoned her. Such was Mother's resolve and thus began a slight
madness, too, in my mother, I have always believed." I didn't break
my stride in taking notes. Karolina lapsed back into the tale as if we'd
never left it and I continued my scrawl.

"Weeks later, arriving for the meeting called for in the letter, a
servant made mother wait in the kitchen for a long time, before finally
showing her into the pastor's study. I remember how angry she
became when she recalled the meeting. She said she felt as if
vallkullor were not fit to meet in the front room of the minister house.
It wasn't unusual for vallkullor to be scorned by house servants,
either. Both felt themselves superior to the other, you see."

The minister's house servants, of whom there were two, were
deferential to Anna-Stina; they respected and possibly even feared her
a little. Though she didn't realize it, it was the minister who made
her wait in the kitchen. Lena, the younger servant, had worked in the
family's fäbod for two summers and had been taught by Anna-Stina.
She'd quickly come to learn Anna-Stina was a force to be reckoned
with, if she was careless or showed signs of shirking her chores, lost
her cows or in any way disrespected any of the other vallkulla, or the
order of the fäbod. She also learned, Anna-Stina could be kind and
patient with her, so long as she applied herself in the work. She'd
seen Anna-Stina perform great feats with lost cows, old milk and

other daily problems of the *fäbod*, which astonished many, beside her. There were some who whispered that Anna-Stina was in league with *Rånda*—or, was herself a witch. But Lena wasn't stupid and after a summer in the forest, thought better, suspecting it was merely jealousy on those women's parts. A witch wouldn't be as kind as Anna-Stina, to her and the other young girls.

The young servant fetched Anna-Stina a stool and then quickly left her, feeling uncomfortable to have to offer such a menial seat. Before she closed the door, she told her to wait while she went to converse with the older servant. She was ashamed to be in such a position with a woman she respected.

Given the news that the expected visitor was in the kitchen, the older servant nodded and went to pastor Johansson's study to notify her employer of Anna-Stina's arrival. Without glancing up from his desk he bade her advise Anna-Stina to wait until he called for her.

She pulled the younger Lena away from the passage as she closed the door quietly and both women returned to the kitchen where the older woman, in as cheery a tone as she could marshal, told Anna-Stina she must continue to wait, that the minister was still busy.

They then attempted to fill the embarrassing wait with idle chatter. Although they were curious about why Anna-Stina had been summoned, they wanted none of the trouble they feared might have arrived with her visit and thus, didn't pry too deeply into her purpose for attending, suspecting it had something to do with her swollen belly.

Both women knew from first hand experience, the bottom limits of Anna-Stina's wrath—and her reputation was even worse. Nervously, they talked at length about the coming child. How was she feeling, was it like the last time, did she wish to have a boy or a girl? The questions rolled forth in rapid succession as, from time to time, their glances passed to the little bell on the kitchen wall that would eventually summon Anna-Stina to the minister's study. They didn't ask what she would name the child but Anna-Stina volunteered that:

"We are still somewhat undecided but have considered that if it's a boy, we would call him Per Gustaf—and if a girl...Karolina."

They were about the go into the history of Anna-Stina's family names as possible choices, when the bell gave a twitch and three pairs of eyes glanced at it, interrupting their exploration. A relieved silence fell abruptly upon the trio. Anna-Stina rose slowly, straightened her simple dress and waited to be escorted to her meeting. The older maid nodded, stepped in front of her and walked down the hallway toward the door of the study.

At the door she paused, rotated the brass handle and before she swung in the door open, smiled sympathetically to Anna-Stina. From inside the room someone cleared his throat impatiently and the woman, glancing at the floor so as not to meet her eyes, stepped aside, allowing Anna-Stina to pass into the room.

Closing the door soundlessly behind her, Anna-Stina surveyed the room; it was small and dominated by a large, polished desk; Pastor Johansson sat with bent head, writing. He was wearing his black frock coat. A large hat lay to one side of the desk, as if he had just arrived, or was just about to depart and decided he must commit something to paper. Two, corner windows were screened by thin curtains. Heavy, damask draperies were drawn open only partially. A pair of candles guttered quietly on either side of the desk, flanking a large ink blotter that was framed in engraved and gilded leather. A twin silver inkwell dominated the center-front of the desk with several steel pens lying in the tray.

Anna-Stina approached the desk but didn't go so near as to divine who he might be writing, or its' subject matter. Nor was she so bold to take one of the two cloth-covered chairs placed symmetrically before the desk. She stood stoic, but patient, her composure resembling someone who might shortly depart unless she was soon dealt with. Her arms were forward, hands clasped, but not fidgeting. She held her head high and backward slightly, giving her the impression she was looking down her nose at the minister. She presented a general air of impatient waiting, but that she was waiting for something from the man…not the reverse, as was the actual case.

Pastor Johansson must have sensed this somehow for, after a moment, he stopped writing and looked up, but didn't rise. Staring at her for a bit, nervously rolling the pen between his fingers, he leaned forward and carefully laid it on the marble base of the inkwell. Leaning backwards again, as if to appraise her, he finally spoke, looking also rather down his nose: "So you have sinned again Anna-Stina Malmberg."

His glance dropped deliberately to the swelling of her belly. He regarded her shape curiously as if it was the first time he had seen her with child. She remained standing, straight and unsmiling, deliberately not gracing him with an answer to what she felt was certainly not a question. By not offering her a chair and by keeping her waiting there, standing in the middle of the room, his rudeness confirmed the course the interview would take.

She returned his stare, defiant only in her silence and posture. Her eyes communicated no emotion that would give him the upper hand in which to begin an argument. If anything, she gave a sense of triumph, knowing she held the ultimate, upper hand. But she also knew she must use care, letting him disclose his devilment, first. She was pregnant again…true. Everyone knew it was Carl Fröman, though, which made it all the worse.

A jewel of the community, mating with a stone in the forest. Nothing could be more unlikely and the pebbles which would result would tumble aimlessly in the stream of life without ever serving in anything constructive, the minister thought, as he took her in. There she stands, he thought, hardly daring to speak for fear his voice would crack with emotion…or passion. God—how beautiful she was, swollen with pending motherhood. She fears—yet shows no respect for this office; but she is humble enough. Or, is that a look of triumph? Over what? I have offered nothing yet and she has not refused it? But surely, she has by now changed her manner: amenable? Obedient? Biddable? A totally humble servant of God and this office? Well, possibly not yet, but I believe she even—yes, I believe she even hangs her head slightly there…possibly this will be easier than I thought.

He finally began speaking, gently and with commitment:

"Anna-Stina, you know the meaning of and the penalty for…fornication." The word rolled from his lips with a sort of relish, almost condescendingly. "You must name the father of your child and declare your sorrow to God, begging forgiveness of the church and of me your pastor. I…we—the church, shall not be any more harsh with you than the sin dictates."

Still, she didn't move, raise her head, or appear to be about to answer.

"This is the second *oäkta* child you have conceived and will bear in sin, outside holy wedlock. This, this freedom, you exercise, must cease, Anna-Stina." He said this with a little more force. He was concerned about this absence of a reaction, from her…that she was going to prove difficult, as in the past, wanting to gain more of a governing hand for herself.

She lowered her head, a little but continued watching him. For those who knew her best, the flush that had slowly come over her countenance would have warned them; she was beginning to burn with rage. But not a flicker, glimmer, or twitch, betrayed the depth of the emotion his comments incited, or the height of the flames being kindled.

What is wrong with her he thought? She is usually so animated. Is she ill? Could it be that she is not really with child—no, there is little doubt of that...he glanced at her belly again. Could she have secretly married? Who would dare marry her outside the parish without our knowledge? Certainly not...*Catholics*? No...never!

"Are you not going to respond, Anna-Stina...why do you not answer the charges I have made?"

But his words began to run down, taper, like a clock, the pendulum's swing slowing, about to stop running. And seeing it coming, now, he finally stopped speaking altogether.

Anna-Stina took a step toward him, dropping her hands as if in readiness to do battle. She also tilted her head to one side, seeming to regard him more seriously...with new attention.

"Carl Fröman and I wish to marry and bring this child—my first child from a union of love, into the world and The Church, with its' true parents as husband and wife, not as an *oäkta* child of an unfavorable union, resulting from an aggressor's forced attack."

What she said didn't surprise him—he knew she would be defiant, but the way she said it shocked him so, he nearly started— the force and commitment of her diction put him off balance. He'd mistakenly imagined the countenance she presented, when she entered the room, would bring a submissive response. For her part, Anna-Stina couldn't resist the taunt—the word unfavorable had been specially selected and she witnessed that its import didn't pass him.

She paused, gauging his reaction before she continued, planning to play her next card. The minister's face, which had earlier borne an evil sneer, was now bent into a crooked smirk of frustration and as he seemed about to interject, she continued to press forward, even stronger.

"You are of course, aware of my terms, Pastor Johansson." It was a statement rather than a question. When he seemed confused, she reiterated: "In the church—on my wedding day—before your fellow souls—you will confess your crime against me and the church. You will admit the sin of assault and rape—and you will claim the parentage of my first—our…" and she struggled with that word, "…our little Augusta—our child, conceived from your frustration and lust. You'll acknowledge her as your own and you shall apologize to me and to the congregation, for being a hypocrite…a mere man— and to God, for your own sin, which is between you and him. And then you will marry us, Carl Fröman and me—immediately after." She hesitated, seeming to be about to add something: "And there will be peace ever after," she added quietly.

As she'd recited her demands the minister's face showed surprise, then disbelief and though he attempted to control himself, feign off her taunt, he finally exploded in anger.

"I imagined, Anna-Stina, that you'd forgotten that stupid conversation," he shouted, leaping to his feet at last, nearly capsizing the tall-back chair. "This time you shall truly regret your impetuosity; I—I—this time you will very much regret your—your wanton nature…."

With the fierceness of his leaping to his feet, some of the ink had tipped from the wells and Anna-Stina calmly watched it creeping toward his newly drafted document and smiled.

He mistook her perceived humor as defiance: "I offer you one last chance, Anna-Stina. Repent—atone of your evil ways, cease your assignations with Carl Fröman and come home to God and His church."

His rage, obvious, his expressions easily read…as from the book that his face had become. I have him now, she thought. Again—like a fish, I have him hooked. He appears about to weep; as a frustrated child who can not have its way.

Without thinking it through, Pastor Johansson tried another tack. "It was not enough…you continue to bring shame to your family Anna-Stina. Now you carry it to the Fröman family. *Fru* Fröman; she was nearly devastated with the news of what you have done to her son Carl…bewitching him."

She fired a last volley: "And who was the bearer of such ill tidings Pastor Johansson—Carl? It was not Carl's belly which was swollen with your sin, so who has done what to whom?"

"What? Why—why must you persist Anna-Stina? Why can you not see the power assembled against you in this misconceived endeavor? Why can't you be reasonable for your actions? The strength that can be garnered against you—force you to comply...it can be tempered, if only you will understand, if only you will acquiesce, bend a little—comply?" With his last words he turned and placed the chair back on its legs and slumped into it, putting one elbow on the chair's arm and bending his forehead to his raised hand, cradling his head.

For a fleeting second, Anna-Stina felt the slightest twinge of pity for him; he was nearly pleading now. Then the recollection of the attack, vivid as ever, slammed her back to the reality of today and she hardened her heart. She witnessed the inward struggle taking place inside him and waited until he finally raised his head; he glanced around the room, not meeting her eyes, appearing trapped by his invited guest and seeking a place to hide.

Still, he hadn't asked that she take a seat in one of the two, available chairs, so she continued to stand, over him now, stoic, waiting, watching him peer from side to side, in obvious anguish, as if searching for his tormentor, or an emancipator.

Taking a long, slow breath and sighing, he began to speak: "Anna-Stina, you must realize if you...are permitted to continue in this manner, the community will come to question your brazen disobedience of The Commandments. The Church does not like disorder, does not regard it as stable or wholesome for the community of man. Therefore we can—will force things—people, to change—changes that even you, I or The Church do not desire, or have the power to control, once they have begun to be instituted. If this should happen, The Church...I...will have no choice but to bring strong measures toward you in punishment." He paused, glancing at the unfinished paperwork on his desk, now ruined by the escaping ink.

"Can you not see reason and accept an alternative? You know, a woman of your...stature, a simple *vallkulla*, can never marry a man like Carl Fröman?"

It was a simple statement of fact...never. What he said next totally shocked her.

"But—Anna-Stina, you—you can marry me...a lowly pastor in The Church...I would yet have you?"

She visibly started, blinking her eyes in disbelief. She almost spoke, standing with her mouth open, but she was unable, knowing if she said anything at all, she'd be unable to control her emotions. If she ever doubted it, he was now hers—hers to the death. She felt she best be silent and retain the final hold she'd striven so hard to achieve. His words had so completely surprised her; marry him now...he wishes to wed me? Here it was, the hold, the grip, the bonds I hadn't yet thought were built, but...he now is truly mine.

Some time passed with neither speaking. The minister deceived himself, thinking her silence meant she was considering his offer. He'd no intention of making the offer of betrothal, though he'd always wished to—dreamed of it, even. But like an impulsive child, the request had had its way, sneaking out in a moment of emotional feebleness. She has enfeebled my mind. This infatuation, he thought.

As the silence lengthened and lacking her response in the positive, he feared he had only shown his weakness. He didn't dare glance upward, knowing he would see the refusal in her eyes; or, even worse, repulsion—condescension. He both hoped and feared she could bring herself to return his affection.

But she did neither. She turned on her heel and in three steps crossed to the paneled door. There she stopped with her hand on the door, standing still for a second, composed, she, turned the handle and as she stepped through the door, glanced back at the beaten man sitting at the desk. He'd raised his head at the sound of her footfall, a look of surprise on his face. He hadn't expected...to have his proposal totally ignored.

What he saw as she turned in the doorway was a smile; a smile of triumph. Even more than triumph, it was a look of lewd torment...a torment which struck him to his heart, to the quick of his being. Open-mouthed, he watched in unbelief as the door closed quietly behind her figure. No violence, no further anger, no emotion. He shuddered, hung his head and began to weep, knowing he'd lost and would have to take the next step, beyond which there would be no returning.

Anna-Stina left the minister's parsonage feeling better than she'd felt months. It had begun to snow heavily as she walked the mile to her cousins' on the bank of the Västerdalälven. She would spend the night and wait, hoping for a ride downstream in the morning, in any of the many rowboats headed down river for Nås and home to the old minister's in Kalebourg.

With the river just beginning to flood it would be a quick journey. And with luck, she'd easily be home tomorrow in time to prepare the old minister's mid-day meal. What ill wind will now blow through me, she wondered, cupping the bulge that lay beneath her stomach? What next...to survive?

After her visit to the minister's, it was more than three weeks before Carl came to call again. But since the meeting with Pastor Johansson, Anna-Stina was no longer worried about Carl's affection. He arrived one evening, well after dark. She'd prepared the old pastor's meal and afterwards, was reading to him in the library. She heard the sleigh's bells and at first thought they'd passed by, but with the sound of someone stamping snow from their feet, on the stoop, she put down her book, causing the old minister to look up in surprise.

"There is someone come, Pastor." She got to here feet with effort and walked along the cold hallway to the door. As always, she was cautious when she answered the knock, fearing what yet unknown evil may come from the thwarted minister. After sliding the bolt, she opened the door only a hand's width, but when she saw Carl, flung it wide and leaped into his arms.

"Oh, Carl—I thought something had happened." She buried her face in the fur of his coat collar. "After my meeting with Pastor Johansson and the way he spoke to me...I didn't know what they would do to you, or to us."

Carl held her for a moment, ecstatic that she was well and seemingly safe, still caring for the old minister. "Let me tend to the horse and I'll return to talk with the old man for a while. We can talk of this later, when there is no one to hear and we can be warm. No one but my mother has yet approached me about the affair. I'll return shortly; we can speak of it later."

He smiled down at her, holding her for a moment more, taking in the beauty of her and letting the pleasure of the sight of her warm smile, her smell and the strong feel of her fill him with pleasure. When she looked up he saw the promise in her eyes. He kissed the top of her head before she shut the door and he returned to the horse and sleigh and she to the kitchen to rekindle the fire, to feed and warm her beloved.

"Pastor—Pastor…Carl has come," she said, excitedly as she passed the library.

Later that evening, after Anna-Stina had prepared a final cup of tea for Carl and the old man, she readied her kitchen for the next day's work as she heated water. When the kitchen was put to bed, she carried the hot water to her room, in two pails, for she and Carl to use to bathe in before bedtime. Waiting for Carl to bring the old man up to his room and then, join her, she stood in the light of the candle, looking down at her belly. We shall have a new Fröman in the world; but will it be able to bear the name? She was afraid of what the church may yet do to punish her for this sin. She hoped Pastor Johansson would relent, himself confess and permit Carl and her to marry, but she doubted it would be soon.

Since his limp proposal Anna-Stina had thought a good deal about their situation. And the more she reflected, the more concerned she'd grown. Pastor Johansson would not take this continued rejection lightly, she thought. Yet, she knew when she set out on this course that it wouldn't be an easy one to follow. She hoped her parents wouldn't suffer, again, from her stubbornness. Her father's health had depreciated considerably in the last two years and her mother was busy all her days, coddling and caring for the old man as best she could, being herself in advanced age.

I should be home helping mother, too, she thought; but that would be even further from Carl and the old pastor. She'd come to love the old man, almost like a father. Selfishly, she though, it would be nearly impossible for her to bring to bear an effective assault on Pastor Johansson from the remoteness of Andersforsbruk.

After wishing the old pastor goodnight, Carl came directly to her room, the door opening quietly and then closing again. She'd been lying in the bed, thinking and waiting for Carl to appear in the candlelight. She'd quickly replaced her own, now-cold, bath water with two warm pails-full for Carl.

"What? Bathe again," he'd whispered loudly, "I just…"

Carl groaned outwardly when she told him he must first bathe before coming to her bed.

"And it's so cold in here," he complained as he undressed.

"Suit yourself," she remonstrated, smiling in the darkness. "I can wake you…in the parlor…when breakfast is ready. Good night."

With that she rolled over, turning her back to him, smiling to herself in the darkness, before pulling up the heavy robe to her chin. She didn't snuff the candle, however, knowing he would need it to see the water for his bath...quick as she knew it would be.

Soon, she heard splashing of water and several groans as the cold air evaporated the water on his body and in moments, he was beneath the robes in her bed, pulling himself against her warm back.

"*Ooouuhhh*," she exclaimed snuggling close to him. "You're cold...now I almost wish you'd remained dirty."

But she soon matched the urgency of his eagerness for her and soon, there was no need for the heavy covering.

Later, Carl was holding her close against him, reaching both arms around to gently caress her swollen abdomen.

"Your belly has gotten much bigger," he said, "...and harder, too."

"And what did you think it would do, Carl. You have planted a healthy seed; this ground is very fertile. Soon we shall harvest a lovely crop and God bless the weather when it comes out for we will need all the help we can get."

He sighed, "Yes, I wanted to speak with you about that possibility. Pastor Johansson had been to see my mother before he summoned you. I'm afraid she's livid. She wants me to deny this child and cast you both out. The pastor has hinted at what he can and will do to punish you, if you refuse, but she won't tell me what it is. They're firm allies in this matter, I'm afraid."

"I know what he wants to do for me, but I don't know what he wants to do to me."

"You do? What did the pastor say?

"I'll tell you in a moment, but first, what more did your mother say, Carl?"

"I've never heard mother so resolute in her conviction that we shall not marry. I had actually thought, possibly...the coming child— she was so angry when she spoke your name, she actually spat it, such was her violence."

"I understand. I believe her fire is being fueled by another source: the minister."

"Really; I thought it might be the other way around...she asking him to prevent our marriage? Why do you believe he's the source?"

"Because he asked me to wed him, himself, Carl; he proposed

marriage to me during our meeting."

"No…he didn't?" Carl stirred beneath the bed clothing, sat up abruptly and turning toward her. "What sort of man is this," he said, touching her shoulder in the darkness. "I didn't suspect this feeling. Was it so strong, even though you told me your own suspicions? I believe we have a strong enemy, Anna-Stina, for…if he can not have you now, he will try to see that no one will have you." This came with a note of sadness, in the darkness. Anna-Stina reached across and hugged Carl tightly, holding him to her for a moment.

"He can't defeat me, Carl," she said with resolution. "I know…that I own him. I know I do, Carl," she said, thinking again of the strange marriage proposal.

"Yes…well…?" was Carl's unfinished reply.

In the darkness she couldn't see the doubt Carl was feeling. He hadn't disclosed all his fears. His mother had hinted to him that, with this second out of wedlock pregnancy, Anna-Stina's fitness as a citizen could come into question by the authorities, especially if her transgressions were fanned further by The Church. He'd asked his mother to be more specific, but she would not. The gravity of what she'd hinted was of great concern to him. His mother wasn't one, at that point, to offer quarter to Anna-Stina, but her son's ultimate happiness concerned her. With this foreboding, she was showing womanly concern she could not help, because he was her son.

She'd suggested Anna-Stina's right to certain functions within the community, church and state could be questioned—denied possibly, but worst of all, the child could be taken from her and she, herself, declared unfit as a mother and a citizen of the community, the latter justifying imprisonment. Carl's heart was sick at the thought. Dear God. I truly have sinned with her, he thought and now she must suffer for what my weakness has brought upon her.

CHAPTER 18

Another Birth

As the snows of March diminished, intermittent storms swept over the community of Nås and Anna-Stina grew larger with child. When the time came in the spring to take the cattle to the *fäbod*, old minister Fröman begged her to remain at the parsonage with him, not for himself, but out of regard for the coming child. But the call of the forest was too much. Throughout the dark winter she'd been confined and now the longer days of spring, the warm rains and first blooms...she just had to escape. The prejudices of the village were evident and weren't pleasant now that people were outside and more active. To exchange that torment, for the impartiality of the forest and her beloved animals was something she couldn't live without. It was truly nourishment for her soul. In *fäbod* it would only be the other *vallkullor* and the animals, both of which she could control, if she needed to.

Thoughts of the annual pilgrimage to Vansberget spurred the *vallkullor* to prepare in advance for the day they'd set out. Preparation of the *fäbod*'s dwellings for summer occupation and once again settling into the daily routine was foremost in all their minds. The cattle and goats were always excited at the onset of the journey; they ran and played along the path for the first hour before finally settling into the long walk.

The path took them northward, over the mountains, following ancient tracks long used by forest animals, following the natural and easy flow of the terrain. Then, striking the Vanån, they trudged beside the river until they were opposite the mountain, Vansberget, at last.

With the end in view across the expanse of the Van, they regrouped and prepared to swim the animals across. Using rowboats left for the purpose, the women ferried children, grandmothers and supplies. Once the passengers were safely on the other side, certain *vallkullor* would take their boss-cows by their halter, pulling them into the water, behind the boats and start them swimming. Remaining villagers would force the other animals to follow their leader to swim the river's expanse. The majority of the goats, too stubborn to swim, would have to be ferried in the boats. Once ashore on the far side, they had only to make the final climb up the steep mountainside, where, the welcome barns and some evening grazing in the yard around the log structures awaited them, before bedding down for the evening. After the magnitude of the day's journey, they would sleep the peaceful sleep of their untroubled and worry-free existence for the next few months, barring a few bear and wolf scares.

From years of prior experience the families immediately began organizing their new quarters. One ancient ritual was setting aside an offering, a small gift of food and milk to the *fäbod* spirits…from the goats to the mountain spirits, the *vittror* and troll, hoping to placate them throughout the summer and protect all the women's summer ventures.

They removed all the assorted utensils from the safety of winter storage, scrubbed them clean in the cold springs, readying them for the week's first *tjôckmjôlk, messsmör,* molded cheeses and butter making.

The men who'd accompanied the women helped clean and sweep all the cabins and barns, remaining the first day only, long enough to make minor repairs to fences and outbuildings. They also repaired any of the neglected tools from the previous fall, sharpening axes, knives and *lie*[92] which they would utilize again later in the summer to cut the hay, when they returned in the middle of summer; others cut firewood. When finished, they spent the last night and departed at dawn for the village and the crops yet to be sown. Even before the men left, the *vallkullor* themselves were already caught up in the fast-paced life at the *fäbod*.

The early summer passed with great pleasure for Anna-Stina. As she expected, the women and girls did not treat her badly; her condition was accepted as women have always accepted others of their sex who were with child. The common concern for the work and the health of the mother and child were primary to all with little regard for who fathered the child. Other than some swelling of her ankles at the end of the day, Anna-Stina experienced little discomfort. She did have a frightening incident when an enthusiastic heifer, rushed toward the spring for a mid-day and knocked her aside with the ease of a blade of grass. Landing in a sitting position atop the thick moss and looking somewhat startled and surprised, Anna-Stina was unharmed. She vowed to be more careful around the animals until her child was born.

Many of the other women and girls, out of their genuine affection and regard for Anna-Stina's reputation, looked for chores to take away from her in order to lighten the usually unequal self-imposed share she took on herself. This resulted in her having a truly beautiful summer at Vansberget. The weather was favorable; the meadow grass grew back again and again after grazing and mowing and the cheeses and butter went down to the village in a continual stream, every other week.

Anna-Stina passed the days in the forest with the cows, when she could, following and sometimes leading the animals to some distant place in the mountains, exploring small valleys and following little brooks, seeping and bubbling everywhere from the stone and tree-covered mountainsides. She didn't know when she would be able to return again, so she wished to take everything from the summer that she could absorb.

Once, when exploring a large cluster of boulders which caught her eye, each the size of a house, she found a *runsten*[93]. Thin and flat and at least the height of a man, it resembled a gravestone. Covered with intricate carvings in *runalfabet*, it had been long forgotten, or possibly even hidden there. She stood amidst the rocks for a while running her fingers along the deep and intricate grooves. The undecipherable glyphs left her completely ignorant as to the mason, or his message. She wondered whether anyone else had ever seen the remote work of the ancient scribe.

With her eyes closed, she tried to fathom the messages in the stones, through her fingertips. Was there something written here to help her with her life situation, she wondered? Could they offer some secret message from the ancients? Stepping back slightly, she suddenly wondered if there was something here from the *vittror*—the, invisible ones living beneath the ground. Could one of them also wish to harm her or the child, possibly casting a spell at some future time?

She began to gather the animals, preparing to leave the place, though she did it with some trepidation. Hurrying the animals around the mountain toward the home pasture, closer to the *fäbod*, she'd succeeded in frightening herself with her own imagination. The animals were unwilling to move; only grudgingly did they begin to leave the fine grazing and then only after some strong prodding from her stick. Again and again she had to force each laggard forward as they stopped to snatch tempting tufts from along the path, trying to get one last sweet mouthful from this place of plenty.

With the end of summer came the reluctant return to the village. Anna-Stina had had a beautiful summer and as usual, was reluctant to depart the *fäbod*. She dreaded the stares and secretive gossip she knew would greet her in the village. Even though she had made her choice and knew it wouldn't be an easy one to endure, her increased size would immediately redirect attention to her husbandless state.

Carl had come to visit only four times during the summer. The other women quietly accepted him. Most people in the community liked Carl. Since he was the squire's son, they knew they'd best show some deference to him, by custom. Many families were tenants to the Fröman family, so their livelihood depended upon friendly and cordial, mutual coexistence. Carl was not a stern person and expected little beyond common respect. His major concern was for Anna-Stina and to be with her. He, too, was suffering the stigma of their yet-unborn child and his continued association with the mother, Anna-Stina, whom he loved dearly.

During his visits Carl didn't pass his fears along to Anna-Stina. He avoided recounting the severe chiding's he'd received from both his mother and Pastor Johansson. Whenever the minister had the opportunity he attempted to persuade Carl to foreswear the unborn child and Anna-Stina and return to the avocation they had chosen for him: the Swedish Church.

He heard their entreaties without comment or outward objection, but didn't capitulate. He hoped to buy time. At first, this action of inaction seemed to frustrate them, but eventually, set both his mother and the pastor to their task with greater earnestness. His mother cried and told him he was ruining the families' reputation. His father, returning from business from a protracted stay in the south, had tried to speak with both Carl and his unreasonable spouse about the situation, hoping to suggest some compromise; Carl felt this probably came at the urging of his mother. But his father's heart was really not in the matter and he failed to really pursue the subject in earnest and, in the end, he and Carl had finally simply discussed the families' general business matters, farming and finally, the weather. Carl's father was helpless in these matters and in his daily life, browbeaten by his domineering spouse on the domestic scene. After the occasion of that discussion, his father had rushed back to his business accounts, which kept him occupied when he wasn't traveling for the family, or the community.

In early November, Anna-Stina received a letter from her mother at Andersfors, written by a neighbor's child.

"Your father's health grows worse." it said. "He's more frail with each day's passing—come home and help me care for him if you can."

None of Anna-Stina's married siblings were able to leave their families. Her mother had gone on to question whether the old minister could spare Anna-Stina to come help her care for her father, thus finishing her confinement in Andersfors, instead of Nås.

Anna-Stina made ready as quickly as she could. She assisted the old minister to arrange one of his younger sister's house girls to come to stay. She knew the promising young girl from the previous summer in the *fäbod*, where she'd proven to be a quick and eager learner and had seemed to have great kindness, something Anna-Stina especially wanted in anyone caring for the old man. She was not a beauty, so wouldn't be too distracted by the young men in Nås. Anna-Stina arranged as quickly as she could to train the girl to the special needs of the old man and prepared, herself, for her return to her family in Andersfors.

Anna-Stina made no specific plans to return to Nås. In order to put her in her place again, she knew Pastor Johansson would probably launch another assault on her and Carl's plan to unite, once the visible evidence presented itself with the birth of their child. She wanted to be close, also, to Carl, in order that he could share in the rearing of his child, even if they could not live together in wedlock. That would require her moving closer to Frömansgården instead of returning to Nås after the child's birth.

The old minister understood the need for her to return to her home, appreciating her past kindness. He hired a sleigh and driver to carry her all the way home to Andersfors. The minister had urged Anna-Stina to go home as soon as she told him of her mother's distress.

"I am not unwell...as is your father," he said, "your place is with him. Though there will always be a place for you here, Anna-Stina— do not forget that; you and your child."

Somehow, he'd also seen that there was a large basket of foodstuffs to accompany her in the sleigh, thanks to a neighbor, who'd packed it at the minister's urging. There was flour, rolled oats, dried fish and even some dried fruit, as well as the wealth of cheeses.

"After all..." he told a neighbor, raising her eyebrows at the cost and for a mere *piga*, "...Anna-Stina could hardly be expected to walk that distance through the snow and cold in her condition." And in a sudden, angry outburst, much unlike himself, he chided the woman for her unchristian behavior. The woman left promptly to tell the tale.

When she reached Andersfors, Anna-Stina found her mother haggard and markedly aged since she visited the previous year; she looked little better than her failing husband, Lars. When Anna-Stina first saw her father she thought he hardly resembled her memory of the once-stout hammer-smith who had swung his hammers with such ringing ferocity.

The old and shrunken man she found beneath the somewhat dirty bedclothes was very weak and hardly recognized her as his daughter. In the following days, as she cared for him, he would whimper and babble incoherently. Her mother told her he had been this way for some time and the revelation struck hard at Anna-Stina's emotional well-being. She tried her best, despite the depressing condition of her parents, to brighten the atmosphere, for her mother's benefit and succeeded somewhat. They spoke often about the yet unborn child and Anna-Stina's own childhood and that of her siblings, bringing a little cheer to both women.

Anna-Stina threw herself into the task of putting right the little house and making both her parents as comfortable as she could. After a week she was exhausted, but her mother, at least, was again well fed and comfortably placed beside the fire, for most of the day. Anna-Stina bathed the old man daily and washed all the soiled bed clothing as best she could, but not without a cost to herself. The food from the minister was a welcome supplement, especially to her mother, who had existed for some time nearly completely on oatmeal porridge. But it little benefited the old man, who ate hardly anything. And Anna-Stina herself was having trouble keeping food in her stomach. She was now big with child, at nearly full term. The heavy work and nightly interruptions to her sleep by her ever-failing parent, were beginning to drag her down.

Of course the neighbors in Andersfors knew of her pregnancy before she came. They didn't outwardly reject her, but she sensed the same distance between these people—people she had grown up with and whose respect she'd once held. Neighbors to her parents looked in from time to time, out of Christian charity, for which Anna-Stina was grateful.

She'd dealt with such people before and was well aware of their mixed and misguided attitudes about her; they didn't concern her. It was the genuine people, people of true goodness who troubled her conscience. Her ulterior motive, her conviction to break the minister's will and have him confess, was of course, unknown to them. But since that was her charted course, she couldn't expect them to understand this behavior, unable as she was to explain why she didn't bow to the will of The Church and common decency.

To leave them with the impression she was a trollop hurt her pride. This role is difficult to play, she thought, even though I'm an actress to some degree, playing another part in real life and after the play is over—that same role again, is difficult nonetheless.

I must again assume the stage role at the end of the performance, whatever that may be, unable to return to the role of gay and carefree actress. I am sincere and committed to it—and I shall triumph—in the end, I know I shall; he will bow to my will...he must.

Every evening Anna-Stina moved her mother from the bunk bed sleeping area along the wall, placing her on a pallet beside the fireplace, she laid for her nightly. Her mother would sleep warm and restful, undisturbed by her husband's fitful slumber.

One evening, a little over three weeks after moving back to Andersfors, Anna-Stina rose for the second time to tend her father. She offered him a drink of water, attempting as best she could to offer comfort. It did little to appease what was now very apparent and he only choked on the liquid. I wish I had some *brännvin* to mix with the water to sooth his sleep. But the cost of it was too dear. She thought the following day she might send the neighbor man to try to trade some of the old minister's cheeses for a small amount of the liquor. The neighbors would probably make insinuations about her being a drunkard, as well as a loose woman, if she attempted to acquire the liquor in person.

Sometime after her first ministrations to the old man, he'd began emitting a rattling sound, as he struggled to draw breath. Anna-Stina smiled a sad and loving smile at the sound of her father's frailty. Death had just entered the room, there in the flickering light of the candle and she touched her father's head. The love felt good inside her, though tinged as it was by the bittersweet pain of reality: her father may not now live out the night. Somehow, though, it gave her comfort, though still posing a feeling of dread of what lay ahead and the change her mother must soon accommodate, living without her life's companion.

To relieve his breathing, Anna-Stina attempted to prop her father upright somewhat in his bed. If he were to awaken, he would now be able to see her across the little room and call, if he needed her.

Half an hour later, as she bent to replace the gourd dipper in the bucket, her first labor pain struck. Deep and strong, the attack came, surprising her with its ferocity and catching her completely off guard. Holding the edge of the table—here I go, she thought. Even though I had expected it, I didn't expect it...and so strong. Unlike the first childbirth pain she had with Augusta, which began as a dull backache that slowly became worse, the onset to this was immediate—extreme and it couldn't have come at a worse time, she thought.

Within an hour she had to awaken her mother; the old woman was very deep in sleep and had difficulty adjusting to the realization that Anna-Stina would soon give birth. Once she was awake, Anna-Stina told her mother her husband would probably also be dying before dawn.

Anna-Stina debated whether to send the old woman for a *barnmorska*[94] or one of the other women who had volunteered to assist her when her time came. Normally, her mother would fetch them. But with the circumstances as they were, being the middle of the night, this was out of the question. If her mother left the cabin on such an errand, Anna-Stina could lose both parents tonight. She thought of going herself, it was only a half hour's walk, but she feared becoming paralyzed by child-birthing pain along the route and birthing the child along the snowy path. In the end she resolved to try to deliver the child herself, with what help her mother might be able to offer. If there were complications, her mother would have to serve, or at worst, go for help.

Between the pains she hastened to add pine chunks to the fire, so the baby wouldn't freeze. As the pains grew more frequent she fetched and poured more water into the copper kettle suspended in the hearth. She found clean linen and removed her own sleeping pallet from beside her unconscious father, placing it closer to her mother's. She then spread a linen cloth on the bare floor in front of one of the bunk beds. Thank God, she thought, we're not at *fäbod* with the earthen floors of the cabins.

Her father began to writhe weakly and occasionally moaned between gasping for breath. "Mother, please go to father..." another pain struck her then, so fierce it made her grimace and grit her teeth with its force. She'd been kneeling as she spread the linen, when another surge washed over her and for a moment, even blocked out her hearing and made stars flash before her eyes. When her vision cleared she saw the distraught look on her mother's face, as she shuffled across the room carrying two candles. She could see her mother's confused anguish, as her mouth moved; but she heard nothing but the ringing in her ears and the roar of the pain, as it wracked her lower body.

Her mother was gesturing, first toward Anna-Stina and then her husband who, though unconscious, faced Anna-Stina from his bed, his mouth was slightly open as if about to protest the impending hold death now had on him. The old woman seemed paralyzed between the two tragedies of the moment: the birth of another *oäkta* grandchild and accepting the impending death of the man she'd loved nearly her whole life.

As soon as the pain subsided, Anna-Stina called to her mother. "Take care of father. Put down the candles and go to father. I'll be all right. You'll be there if he..." the pain came again so suddenly, she toppled backwards, landing on her backside, clutching her abdomen. There she lay, rocking forward and back with each wave of cramping. Attempting to turn toward her parents, another contraction gripped her, almost in slow motion. Through the roar of the pain in her ears she could see her mother tottering beside her father's bed.

The old woman had placed the candles on the rough bench, serving as a bedside table and bending, climbed into the bunk bed, laying down beside her dying husband. As Anna-Stina watched— unseen and unnoticed—the old woman encircled her lifelong mate in her frail arms and drew him gently to her, holding him in the same comfort she must have done a thousand times, easing for him one, last fearful affliction, until it too would pass.

As one contraction eased, Anna-Stina could feel another mounting. She rolled her body, pivoting clumsily into a squatting position. The pallet was now soaked with her birth waters and she could smell human excrement and wondered if it were her father's, or her own. Bracing herself between the corner wall with one hand, her back against another she reached for the bench beside her father with her other, steadying herself, just as another pain came. Their faces were a mere body's length apart.

She didn't feel the tearing of her groin as the baby's head emerged. Her mother watched her calmly over her husband's shoulder, powerless to redress the pain emanating from Anna-Stina's scowling face as in the eerie, half-light of the fluttering candles, she grimaced and bared her teeth in the smile as old as time itself.

As Anna Helgsten watched the contortions of her daughter's birth giving, wave after wave of contractions swept over Anna-Stina. In the relief between the rushes, Anna-Stina and her mother silently looked at each other. At times, paralyzed, beyond speech, the daughter alternately steadied herself, hugged the unborn child within her abdomen—a life about to be given to them, while the old woman hugged the living remnants of the past five decades of marriage, which she would soon lose.

Without the need for words, their eyes communicated a mutual sympathy. In the short duration between her world of pain, Anna-Stina tried to smile in reassurance as her mother's bright eyes burned back, beside the gray of her father's matted hair.

Another searing wave nearly overwhelmed Anna-Stina. Peering between the slits of her eyes she could see her mother smiling sadly over the form of her husband. She spoke to him and stroked his brow and, surprisingly, her father had opened his eyes...momentarily back among the living and had taken his wife's hand, or she his, but he was still alive and looked across at the sight of his daughter, squatting on the floor before him.

Anna-Stina's body contorted in a final, mighty contraction, driving to rid itself of the infant. There followed another surge and the child passed through the opening from whence half of it had entered, in such joy. Anna-Stina's eyes and the eyes of her father, momentarily locked together in the last, flickering light of his life and her pain.

As the ultimate rush of birthing deposited his grandson onto the wet and bloody pallet in front of him, Anna-Stina watched the light go from her father's eyes and his stare at the child slowly became blind.

Little Per Gustaf was born well before morning dawned on the twenty-sixth day of November, 1854 and he was the last thing his grandfather's eyes saw...on this earth.

CHAPTER 19

Unwelcome Revelation

"As you can see," Karolina said, taking a deep breath, "trouble for mother seemed always ready to rear its ugly head. She would just begin to disinherit one burden and another would come along to be heaped on top again. When her father died—the day my older brother Per Gustaf was born, grandmother seemed to gain new strength, shaking off whatever had been ailing her. Whether it was relief or rest from the fatigue of caring for Grandfather, or the new interest of a baby in the house, Mother never knew. Grandmother lived on for more than a decade, until around 1870, I believe. Of course, I never knew her...but my older brother Carl did. He always said she was a spicy one and would pull his ear when he misbehaved."

I was shaken, as usual, at Karolina's revelations. Her own stamina was nothing to scoff at—I don't know who tired sooner during our sessions; she, from the telling, or I, from the emotion of the hearing.

"You've been at it over two hours and a half, Karolina. Do you think you should have a little break?"

"Really? I thought I just got started. Time goes so fast when we get into mother's story. Do you think we should stop, Alex...are you tired?"

"No, *I'm* fine, but I think you should have your lunch now."

"Oh...well, I suppose I could. I've passed the point that I'd organized in my head, anyway...my thoughts? I'll need another day or so to put things right in my mind again. I believe you're right, Alex this is a good point to stop. You go ahead—be off..." she said, waving her hand toward the street with a smile. "Go and find the one you were thinking about anyway."

I stood and began gathering my papers. "I don't know if she's still here, Karolina. Wouldn't you like to go inside before I take off?

"The sun's still warm. I'll stay here for a while—possibly have a little rest…then get myself a treat…lunch, maybe." She smiled, leaned back in the chair and closed her eyes. Will you come back this afternoon, then…?"

"I'll see how I feel, Karolina. I'll call and let the nurses know either way, Karolina."

She didn't open her eyes though she smiled and nodded, indicating she was OK with whatever I did. I left her then, still without a specific decision as to what I would do myself.

I really didn't want to face Karolina after lunch, or work on the book. I called the hospital asking after her condition. They reassured me that she was well—improving, so I asked them to tell Karolina I had an upset stomach and I wouldn't be visiting her again today.

As I took the Volvo for a long drive to the southwest coast, I felt guilty for lying. There were a lot of people, everywhere I went and it was difficult to really get away and find any privacy, like in the north; I was frustrated and wanted to think. Finally, I turned the car to the side of the highway and parked it on a lakeside pull-off. I wished there were dense forest, where I could take a walk. There, I could be completely alone and out of sight. I longed for the deep, moss-draped conifers surrounded by the giant stones of Dalarna. Many was the time I'd trudged into a forest, found a sunny spot, lain down and sank into the deep, mossy carpet, to doze or stare up at the scurrying clouds.

Staring out the windshield now, across the tossing gray water of the lake, I felt depressed. Sweden, Karolina and the story had all lost the mystery and appeal that had carried me to this point with such strength…for so long. There was no use denying it, Anna and my affection for her, had carried the load. Now, she was the cause. Or, the fact that I'd allowed myself to fall in love with her…was. How could I have been so stupid with Anna? Permitting myself to be so taken up; it wasn't as if she was plotting. But I think, probably without knowing it, she was using me to break free from the self-confinement of her failed marriage; or, maybe it was totally subconscious. After an hour, I realized I was getting nowhere with myself, so started the car, turned around and headed back.

Within a few miles of the apartment, I turned left, following the eastern road around the area of new industry that seemed to be fairly newly built. The country was growing quickly, I thought, lots of opportunity and money was being made around here.

A low-wing airplane glided over the highway, just then, at tree-top height. I slowed and watched it flare and settle onto the small runway. I didn't know there was a strip nearby. I drove a little further. Then on an impulse, checked the mirrors and abruptly swung the Volvo in a U-turn and worked my way back, stopping directly adjacent the runway.

I studied the layout, figuring where the office might be. I concluded it was probably at the other end of the airstrip, so I swung the car around again and as I approached a fairly busy intersection, hung a right. After another six blocks I turned right again when I spotted the tail-planes of a couple of aircraft jutting over a fence. I drove in that direction, finally stopping again beside one of the only two buildings along the runway. One, the larger one, must have served as a hangar and garage combination and there was a sign on the smaller building that said *Skata Landningsbana*.

"Magpie Airstrip" I thought, reading the sign as I got out of the car.

There wasn't anyone in the smaller building. It was fairly neat, both inside and out, always a good sign when you are considering renting an airplane, which I now was. Cleanliness and neatness are next to safety in importance and usually went together. Large maps neatly covered the wall in one area, consistent with the other small aircraft facilities I had visited around the world. Local air charts showing navigational—guidance beacons and all airports for Sweden and Norway. There was a larger map of Scandinavia with a measuring string dangling from an attachment point (my current location) which would give a rough estimate of distance from the attachment point. I grabbed the string and stretched it up to Dalarna and an airstrip near my cousins' farm. I compared it to the highway distance that I recalled from the drive, did a quick calculation in my head for the estimated flying time. Interesting, I thought—about a third of the time to fly there, as drive. That would make an easy trip, given good weather.

I strolled back outside, walking around a couple of aircraft tie-down rings imbedded in the turf and crossed to another of the buildings. There wasn't anyone inside this building—a makeshift hangar. Back outside, I walked out on the taxiway toward the strip. I was about to give up when I heard an aircraft and glanced up as a plane crossed overhead. It was the same low-wing Beech I'd seen from the highway—maybe a Bonanza; he was crossing mid-field, a little below pattern altitude, probably to land.

Maybe that's the operator, I thought deciding to stick around to see. I'd ruined the morning for any productive work (or Anna's confession, the night before, had) and I still didn't feel like facing Karolina's probable questions about the picnic, the day before, with Anna. I knew she'd see straight through any evasions I might proffer. My mood was still too sour to be any good company around her.

As the airplane turned from base to final approach, I saw it was a Beech—and fairly new from the look of it. I was surprised to see an aircraft that new in Sweden. They had to be flown from The States, across the Atlantic non-stop—no mean trip for a single pilot, having to stay awake. The seats were usually removed and additional, rubber fuel balloons replacing the seats to extend the aircraft's range. Being a single engine aircraft, if the engine stopped, you were definitely going to try out the rubber raft, assuming you survived a 60-70 mph water landing and got the raft and yourself, out of the aircraft before it sank. Brave fellows; those who brought the singles across.

I watched the aircraft settle in for its' final approach. The set up was smooth and the descent likewise. The pilot was rock-steady, despite the crosswind, maintaining the glide descent perfectly. Over the runway numbers, there was a little flair as the nose came up and the plane settled down for a perfect landing. I saw the little smoke puffs from the tires and a split second later, heard the yelp of rubber on asphalt.

The pilot taxied straight down the runway, left at the exit to the taxiway, continuing in my direction. I moved into the doorway of the operations building to clear the way for him to the hangar, should he want to power it inside. But he didn't; he shut the plane's engine down over one of the tie-downs, after pivoting the aircraft around so the wings were just aft of the rings. After ten seconds, running out the fuel, the engine sputtered and died.

When he opened his door I noticed the pilot was smiling and looked to be only a few years older than I. Gathering a clipboard from the empty passenger seat, before stepping out on the wing, he jumped down lightly and waved at me as he approached.

"*Hej—hej...,*" he greeted me.

"*Hej...hur mår ni,*" I answered. I thought I might as well switch to English now before he thought I was trying to prove something with my poor Swedish. "*Jag talar inte så bra Svenska*" I speak not so well, Swedish.

"I thought you were doing pretty well," he responded in English with a strong accent, looking surprised but grinning. "In fact, with your Norland accent, I would have guessed we're related. Karlson's the name, Per Karlson and welcome to the Magpie. Sorry I wasn't here when you arrived...hope you haven't been waiting long?" We shook hands and he turned toward the office gesturing that I should follow.

"That's all right, I didn't have anywhere to go, so I watched you bring the Beech around and down. Good job."

"Thanks. You an aviator?" he responded, interested.

"Yeah, in The States, I fly a little. Not as much lately and I haven't been up non-commercial, for over a year."

"Want to get checked out, again? Your ticket's good in Sweden you know—assuming your medical is current?"

"Yes, the medical's still OK. I've been thinking about taking something up to Järna—in Dalarna, for a long weekend to save that seven-hour drive. Got anything I can rent?"

"Oh, I know the strip there; sure, everything's for rent. What are your typed for—single engine—high performance? Can you fly this thing?" He gestured behind at the gleaming, new airplane.

"Yes, single engine, high performance, but I've never been in one of these newer Beeches, though I've flown the older ones. How long have you had it?"

"Less than six months; someone brought it over for short hop— corporate stuff and it turned out to be too small for them. Payload's around four hundred kilos after fuel. It is certainly nice. I just did a hundred hour check and it looks pretty good. When do you want to get checked out?"

"Doesn't matter to me—afternoons are good...or early morning's?"

"You instrument rated?"

"Oh, yeah, but not current of course."

"I can take care of that for you too, easily enough. What about tomorrow morning—say, seven?"

"Fine with me."

"Good...I'll be here.

"Anything you need to know before hand?"

"Well, is there any chance of borrowing the Beech's manual for the evening, so I can familiarize myself with her systems a little—be glad to give you a cash deposit in case I loose it?"

"Sure, I think I can do that. Got any identification—your permit to fly—something like that?"

"Yes—I have a pilot's license from The States; that OK?"

"Let's have a look—I have to, anyway, to certify you. Come inside and let me take a couple numbers down."

By the time, we were in the little operations building I'd fished out my wallet-sized pilots license and medical certificates. We crossed to the office area and I plunked the documents on the glass counter. Per looked at them, turned them over, and finally copied the certificate number.

"OK—you look like a trustful person; a deposit for the Beech's manual won't be required. Where are you living—staying in Sweden?"

I told him and gave him the address.

"Thanks," he said. "Here you are." From a neat shelf, Per pulled out a new, ring binder with Beechcraft lettered in white on the gray spine.

"Thanks again. That ought to keep me awake for a little bedtime reading. I'll see you in the morning...seven."

I turned to leave and then had second thoughts and returned. "Any problem if it's low ceilings tomorrow—should I call you first, or...?"

"Only if it's zero-zero visibility; then don't even bother coming. You can call to reschedule if you wish, though. If it isn't too foggy, we can still file IFR[95] and you can get checked out in the real stuff—if that won't bother you, that is, for the first time in Sweden?"

"No...all right with me...*thanks.* See you Per," I said shaking his hand and then leaving.

Passing the window outside, I glanced in to see Per wave without looking up from his document and I carried the borrowed operator's manual out to the Volvo and started for home.

I felt better. Good to break the routine, I thought. And I can sure do without that long drive the next time I go back to visit the cousins in Dalarna. They might even enjoy a ride, I thought, smiling to myself for the first time since leaving Anna.

Driving back to the apartment, I was thinking to myself: I'll bet Anna—and then I paused. Was there going to be an Anna in my future? At this point I wasn't sure. It would be nice to take her with me—up north. We could be anywhere in Sweden in a little more than two hours; even go elsewhere, airport hopping—see some of Sweden, Norway, Denmark…I wasn't sure about Finland. I'd never been there before. All was of course, if, there was going to be an Anna.

I found the thought exciting, of her accompanying me in the airplane. I realized the momentary diversion of the airport and flying had made my concern for her marriage and our future, even more poignant.

I drove past her house on the way home, but it looked deserted and her Volvo wasn't in the driveway. Probably had to work late again, I thought, feeling let down, somehow as I turned the corner and headed home.

I had bread, cheese and a bottle of beer for my supper, while I looked over the operation manual for the airplane. It was pretty standard stuff, being an American publication. I didn't really see anything different: weight and balance information, maximum load, take-off/landing airspeeds were different, but not new. Just another airplane…but a little bigger and faster than I was accustomed to.

I wrote a couple of figures on a pad for review before my checkout with Per in the morning; then I put the manual away and began transcribing some notes gathered with Karolina, before finally going to bed.

I awoke after a couple of hours, dreaming. I tossed around again for a while before finally settling down to deeper sleep.

I was deep in sleep at 5:30 a.m. when the alarm went off. I was confused at first, wondering what I was doing up so early, before it occurred to me that I was going flying. I wished I hadn't made the appointment so early and grumbled my way to the bathroom. I still didn't feel much better when I went outside to check the weather. It was foggy, but it didn't look bad enough to cancel and it might occur to Per that I wasn't really serious about flying. He might think twice about turning me loose in his new Bonanza, in instrument conditions. I was beginning to feel better as I got a cup of coffee and some bread, cheese and cold sausage down.

I was ten minutes early for the appointment but Per was there and already on the telephone. Cupping one hand over the phone, "I'm waiting to talk to weather and file our flight," he said waving toward the open door. "I think we can make it out of here. We can get a void-time clearance—do you have those—in the states?"

"Yup, we do…but, why don't you let me do that," I said, gesturing to the phone, "I've never filed and gotten a clearance in Sweden and I can use the practice."

Per stepped back and held out the phone.

"They're supposed to be able to do this in English—right? I want to see if I hit any snags with the regs or anything else special…if that's OK."

"I was hoping you would ask that," he said. "You're on hold for the next reporter. I'll pull the Beech over and gas it up. Yell if you have any problem on the telephone. I'll be around the corner at the fueling pump."

He waved to the left as he trotted out of the office. I held on the phone another couple of minutes wondering how long Per had been waiting. I leaned sideways and glanced out the window. Looks like about a thousand foot ceilings—let's see, what's that in meters. The flight briefer would want to know that…around 300 meters, I guessed and was interrupted by a noise on the telephone.

"*Hej-hej…?*" a female voice answered.

"Do you speak English," I asked, fearful I wouldn't be able to receive a flight briefing in Swedish.

"Absolutely sir, how can I help you?"

"I am flying for the first time in Sweden and I may need a little help with the briefing, if you don't mind. I'm departing from…" I glanced around the office frantically searching for something with the numbers of the airfield identifier. How terrible…my first time filing and I didn't know where I was. Then, I spied the four-character, airfield identifier WCAC, above the map.

…could it be Whiskey—Charley—Alfa—Charley—Skata Landningsbana?

There was a pause, "Yes, sir, those match."

"Good. I wish to get a full weather briefing and then file an IFR flight plan for a check-out flight to somewhere where there is sunshine. I'm sorry; I don't know where we are going yet. My examiner has left the room to fuel the aircraft, but by the time I get the full briefing I should know where we are going." I crossed my fingers, thinking how stupid not to have asked Per.

"Well, sir, I can give you a full briefing but I don't believe I will be able to help you with the sunshine, unless you can get on top at five thousand meters..."

And so the briefing went...not that much different from in America. As I hung up and jotted a couple of notes, Per returned.

"Sorry, Alex, about not giving you the layout before I went to fuel up—stupid of me. Was he upset with you?"

"No, *she* wasn't—a perfect lady about it; very professional. Are all the briefers that good?"

"Well...you get good ones and bad ones. I assume it's the same in The States? The ladies are usually best since they're pushing the upper limit, trying to break into the system. I knew it wouldn't be long before we had female airline pilots. Sweden is pretty liberal about the ladies, or they're pretty pushy about demanding their share...unwilling to take a back seat to any man. Or, have you already noticed that about our women?"

"It had occurred to me on the odd occasion," I laughed.

"Did you get a void-time clearance?" he asked.

"Yup and we have another forty-five minutes; I thought you might want to go over some things first."

"Good thinking; just time to get you checked out on the panel and answer questions. Have any problem with the manual last night?" he said, hefting the book I'd returned and putting it back on the shelf.

"None at all; standard stuff from the looks of it," I said, "she's pretty fast, isn't she?"

"Few can beat her with her full payload," he quipped, gathering up the charts and folding them. "The manual's almost always right here if you have any questions later. Shall we go do it?"

"Right."

We walked out. He closed the door and I followed him out to

the plane. On the walk out he said: "Will it make you nervous if I let you do all the check out, without prompting you, or would you rather I take you through it first?"

"No, that won't bother me; let's see how far I can get before I'm stuck. Where's the check list?" We'd reached the beautiful new Bonanza.

"Should be in the pilot-side door pockets," he said, walking back toward the hangar. "I'll be right back...go ahead and get started."

I wanted to get going and get this over with. I climbed up on the wing, popped the door and knelt on the pilot seat searching the unfamiliar instrument panel. Then I located and turned on the master power switch. I heard the gyro begin to wind up and saw the radio panels light up. I flipped the peto-static switch to ON so it would warm up while I did my exterior, walk-around check.

I did my best to work my way around the other items using the checklist and faking it where I couldn't make out the abbreviated technical Swedish. Surprising myself, I was able to remember a good bit of detail, since most aircraft are much alike in the items the pilot must always go over without fail in a pre-flight check. Apparently it satisfied Per, who had returned and leaned on a wing watching me.

When I said "OK?" he nodded and climbed in the passenger side without comment.

Settled inside and strapped in, I flipped off the master and peto-static switches, Per strapped in and again I scanned the checklist. I decided to toss it and ask Per when and if I got stuck.

"Altimeters' in meters," I commented, "guess I'm not surprised there."

"Right. The chart will also be as well and the approach plates, too. Before we depart, I'll go over a couple of the plates with you."

"Fine—that's why I'm here."

"Do you feel confident enough working in metric measurement? See..." he pointed to the altimeter, "...the pressure's different, too."

I looked where he indicated the altimeter-setting window, showing the pressure in some form of measurement I'd never encountered before.

"If they give me the correct reading, I can't see how I could get it wrong; no, I don't think that'll be any problem. Let's see...the radios...OK, vacuum, fuel pressure—a green band to stay inside—oil pressure, again…colored—temperature…same. Looks OK to me, Per." I said, meaning it and feeling satisfied with my ability to safely fly the airplane.

"Ok, ready to take her out?"

"Let's do it," I said and we each donned radio headsets, consisting of earphones with a microphone built in the front. Per adjusted his own earphones.

"What're the runway numbers here, Per?"

"Nine-zero and two-seven," he answered, me, indicating an east-west runway.

"Ok, then it's two-seven for us," I said, glancing at the wind sock which indicated a generally westerly breeze. We would be taking off into the wind.

We taxied to the edge of the runway and went through another check of the engine before announcing departure, throttling up and taking off.

The plane climbed steadily. Just before we entered the cloud bottom I raised the landing gear, brought in the flaps and began easing back on the mixture control to lean the fuel flow to maintain the proper manifold temperature. Getting that, I then adjusted the prop pitch to trim it out to the proper engine rpm's.

We entered dense cloud at seven hundred meters and I switched on the peto-static tube heater to insure continued instrumentation function when and if we ` altitude. At fourteen hundred meters, I checked the local approach plate and dialed the indicated frequency on the other radio. I switched to the number one radio and called Stockholm Center Control, as Per had instructed.

We flew for an hour and a half, working our way through the landing approaches, down through the cloud using the plane's instruments and the air controller's instructions. Finally, we received clearance from Flight Center to make the last instrument approach, down. From there, once we were below cloud and could see the ground, we canceled the flight plan and scuttled back to the home airport at Magpie under VFR[96], because Magpie was too small to have its' own instrument approach. The Bonanza landed faster than I was accustomed to, but I didn't have any problem—the wheels just touched before I expected it, bouncing once, slightly and settled into a

Inside the little building that served as the office, I sipped on a cup of coffee as Per wrote me up an approval to fly on my own, with a temporary logbook for me to record my flights.

CHAPTER 20

A Journey That Ends

Karolina appeared to be dozing when I strolled across the stone flags of the garden and entered the ward. So I sat down a little behind her and began to sort through my notes from the previous evening, trying to make up for the lack of organization from the long weekend with Anna and a day of playing airplanes.

After a quarter hour, I noticed Karolina stir. Her head had been bent forward; now she looked around and finally took a sip of water from the carafe on the small table beside her bed. She couldn't see me without turning around. I gave her a few minutes more to organize herself after her nap. She finally leaned her head back, holding her face toward the afternoon sunlight. I got up and sauntered over as if I'd just arrived.

"Oh…" she said, startled, "I didn't know whether you would be coming today. I was just having a short cat-nap…*sätt där…*," she indicated the chair beside her, patting the cushion, smiling and happy to see me it seemed.

"I'm feeling better," I lied. "So I thought I'd see how you were today."

"Dr. Olsson was here this morning for a little while. She seemed concerned that you didn't come yesterday and we both thought you weren't coming, again, today. I think she was even going to go to your apartment…to see if all was well with your stomach upset. But…here you are and all is fine—*yes?*"

"Yes, just a mild headache, out of sorts—something, I'm not sure."

"I saw Dr. Olsson and asked if you two overdid it last weekend.

You know—youthful zest? But she reassured me you behaved yourselves."

"Not much danger at our ages I guess." I tried to be cheerful. I didn't want to bring my problem with Anna to this old lady.

"Feel like catching me up on a few holes in my notes this afternoon?"

"Certainly. I hadn't planned, or organized my thoughts, but if you want to give me the questions, I'll try to answer them."

"OK," I said, sorting through my notebook. "I was curious about some of the ceremonies that were normally carried out among the church and community members in your mother's time. I know they—men and women, sat on separate sides of the church during the service…but what about the very old customs? I know the church didn't appreciate most of the old ways of celebrating, you know, *Midsommar*…the Easter Witches…*blåkullor* and the Easter rabbit—and so forth. I learned that they also condemned many of the songs and musical instruments, like the violin, bagpipe and the keyed fiddle. I wondered if your mother ever spoke about any of the special occasions—ceremonies in the community, or the church. You mentioned the cart ride ceremony was a sort of joking tradition and how your mother and the other *vallkullor* were sort of, celebrated within the families that she and others served—were there other occasions?"

Karolina sat pensive for a few seconds. "Well…you know that Mother played the fiddle and also the *säckpipa*. Of course there was the holiday…*Jul*[97] which was always special—and *Midsommar*, that was probably second most celebrated—still is, I believe. After that came *Påsk*[98] and some of the church days—*Whitsun*[99], Advent…. She sat for a moment looking at her lap and then looked up at me and smiled a little bitter smile.

"Only those celebrating birth and Christian holidays. I've already spoken of the one bad one that celebrated the birth of Mother's first child. They had other things in mind for her, after that, you see…."

Anna-Stina literally collapsed for a few moments, immediately after the child was born. But she found herself returning to consciousness as the cramping returned with the passing of the *moderkaka*[100]. Her mother had risen when she saw the bloody child lying squirming, on the floor. She knew her husband's final breath meant he had died. She covered him tenderly before slowly shuffling across the room to tend the kicking, mewing newborn.

First she examined her daughter, reassuring herself Anna-Stina had merely collapsed of exhaustion from birthing. She looked to see whether there was also any abnormal bleeding; but Anna-Stina was not yet out of danger. She opened her eyes as her mother wobbled toward her. She had a long piece of string dangling from each side of her toothless mouth and was carrying a long kitchen knife. She looked pale and weak, but appeared as if she had sufficient resolve to administer the cord tying and severance, before tying and severing the cord before wrapping the child. When she finished, she helped her daughter up from the soaked pallet. It had begun to be cold to Anna-Stina, as her wits began to return. Her mother didn't speak, but went about her work with resolve, though apparent fatigue and returning exhaustion were beginning to show.

Later, Anna-Stina finally stood up, with difficulty and went on shaky legs to the next room to add wood to the fire, only to find her mother already had. She thought about her dead father and what to do about preparing the body. She knew she'd be unable to do much herself, at least not for a day. Possibly by this afternoon, she thought, I might be able to walk up the path and summon a neighbor to fetch someone to come. I shall see; father will be cool enough there, covered as he is.

Later that day there came a knock on the door, waking her from the intermittent slumber that had overtaken her after she passed the afterbirth. Her mother had wrapped this in one of the bloody linen rags and placed it just outside the door. It was well into the morning by this time, so someone had been considerate enough to look in on them. She sat up with effort as the door swinging open. It was her brother's wife, Lena, dropped off on the corner of the main road by her husband. Lena was a welcome sight to the two women. Taking in Anna-Stina's appearance, she knew immediately what had happened and extended a hand in concern.

"Are you all right? Where is the child? Is it healthy?"

"Yes...we're both fine, Lena. Mother is more in need of help than I. Father has passed during the night, just as I birthed a son. Mother is trying to cope with both, now. Would you please go to them? I'll just sit by the fire for a moment and then make us some tea. Possibly, in a little while, you will fix us something else to eat."

Lena stepped toward the other chamber and hesitated as Anna-Stina took a tottering step toward the fireplace.

"I'm all right, Lena," she said, waving her sister-in-law into the next room, as she walked to the dying fire.

Soon Lena appeared with the blood-soaked linen pallet rolled between her hands, a questioning expression on her face.

"For now, just put it outside beside the door; there should be another bundle there. But, do not put it on the ground, or it will freeze, so I won't be able to free it up until spring. When I'm stronger I will boil the washing outside and I'll tend to it then."

Returning, Lena closed the door; the draft of cold air was fresh and invigorating to Anna-Stina, though it made her shiver slightly. She clutched her woolen shawl more tightly. I must not come down with childbed fever, she thought. Mother needs me now, as does the child. I must be strong. There are still two to care for. She'd not yet looked closely at her new son; her mother was holding him against her chest, still wrapped in a rag.

"Mother, how is he?"

Her mother smiled weakly and held the child out toward her, proudly showing Lena the bottom of the infant's feet.

Lena came across and took the infant, helping her mother-in-law to stand.

"Come, sit beside Anna-Stina. You two can look at him together while I prepare *Farfar*[101]. She handed Anna-Stina the infant, pink in all the right places. Lena had cleaned the child and wrapped it in her own clean shawl. Her mother leaned close and together, the three women touched and examined the child thoroughly.

After they had made over the infant for several minutes, Anna-Stina told Anna: "Take him for a moment, Mother." I'll get something more suitable to wrap him in. Lena's beautiful shawl will be ruined if we leave him in it."

She stood, searching the room for something to cover the child. Finally spying an apron hanging on a peg beside the only cupboard, she shuffled over and brought that back. Her mother helped her wrap the infant in the coarse linen. The old woman seemed to be growing stronger and was making cooing noises to the infant.

"Poor little one...you must wear but an apron for your first day of life on this earth. I pray it and God will give you more in the future and a long life to enjoy the earth's wonders and you can grow to be a man, despite your first clothes."

"He came before I had time to sew something for him," Anna-Stina spoke to her mother, knowing it was because her parents had required so much of her effort that she'd no time to think of herself and the coming child.

"I must find some goods and make some things for him to wear."

"There will be time enough for that," her mother smiled weakly. "We have many things to plan for before that becomes important. Have you chosen a name for this child Anna-Stina?"

"Yes. He shall be Per Gustaf," Anna-Stina answered.

"A noble name, I should think," Lena nodded, "let us hope he grows to be a strong and considerate man."

"Like his father," Anna-Stina replied without glancing up.

Around ten in the morning, I left Karolina and walked up to the ward desk and asked the nurses when Dr. Olsson would return. They told me she'd taken the remainder of her holiday...four days, actually, they said, at least with an indication of more to be added later. The nurses weren't sure how long she would be away.

"Something with her family..." they'd said, vaguely.

I left the hospital with a sunken feeling, realizing I was too late and would now spend a very lonely fortnight alone. On the way out to the parking lot, I decided to pass by Anna's, not knowing what I was going to say if she was there, but I definitely wanted to see and to speak with her.

Rounding the turn on her street, I could see her car almost a block away, still parked in the driveway. Hesitant, I pulled in behind her. The trunk was open and there were a couple of boxes on the gravel and a suitcase nearby.

As I opened my door, Anna came out of the house carrying a couple of boxes. I slammed the door and she glanced in my direction. At the instant of recognition, her face lit up.

"Hi," I said, walking up and taking the box from her and stopping beside her car. "Let me help."

"Hello—thanks, you don't have to do that."

"I don't know what else to do." I said, standing there with the box and not knowing where to put it "Heard you were going home?"

"Yes, as I told you, I need to visit my parents...Father is...well, not doing very well and Mother needs me, I think, whether she will admit it or not."

Straightening after putting the second box in the trunk, she stepped toward me, took the second box and turned to go but, as if on second thought, standing on tiptoe, she gave me a peck on the cheek.

"I'm happy to see you—I didn't wish to go without talking to you again. I feel really horrible about what I did. But I didn't know any other way to tell you. It had already gone too far. I didn't want to deceive you and we were going so fast, you know?"

Sort of ignoring her, I said: "Can I help you with something else?" I asked, still a little upset when she brought it up again. It stung anew.

"Sure, always glad to have a big strong man around—oh, I'm sorry...did I do it again?"

"No, not a bit. This strong man's got something to propose to you—got a beer, while I tell you about it?"

She looked surprised and nodded. "Sure, come inside."

I followed her into the kitchen and took a seat at the small, pine table with the yellow, flowered runner and vase, still containing my day-before-yesterday's flowers. Fetching a bottle of beer for me from the refrigerator, Anna poured milk for herself and returned the bottle.

"I—sorry, maybe I'll just have milk too. It's a little early for beer, I guess."

She nodded, returned the beer and poured another glass of milk before she sat down, crossed her slim legs brusquely and leaned back, smiling.

"I'm all ears," she said, serious but letting the smile lurk just beneath the perky face.

"Want you to fly back home with me...take you to Jämpland, I mean?" I popped the plan that I'd been hatching, as I drove from the hospital.

"Fly...with you—to Jämpland...? You mean...in an airplane?" She seemed taken aback by the idea.

"Yup. Save you hours and hours on the road, dodging the moose. And it'll give you even more time to spend, doing whatever you have to do with your folks, once you get there."

"When would we leave? I'm already late in getting started and my mother…and father, are expecting me tonight."

"We can leave anytime, I think. I'll have to make sure I can get the airplane, but I don't expect that will be a problem. I don't know where you have to go, but the Dalarna-Jämtland border is probably only three hours from here, depending upon the winds." I'd forgotten about that, too. I wished I'd thought to see what the schedule for Per's Beech was, before asking her. I didn't want to disappoint her, now that I'd asked.

Still, she seemed to hesitate. She was thinking. I hoped, not for an excuse not to go with me. Silently, I crossed my fingers.

"Where will you land—when we get there?"

"Where do you have to go? There are usually lots of small airfields available that would be close—unless you are going to the Arctic Circle; in either case, we can rent a car, once we're there…or close."

I added the latter for reassurance, definitely reaching now. God, what were the landing/take-off distances for that airplane—my mind raced to recall the statistics I'd studied a couple of nights before? Would we be able get close enough to where she was going?

"There's an airport there, but, I don't know…?"

What was she worried about? Was it such a small field?

"I mean…can you land at the same airports the bigger planes land at? There's a large one at Östersund, where my parents live; the large airplanes land there all the time, but can you too?"

"Oh, what a relief." She was worried the bigger airplanes would run over us, or something. "Yes, we can land there and in almost in any weather, too. I'm certain they'll have an instrument approach." I thought I'd recalled seeing an approach on the chart at Per's.

"I'm not sure," she said, looking a little worried, "they do have a very large runway—compared to here." She continued to seem to ponder.

"You're hesitating Anna…is it because you're afraid of flying with me?"

"Oh—no, not at all. But I was just wondering…why—what…going home with me? Why do you want to continue to rub the wounds?"

"Well…" reaching again, "…I thought I could drop you there—Östersund, then go down to Dalarna to the cousins—probably a three-quarters of an hour's flight and spend some time with my cousins for a change. Maybe you and I could even get away and do something together, you know, eat or—I don't know…it was only a thought."

She seemed to realize she was trying my patience and put her hand on my arm, across the table.

"I think that would be just wonderful." She seemed to be thinking for a moment. Then she brightened. "I can get my father's car so we would have transport while there and—getting there faster would be nice. I always get so tired, when I drive home all that way and at night. I think it's the emotion of having seen my mother and—Harald's—ill…you know? It depresses me."

"I think I understand. Let me use your telephone to call the airport. I have to check something quickly." My mind raced ahead for a back-up plan in case the plane was rented for the next few days.

When he answered, "Per? It's Alex—the American…from the day before yesterday, right? The Beech—is it still available for a week or so? You see, I was thinking about a little trip for several days. Do you have any restrictions about time away versus time on the machine? Yeah—Jämpland and then back and forth to central Dalarna a couple of times?"

There was a pause as he thought about it.

"Right; a little over a week," I said this, cringing, just knowing he'd say no. But he didn't.

"It is…*great*…yes, fill it up and add anything else you think I might need…right…no, first land at Östersund…then down to Dalarna after a day or so. Good, I'll expect it. And don't forget…if you have a set of approach plates for the area."

Anna came up and whispered something. "Just a second, Per. What…?"

"I'll finish getting my things together, Alex. How much room will we have?" I thought of the pile of boxes outside and what she might have yet to come. "Not an awful lot more," I answered making a wry face.

"I don't have much more, anyway," she said, "go ahead, back to your call. I'll finish packing. Uh…should I put it in my car?"

"No—yes…I'm not sure but maybe we'll take mine. We'll leave it here, at the airport. Just put your things on the drive beside my car and I'll see if it will all fit in the airplane."

She disappeared down the hallway, singing lightly.

"Sorry, Per. Anything else I need to tell you? Parts...sure, no problem? OK, we'll see you in a half hour. I hung up, thrilled that my luck had held. Per had said keeping the plane wasn't a problem and there was a spare part that I could pick up for him in Östersund. Perfect! I went out and found Anna standing beside the car.

"It's all set. We can take the plane."

"Do we take both cars, or only yours?" she asked still puzzled by the change of plan and the amount of luggage.

"Let's take yours to my apartment and mine from there." I helped her pack the items in the car. "I don't believe we can carry much more, Anna. The plane's not that large."

"This is it...what's here?" she indicated the mound of cardboard boxes and one suitcase. "I could probably consolidate a couple."

I hefted each of the boxes. They weren't that heavy, the worst problem for airplanes was weight. I thought I'd be able to repack and fit it all in.

"Good idea; see what you can do. I'm leaving now to pack my stuff and I have to call Karolina to let her know I won't be there for a few days."

"Maybe we should stop and tell her—I'd feel better if we did that. Would there be enough time?"

"You're right. I shouldn't be so inconsiderate. I'll meet you at my apartment. After I pack, we can finish loading my car and stop quickly at the hospital to say goodbye—then to the airport.

When we got there, Karolina seemed happy enough to see us off. She said skipping a few days would give her a chance to organize her thoughts and that I should come prepared at my next visit with lots of paper in my tablet. She also wanted us to remain long enough to take coffee, but we declined. Rest rooms were scarce in the air and none, of course, in small airplanes; so it wouldn't be wise to take in any more liquid than necessary. I wanted to get to the airstrip and get the Beech in the air so we could arrive well before dark. Per had said the metro people had forecast a fine day for most of Sweden and Norway. I hoped the weather would hold.

We arrived at the airstrip to find Per, pulling the Bonanza away from the fueling tank.

"*Hej*," he greeted us with a smile and a nod, requiring both hands to pull the airplane by a yoke connected to the nose wheel. I

got in front of a wing and helped maneuver while I introduced him to
Anna. She watched rather helpless, as we pushed and pulled the
heavy aircraft out and around front. We chatted continuously and I
could soon see that Anna had completely captivated Per with her
smile and cheery manner.

"I put extra oil in the baggage compartment. Where is your
luggage? I'll help you stow it. Have you called for weather?"

"There…," I said indicating the parked car. "and…no—I've not
called, yet. But you said it was to be a fine day."

"Right, but this is Scandinavia…not central USA. Our weather
can change in half an hour. Are you going VFR?"

"I thought we should be able to, why."

"No…I agree…and you can always file IFR from the air, if you
find you must."

We got the plane in position and Per removed the push/pull
handle and tossed it in the back.

"You go call metro while I help Anna with the baggage. I spoke
with the weather briefer earlier this morning. They were forecasting a
fine day…through tomorrow. There is a front moving into Norway
though. But then, you will get an update on that. Go ahead
Alex…come, Anna, let us look at your baggage and see what we have
to leave behind."

"Leave—behind," I heard her confusion.

"Everyone packs too much for small airplanes—too much weight."

I left him explaining weight and balance to Anna. I figured we
were all right on weight but it would take some master packing skills
to fit the bulk in the back seats and luggage area. I went in the office
and rang up weather. The report was pretty much the same as Per
had recounted. A front coming up the North Sea into Norway
tomorrow, late, might bring in low ceilings with the possibility of
thunderstorms the following day. I definitely didn't want to deal with
those, but we would be all right—all day.

"Are there tie down ropes in the airplane, Per?"

"No, I've forgotten. It's good you remembered. I'll go to find
some. Oh, I took out the back seats to fit in your boxes. Do you
think you will have more than two passengers?"

"No, that should be OK."

"Good…then you are all set." He ducked in the hanger and

quickly emerged carrying a fist-full of ropes. Handing them over, he
waved, "see you when you get back."

I tossed the ropes in the baggage area in the Beech before
returning to the Volvo to check that the entire luggage was out of the
car. I'd gotten directions on where to park the car and moved it then.

"Ok," I said to Anna, a little breathless from the trot back. I
grinned, "I guess we're ready." I climbed up on the wing and helped
Anna on the step, showed her where to step on the wing and inside
the aircraft, saw her seatbelts were fastened.

"Oh, this should be fun...I hope," she said. She had a little
trouble getting the seat slid forward. I helped her and once she was
settled, slammed her door and walked around the rear of the plane. I
carefully began working through the mental checklist in the walk-
around, outside the airplane: brakes, flaps, nav lights, oil...and finally
finishing by draining the wings and engine fuel sump of any
accumulated water.

I opened the baggage door and took a last look at the luggage.
Per had done a good joy stowing it, adding a fish net stretched over it
all, well secured against bad weather. The last thing we needed was
luggage bouncing around inside the aircraft, threatening to go
through the roof.

Flying VFR, we could fly as low as we wanted and Anna could see
the sights from the air. We could turn around, or look at whatever we
wanted, go up or go down. But if we encountered low cloud, I'd
have to call the control center to file IFR and go on instruments from
there to Östersund.

Per came out again and waved good-by. I climbed onto the
wing, opened my door and slid into my seat. Per did a thumbs-up
gesture to Anna and stood watching as I buckled up, fitted our
respective headphone sets and began doing the cockpit pre-flight.

Anna loved the pre-flight check procedure and asked questions
constantly through her headset mike, wanting to help. At last it was
finished and we waved one last time to Per and I started the Beech.

All we had to do now was enjoy ourselves and we did. Anna was
like a child once she realized she wouldn't fall out of the aircraft when
I tipped a wing low, as we would bank to get a better look at
something on the ground.

Anna even took a turn at the yoke, "driving" as she called it. Like most beginners, she had trouble holding a straight course and maintaining consistent altitude. But it didn't matter, we weren't under any strict rules. She seemed to enjoy the challenge and soon realized there was no real mystery to piloting an airplane, at least the keeping it in the air, part.

We headed straight up the middle of Sweden, passing Jönköping in less than an hour; then crossing kitty-corner, the big lakes of Vättern and Vänern, past the city of Karlstad and into Värmland Province, before finally striking Dalarna Province. Anna had the chart and identified each landmark wondrously, as we passed them.

Through the eyes of her bubbling enthusiasm and excitement, I saw the Swedish landscape anew. She marveled at each new mountain lake and asked several times if we could circle one, to take in splendor of the bolder-encrusted shores. I gave up on maintaining any kind of altitude and bounced in the heated air that rose to meet us as we skimmed first the mountain tops and then another bog or lake.

"Oh, Alex, can we be there already?" she would remark as we passed a town that took an hour to reach by road. She became very good at following our way on the air chart and could even call out some of the highway numbers, having traveled them frequently. Then we slowed once more, circling a couple of moose which were feeding nonchalantly in a field of oats. They didn't seem to know where the noisy threat was coming from.

They trotted toward the cover of the woods as we turned round them, passing over the farmer's timberhouse. A woman in the yard, hanging her bright wash on the clothesline, waved enthusiastically and pointed to us with extended arm, for her child to see.

Anna waved back with equal fervor and after I'd leveled our wings and gotten us back on course, Anna smiled brilliantly, beside herself with care-free bliss and mouthed the word "fantastic" above the noise of the engine, smiling broadly, literally loving the flight.

Before we knew it, the radio direction signal indicated we were nearing Östersund. I started our descent, called the control tower and received instructions to circle the city to the north and approach the single runway for a landing toward the south. Anna tried to find her parent's house as we turned, but got lost in the maze of blocks and streets and red roofed houses.

She seemed to hold her breath as the Beech sank lower and lower and finally bounced once, slightly and we were rolling along the runway, safe on the ground again. I gently applied the foot brakes and, once off the runway, switched radio to the ground control frequency and got taxi and parking instructions from that controller.

"Oh, Alex, that was wonderful. Thank you so much for that." Anna and I stood beside the parked aircraft as I tied down the plane. Walking toward the terminal, we discussed the thought of using her parent's car while we were there; she was having second thoughts. She wasn't sure what shape it would be in. Her mother didn't drive and since her father had become incapacitated, it might not be usable. I suggested a taxi to her house, or renting a car for a day or two until we could get some idea of the overall need and get her up and running in her parent's car, before I left for my relatives in Dalarna.

We found there was no one at the rental car stall in the airport, so we had to call a taxi. Soon, we were puffing with the exertion of carrying the boxes to the curb, to await the taxi.

"What will your mother think," I later asked as we rode in the cab; I was concerned.

"About what," Anna asked, knitting her brow.

"Well, about us—me, coming home with you."

"What would she think? Is there something to think?"

"Your husband—Harald. I'm not him—I'm a stranger. Won't people talk?"

"Oh, now I understand; another American Puri—tan concern." She smiled at me. "No, no one will talk or think anything. It's just you, giving me a ride in your airplane, before you go visit your own relatives. Honestly…!" I think she was becoming a little exasperated with me.

"I didn't know," was all I could muster.

The city of Östersund was located on a large lake, of which we'd had a beautiful view on the landing approach.

In the cab, the driver skirted the lake as he drove silently through the downtown area and into the suburbs. Anna pointed out various civic buildings and parks, naming them for my edification and calling out places of interest from her childhood.

The architecture was different here, from southern Sweden or Dalarna. The houses had more double balconies and even a sort of

Swedish gingerbread trim, like on the turn-of-the-century houses in Midwest America, but different.

Before long the cab drew up to a medium-sized, brick bungalow with a large yard. Together, the driver and I carried the luggage and then the boxes to the front door. Anna located her mother, happily working along the side of the house, gathering flowers.

I paid the driver and went back to the house and met her mother. Presently her father came out of the house, looking rather confused, apparently searching for his wife.

"Oh, hello Anna," he said in Swedish, "where has your mother gone to..."

Turning to me, he looked puzzled for a moment and then said: "Harald...? Do you know where my wife disappeared to?"

"Father..." Anna smiled at me sadly, "...Mother's out in the yard...around the corner with her flowers," Anna spoke kindly, but there was a small edge in her voice I'd not heard before. She hugged and then gently turned her father back into the house and putting an arm around his waist accompanied him, smiling at me over her shoulder as I followed with the first of the bags.

"And where is my hello kiss," she asked hugging him as we walked.

"This is my father—Alfred," she said, a little sadly over her shoulder. I felt sorry for her. All the king's men, I thought, couldn't put Humpty Dumpty together again.

The evening meal was tedious; it was very nearly like having to deal patiently with a misbehaving child. I could see Anna was caught in the middle, between her mother's constantly correcting her father's confusion and herself trying to comfort her father's frustration at misunderstanding everything. I don't know how she bore it. It wouldn't have been so bad if her mother hadn't kept trying to bring the old man back—make him remember everything. I thought she would have been better off to go with the flow of his behavior, as long as it wasn't belligerent. That's what Anna did and it seemed to cause far less anxiety in him.

After an hour, I'd begun to believe Anna regretted coming to see her parents; I couldn't visualize how she would be able to bear two days of this—let alone two weeks. I found it extremely frustrating watching her suffering and was relieved when, around seven thirty her mother announced it was her husband's and her bedtime. Anna helped her mother with her father's bath while I did the dishes alone, by then, very welcome diversion.

When I finished, I went up to the room I had been assigned and having nothing else to do, lay down and started reading a novel I'd bought on the first flight over, but never finished. From time to time, I could hear Anna and her parents as they worked through a bedtime ritual with her father. After an hour, I was still struggling with the same chapter. It was still bright outdoors, not being that far from the longest day of the year, Midsommar.

There was as gentle knock on my door and Anna quietly opened it and stuck her head in. She smiled a weary smile, rolled her eyes and said: "I need to go for a walk or something; care to see the neighborhood?"

"You bet," I jumped off the bed. "I wasn't that interested in this book, anyway...let me grab my jacket."

We strolled toward the city center. After two blocks, Anna took my hand, I assumed, comforted that by now the street's occupants lived far enough from her parents not to recognize her, or me, as someone who wasn't her husband. I felt a little guilty, then perturbed.

"Quite a meal," she finally said, without turning.

"Uh-huh." She seemed quiet and pensive.

We walked a couple more blocks in silence.

"Alex...how old do you wish to live...to be?"

I glanced over and seeing her a little tearful, dropped her hand and cupped her shoulder, giving her a squeeze in the process.

"As long as I can still get far enough away to die, before I reach the condition of your father, what ever that age will be; just walk over the edge of a cliff or something...the way the American Indians used to do."

"Yes, I feel the same...mother doesn't seem to understand, though I've explained it several times. She seems to comprehend what I tell her about father's medical condition, but then she immediately persists again with father—as if I'd said nothing, constantly trying to fix him. She makes it worse."

"Have you noticed any change since you were last here...his condition? When was that, anyway?"

"I was home for Christmas for a week and yes, there is definitely a change...possibly not so much in Father, but Mother. She seems…less patient. I'm afraid for her—for her health."

We chatted for a while after that without Anna making or revealing any definite plans she'd made. By then we'd circled the blocks and returned to the house. Upstairs, all was quiet and we said good night outside my door with a long kiss.

Lying in bed, I wondered what the following day would bring. I assumed Anna would probably visit her husband. I knew he was in a local asylum; we hadn't spoken of it that day or evening. Her mother seemed little concerned that I was there, which was a relief to me. She was polite and went out of her way to be helpful. When she didn't have her hands full with her husband, she seemed rather absent and welcomed not to have to deal with any additional complications I might have presented.

The next morning I was up by six and could already hear Anna's mother fussing at her husband behind the door of their bedroom. I paused in the hallway, planning to go for a walk before the house was totally awake, but it appeared to be too late for that. Anna would also be up soon, it would seem, with the ruckus.

There didn't seem to be any crisis from the sound of it so I decided to go anyway and went downstairs. Out on the sidewalk the air was crisp, with a little fog lingering in the high, early morning sun, eager to burn it off. I walked briskly to the south and within half an hour, I was nearing the edge of the metro part of city and turned right, crossed one block over and repeated my trek back.

In that single hour the house became alive and returned to the stage it had left off the previous evening. It sounded like her parents had taken up where they'd left off the previous evening. Anna was frustrated. She'd put her hair up and a couple of strands had already escaped and flew about her head as she tried to reconcile the current dispute between her parents; she was patiently trying to explain to her mother to just let her father forget. As she did, she alternately brushed aside the stray wisps as she helped with the breakfast.

She hardly acknowledged me as I came into the kitchen. Listening, it seemed most of the ruckus concentrated around refereeing. I could see she had bought right in to their problem again, herself...or, rather, her mother's problem and only exacerbated the whole affair.

Listening, I could see that both her mother's and Anna's actions further complicated the whole situation, adding confusion to confusion for the old man. I wasn't also going to be hooked in and further complicate the dispute, so tried to remain out of the way and helped them where I could with the food prep.

After the ordeal of breakfast was over, Anna and I did the dishes while the old folks went for a walk. Her mother was harping on her husband about wearing the wrong jacket—he'd actually grabbed mine.

Working together at the sink, for a few moments, we welcomed the peace and quiet. During the meal Anna's father had continued to address me as Harald.

Anna handed me a soapy plate to rinse: "I'm going to ask Mother if she wants to go visit some of her friends for the day. She needs to see some other people for a change. I've been in correspondence with this particular couple and being old friends, they're sympathetic. I want to take her there as soon as I can."

The only sound was the rattle of flatware as Anna worked through each piece like it was surgery tools.

"Father must be taken out of the house for both my parent's well being; I know Mother hasn't had a moment with anyone other than Father. It will do her a world of good to be with them and I know they'll help me to persuade her to agree to put him in the institution. We'll leave when he has his nap. Would you mind remaining with him, Alex, while we go? He seems comfortable with you and I really hate asking you?"

"Of course not."

"Thanks. Father won't even know we are somewhere else anyway and maybe it will distract him for part of the day.

"That's not a bad idea, either. From the looks of it you could already use a little rest."

"Does it show that much? I'm sorry to be neglecting you, Alex. You've been so good…and you're right, I am tense; I can't believe the change in Father since Christmas. I believe I'll have to reconsider the length of my stay, now."

"What do you mean? You'll remain longer than you planned?"

"No, I can't be away from the hospital that long. I mean…I can't bear to watch and listen to this any longer. It's not good for either of my parents. Father doesn't understand and Mother won't accept the fact she's unable to turn back the disease. I'll ring my Father's physician today to see if I can meet him for consultation. Depending upon how it goes, I may or may not take Mother."

"I'll hang around as long as you like. I told the cousins I would be there when I showed up...so go ahead, make your arrangements. If you wish, I'll remain here with either of them while you do what you must do."

That got me a kiss as we finished the dishes.

"I'm going to telephone him right now."

She returned a few moments later, her brows knitted. "He can see me anytime I come down, given the fact I've traveled so far. Would you mind if I took a taxi and left for an hour to speak with him?"

"Certainly not, go ahead. While you're gone why don't I take a look at your folk's car and see how it's surviving. Maybe your mother will find a neighbor to drive her in it, if she knows it's OK."

"Are you sure you do not mind? I seem to find myself depending on you for more and more things, Alex. I'm sorry it has worked out this way," she squeezed my hand. "I'd better go find the car keys, or you won't be able to do anything with it."

She returned a minute later with a string of several keys. "It may take a while to find the right one," she said, shaking the bunch before me, "but Mother assured me it is on here—one of the—fifty, at least, in the ring.

When they got home they put her father down for a nap, just as if he was a child. Anna and her mother didn't waste any time and were soon off again to visit their family friends and then the physician's office, leaving me to see to her father, should he awaken before their return. Strike while the iron is hot, Anna had said. After the friends helped convinced her mother, she would get her right to the family doctor before her mother could reconsider.

Out in the garage, I opened the large door and looked around, blinded momentarily by the daylight. Everything was neatly hung, stacked or sorted on assorted hangers, nails, shelves and boxes. Her father was a careful and neat man in his best days.

I sorted key after key until a likely looking one went right into the ignition. I turned it on and pressed the starter button: nothing. I tried the radio with the same result...then the headlights. No juice. I put the shift lever in neutral, got out and with some effort, pushed the car out, into the daylight; I lifted the hood and shorted a pair of pliers across the battery terminals: nothing. The battery was definitely dead.

I poked around the garage in vain for a charger. A neighbor had seen me pushing the car out and finally sauntered over, introduced himself and asked whether he could help. He was holding hedge trimmers.

"Thanks, but no…unless you happen to have a battery charger," I asked.

He nodded: "*Ja…komma….*"

We walked across the short space of lawn dividing the two properties, through a narrow gate and into another well-organized garage. There was something resembling the shape of an automobile beneath a large drapery. Lifting one corner of the canvas, he showed me a newer Volvo.

"I just brought it home," he said, unusually proud for a Swede. "My wife and are taking a road trip in it next week, so I must keep it clean. In past years Anna's parents have often come with us, but…."

I nodded my understanding. "Yes. It is sad." As we carried the heavy charger back across the yard, he sympathized with the family for Anna's father's condition.

Under the hood, we rigged the alligator clips on the proper battery posts, corroded somewhat from disuse. Like his Volvo, the neighbor's charger was relatively new and even had a rapid-charge setting. I remembered seeing an extension cord hanging on the garage wall and quickly retrieved and connected it. I then loosened the battery's reservoir caps. The neighbor turned the charger setting to high. The liquid in the battery wells began to bubble slowly.

"It should not take too long; it is a good charger," he said, stepping back and nodding satisfactorily. "Maybe you should add some water and, once the engine starts, I would reduce the charger setting to…here…" he pointed to the dial, "…and leave it on the battery all the day, unless you wish to go for an extended drive to bring up the charge."

"No, I don't believe we will be doing that." I thanked him and he went back across the lawn. Soon I heard the snip-snip-snip of his hedge clipper again.

When Anna's father awoke an hour later, he came down to find me working on his old Volvo.

"Where is…oh, Harald…?" he asked, looking confused and glancing around the yard.

"They went to buy food, father," I said. "Want to help me? I'm working on the car."

"Whose car is it...?" he asked "...what's wrong with it?"

"The battery's dead. I can't tell if there is anything else the matter until I can get it started."

"Oh...looks like a pretty good car...I think...I had one like it a long time ago."

We puttered around, checking the fluids—oil, water, brake fluid. Anna's father had opened the trunk and was occupying himself in cleaning the toolkit he'd found there. He didn't seem to stay with any single task for long, but did keep himself occupied. After another hour the women returned, chatting a mile a minute.

"Oh, you're up Father," Anna exclaimed when our heads popped up from under the hood. "How was your nap?"

"Nap? I've been working—not sleeping," he said having completely forgotten the morning. Anna raised her eyebrows at me, then gave me a big smile

"Let's see if it will start," I said. "Get in and give her a try Father."

Anna looked at me when I called him father and smiled, but with a hint of concern.

"OK," he said, "where are the keys?"

"They're in the ignition."

"Oh..." he walked around and got behind the wheel. "You're right. They're here."

Anna stepped closer and put a hand on my arm, looking a little anxious.

"Alex, do you think you should let him do this," she said, obviously worried, "he might get hurt, or hurt someone else."

"I don't think he can do much damage. He's been helping me— well, keeping me company. He seems to have enjoyed it and I think it has done him good. I haven't had one argument with him. I just gently steer him, or the conversation, to keep him interested."

"Who is the doctor, here," she said, reaching behind me and pinching my buttock.

"Don't you think he has a little more color and he's certainly been enthusiastic?"

About that time the engine starter turned over a little and stopped. I pulled her aside. "Move away from the front, Anna."

"It will not go," he shouted, having stuck one leg onto the

driveway, starting to get out of the car.

"Keep trying, I shouted around the hood, waving one arm. Maybe you should choke it a little more."

I waited and then saw the choke lever on the carburetor go closed. The engine turned over again. I began to think it wouldn't go either, but just when I was going to tell the old man to stop, it suddenly caught and the engine raced. He took his foot off the gas and pushed in the choke and it slowed to a fast, but rather rough idle.

Anna had retreated back and to one side and was frowning. When the engine slowed, we heard enthusiasm in her father's voice and she half smiled at me and gave me another hug.

"See, he's having the time of his life I yelled over the engine as, pressing the accelerator, he began to race it again.

"He remembers everything, from the sound of it."

"Don't believe it for a minute," she said and the engine began to race again to prove it. "And do not get in front or behind him in case he engages the gears."

As if to prove her correct, beneath the hood, I saw the clutch pedal lever suddenly depress. Her father was getting ready to drive somewhere. I leaned forward quickly and yanked the ignition coil wire out and the engine rolled harmlessly to a stop. I was afraid her father would put the car through the back of the garage wall, or worse and Anna's fears would materialize.

"What happened," her father said poking his head out the drivers side window and holding both hands palm upwards in frustration. "It just stopped?"

"Yes…," I said, "I stopped it. You did a good job—got it running now. You can get out if you want and look at the engine with me again."

I felt the car shake slightly and he climbed out and slammed the door with an air of satisfaction.

"Did we get it?" he said, coming around the front at a slow trot, grinning broadly.

"Yup…we got it," I said, "…you got it to start."

"Good, it always was hard to start." he turned to Anna, "I'm hungry. I'm going in to see if supper's ready. Put away the car, will you…Harald." he said and abandoned me for the kitchen without even a backward glance.

I shook my head, "Yes Sir." Smiling to myself, I lowered the hood with care so as not to damage the charger cord. I put away the tools I'd removed from the garage, then checked the charger once again; the needle indicated a steady charge. About all Anna, or whoever would have to do now, was have the oil changed. I could do it if I stayed long enough, but I didn't know the plan yet. I figured I'd be taking off for Dalarna in a day or so.

Anna had disappeared after I'd yanked the coil wire. But now she came through from the back door, slowly carrying a large glass of beer.

"Thirsty work, I'll bet," she said, handing the glass to me and standing on tiptoe to kiss me. "Thanks for being such a dear with Father."

"You're welcome," I said returning her smile. "Did you get another one for your dad?" I said, taking the welcome refreshments. "He worked too, you know."

"I gave him half a glass in the house, over mother's protests. Even at that he complained, asking who this full one was for. I told him it was for you and then he seemed to think about it and said that was OK that you had worked hard on your car and needed his help."

We laughed about that and I got another kiss behind the garage door before we went inside to join the melee we could hear already beginning inside.

Anna stopped me outside the doorway again. "I believe this actually benefited him, don't you?" she said. "He seems livelier and more passively accepting of mother's nagging—even patient."

"Sure it isn't the beer?" I joked.

"No...a little while ago, she corrected him about something and he just waved his hand at her and smiled into his beer. I haven't seen him like that since before Christmas. You are so kind and understanding to him, Alex. Thanks again...so much. I don't know how I'll ever repay you for coming along to help me."

"Oh—they're both OK. They can't help the predicament life has put them in. And neither can you. I'm sorry; I forgot to ask, what did the doctor say?"

"We discussed both Mother and Father. I had an awful time keeping her from coming in until we were ready for her. As it happened, a friend of hers came in at that time for an appointment and she and mother had a good visit in the waiting room; meanwhile the doctor and I discussed Father and their condition."

"And her friends...were they convincing to her?"

"Not at first, but then they were able to persuade Mother just to try it and she finally saw the reasoning behind it, especially when they and I shouldered some of the blame for what she called betraying Father.

Dr. Tellander said he felt both Father and Mother would be far better off if Father were moved to the nursing home. After seeing the result of your afternoon with Father, I have a tendency now, to agree, because Dr. Tellander explained all about the ongoing rehabilitation program they have there...things to keep him stimulated and active. Mother never did that; she just tried to fix him. But you did. The doctor said Father could remain occupied as long as he wished—with time out for naps and meals. I believe he will feel happy there. Of course rehabilitation is really misnamed...there's no help at this point to get his memory back. We can only hope to keep him comfortable for the time he has remaining to him."

"I agree."

"They have so many activities; they will keep him entertained, for as long as he's able to interact. It's after that...well, I talked to Mother about it and asked her to come live with me in Karlskrona for a while. At first she protested that we weren't going to do that to Father and she wasn't about to abandon him in his hour of need. But I then explained that if she enrolled him, she could go to the home every day to be with him—and they even have live-in rooms if she wanted to remain overnight, sometime. She's thinking about it now; I think the work and worry has gotten to her and if she sees a chance like this she may agree. I told her what you and Father were doing— with the car—was just like what would happen in the home. I believe she saw the little time we were gone—he was calmer, possibly more satisfied...with himself."

"I hope she begins to feel comfortable with the idea—for all your sakes."

"Me too. We're able to arrange a visit to her friend's again this afternoon. You and I can have the afternoon free, if father takes his nap—free to hang around here, that is, while he sleeps, we can't leave him."

"Fine with me," I said finishing my beer. "What's for lunch?" I said, imitating her father's tone, for which she feigned a kick in my direction.

Lunch didn't go well either and then her Father went for a nap immediately after. Anna was becoming stressed again. She said she'd like to make the arrangements for the nursing home herself, but that Dr. Tellander had promised to have his staff take care of them. I could tell Anna was still fretting about something; I assumed it was her husband and that whole quandary. She still hadn't mentioned going to see him since we arrived. I knew it had to be on her mind. But it came out while her mother was putting her Father down for his nap.

"I should go to see Harald and check his progress one last time with the psychiatrists." This seemed to be troubling her to distraction.

"Why don't you call and set up the appointment as long as you are in the mood for getting things done." I was curious about what she meant, one last time. Seeming to have been awaiting my approval, she went into the hallway to make the call.

"I can go tomorrow," she said, returning five minutes later, "...at nine. I spoke with the chief psychiatrist. He wasn't very enlightening; in fact, he was rather closed-mouthed. He said we would discuss everything tomorrow and no need to get into it on the telephone."

"Makes sense, coming so soon, I mean. And they didn't even know you were in town. That's pretty quick—the appointment, I mean."

She seemed to be mulling something over. "Are other physicians that annoying to you, when they do that? He seemed so—to me, at least?"

"Usually," I said, "sometimes worse; sort of controlling," I feigned, having absolutely no experience with physicians...I was never ill, "especially the female ones."

Quick as a flash I ducked a dinner roll she'd been nibbling on. That got her giggling again, at last. The past two days were taking their toll on her sense of humor.

The next morning the phone rang and the nursing home informed her that the arrangements for her father were in the process. He could move in the following week. Anna apologized again for the turmoil saying I should go on to Dalarna immediately, or I wouldn't get to see any of my relations.

"If you want me to go, I will," I said, "but I thought you could use the help from the looks of it, at least in the beginning."

"I just don't want to ruin your holiday too; I've already imposed enough."

"If I didn't enjoy being here with you, I'd leave, Anna. I enjoy being a part of your family, Anna, pretty much lacking one of my own. Maybe I'm getting homesick for The States, or something—getting nostalgic in my old age!"

"You are sweet," she said, flashing me a million dollar smile. My heart was definitely in this—no matter what my head tried to tell me.

"Do you want me to leave, because of Harald, I mean. Would you rather be alone when you work that out?"

"I've thought about that…in the past, of course I'd have had Harald around to—act as a sounding board for things—things like this. Someone I lo..urr—like, to help me with the really hard decisions. You've done that now, Alex; been a—what do the British call it—*a stick*, for me? It helps to maintain the stability. I don't know what I'd have done? Just let nature take the proper course, I guess."

"I'm happy to help and anything you want—just ask. I believe you know that by now, or at least I hope you do."

"Thanks, I think I'll need some time while I deal with the problem I have in my marriage. The doctors...I want to see what they recommend. Maybe I should handle this with a clear mind. If you're around, I—will be distracted. I want to be able to react on my own...no influential—tempting influences. Do you mind, Alex?"

"No, I don't. It's probably a good idea. I'll head for Dalarna and you can keep me posted."

In my heart, I was disappointed; there was no getting around it. I wanted to tell Anna. Maybe my face showed it, though I tried not to let it. She was watching me intently; scrutinizing me. It was what she thought she wanted and would probably be best for her. I didn't want to be held accountable for influencing her with something this serious.

"I'd better give you the telephone number there so we can stay in touch. And if you want anything, I can be here in a little over an hour, with the plane, once summoned."

That afternoon, my cousin picked me up at Dala-Järna's grass airstrip. I'd telephoned a couple times, but received no answer and I didn't know how else to notify them in advance. They were always either in the barn or the fields, unless it was mealtime, so there wasn't anyone around to answer the phone.

Finally, Lisa answered and I let her know I was coming down in an airplane. As if that was normal, she said to just buzz their barn, or the fields—I'd be able to see the men around somewhere and they'd come to fetch me when they saw the airplane.

I did and they came in less than a half hour. We rode back to the farmstead with my cousin chatting away happily about the sad state of farming in Sweden...of course; all conditions were bad—weather, prices and the government. I'm afraid I was mostly silent during the ride—even morose, preoccupied with Anna and her problem. Her quandary made it my quandary. My cousin glanced askance at me once or twice, but I still could only contribute to the conversation in monosyllables.

After two days at the farm in Skålbyn, I'd become a very bad guest. I milled about when there wasn't anything directly that I could help them with. I felt they were beginning to have to make work for me—find stuff to do. I didn't know how to manage much of the agriculture machinery they had to operate on a daily basis, though I'd offered to learn. They protested that they had more than enough help with that side of the farming.

I was able to help with the daily milking and did. They had some of the new milking machines, which made the job go pretty fast. I was relieved that, if I was going to be such a morose guest, I at least could relieve the family of the burden of some of the endless, repetitive barn chores. These were the most tiresome to any farmer—having to be repeated twice daily, seven days each week, every day of the month and year. My cousin and her husband were even able to take off an evening or two and take in a movie as a result of my small effort. I couldn't get them to forego the morning milking, however, which meant a six a.m. appointment with thirty cows, every day.

On the fourth day my curiosity got the better of me. I borrowed my cousin's car and drove into town to call Anna from the more private telephone both outside the small store. No one answered, so I drove around for a half-hour and then tried again, with the same result.

That evening I relented on my promise to myself not to let my cousins in on my infatuation with a female Swedish physician. I telephoned from the hallway where their phone was located. I got her mother this time. Anna wasn't there and it was a struggle to explain to her mother, just who I was. I finally told her at the end to tell Anna to call the man with the airplane, thinking that might jog her memory enough to mention something to Anna. I knew if she did, Anna would know I'd called.

It wasn't until two days later that she telephoned back. It was during the day and I was in the forest, out of boredom, having ridden along with my cousin's husband. By this time I'd already begun wishing I'd brought the little typewriter I'd purchased to transcribe Karolina's notes, deluding myself that I might be able to concentrate on the pile of notes I packed along.

I tried calling Anna back after the evening milking. There was no answer again. Damn, I thought, disappointed. I was getting frustrated. I guess I didn't really have a right to that behavior, but I was, nevertheless. I wasn't worried about Anna, but I was bored on the farm and wanted more of Anna's undivided company. I was selfish and knew it. My curiosity about the relationship with her husband was getting to me. The next day I tried calling twice; no answer. Finally after being at the farm for over a week, I caught her by calling late, around eleven. She answered on the seventh ring.

"Anna...," I said, relief flooding over me at the sound of her voice. I'd forgotten how its sound thrilled me, "...it's me."

"Oh—Alex...how good to hear your voice. I've tried to call but you weren't there."

She was making excuses, or sounds, like she had to apologize. That bothered me immediately. "What's been going on there?"

"Your call...it wasn't anything important, was it?

"No...I guess I've gotten a little bored and I thought we might get together for a couple days, if you can somehow get away."

There was a few seconds of silence like she was thinking. I hastened to fill in the pause lest she tell me something I didn't want to hear.

"How's your dad doing...and your...your mother?"

I couldn't bring myself to say husband, though that was my reason for calling.

"They're fine. Father's adjusted Quite well. In fact, already, I believe he resents our—mother's and my visits. He's made new friends, when he can remember them. And he's not resisting as I thought he might. But Mother is having a more difficult time. She feels guilty. I've tried to show her how well he's doing and how much better it is for both of them, but I'm afraid it's not doing much good. I suppose she'll adjust after a while."

"Well, that's wonderful." I tried to keep a light-hearted note in my voice. "Any chance we can snatch a day or two? My cousin's been telling me about this great lodge in the northwest of Dalarna—near the border with Norway, in the mountains. It really sounds great...and there's an airstrip. We could be there before you knew it?"

There was a second's too long hesitation. "Yes, I'd like that Alex. I can tell, from the sound of your voice, you would too...but...not right now, thanks though."

"Ok, sure...I understand..."

"Alex—can you come back up here again?"

I didn't take a second to answer. "Well, certainly, if that's what you'd rather do. I thought you might need to get away by now and your father seems to be doing pretty well.

"He is but that's not what...why I want you to come." Again...that hesitation. "Alex—Harald...it's Harald. They've been giving him some different medication for the past year. Medicine that has—he has really improved, they say and I've seen him. You wouldn't, I mean one wouldn't recognize him; he's changed so much, made excellent progress. He's back to the—back to who he was...before, when we were ma—when we were together." She faltered. "I'm so confused, Alex. I guess I need a voice of reason. And lately, that seems to have been yours. His physicians are thinking of discharging him already, on his own recognizance, but they'd prefer releasing him to someone related to him...someone who can help him to be...to remain responsible and continue to...to improve."

My ears were ringing and I tasted brass in my mouth. I hurt so much I could hardly form the words to reply. This was the second time—since she'd told me she was married.

"Well...that's wonderful news Anna," I finally choked a reply.

"Come up? It sounds as if you've been accomplishing more that you had expected. Sure I can come up, but, do you really need me?" My attempt at casualness sounded hollow.

"I know I don't have the right to expect it, Alex. You've already been so kind."

I really wished she'd quit saying that, it sounded so...patronizing.

"You need to do things to continue...your own life."

There was a long pause; I didn't know what else to say.

"Alex—Harald has been out of the hospital on pass with me; he goes to visit my father with me. It's frightening, I feel like I've been caught, trying to figure out a way to separate and I wonder if he—Harald, can make it alone, without someone. Without me?"

I couldn't speak again for several seconds. Anna must have sensed by my silence that she'd hit me pretty hard.

"Alex...."

I hoped she wasn't going to tell me again how kind I'd been.

"We—I have to figure this thing out. Harald? It is uncanny, but, he's not the same person—I mean he's—it's as if we've turned the clock backward—ten years back. He claims he is in love all over again—he says this, over and over—and with me...still. And it feels—it feels just like it did years ago, except I'm not in love with him any more—but I'm afraid to...I feel responsible—I'm still *legally*...his wife."

I brushed away tears of anger and frustration, hoping none of the cousins came into the hall.

"Oh...Alex. I can't endure this. Please come. Can you?"

I could hear her sobbing quietly, even over the poor line connection. My heard ached and I wished I could be there to comfort her and peel the big tears off her cheeks with my thumb. My heart ached for the smell of her.

"Alex, I love you; I know that now. I wanted you to know that, but I feel a responsibility to my husband. I feel love so very strongly for you. But as his wife, I feel responsible for Harald...like a child and I can't stop—with either one of you!"

My hurt had turned to anger. But I didn't want her to hear it in my voice.

"What do you really want me to do Anna...just come up there? Then what?"

She didn't reply.

"And what are we going to do then?" I repeated, having almost said: "double date." But I loved her too much to take the chance of losing what little I had left of her.

"Anna, do you just want to talk? Do you want me to just go back to Karlskoga...without you?"

I expected her to blurt: "No...don't leave." But instead, she was silent...God...she was hesitating...considering it. Finally she replied.

"Alex—I want you to come up here and—come up here and hold me for a minute. I need to feel your—your strength."

"I can do that Anna. I can come up—and I can hold you. I can come up and make love to you. But I can't make you fall out of love with Harald, if you still love him. After all, he's your legal husband. I don't want to do that. You know my—my reluctance to interfere with someone who's married."

"You're honorable, I know that, but I'm so confused right now. If you come, you'll not make me do anything I don't want to, or need to do. But I do know I really miss and need you now and the sooner you come...the better."

"All right, I'll come tomorrow. Will you meet me if I call first?"

"I'll be home in the morning. What time will you come—take off?" If you call before you leave and tell me how long it will take, I will be at the airport waiting for you."

"Ok...I'll call you around seven, ready to leave; is that too early, at your mother's?"

"No, I will be waiting, Alex. Alex...?"

"Yes?"

"Thank you for your...for being who you are."

Yeah, I thought. Thank me for being a fool and disregarding the little voice that had whispered to me in the car, on our first date? The voice had said: "be careful stupid." It hadn't said stupid, but the one that spoke from my unconscious now, was shouting: ..."stupid!"

"I'll call you at seven, Anna...good night."

I had trouble sleeping after I'd told my cousins I'd be leaving in the morning. They'd told me to go ahead and take the ancient Volvo and just leave it at the strip. One of them could bring it back later in the day. Seven in the morning would be right in the middle of the morning chores.

Before turning in, I'd called weather and learned there was some real stuff coming from Norway and the North Sea, due to cover Sweden most all week. Did this ever let up, I wondered as I considered my options? I could easily get off the strip and probably land again in Östersund.

In my little downstairs bedroom I seemed to waken every hour, glance out the window, roll over and doze again. Once I heard rain on the window and wondered again, just before I gave in to the welcome rest, whether the weather would be too bad to fly. There wouldn't be any thunderstorms, I didn't think, so I should be able to get away without any hitches...should. What if I couldn't make an approach at Östersund because of the low cloud, once I was there? I thought they had an ILS[102]. or, was it the lesser approach beacon, a VOR? But in my drowsiness, I couldn't remember the charts, or the approach plate for the airport...and so my sleep went.

But with morning, I was able to get off in the patchy fog. My cousin's husband Olle decided to drive and dropped me off in the rain, beside the dripping Beech. While I untied the tie-down ropes, I promised to return if and when I could. I don't think he understood what was happening, but he knew me well enough to know I was troubled about something and that it was serious, at least to me. He'd said thanks for the work, take care of myself and come back soon—that I was always welcome. I knew that and loved him and his family for their generosity and understanding; they knew I'd never behaved like this before. As he let me out of the car, he'd squeezed my arm and asked me if there was anything he could do. I really appreciated that, smiled and shook my head.

Before I'd left the house, I'd called weather and got a flight briefing. It'd changed little from the previous day, though there were now possible thunderstorm warnings issued for southern Scandinavia...far from my worry, fortunately. After the briefing I'd set up a void-time clearance for the airstrip at Järna, providing me a time window to check out the Beech and take off up into the clouds without hitting another airplane. They'd keep the airspace over the airport clear of traffic until the void-time departure expired, or I radioed them from the air, asking instructions to proceed to Östersund.

I didn't think I would, or could return, that is, at the time. After the fitful night's sleep, I guess I decided to go to Jämpland and tell Anna goodbye. I wasn't able to be the yo-yo to her waving hand and planned to end it quickly, before she hurt me any more.

This I mulled over on the way, as I methodically monitored the Beech's instruments and operated the controls up into the cloud and rain. Unconsciously, I spoke to the Center controller in Oslo and then before I knew it, he was letting me down for the ILS approach. I broke out of the cloud bottoms to see the dark green forests and lakes at around 400 meters, ample room to spare above the minimum approach altitude and a safe landing.

CHAPTER 21

A Finish—A Beginning

True to her word Anna was waiting, standing just out of the rain beside the terminal. I taxied the Beech over to the parking tie-downs, near the terminal. After the previous day's telephone conversation with her, I hadn't derived even a glimmer of enjoyment from flying the nearly-new airplane back up from Dalarna. The dream trip, with the woman I begun to love, had turned into one of the biggest let-downs of my entire life. It was a shame—the whole thing was a damn shame.

And coward that I had turned into—all those brave plans I'd made on the flight over in the Beech...to ditch Anna—*show her*—and return to Karlskoga? They washed away the moment I saw her anxious face through the window of the Beech. I climbed down, locked the airplane and I secured the ropes, two beneath the wings and then the tail cone, grabbed my satchel and started for the row of windows blurred by the running rain.

Anna had worn a scarf knotted neatly beneath her chin and she had on what looked like her mother's raincoat. She'd undoubtedly dressed in a hurry, no longer trying to look good for me or for anyone else. She was suffering; it was easy to see when I got close up.

I held the terminal door for her and she paused, glancing up at me. Her breath was warm as were her lips as she pecked my rain-wet cheek before passing through the door. Turning toward the car, she smiled and linked arms with me, ducking her head as we sloshed across the small lot beside the building.

"How was the flight?"

I opened her door and then circled the car. She waited while I climbed in my side, unzipped my jacket and settled back in the seat. The car smelled damp—dank and as unused as it obviously was. When I glanced at Anna, she was slowly removing her wet scarf before shaking out her hair. We looked at each other for a bit without speaking. And then, as if she'd been waiting, Anna slid across the narrow seat and reaching both arms up and around my neck, gave me a long, lingering, tender kiss. Nothing sexy—no passion…simply giving and taking comfort. She then pulled her arms down and put her palms against my chest, hid her forehead in my collar and began to sob very hard.

I held her and waited, one arm on hers, the other around her shoulder, just sitting there, smelling her wet hair and the clean, body smell of her. I rested my chin lightly above her ear and stared at the little rivulets—blurry streaks of rainwater, coursing erratically down the windshield, focusing and refocusing the crazy-striped scene outside. She was really hurting. The car nearly shook with the fierceness of her sobs.

After a while she caught her breath: "Oh…Alex—what must I do," and then fell back into shaking hiccups, crying harder. I patted her on her back, holding my cheek against the top of her head. The rainy wetness of her hair was strong…so much so, I could almost taste the herbal smell of the soap, sweat and body oil.

I held her there for at least five minutes while she cried herself out and finally relaxed, probably the first time since I'd left. I believed she needed to let it out so I was patient, sitting, waiting for her to speak first. Hard as it hurt, I was glad she'd unburdened herself with me and not someone else.

As she leaned against me, I examined the part, in the top of her head. I could see every strand of hair, every small sweep of every wave and slight curl of the beautifully shiny locks. I was so close to her—and I seriously feared that I would never be able to observe her like this again, hold her so close—ever. Something ominous pending, but I didn't know what.

She finally stirred and sat up, took a handkerchief from her coat pocket and blew her nose, smiling over at me with red nose and swollen eyes.

"Now aren't I a pretty sight. You've now seen the very worst of me Alex. I'll get control in a moment," she said, pulling the rear-view mirror down. Giving it a twist, she craned her neck to peer into it—frowned and cocking her head.

Giving it another twist in disgust, she exclaimed. "God, I really look awful. But I'll maintain control now, Alex. It's just that I felt happy to have you here again, safe and—well, just here." She moved to the right, back beneath the wheel, and I was immediately sorry she had.

"So...you didn't elaborate; how was your flight over? I was watching and I didn't even see you come down out of the clouds."

Without waiting for my answer, she slid back over and gave me another kiss and I gladly returned it, with a new reassurance in my heart as it carried me to new heights again, despite my little head voice still shouting fool.

Then she started the car, maneuvered through the parking lot and the entrance onto the highway and drove direct to her parent's house. On the way, Anna told me she'd taken her mother to the nursing home, where she usually remained for part of the day, now, her father was lodged there. The accommodations were wonderful, she said, for such babysitting; almost like parents dropping off children she recounted and her mother could eat there also. I only half-listened as I thought she was only stalling me.

When we arrived, I jumped out and opened the garage door, let her get out and then pulled the car in, closing the door. We had the house to ourselves. Anna went directly to the kitchen and I heard her rummaging among the coffee things as I came out of the bathroom and headed upstairs to my room. I had no intention of staying the night—none at all: fool...

I tossed my bag on the settee in my room and popped the lock on the lid and tipped it open. I wanted some dry slacks and shirt, but in the jumble I'd thrown together the previous night, a coordinated pair eluded me. I began unbuckling my belt. I was unbuttoning the last button of my shirt when I heard a sound behind me, thinking Anna'd also come up to her room to change.

She had. She stood on one leg, leaning against the doorframe, one leg in the air as she removed her underpants from around her upraised ankle.

Completely naked, she straightened and looked directly at me. She very deliberately brought both hands up and rummaged her hair brusquely with her fingers, then shook her head vigorously, fluffing out her hair.

I swallowed hard, my mouth constricting at the beautiful sight of her nakedness. I'd forgotten to unbutton my shirt, watching her, too surprised to react. Anna walked slowly toward me, smiling as she approached, letting me savor the loveliness of her. She began unbuttoning my shirt and after pulling it from my slacks, reached for my belt buckle and let my slacks fall around my ankles. Then, she slowly pulled my shirt off my shoulders and put both her arms around my back and drew herself up tight against me in a tight, warm hug, her breasts, still cold from the outing, hard and flattened against my chest and I could feel my heart hammering against the cushion of her soft flesh.

I reached behind her, letting my hands rest lightly along the small of her back, just above her buttocks. My cheek against her ear, again and I inhaled the sweetness of her damp hair. God—I loved her—so much already.

Finally Anna leaned back and put her arms up around my neck, stood on tiptoe and began a long, lingering kiss. She moaned slightly. After a few seconds her tongue began to probe, parting my lips as she explored my mouth, almost as an apology—a request. The kiss seemed to last forever; when she finally leaned her head back and looked up into my eyes, she was very serious—unsmiling for a moment, the joking girl now gone. Then as her lips opened slightly again in a partial smile, she closed her eyes, rose on tiptoe and kissed me again: another invitation.

The kiss went on and on; I tightened my arms around her waist. I could feel the muscled hardness of her lower back, the valley running up from between her buttocks to her shoulder blades was deep and well defined, firm on each side of her spine. She arched her back and slowly and ever-so-gently undulated her pelvis against me, as I trailed my fingers along the strong curve.

She stretched again—pulling her body upward, tightening her arms around my neck, even more insistent. As one hand massaged the back of my head with the other, she controlled the pressure and the intensity of the kiss. Her tongue became insistent. I pulled her body even tighter to me, becoming lost in my own desire. I realized then that my scruples were easily discarded and now lay at our feet with my shirt, shorts and her underwear in the doorway; they all had so easily fallen away at the sight of her nakedness.

Anna sank back onto the soles of her feet and with one arm still around my neck, reached behind me running her hand around my hip, pulling me to her with more urgency. She also punctuated it with an insistent whimper, probing harder with her tongue. She suddenly leaned sideways and we both tipped conveniently onto the bed. Still in the kiss, Anna rolled me to one side and pulled the bedspread and pillows away with her free hand, then rolled us the other direction and did the same thing; even in her passion, she was mindful of the linens. I almost had time to smile to myself.

We lay the way we'd finished, for a while—wrapped in each other's arms and legs. I began to wonder whether Anna had fallen asleep, nuzzled into my neck, breathing steadily—deeply. But finally, she sighed, stirred and began nibbling my ear. But in vain; I was vented, for the time being, anyway. After a couple of moments, she gently rolled off me, turning on her side to face me.

"You'd planned to leave me today, didn't you Alex…go back to Järna?"

I looked into the face I'd come to love so much.

"Yes, I did."

"I thought so," she said toying with the nipple on my right breast. "I was afraid you'd try to say goodby at the airport and I wouldn't have had a chance to—well, to do this with you. I wanted to give you—give *us* this…so we, or I, would have something to think about if you left me."

"I see," was all I could think to say, though reward had come to mind.

"I know that you believe something has changed about us—and I guess it has. Since I've seen Harald's doctors and the remarkable alteration in his behavior—I wanted to do this to…to sort of, mark our place in life. The place where we were when, well, when it began to get too complicated."

"Unraveling…" I said, not looking at her. "…when it began coming apart."

"I feel a little remorse, as if I have cheated on Harald now. Less remorse, for the sorrow I have for misleading you, but I have absolutely no guilt. He cheated on me, by doing—by what happened to him—what he did to our life through…well, he left—left me for somewhere else he would rather have been and he went by his own choice, where I could not go—where I would not go. He abandoned me without anything or anyone to love or comfort me in his absence."

"And now he's come back… and you don't know who to abandon…" I offered, sorry the second I'd said it.

"Yes, you could say that. He has come back. Or, the medication and psychotherapy have brought him back. And with his return, he's opened the wound—the old romance—the love, we felt—he felt, before; the love that he left. But, so he says—that he has a right to, today."

"I see. So—so why this—why this *now?*" I asked, gesturing to her beautiful nakedness.

"I wanted to have sex with you and I knew you wanted to have sex with me. But I knew you'd never ask me—I knew you'd leave first. I knew the reasons for your reservations and I hope I haven't forced you to compromise them…your American principles?"

"No one's forced me to do any of this, Anna—I have my eyes open—as far as I was allowed to see ahead, anyway."

"I know, I deserved that; I haven't always let you see ahead…I should have told you, up front, right away, but I didn't—my weakness and your suffering. I'm so sorry, but now…today, I felt we owed each other this." She squeezed my arm, "I hope it can hold…*mark* the place while—while I try to sort out my past life with Harald and get him moving on again, but eventually, alone."

"Like a bookmark. Return to the story after a while and read further—or decide the story's not worth pursuing and forget where you left the book; which dusty shelf; never bothering to pick it up again?"

"No, not like that, Alex," she said, reaching up and caressing my cheek. "Not at all like that. I wanted to give you a—a promise—a fulfillment—a contract of what had come to be, with us, so you would wait—hoping you'd be patient with me."

"Wait? Wait for what, Anna?

She looked at me but didn't reply.

And if I didn't, or couldn't…?"

"Then—I guess we'd still have this, hopefully something more—not more, or better, just something in addition to what we've shared up until now. No one can ever take this away, Alex. No one."

"What if it isn't—wasn't enough for me to wait?"

"We can't talk about that future, now. If you wish to get up and leave now, then you have a right to. It's your choice. But I hope you won't. I need time, Alex. Time to sort this out; if this...his change is truly real, or whether the medication will wear off in a week, a month."

"Or a year...two? Never?" I said, unable to control my sarcasm because of the hurt of losing her.

She was showing endless patience at my anger and hurt.

"No—not *that* long."

"How long then, Anna...you're the doctor?"

"Oh, I don't know; it's not my field and right now...I'm so mixed up. Surely, Alex, you don't expect me to just...guess?"

"A year—two years?" I said, not relenting. "I'm afraid I don't work that way, Anna. I can't—won't wait that long. I just..."

"Please don't say that yet, Alex. Please try to go along with me—just for a while. I'll have to go back to work. Harald's physicians have asked me to transfer back up here. But I have too much at stake back in Karlskoga, too much to throw away with no more reassurance. Am I against a few, or many days of torment."

I shook my head.

"I'm sorry, Alex, that I'm so torn. I know I'm being selfish—*damn selfish*, because Harald can't be, I don't believe. And I know it's not fair to you—I know that," she almost shouted, "that it's grossly unfair of me to ask. But it's what fate has dealt me and I'm trying to be honest with you—and hope you can find it—respect me...and wait a while—just a while, Alex."

"I can see that...you just want me to park my affection and wait," I said, sarcastically.

"I deserve that, I know, Alex, but—again, I ask—I beg you—just try to be patient a little longer. Don't throw away what we had—have. If I left Harald now and we, well, if I left him...and if something did change with him, wouldn't I forever be wondering if I cheated him—my legal husband, or cheated us by leaving him and being—remaining with you? And if I gave up what we have here, now at this moment and went with Harald, would I forever wonder if it would have been better with you? Can you not see the problem of responsibility and guilt I also have, Alex? He's my sworn husband and you're the man I love."

"Now who's sitting on their scruples. Anna, I believe your husband, as you call him, is a husband on paper only. He gave up the husband's right to loyalty or sincerity when he started—when he did what he did to all those children. He has no rights, in my book, Anna. I can't have a love affair with you—I'm not built that way…emotionally."

"Or, morally," she offered and kissed me. "It's so basically earthy, on my part. So seemingly childishly selfish, I know, but it is the way it is. No amount of education, sophistication, maturity—*nothing* can change our—my emotions. I must be sure it's finished with Harald. That a corner has been turned, a door closed and I've done all I can have done for him, as is my responsibility as his wife and legal mate. And all the while, I'm punishing you Alex—asking you to take it— stand it—on the chin, as your American movies say…and wait. Oh, Alex…." She put her arms around me and held me closely. "I'm so awfully, awfully sorry for you and so confused for us."

Then we kissed again and she began to caress me. Before long we were well underway. I thought, Hell, why not…one last time. I felt really mean and cruel toward her then. I was angry and wanted to screw her hard…to hurt her—not physically—emotionally, and I was beginning to put that energy into our lovemaking.

She must have sensed the new urgency because she slid from beside me again, rolling on top. Sitting there astride, her thighs pressed close to my waist, the backs of her soles curled and wrinkled. She placed her palms on top of her thighs. Her stomach muscles beneath her deep navel undulated slightly as she rolled her hips forward, up, down and back again. There was a slight hollow beneath the navel that went down to her pubic hair.

Then, she began a slow easy rocking—rolling her hips forward, while she looked into my face. Neither of us spoke, but we maintained perfect eye contact. Anna smiled ever so slightly, looking directly down into my eyes all the while. I could see and feel she was getting closer to orgasm. Her knees began to tremble and her lower lip too. Then something around her eyes gave way that it was near and her mouth clenched into a fixed smile. Her eyes began to change and I saw both the passion and then the same anger in them, that I felt. But then she closed them tightly, unwilling to show me more of the emotion I knew was there. She rocked, rising and falling, still with a slow, rhythmic control. The anger was not for me—I knew that— but it was there, nevertheless.

Then her urgency increased—and increased yet again. And just as our mutual orgasm was eminent, she opened her eyes and looked directly into mine, baring her very soul. And I saw there in that instant the empty confusion, the hurt, the pain—the loneliness and uncertainty and in a final, extended thrashing frenzy—finalizing, in a sustained rigidity as we became one again in sensation, if not purpose. She screamed a long, long scream of agony and ecstasy, remaining firmly astride me, gripping my thighs with hers, quivering through two more smaller orgasms before she collapsed forward, atop me, her mouth against my neck, breathing heavily in my ear. I never felt as close to any woman as I did to Anna, then. All the wraps were off— both of us. We were like brother and sister—twins. And if I could have crawled inside her—literally and turned myself outside, looking out through her eyes, become as one body—one mind—one love, I would have done so at that moment, so we could always be one— together. One love, one mind—one heart—I loved her so much.

Afterward, we bathed and went to lunch at a small restaurant, nearby; she continued talking all the while, mostly about her parents and the nursing home back in Karlskoga and how she had to make arrangements for her replacement. Small talk, filling in the time; ignoring the awkwardness between what wed finally had in bed and the finality of an uncertain finish. We discussed the situation at length, almost clinically. Anna said she felt she must give her Harald another chance to prove himself fit for living outside an institution; that final chance would forever rid her of any guilt which might likely follow if…well, just if. I didn't know until then, she'd planned, she said, to file for her divorce when we flew up. But now—the change in Harald's emotional and physical state had taken her aback. The doctors had urged her to do nothing but encourage her husband for the time being and attempt to return as near as possible to their former state. Of course they knew nothing of her budding relationship with me. They told her there might be a chance, between the medications and therapy, if their relationship remained solid, that he would get well. She told me—then, she said, she could leave him without guilt.

I thought, if she chose to do that, in the end, then there might be something.

For the days I was in Dalarna, she and Harald had everything, she said, but sex. She'd refused him that intimacy, even though his psychiatrists had urged her to accept his advances, if he made them. He, she said, had quietly resigned himself to accept her decision, telling her he knew he had to earn back the respect he, himself, had destroyed between them and that he could be patient waiting for the day she would take him back into her bed.

I don't know why but this made me bristle inside; I felt like shouting: "bullshit," to her. Of course, Anna didn't become aware of it. It was too aching and deep to show that easily. Something just didn't ring true with this whole thing, but I believed Anna was enough of an altruist at heart that she'd give everything a fair chance, even sex, if it finally came that far. I thought about it in between our conversations. It was nagging.

Something...something was queer about all this. I don't believe Anna was sufficiently detached, emotionally, to be able to trouble-shoot the situation alone. Maybe, as time went on, she'd find a chink. Or, maybe she wouldn't. The revelation that she might get back with her husband never crossed my mind. I guess I never thought anything, either way; but now, it really frightened me. Especially, because it sounded as if he was really getting well. I couldn't fault him for that, or her, at the time. I didn't want to come between them...hadn't since the time she told me she was married. But there was no denying it, I loved her and now I smelled a rat.

I guessed, in those few moments that I would quietly (but angrily at the hand fate had dealt me), fade into the background and let her resume her marriage. After considering it, I didn't feel guilty now that we'd had sex; I guess I felt more selfish, like it was owed me and that I'd somehow gotten them...*him*...*her*, back. A typical male presumption, I thought to myself, feeling a little guilty about that. The whole thing had gotten me down.

I thought about Karolina and our mutual project, which had taken us so far and brought Anna and me together. I didn't, in that moment, feel like I wanted to resume the interviews. I felt like giving it up—throwing in the towel, even going back home to The States. Anna really had me confused, but so much in love.

Around three in the afternoon, I asked Anna to drive me to the airport. Rather than endure further discussion, I asked her not to come around to the plane, because I had to file a flight plan, fuel and perform a pre-flight check on the aircraft and would be at least an hour at it. It would be torture, trying to make conversation about everything except what I wanted to talk about, I thought, but I didn't say it.

So we said our good-byes there in the parking lot. Like me, Anna seemed reticent about any further discussions, so neither of us said anything further about the us; she'd already apologized for what she'd done. I knew where I stood. I guess I was as much to blame as she for falling for her. So I slammed the door and bending down, waved at her through the window on my side of the car, stepped back and waited. She stared seriously at me one last time before putting the car in gear. Wondering what she was thinking, I watched her back out and drive away without a backward glance.

I fueled the Beech for the flight, but not back to my cousin's in Dalarna; I knew I would be a poor house guest and flew back to Karlskoga, instead.

It was an uneventful flight. And I picked up the little field before I knew it, methodically descending to pattern altitude and working my way, downwind around the airport pattern in the descent, adding flaps, mixture, and on final, throttled the airplane's pitch and power back and settled onto the strip without a bump.

My mind had played with all the possible permutations of my relationship with Anna, during the flight; I thought, as I taxied to the little hangar, all it had gotten me was back in another place where I didn't think I really wanted to be.

Per wasn't at the strip when I parked the Beech beside the hangar, not expecting me of course and it was past normal business hours, so there was no one around. I secured the airplane with tie-downs, locked it up and flipped the keys through the trap door of the office, along with a quickly scribbled note to Per that I was back and would be in the next day to pay him for the rental. I also told him the plane had functioned flawlessly. Too bad I was too depressed to have enjoyed flying it. I walked over and fired up the Volvo and drove to the hotel. I remember thinking, for some reason, thank God it had stopped raining. I had a beer, made a snack from what I could find; the milk was sour and the bread moldy. Everything matched my disposition.

End of Vallkulla Book One

CONTINUED IN BOOK TWO...

Prelude to Vallkulla, Book Two

Both Anna and Alex meet challenges in *Vallkulla*, Book Two. Anna returns to her former life with Harald, after he's released from psychiatric confinement; but she soon suspects her husband is returning to his old habits.

Alex has a challenge of his own involving his business in America and finds he must bid farewell to a stern and near-tearful Karolina and deal with the unexpected problem at back in America. Unknowingly, he has left Anna with a gift.

Anna deals with the result of her husband's criminal misbehavior one last time and seeks an immediate divorce. Winding up her affairs in Jämpland, she returns to Karlskoga and the nursing home for a short visit, hopeful that Alex is there, still interviewing Karolina. Sadly, she learns he's returned to America over a year previously. Her former colleague Birgitta, informs her about a job posting for a supervisory physician at an institution in South Africa. After an whirlwind interview in Stockholm, she accepts the position.

Alex winds up his business affairs and returns to Sweden at the same time she's in Stockholm, interviewing. On the day of his arrival, Alex catches sight of Anna in a crowd, during a large convention in the hotel where he's staying; but he's unable to catch her, before her cab speeds away.

Heartbroken, Alex arrives at the nursing home and a very depressed Karolina informs him that Anna's moved to Africa. Alex considers giving up his book idea and returning to America. But his strong sense of duty tells him he's already invested so much time in Karolina's tale of their family, that he should remain and hear her out. He also feels a strong sense of guilt and decides it will pick up both their spirits.

The first thing Anna does in Johannesburg is locate the perfect apartment; the second is to begin interviewing prospective governesses…for she didn't travel to Africa alone.

Vallkulla, Book Two

PRONUNCIATION HELP

ä= fah (fat)
å= oh (hoe)
o= oo (shoe)
ö= (not in English)

FOOTNOTES

[1] *Oäkta* — in local dialect, illegitimate...a bastard child.

[2] *Halsduk* — Head scarf.

[3] *Stockholmska* — Someone from the city Stockholm, meant to be a slur on city people.

[4] *Gårdsnamn* — A farm's name, put before a first name, similar to surname.

[5] *Kristiania* — previous name for Oslo Norway.

[6] *Fäbod* — Literally, (fä) animal (bod) place, a place in the forest — high-forest settlement where young girls and grandmothers cared for cows and goats while pasturing them on marsh and wild grasses, and leaves stripped from the birch trees. Butter and cheese were made at these locations and sent home. Fields in the primary farm, below, in the valley, were too valuable for growing grain.

[7] *Hjortronbär* — Cloud berries, a yellow berry thriving in the northern marshes used for jam.

[8] *Tjöckmjölk* — fermented milk, similar to yogurt, now called tetmjölk or filmjölk in the Nordic countries..

[9] *Smultron* — wild strawberries.

[10] *Vansberget* — A mountain, west of Vanan, where the Fröman's *fäbod* was located.

[11] *Andersfors Bruk* — Probably named for Anders Fröman, an early manager of Bergslaget's operations in Vansbro Kommun.

[12] *Blåbär and lingonbär* — blueberry and lingonberry (the latter, similar to cranberries in taste).

[13] *Kyrkbåt* — Church boat. Literally, a long, lapstake constructed wood boat used to transport parishioners along river banks and lakeshores to the central church.

[14] *Ny potatis* — new potatoes

[15] *Råg* — rye

[16] *Korn* — barley

[17] *Välling* — A gravy-like slurry made from liquid fat or juices, flour and milk.

[18] *Head* — the distance water fell from the top of the millpond to the wheel. The greater the distance and volume, the more potential power to drive the wheel.

[19] *Dräng* — farm hand.

[20] *Vallkulla* — one of the women or girls who went to the *fäbod* (see 17) to pasture the cattle and goats.

[21] *Fiol* — violin.

[22] *Säckpipa* — Swedish bagpipe (sack-pipe) consisting of a goatskin or calfskin leather bag, with one drone pipe, and a chanter, usually tuned in A, each with a reed made from *vass*, a local plant (reed) growing along lakeshores.

[23] *Midsommar* — June 21, the longest day of the year in Scandinavia…when the sun shines all night in the north.

[24] *Kyrktagning* — A 'cleansing' ceremony which 'welcomed' a new mother back into the church. New mother's were considered to be contaminated by the Swedish Lutheran church. Meant to be rather celebratory for a woman giving 'legitimate' birth, for an unwed mother, it was considered very unpleasant. Use of pillories or stocks for this purpose have yet to be documented and the occurrence in this work is fiction.

[25] The author was unable to find factual evidence to validate or substantiate this practice, though some old drawings exist.

[26] *Smedja* — Blacksmith shop

[27] *Järnamål* — Mål means talk or tialect. Järna is the community.

[28] *Kullor* — Girls

[29] *Vind* — attic or loft.

[30] *Troll* — Small, human-like creatures reputed to live in caves, or beneath the ground, who could cause much mischief in one's life. They had a deathly fear of iron. Troll is both the singular and plural name.

[31] *Rånda* — Imaginary woman, rumored to be very beautiful, wearing a long dress which she pulled down to cover her tail, which was that of a fox. She was rumored to have a large hole in her back so you could a cave-like depression. She could help or hinder a *Vallkulla* in her daily life.

[32] *Dalkulla* — Girl from Dalarna province.

[33] *Stugo* — Small, log house or cabin.

[34] *Källa* — spring, well or spring house.

[35] *Vell* — a piece cut from the fourth stomach of a newly-slaughtered calf which has never been allowed to eat or drink anything but milk. A bacterial culture is present in this stomach which will start the

milk's fermentation, thickening it in order to preserve it or start
cheese (*tjôckmjölk'thick-milk'*).

[36] *Lur* — a long, conical horn fabricated by wrapping birch bark around
to form several layers. *Lur* were used to communicate in the *fäbod* or to
frighten wolves, bears and spirits. Sometimes they were used to call the
goats and cows, but usually that was done by voice with *kuja (kulning)*.

[37] *Gärdesgård* – a running fence constructed from old growth fir
(gran) trees about 2" in diameter, lashed diagonally with twisted bark
strips between two upright poles, the bottoms buried in the ground
interspersed every 10' feet or so.

[38] *Budar* — to be in the *fäbod*. *Buan*—to make the trek to the *fäbod*.

[39] *Kuja, kulning, or kolning* — A pitched, throaty, often singing call,
issued to the animals to control them. It was also a form of
endearing call or conversation with them. Kulning is the modern
Swedish, *kuja* is the dialect form of the verb, *järnamål (järna=district,
mål=dialect-of Dalarna.)*

[40] *Frömansgården* — Frömans (a family name), *gård* or *gården*, a yard
or farm.

[41] *Skrymt* — one of the many superstitions of the country people—
haunts or ghosts who could do evil.

[42] *Troll* — Little reatures who lived in caves or under the ground who
could cause much mischief in one's life.

[43] *Vittror* — Invisible little persons who coexisted with humans, above
the ground who could also do much mischief

[44] *Naken* — A naked young man who played violin while standing in a
stream or lakeshore. He could play so sweetly, listeners were unable
to cease dancing.

[45] *Lax* — salmon

[46] *Lapplander (Sami)* — Indigenous peoples of northern Scandinavia, commonly known as Lapplanders in the west; they prefer *Sami.*

[47] *Mål* — any local dialect.

[48] *Kyrktagning* — a ceremony abandoned in most churches at the turn of the 20th Century.

[49] *Vapenhus* — literally, weapon's room. The area the congregation first enters when proceeding through the front doors of the church. From Viking times, swords, spears and pikes were left there, least fighting and murder break out during the worship service.

[50] *Mörksuga* — Meaning dark sow, the creature is totally imaginary, since no one has ever seen one.

[51] *Järn* — iron.

[52] *Söndag* — Sunday

[53] *Knäckebröd* — A rye-based bread, rolled very thin and cut in the form of a wheel with a hole in the center. The bread was baked, then stacked on a long pole and suspended from the ceiling for storage. These horizontal poles were sometimes used for boundaries of etiquette when visitors came to call, each pole 'admitting' visitors closer to the intimate family area.

[54] *Stråke* — violin bow (stroke with a bow)

[55] *Gånglåtar* — gång (walking) låta (tune)...walking tune, a march.

[56] *Björsköttens* — Bear hunter's (bear-shooter's)

[57] *Pols* — very old *Scandinavian dance,hambo*-specialized Swedish turning dance, Schottis-skipping dance, vals waltz

[58] *Flöjter* — wooden flute

⁵⁹ *Spelåpipa* — wooden flute

⁶⁰ *Gärdesgård* — Typical Dalarna fence, constructed of very old (dense) fir poles, lain horizontally, but diagonal, strapped with bark strips to vertical poles on ten foot centers.

⁶¹ *Dalecarlian* — of or being from, Dalarna.

⁶² The *säckpipa* was dichromatic, having only eight notes. J.S. Bach invented the dichromatic scale, having 12 notes to the octave.

⁶³ *Uppläns* — Uppland, the southern Swedish province where the nyckelharpa originated.

⁶⁴ *Kaka* — cake.

⁶⁵ *Smultron* — wild strawberries.

⁶⁶ *Vispgrädde* — whipped cream (visp=whip)

⁶⁷ *Var så god* — literally, "you are welcome…," here, "help yourself"

⁶⁸ *Järnafolke* — Residents of the community of Järna.

⁶⁹ *Drangar* — landless, peasant farmers.

⁷⁰ *Domkyrka* — literally, dome-church, the large Swedish Lutheran cathedral in Uppsala Sweden

⁷¹ *Piga* — scullery maid.

⁷² *Tall* — pine tree

⁷³ *Gran* — fir tree

⁷⁴ *Korn* — barley

⁷⁵ *Hempiga* — *(hem=home-piga=maid, house girl)* the house girl

[76] *Sovhol* — a place in the *fäbod* forest or meadow where both the cows and the *vallkulla* rested during the warmest part of the day. She would build a fire to drive off flies and mosquitoes while the cows rested and chewed their cuds; the *vallkulla* might sew, knit or do other handy-work to occupy her time, which was paid for by her employer. *Sovhol* were also places where messages could be left and transmitted to other *fäbodar*, passed from *sovhol* to *sovhol* by individual *vallkullor*.

[77] *Nålhus*— or, *nålhylsa*, needle house, a small, cylindrical container, usually suspended from the *vallkulla's* belt, where she kept her scarce and valuable sewing needles.

[78] *Kyrkabåtar* — church boats

[79] *Lördag* — Saturday

[80] *Satkärring* — bitch

[81] *Körttbullar* — meatballs.

[82] *Sill* — potatoes in creamed (salted) herring

[83] *Älg* — European moose, somewhat smaller than the in North America.

[84] *Punsch* — a sweet, thick yellowish liquor, flavored with aarak, traditionally drunk in Sweden at pea soup meals on Thursdays.

[85] *Rödvinbär/svartavinbä* — red and black currants, respectively. They make a jam and serve it as a meat sauce.

[86] *Lingon* — similar to cranberries, but instead of in the bog, they grown in a shaded forest.

[87] *Fjäll* — mountain.

[88] *Åska* — thunder

[89] *Fan* — the devil (an oath, similar to "Oh hell...")

[90] *Korv* — wiener...hot dog (without the bun)

[91] *Stårbrittania* — Great Britain

[92] *Lie* — scythe for cutting hay or grass.

[93] *Runstenar* — rune stones, flat stones with tributes carved by Viking-era people, using the runic alphabet *(runalfabet)*.

[94] *Barnmorska* — midwife

[95] *IFR* — instrument flight rules

[96] *VFR* — Visual Flight Rules (out of and away from the clouds) and not in communication with Traffic Control Center.

[97] *Jul* — Christmas

[98] *Påsk* — Easter

[99] *Whitsun* — The day takes place 50 days after Easter, with roots in Jewish tradition. The birth of the Christian Church is often said to date from the first *Whitsun*.

[100] *Moderkaka* — placenta...afterbirth.

[101] *Farfar*– father's father, grandfather.

[102] *ILS* — Instrument Landing System, an electronic system which transmits a "beam" (radio signals) from the airport runway that the pilot sees on an instrument on his panel which helps him turn to right or left and climb and descend as needed to come down through clouds to within about 200 feet of the ground, right over the approach-end of an ILS-equipped runway.

ABOUT THE AUTHOR...

Born in 1941, in Ohio; when Gerald was three, his father moved the family to his boyhood home in Southeastern Missouri's Bootheel. Gerald left home at seventeen, working his way around America before eventually marrying and studying English at the University of Minnesota. He decided he didn't wish to teach, so continued to use engineering skills, as his family grew to four children. This included time as a designer in the aerospace industry, during the Apollo years. These skills eventually stood him in good stead when he formed a high technology company and changed careers yet again.

An instrument pilot, avid sailor and outdoorsman, Gerald's experiences and hobbies surface often in his writing. The urge to write never left him and Gerald continued creating short stories and poems, though he didn't attempt to publish until his late fifties. Around this time he began an epic novel, *Vallkulla*, about his early ancestors in 1800's Sweden which took many years to complete.

"The second novel, *My Enemy's Child*, was written for fun," Gerald quips, following the rigorous emotional demands of *Vallkulla*. "It nearly wrote itself...," he remarked, enjoying the change-of-pace, espionage theme. Scandinavia is a recurrent theme in the Gerald's art, albeit video production, photography, music, or writing. He travels to Scandinavia nearly every year, filming, interviewing and gathering experiences from others. "Any of these might make for a great novel some day."

Gerald enjoys playing fiddle and harmonica with his many musician friends on both sides of the Atlantic. Growing up in the "northern south" his early blues exposure sometimes tries to creep into his Scandinavian fiddling, when, Gerald says, "...the catfish are swimming with the lutefisk again."

Still a businessman, G. R. Revelle continues to write from his home in Wisconsin. Watch your books-seller's shelves for continuations of the three volume romantic epic *Vallkulla*, or check Smultron Publication's website at: www.smultron-pub.com.